The Banished
A Swabian Historical Tale

By

Wilhelm Hauff

The Banished
A Swabian Historical Tale
by Wilhelm Hauff

Copyright © 2023

All Rights reserved.

ISBN: 978-93-60464-73-8
Published by

DOUBLE 9 BOOKS

2/13-B, Ansari Road
Daryaganj, New Delhi – 110002
info@double9books.com
www.double9books.com
Tel. 011-40042856

This book is under public domain

ABOUT THE AUTHOR

The Württemberger artist and author Wilhelm Hauff was born on November 29, 1802, and died on November 18, 1827. Hauff was born in Stuttgart. His father, August Friedrich Hauff, was a secretary in the Württemberg ministry of foreign affairs, and his mother, Hedwig Wilhelmine Elsaesser Hauff, was a teacher. He was the second of four kids. When Hauff was seven years old, he lost his father. He learned most of what he knew in the library of his maternal grandfather in Tübingen, where his mother had moved after her husband died. From 1818 to 1820, he went to school at the University of Tübingen. In 1818, he was sent to the Klosterschule at Blaubeuren. He studied philosophy and theology at the Tübinger Stift for four years and was done. After graduating from college, Hauff worked as a tutor for the children of General Baron Ernst Eugen von Hugel (1774–1849), who was the minister of war for Württemberg. It was for these children that he wrote his Marchen (fairy tales), which were later collected in the Marchen Almanach auf das Jahr 1826 (Fairytale Almanac of 1826, also known as Tales of the Caravan, Inn, and Palace in the US).

CONTENTS

INTRODUCTION

"His varied life is toss'd on Faction's wave,
A leader now, and now a party's slave;
And shall his character a waverer's seem?
If that's a fault, impute it not to him;
He play'd a stake, and fortune threw the die;
So look upon him with a brother's eye.
We would for him an interest create,
His own his virtues, and his faults his fate."

Schiller.

The events which are recorded in the following pages, took place in that part of Southern Germany situated between the mountainous district of the Alb and the Black Forest. That portion of territory is bounded by the former on the north-west, by a long chain of hills of unequal height and breadth, extending southward, whilst the forest, commencing from the sources of the Danube, stretches uninterruptedly to the banks of the Rhine. Being composed of woods of black pine, it forms a dark background to the beautiful picture produced by a luxuriant country, rich in vineyards and watered by the Neckar, which flows through it.

This country, which is the "Würtemberg" treated of in these volumes, was originally of small compass. Its previous history, which is enveloped in darkness, tells us that it rose through various conflicting struggles to its present position among the neighbouring states. When we reflect on the time when it was surrounded by such powerful frontier neighbours as the Stauffens, the Dukes of Teck and the Counts of Zollern, we are astonished that its name should still exist as a nation; for the repeated storms of internal as well as external violence often threatened to erase it from the annals of history. There was a time, indeed, when the head of the reigning family was, to all appearance, driven for ever from the halls of his ancestors. Duke Ulerich von Würtemberg being obliged to fly his country and seek shelter in painful exile from the fury of his enemies, left his castles in the possession of foreign masters, his lands being occupied by their mercenaries. Little more was wanting to complete the extinction of the name of Würtemberg, than the parcelling out of the spoil of its blooming fields among the many, or the whole becoming a province of the house of Austria.

Among the many events related by the Swabians of their country and their ancestors, there is none more fraught with romantic interest than the struggles of that period, which are closely connected with the extraordinary fate of their unfortunate prince. We have attempted to bring them to life again, as they have been related to us on the heights of Lichtenstein and the banks of the Neckar, at the risk, however, of being misapprehended. We shall probably be told that the character of Ulerich1 is one not fit to be exhibited in a favourable point of view in an historical romance. He has been calumniated in many instances, and it has been even the custom, when reviewing the long list of Dukes of Würtemberg, to pass over in silence the descendant between Eberhard2 and Christoph, and to look upon him with a kind of horror, as if the troubles of a country were to be attributed solely to the conduct of its ruler, or that it were better to bury in oblivion the days of its misfortunes.

It may, however, be a question, whether the condemnation pronounced on the name of Ulerich, by his bitterest enemy Ulerich von Hutten, has not been exaggerated; for, to say the least of it, he was too much a party concerned to be trusted as an impartial judge. The voice which the Duke and his family raised in vindication of his innocence of the crimes imputed to him, having been too feeble to withstand the accusations and calumnies of his enemies, contained in the flagitious publication "Philippica in Ducem Ulericum," has been silenced by the revolutions of time.

We have conscientiously compared most of the contemporaneous writers of that most boisterous period, and have not met with one who absolutely condemns him. It is but just to keep in view the powerful influence which time and circumstances produce upon the minds of men. Ulerich von Würtemberg was brought up under the guardianship of bad counsellors, who, for the purpose of making him subservient to their views, fostered the evil propensities of his mind. As he took the reins of government into his own hands when boyhood is scarcely ripened into youth, justice at least compels us to make allowances, and though we cannot extenuate the outrages he committed during the course of his career, we are bound to look to the noble side of his character, in which we shall discover strength of mind and undaunted courage, in circumstances of extreme difficulty.

The year 1519, the date of our narrative, decided his fate and saw the beginning of his misfortunes. Posterity, however, may date it as the era of his prosperity; for, having passed through the ordeal of a long banishment, in which he learnt to know himself, he came out of it a wiser man and a more powerful Prince. From that period fortune favoured him, and each Würtemberger has cause to prize the latter years of his government, esteeming the religious reformation which this prince effected in his country, as the greatest blessing conferred on his countrymen.

The public mind, in the year 1519, was still in a state of great excitement. The insurrection of "poor Conrad,3" six years before, had been partially quelled, though with difficulty. The country people in many places still shewed symptoms of discontent. The Duke, among his many failings, had not the method of gaining the affections of his subjects, for they were oppressed by his men in office, under his own eye, and burdened with accumulated taxes to satisfy the wants of the court. The Swabian League, composed of a formidable confederacy of princes, counts, knights, and free cities of Swabia and Franconia, formed originally for the mutual protection of their rights, was treated with contempt by the Duke, particularly owing to his refusal to become a member of it. His frontier neighbours, therefore, watched his actions with the eye of enmity, appearing to wait for an opportunity to let him feel the weight of the power which he had despised. Neither was the Emperor Maximilian, who reigned at that period; very well inclined towards him, since he was suspected of having supported the knight Götz von Berlichingen, for the purpose of avenging himself on the Elector of Mains.

A coolness had subsisted for some time between him and the Duke of Bavaria, his brother-in-law, a powerful neighbour, owing to his having ill-treated his wife Sabina, the Duke's sister. Added to that (and which hastened his downfall) was the supposed murder of a Franconian knight who lived at his court. Chronicles of undoubted authority mention, that the intimacy between Johann yon Hutten and Sabina was such that the Duke could not behold it with indifference. One day at a hunt, the Duke taxed him with, and upbraided him for his treacherous conduct, and calling upon him to defend his life, run him through the body. The family of Hutten, and particularly Ulerich, Johann's cousin, raised their voices against the supposed murderer; and their complaints and the cry of vengeance resounded throughout Germany. The Duchess also, whose imperious querulous temper had, even as a bride, irritated the Duke, now broke all ties with him; and flying with the aid of Dieterich von Spät, appeared before the Emperor as his accuser and bitterest enemy. Agreements between the contending parties were concluded and not held; peaceable adjustments of their grievances were no sooner proposed than broken off again. The Duke's troubles augmented from month to month; but his proud mind would not bend to submission, for he believed himself in the right. The Emperor died in the midst of these altercations. He was a prince who had manifested much forbearance and mildness of character towards Ulerich, in spite of the many complaints of his enemies. The Duke lost in him an impartial judge, to whom he could alone look for aid in his present troubles.

The funeral service for the Emperor was being performed in the Castle of Stuttgardt, when a messenger suddenly arrived, seeking the Duke, with the intelligence that some people of the imperial town of Reutlingen, which lay within his frontier, had slain the administrator of his woods and forests on the Achalm. The townsfolk had, on some former occasion, insulted him very keenly. He entertained a bitter hatred of them; and this circumstance now gave him an opportunity to satisfy his revenge. Easily excited by anger, he sprang upon his horse, ordered the drums to beat the alarm throughout the country, besieged the city, and gaining possession of it, compelled its inhabitants to swear allegiance to him, whereby the imperial town became part of Würtemberg.

This was the signal for the Swabian League to assemble their forces, Reutlingen being a member of the confederacy. Difficult as it might otherwise have been to summon these princes, counts, and cities together, they did not hesitate, in the present instance, to obey the call, for hatred and revenge form a strong cement. In vain did Ulerich defend his conduct by written proclamations; in vain did he attempt to justify it in the defence of his rights; the army of the League assembled in Ulm, and threatened his country with invasion.

Such was the state of affairs in Würtemberg at the commencement of the year 1519. There was no doubt of the Duke gaining many adherents, could he have maintained the superiority in the field; but woe to him if he were discomfited by the League. There was too heavy a debt of revenge to be paid before he could expect mercy at their hands.

All eyes in Germany looked anxiously to the result of this contest. They essayed to pierce the curtain of fate, and to prognosticate what the coming days were likely to bring forth, whether Würtemberg or the League should remain master of the field. The following pages will withdraw this curtain, and expose the principal characters, who took a leading part, in due order; and we trust the eye of the reader will not turn away too soon fatigued with the narrative.

It surely is not an uninteresting occupation to peruse, in our days, an historical tale of olden times; and therefore it is our hope, as it has been our aim, to excite the interest of our readers in one, the events of which, though they occurred in so secluded a spot as the Swabian Alb, and in the remote, but delightful, vallies of the Neckar, we trust that the few hours spent in their perusal will not be thrown away.

Germany is not less rife in romantic events than other countries; and she can likewise draw largely upon the history of civil strife, equally interesting to our mind, as those recorded in the pages of more well-known states. We have, consequently, ventured to unroll an historical Swabian painting, which, if it does not exhibit the bold outline of figures, the same enchanting composition of landscape--if the colouring be less brilliant, and the pencilling less clearly defined--than the works of other authors, the artist may safely shelter himself under its historical truth, to make up for the deficiencies of composition.

FOOTNOTES TO THE "INTRODUCTION":

Footnote 1: Ulerich von Würtemberg was born in 1487, was invested in 1498 as Duke, with a Co-regency, which he dissolved in his sixteenth year, and reigned alone from the year 1508. He died in 1550.

Footnote 2: Eberhard with the beard was born in 1445, and died 1469. He was the first Duke of Würtemberg, and founded the University of Tübingen in 1477. Christoph, born in 1515, and died in 1568, was a prince whose remembrance is not only blessed in Würtemberg, but also in all Germany. He was the founder of the constitution of Würtemberg.

Footnote 3: So called from the name of a poor peasant, who headed his oppressed fellow-sufferers, in an insurrection for the redress of their wrongs, calling themselves the "League of poor Conrad."

VOL. I

CHAPTER I

What means the drum, that deeply rolls?
What means this warlike cry?
I'll to the casement, tho' my soul's
Misgivings tell me why.

L. Uhland.

After a succession of gloomy days the imperial town of Ulm, on the 12th of March 1519, at length was enlivened by a fine bright morning. Mists from the Danube, which at such a season generally hung heavily over the town, had on this occasion been dispelled before noon by the sun, and as it rose, the view of the plain on the opposite side of the river became gradually clearer and more extended. The narrow, cold streets, inclosed by their dark gable-ended houses, were also lighted up more bright than usual, and shone with a brilliancy and cheerfulness which accorded well with the festive appearance of the town on that day. The main street, called the Herdbrucker street, leading from the Danube gate to the town hall, was on this morning thronged with people, whose heads were so closely packed on either side against the houses (like stones of a wall) that they left but a narrow passage through the middle. A hollow murmur, the indication of great expectation, which issued from the crowd, was only occasionally interrupted by a loud laugh, caused by the severity of the city guard, celebrated for its strictness and its antiquity, who, using their long halberds, pushed back with appropriate rudeness whoever was unfortunate enough to be squeezed out of his place into the middle of the street; or perchance by some wag, who, by way of joke, would exclaim, "Here they come, here they come!" causing disappointment to the anxious assemblage of spectators.

The throng was still more dense in the spot where the termination of the Herdbrucker street enters the square before the town hall. It was there that the different trades were posted; the guild of boatmen, with their masters at their head, the weavers, the carpenters, the brewers, all displaying their banners and the emblems of their vocation, were drawn up, clad in their Sunday dresses and well armed.

But if the multitude in the streets presented a jovial holiday spectacle, much more was that the case in the lofty surrounding houses. Well dressed women and young girls crowded the windows, which were adorned with many-coloured carpets and floating drapery, giving to the whole an appearance of beautiful paintings set in splendid frames.

The corner bow-window of the house of Hans von Besserer presented the greatest attraction. Within it stood two young maidens, each strikingly conspicuous by their uncommon beauty, but so much differing in looks, height, and dress, that whoever remarked them from the street, might remain some time in doubt to which to give the preference.

Both appeared to be under eighteen years of age: the tallest of the two was delicately made; rich auburn hair encircled a fine open forehead, the vaulted arch of her dark eyebrows, the placid blue eye, the delicately turned mouth, the soft colour of her cheek, were unrivalled. She altogether formed a picture, which, among the beauties of the present day, would not have failed to be distinguished; but in those times, when a higher colour, upon a face partaking of the form of an apple, was more admired, it was principally by her graceful demeanor that she drew attention.

The other, smaller, and possessing in a greater degree the attractive qualities suited to the times, was one of those thoughtless, merry beings, who are conscious that they possess the power of pleasing. Her brilliant fair hair, according to the fashion of the ladies of Ulm, fell in long braids behind and in ringlets in front, and was partly covered by a neat white cap, full of small tasteful plaits. Her round fresh face was ever in motion: her lively eyes, still more restless, wandered through the crowd below; and her laughing mouth, exhibiting at every moment a set of beautiful teeth, evidently showed that objects were not wanting, among the numerous groups and figures of adventurers, upon which to exercise the playfulness of her wit.

Behind them stood a large, broad-shouldered, elderly man, with deep, stern features, thick eyebrows, long thin beard, already sprinkled with grey hairs, and his dress so entirely black, that its hue contrasted strangely with the rich and lively colours of those about him. He wore a thoughtful, almost a sorrowful look, scarcely ever relaxing into one more cheerful, excepting when a momentary gleam of kindness would shoot through his countenance, like a flash of lightning, at some happy remark of the merry fair one. This group, so varied in colours and dress as well as in character, attracted much of the attention of the bystanders immediately beneath them. Many an eye gazed upon the pretty girls, whose fascinating appearance helped to beguile the time of the idle and staring multitude, now growing impatient to witness the sight for which they were assembled.

The time was now approaching the hour of noon. The crowd became restless at the long delay, and manifested an increased impatience, by pressing and pushing upon each other in rather a turbulent manner; whilst here and there, tired of standing, several of the more sober members of the trades seated themselves on the ground. When, however, the report of three guns, fired from the fort on the hill on the furthermost side of the river, and the sound of the cathedral bells in deep tones began to echo over the town, order was speedily restored throughout the anxious ranks.

"They are coming, Bertha, they are coming!" said the fair girl in the balcony window, and put her arm around the waist of her companion, as she stretched out her neck to the utmost.

The house of the Herrn von Besserer formed the corner of the forenamed street, having a window on one side of it looking towards the Danube gate, and another on the other side commanding a view of the town hall, by which means the party were in a good position to see the expected sight.

The space between the two rows of the people was, in the meantime, with difficulty kept sufficiently open by the town guards. Anxious stillness now reigned throughout the immense crowd, whilst the deep tolling of the bells alone broke the silence.

The deadened sound of drums, blended with the shrill clang of trumpets, was shortly after heard, and a long brilliant train of horsemen moved slowly through the gate. The appearance of the town drummers and trumpeters, and the mounted body of the sons of the patricians of Ulm, was too much of an everyday occurrence to excite any great sensation on the present occasion; but when the black and white banners of the town, emblazoned with the imperial eagle, accompanied by flags and standards of all sizes and colours, came floating in the breeze through the gate, the spectators then became sure that the long wished-for moment was arrived.

The curiosity of our two young beauties in the balcony became doubly excited when they observed the crowd in the lower part of the street respectfully take off their caps.

Mounted upon a strong bony horse a man approached, whose stately carriage, affable and open countenance, contrasted strangely with a deep stern brow, and whose hair and beard were slightly tinged with grey. He wore a hat pointed at the crown, adorned with many feathers, a cuirass over a close-fitted red jacket, and leather buskins slashed with silk, which might have been handsome when new, but by dint of bad weather and hard work had now assumed an uninterrupted dark-brown colour,--large heavy riding boots came up to his knees; his only weapon, a singularly large sword, with a long handle, and without basket-guard, completed the figure of the warrior. The sole ornament worn by this man was a long gold chain of massive rings, twisted five times around his neck, having a medallion of merit of the same metal attached to it, which hung upon his breast.

"Tell me, quickly, uncle, who is that stately man, who at once looks so young and so old?" said the fair girl, as she turned her head a little towards the man in black standing behind her.

"I can tell you, Marie," he answered; "that is George von Fronsberg, commander of the confederate infantry; an honourable man, did he but serve a better cause."

"Keep your remarks to yourself, Mr. Würtemberger," she replied, whilst she playfully threatened him with her finger; "you know that the maidens of Ulm are staunch confederates."

Her uncle, however, not heeding her reply, proceeded: "That one on the grey horse is Truchses von Waldburg, second in command. He also owes a debt of gratitude to our Würtemberg. Behind him come the colonels of the League. By heaven! they look like hungry wolves seeking for prey."

"Oh! what a set of miserable figures," remarked Marie to her cousin Bertha, "they surely are not worth the trouble we have taken of dressing; but hold, who is that young man in black on the brown horse? just look at his pale countenance, with his fiery black eyes; on his shield is written, 'I have ventured.'"

"That is the knight Ulerich von Hutten," replied the old man. "May God forgive his calumny against our Duke. Children! he is a learned, pious man, but the Duke's bitterest enemy; and I say so, for what is true must remain true. And there, those are Sickingen's colours. Truly, he is there himself! Look this way, girls; that is Franz von Sickingen. It is said he brings a thousand horsemen into the field; that is him, with the plain cuirass and red feather."

"But tell me, uncle," asked Marie again, "which of them is Götz von Berlichingen, of whom cousin Kraft has related so much to us; he is a powerful man, by all accounts, and has a hand of iron; does not he ride among the burghers?"

"Do not name Götz and the burghers in the same breath," said the old man, seriously; "he holds for Würtemberg."

The greatest part of the procession had, during this conversation, passed by under the windows; and Marie remarked, with astonishment, the indifference and unconcern with which her relation Bertha viewed it. The usual manner of her cousin was thoughtful; indeed, at times she appeared in a state of absence to all surrounding objects; but on such a day as this, to be so perfectly insensible to the brilliancy of the passing scene, was, in Marie's mind, to be guilty almost of impropriety.

She was just on the point of upbraiding her, when her attention was called to a sudden noise in the street. A large, powerful horse was prancing immediately under their window, having probably taken fright at the waving ensigns of the trades. The high crest and flowing main of the steed sheltered the rider's face, and the feathers only of his cap were visible to the spectators at the window; but the adroitness and ease with which he managed his horse and kept him under command, proved him to be a skilful cavalier. In his exertion to quiet him, his light-brown hair had fallen over his face, and as he threw it back, his look fell on the bow-window of the corner house.

"Well at last there is a handsome young man," whispered Marie to her neighbour, so softly and secretly as if she feared to be overheard by him; "and how polite and courteous he is! Look! I really think he has saluted us, without knowing who we are."

Marie's curiosity was too much excited at the moment to notice the sudden change which her remark had produced on her cousin's countenance, who, to conceal her embarrassment, feigned to pay no attention to what she said. Bertha had hitherto sat unconcerned, viewing the passing procession with apparent cold indifference; but when she recognised the young cavalier, and returned his salutation with a slight inclination of the head, her cheek was suddenly suffused with a burning blush, her thoughtful eye was animated into an expression in which tender love and fearful anticipation predominated; and though the smile about her mouth might bespeak joy at the sight of the unexpected apparition, a keen observer could not have failed to discover, that it betrayed somewhat of pain and regret. Her accustomed self-possession, however, quickly regained the ascendancy over these conflicting feelings, and thus her merry cousin, whose quick penetration at any other moment would have been startled into surprise at the alteration exhibited on the features of her whom she considered wanting in tender sentiment, lost the opportunity of rallying her upon this occasion.

Marie, pulling the old man by the cloak, cried, "Here, quickly, uncle; tell me who is this with the light-brown scarf trimmed with silver?--well?"

"Dear child," answered her uncle, "I have never seen him before. Judging from his colours, he is in no particular service, but he, as well as many others, wages war against the Duke my Lord for his own individual pleasure and profit."

"Ah! there is no getting anything out of you," said Marie, and turned away, annoyed at her uncle's indifference; "you can distinguish all the old and learned men more than at a hundred yards off; but when one asks you a question about a young and polite cavalier, you can tell one nothing. And you too, Bertha, you open your eyes upon the procession below as if the host were passing. I'll wager you did not see the handsomest man of all; and thought only of old Fronsberg, when quite a different set of men rode by."

By the time she had finished these her angry remarks, the principal part of the procession had reached their station before the town hall; the few remaining cavalry of the league which came up the street possessed little interest for the two damsels. When the officers had dismounted and gone into the town-hall for refreshment, and when the members of the trades had been dismissed, the people by degrees began to separate, and then the party in the balcony withdrew also from the window.

Marie did not appear perfectly pleased. Her curiosity was only half satisfied. She took care, however, not to let her stern old uncle remark her disappointment; but when he left the room, she turned to Bertha, who had retired to the window again, and stood there in deep thought.

"Well," she said, "after all our anticipated expectations about this procession, there was nothing worth making such a fuss about. But I wonder who that handsome young cavalier was? I should like very much to know his name! How very stupid it was of you, Bertha, not to notice him; did I not push you when he saluted us? Light-brown hair, very long and smooth,--friendly dark eyes,--the countenance a little tanned, but handsome, very handsome! Small mustachios on the upper lip. No; I tell you----but how red you get again all of a sudden, as if two maidens, when they are alone, dare not speak of the pretty mouth of a young man. We often converse upon such topics here in Ulm; but I suppose at your good aunt's at Tübingen, and your strict father's in Lichtenstein, such things were never mentioned; but I see you are dreaming again about something or other, so I must look out for some thorough Ulmer girl when I want to have a little gossip."

Bertha answered only by a smile, which expressed more than she dared to utter; and Marie, taking a large bunch of keys which hung on the door, hummed a song, and went to prepare for dinner. Though she might have been accused of being rather over curious at the momentary appearance of a courteous young cavalier, still that did not make her neglectful of the important duties of a housekeeper.

She skipped out of the room, and left Bertha to her thoughts, which we also will not disturb, whilst she now recalls to her mind the endearing remembrance at gone-by days, which the appearance of the afore-mentioned young cavalier called up at once from the depth of her faithful heart. She dwelt on that time, when a hasty glance from him would cheer the passing hours; she pondered on those nights when in her retired room, undisturbed by her good aunt, she worked that scarf, whose well-known colours awoke her now as out of a dream. We will not at present pause to inquire the reason why, when blushing and with downcast eyes, she asked herself, whether cousin Marie had rightly described the sweet mouth of her beloved?

CHAPTER II

And don't your heart now burn

While hope succeeds to fear?

Don't even youth return

To Swabia's land so dear?

J. Schwab.

The reader will have learned from the introductory preface the state of affairs. Duke Ulerich of Würtemberg had brought upon himself the bitter hatred of the Swabian League, by the obstinacy with which he braved so many confederated princes and knights, by the furious expression of his rage and threats of revenge, by the boldness with which he alone bid them defiance, and last of all by the sudden military occupation of the imperial town of Reutlingen. These were some of the principal circumstances which led to the rupture. Others of a more private nature fostered the bloody thoughts and thirst for revenge and plunder of those who made a plea of individual insult the cause of uniting their banners, for the downfall of the Duke and the partition of his possessions.

The principal officers of the Swabian League were the Duke of Bavaria, whose object was to procure satisfaction for the ill treatment of his sister Sabina, Ulerich's wife--the knights of the Huttens to revenge the supposed murder of the cousin of their ancestor--Dieterich von Spät and his companions to wash out the disgrace of family insult in Würtemberg's misfortunes--and to these were added the authorities of the towns and boroughs, who desired to recover Reutlingen again from the occupation of Duke Ulerich's troops. They headed the pompous entry into Ulm we have described in the foregoing pages, and arrived on the same day from Augsburg, where they had assembled. War was therefore now inevitable, for it was not to be supposed that they would propose terms of peace to the Duke, after having proceeded thus far.

But of a much more peaceable and cheerful cast were the ideas of Albert von Sturmfeder, that "courteous, polite cavalier," who had so highly awaken Marie's curiosity, and whose unexpected appearance had coloured the cheeks of Bertha with so deep a red. He scarcely knew himself how he came to take part in this campaign; for though he was acquainted with the use of arms, yet he had not been trained to them. Sprung from a poor but not obscure family of Franconia, he became an orphan at an early age, and was brought up by his father's brother. A learned education began even in those days to be considered an ornament to the nobility, and his uncle, therefore, chose the path of literature for him. It is not mentioned whether he made much progress in learning in the university of Tübingen, then in its infancy; thus much, however, is known, that he took a warmer interest in the daughter of the knight of Lichtenstein, who lived with her aunt in that town of the Muses, than in the lectures of the most celebrated doctors. It is also related that she resisted with pertinacious determination the different attacks with which many a young student assailed her heart. But although all kinds of manœuvres to conquer a hard heart were well understood in those days, (for the youth of ancient Tübingen had, perhaps, studied their Ovid better than those of the present), neither nocturnal love-complaints, nor yet furious encounters between rivals to gain possession of her, could soften the maiden's apparent obduracy. One only succeeded in winning this heart, and that one was Albert. The lovers, indeed, divulged to no one when and where the first ray of tender feeling dawned in their hearts, and far be it from us to wish to penetrate the veil of mystery of first love, or even to relate things which we cannot substantiate; we can nevertheless assert this much, that they had already reached to that degree of love, when true lovers swear eternal fidelity, amidst the interruptions of external circumstances, and which, in the painful hour of separation, proved their only consolation. Her much-loved aunt having died, the knight of Lichtenstein sent for his daughter to Ulm, for the purpose of finishing her education there, under the roof of a married sister. Bertha's nurse, old Rosel, remarked that the burning tears which she shed, and the longing eyes with which Bertha over and over again looked back as they left the town, could not have been given alone to the hilly country to which she was bidding adieu.

Shortly after Bertha's departure, Albert received a communication from his uncle, in which the question was put to him, whether after four years' study he was not now learned enough? He readily complied with this hint, and, without a moment's hesitation, prepared to quit the university; for since Bertha's absence, the lectures of the learned doctors, and even the charming valley of the Neckar, were become hateful to him.

The fresh air from the hills invigorated him with renewed force, as he rode through the gate of Tübingen towards his home, on a fine morning in February. In proportion as his bodily frame was braced by the freshness of the morning, so was his soul raised to that cheerful elevation of spirits so natural to his age. Youth vainly imagines itself capable, by its own powers, to bring about its most anxious wishes, and it is this reliance on self which inspires more confidence than assistance from others.

When Albert was left to his own thoughts as he paced his lonely way homewards, the contemplation of his future prospects were wrapped in mysterious uncertainty, which led his mind to compare his present position with the clear lake which reflects on its surface the cheerful objects rising around its banks, but veils the treacherous depth of its waters by its bright colours.

Such was the feeling of Albert von Sturmfeder as he rode through the beechwood forest towards his home. This road did not, indeed, lead him nearer to his beloved; neither could he properly call anything his own besides the horse which he bestrode, and the ruined castle of his ancestors. Upon this castle there was a popular joke, which ran thus:--

A house on three props you'll find:

Whoever enters in front,

Has no room to sit behind.

But although he was well aware of his poverty, and was awake to his needy circumstances, still he knew that with a determined will a hundred paths were open to him by which he might attain his object, and that the old Roman saying, *Fortes fortuna juvat*, had never yet deceived him. The present state of excitement in the country appeared to afford him an opportunity by which, after some active employment, he might hope soon to realise the object of his wishes.

The result of the contest which was about to commence, appeared at that time very uncertain. The Swabian League, though it possessed experienced commanders and disciplined soldiers, was nevertheless weakened through disunion. Duke Ulerich, on his side, had enlisted 14,000 Swiss, brave and experienced warriors; he could bring into the field, out of his own country, numerous and hardy troops, but not so experienced as the others; and thus stood the state of affairs in February 1519.

When every one around him was taking an active part, Albert also determined not to remain an idle spectator: a war, he thought, might open a path to lead him sooner towards the object of his desire than any other, and by which he might hope to render himself worthy of meriting the hand of his beloved.

Neither of the contending parties had, indeed, any claim upon his heart. People of the country spoke ill of the duke, whilst the views of the League did not appear to be influenced by the purest motives. But when he heard that several knights and counts, whose properties adjoined the duke's, urged by the loud, and, as he thought, just complaints of the Huttens, against the tyrannical conduct of Ulerich, had withdrawn their allegiance from him, he was induced to join the League; being unaware that they had been corrupted by money, and the seductive prospect of rich plunder, to overrun his country. But the news of the count of Lichtenstein being in Ulm with his daughter was, in truth, the mainspring which influenced and confirmed his determination; for he thought he could not be far wrong if he took the side on which Bertha's father acted, and therefore tendered his services to the confederates.

The knights of Franconia, headed by Ludwig von Hutten, approached Augsburg at the beginning of March, for the purpose of joining Ludwig von Baiern, and the rest of the members of the League. The army being collected, their march resembled more a triumphal procession as they approached the territory of their enemy, than regular military proceedings.

Duke Ulerich was encamped at Blaubeuren, the frontier town of his possessions towards Bavaria and Ulm. In the latter place the great council of war of the League was appointed to deliberate upon the plan of the campaign, and they then hoped, in a short time, to force the Würtembergers to a decisive battle. Things having gone thus far, negotiations for peace were out of the question: war was the watchword, and victory the only thought of the army.

Albert's heart beat high when he thought that his first trial in the career of arms would soon be put to the test; but whoever may have been placed in a similar situation will readily find excuses for him, if feelings of a more tender nature at times possessed his soul, and made him forget his dreams of battle and victory.

As the army approached the town, a fresh east wind wafted towards them the salute of the heavy artillery on the walls, and the sound of all the bells ringing to welcome their arrival from the opposite side of the river. He first obtained sight of the lofty cathedral in the distance, emerging from a fog, which, gradually clearing away as he drew near, displayed the town with its dark brick houses and high entrance-towers to his view. At that moment the conflicting doubts and anxieties which had long assailed his breast oppressed him more than ever. "Do those walls indeed inclose my beloved? May not her father, perhaps, contrary to my hopes, be the faithful friend of the duke, and concealed among his enemies? and if such be the case, dare I, whose only hope is to gain his good will--dare I stand opposed to him without blasting my own happiness? And should her father have really taken part with the enemy, can his daughter possibly be with him? But even were my best hopes realised, and should she be among the spectators assembled to witness the entry of the army, shall I find her still true to that faith she has plighted?" These and many other anxious thoughts passed through his mind in rapid succession.

The last distressing thought, however, gave way to a pleasing certainty; for if all kind of disaster were leagued against him Bertha's fidelity, he felt convinced, remained unaltered. He pressed the scarf she had given him to his breast; and now, as the Ulm cavalry fell into the line, their trumpets and cornets playing martial music, his natural cheerfulness returned, he rose prouder in his saddle, and as they passed up the gaily adorned streets, his quick eye examined all the windows of the lofty houses, seeking her alone.

There he perceived her, serious and thoughtful, as she viewed the passing scene. He fancied her thoughts might be occupied with him, whom she supposed to be far distant from her. He gave his horse the spur, which made him bound in the air, and the pavement resound under the clash of his hoofs. But as she turned towards him, and their eyes met, and judging by the joyful blush which animated her features, that she assured him he was recognised and still beloved, then it was that poor Albert nearly lost all recollection of his situation; for though he followed the march to the town-hall, so great was his desire to linger in the neighbourhood of his beloved, that little was wanting to make him forget all other considerations, and be irresistibly drawn to the corner house with the bow window.

He had already made the first step in that direction, when he felt his arm grasped by a powerful hand. "What drives you in this direction, young man?" said a deep, well-known voice; "this is not the way to the town-hall. Hallo! I really believe you are faint from fatigue: no wonder, indeed, that you should be, for the breakfast was a very meagre one. But never mind, my lad, come along. The Ulmers give good wine, and we will treat you to some of the best sort, old Remsthaler."

Though the transition from the raptured joy in which his mind for some moments floated, when he first saw his love, to the bustle before the town-hall in Ulm, was somewhat sudden, he could not help being thankful to his friend, old Herrn von Breitenstein, his nearest neighbour on the frontier of Franconia, for awakening him out of his momentary dream, and saving him from making a precipitate, foolish step.

He therefore took the advice of the old gentleman in a friendly way, and with him followed the rest of the knights and nobles, whose appetites were well sharpened by their long morning ride for the good mid-day meal, which was prepared for them by the imperial free city in the town-hall.

CHAPTER III

The sound or music greets my ear,
The castle glares with light:
What means these varied sounds I hear?
Who banquets here to-night?

SCHILLER.

The saloon of the town-hall, into which the guests were ushered, formed a large oblong. The walls, and the ceiling, low in proportion to the size of the room, were wainscoted with brown wood; numerous round windows, on which were painted the arms of the nobles of Ulm in bright colors, occupied one side of it; whilst on the walls opposite were suspended the portraits of renowned burgomasters and councillors of the town. They were all painted in the same position, that is, the left hand supported on the hip, the right resting on a table covered with rich cloth, and looking down on the guests of their descendants with grave and solemn, aspect. The assembled company crowded in mixed groups about the table, which being in the form of a horseshoe, occupied nearly the whole length of the apartment. The brilliant festive costume of the grand council and patricians, who were to do the honours of the day in the name of the town, was not in keeping when compared with that of their guests, who, covered with dust, and clad in leather and steel, discomposed the silk cloaks and velvet dresses of their entertainers in no very ceremonious manner, and much to their annoyance.

They waited some time for the Duke of Bavaria, who, having arrived in Ulm a few days before, had accepted the invitation to this brilliant feast; but when his page brought an excuse that he could not attend, the signal by sound of trumpet was given to take places. The rush to the table in consequence was so impetuous that it was impossible to put the preconcerted friendly intentions of the council into execution, by which a citizen of Ulm was to sit between each two of their guests.

Breitenstein secured a seat for Albert at the lower end of the table, which he said was one of the best places. "I could have put you," said the old man, "among our seniors, near Fronsberg, Sickingen, Hutten, and Waldburg at the head of the table, but in such company etiquette and reserve will infringe upon the more important consideration of gratifying the cravings of hunger with ease and comfort. We might have gone further up also, among the Nürnbergers and Augsburgers; there where the roasted peacock is, which I declare is not a bad place; but I know you do not like such townsfolk, and therefore brought you here. Look around you, is it not a capital position? As we do not know the faces hereabouts it will not be necessary to talk much. On the right we have a smoking hot pig's head, with a lemon stuck in its mouth; on the left a magnificent trout biting its tail for joy; and in our front a roebuck, not to be matched for its tender meat and quantity of fat the whole length of the table or elsewhere."

Albert thanked him for his kindness, and took a hasty glance at those immediately about him. On his right sat a good-looking young man about twenty-five or twenty-six years of age. His neat-combed hair, throwing out a perfume of some highly-scented ointment, his small beard, evidently having just gone through the ordeal of warm curling irons, made Albert suspect, even before he was further convinced of it by his dialect, that he was a gay Ulmer citizen. The young man, perceiving himself to be the object of his neighbour's observation, made himself very officious. He filled Albert's glass from a large silver tankard, and pledged him to drink to a better acquaintance and good fellowship; he then offered to help him the best slices of roebuck, hare, pork, pheasant, and wild duck, which lay before them in great profusion on large silver dishes.

But neither the officious kindness of his neighbour, nor the uncommon appetite of Breitenstein, could provoke Albert to eat. His mind was too much occupied with the beloved object he had seen in entering the town to follow the example of his neighbours. He sat full of thought, looking into his tankard, which he still held in his hand; and as the bubbles on the surface of the sparkling wine dispersed, he fancied he saw the portrait of his love in the gilded bottom of it. No wonder then that his sociable friend on his right, seeing how his guest held his tankard, and refused every dish which he offered him, took him for an incorrigible wine-bibber. His keen eye, which was fixed upon the object before him, appeared to point the youth out as one of those perfect connoisseurs of wine, whose refined taste liked to dwell upon the quality of the noble beverage.

For the purpose of seconding the good intentions of the grand council, namely, that of rendering the feast as pleasant as possible to their guests, the young Ulmer sought all means to discover the weak point of his neighbour. It was, indeed, contrary to his moderate habits to drink much wine; but, in the hopes of rendering himself agreeable to Albert, he thought he would stretch a point this once. He filled his goblet full, and said, "Don't you think, neighbour, this wine has fire in it, and is high flavoured? It is not, indeed, Würtemberger wine, such as you are accustomed to drink in Franconia, but it is real Elfinger, out of the cellar of the senate, and calls itself eighty years old."

Astonished at this address, Albert put down his tankard, and answered with a short, "Yes, yes." His neighbour, however, would not let him off so easily. "It appears, nevertheless," he went on to say, "that it is not quite the thing you like, but I know a remedy. Holloa, there!" he called to a servant, "bring a can of Uhlbacher here. Now just taste this; it grows hard by the castle of Würtemberg. You must pledge me in this toast: 'A short war and glorious victory.'"

Albert, to whom this conversation was in no wise agreeable, thought to turn it to something which might lead to a more interesting topic. "You have much beauty here in Ulm," said he; "at least, in passing through the town, I remarked many pretty faces at the windows."

"Yes, in truth," answered the Ulmer, "the streets might be paved with them."

"That would not be amiss," replied Albert, "for the pavement of your streets is bad indeed. But tell me who lives in that corner house with the bow-window?" pointing to the situation of it: "if I do not mistake, two young ladies were looking out of the window as we rode by."

"So! you have remarked them already?" laughed the other: "upon my word, you have a quick eye, and are a good judge. They are my pretty cousins, on my mother's side: the little blonde is the daughter of the Herrn von Besserer, the other is the lady of Lichtenstein, a Würtemberger, staying with her on a visit."

Albert thanked heaven for having been placed so near a relation of Bertha, and determined at once to take advantage of his good fortune. He turned to him, and in the most friendly manner said, "You have a couple of pretty cousins, Herr von Besserer."

"I call myself Dieterick von Kraft, secretary to the grand council, with your permission."

"A pair of pretty cousins, Herr von Kraft; do you visit them often?"

"Yes, I do," answered the secretary, "and particularly since the daughter of Lichtenstein is in the house. Before her arrival, cousin Marie and I were one heart and soul, but she is somewhat jealous now, being piqued by the attentions I bestow upon her charming cousin, Bertha von Lichtenstein, which she thinks belong to her alone."

This confidential communication of the secretary to a perfect stranger, was not a little surprising to Albert, who very soon discovered that a certain portion of vanity was one of his weak points, though in other respects there was much to like in him.

This avowal, however, on the part of his new acquaintance, did not sound agreeable to Albert's ear, which caused him to press his lips together, whilst his cheeks assumed a deeper colour.

"Laugh as you will," proceeded the scribe, whose head began to feel the effects of the wine, to which he was unaccustomed; "if you only knew how they pull caps about me! My Lichtenstein cousin has, however, a disagreeable, odd way of showing her friendship; she is so ladylike and reserved, that one is afraid to joke in her presence, much less to be as familiar with her as with Marie; but it is just that which renders her so attractive in my eyes, for if she sends me away ten times, I am sure to return to her the eleventh:--the reason is," he murmured to himself, "that her old strict father is present, of whom she is rather shy; let him but once cross the boundary of Ulm, and I'll soon tame her."

Finding his new acquaintance so very communicative, Albert resolved to question him respecting the knight of Lichtenstein's view of the coming struggle, because that was an essential point, upon which his dearest hopes turned, and one upon which he had his doubts; but just as he was about to begin, he was interrupted by the sound of peculiar strange voices near him. He thought he had heard them before amidst the noise and clatter of the ghosts, as they recited in a drawling uniform tone a couple of short sentences, the purport of which he could not well understand. But now that he heard them repeated close to him, he soon learnt the subject of their monotonous import. It was the fashion in those good old times, particularly in the imperial towns, for the father of the family and his wife, when they entertained company, to rise about the middle of the repast, go round to each individual guest, and in a short sentence of customary usage press him to eat and drink.

This fashion was one of such old standing in Ulm, that the grand council would on no account dispense with it on the present occasion, and, therefore, appointed the father of a family and his wife, in the persons of the burgomaster and the oldest of the councillors, to perform the office.

Having gone round two sides of the table on their "*pressing*" embassy, it was not to be wondered at, that their voices became, by their efforts, rather husky, so that at last their friendly exhortation assumed almost the tone of a threat. A rough voice sounded in Albert's ear, "Why don't you eat, why don't you drink?" Startling, he turned round, and beheld a large man with a red face, who had addressed these words to him, and before he had time to give an answer, a little short man, with a high shrill voice saluted his ear, on the other side.

"But eat and drink and take your fill--
Such is our magisterial will."

"I have long thought it would come to that," said old Breitenstein, as he took breath for a moment from the vigorous attack he had been making on a haunch of roebuck; "there he sits and talks, instead of enjoying the excellent dishes of roast meats, which have been put before us in such profusion."

"With your permission," said Dieterick von Kraft, interrupting him, "though the young man eats nothing, he is a lover o£ wine, and a capital judge of it; I found it out immediately, for he cannot keep his eyes from the bottom of his cup; therefore do not blame him if he prefers old Uhlbacher before anything else."

Albert had no idea how he had become the subject of this extraordinary apology; he was on the point of making an excuse, when another event drew his attention. Breitenstein had now taken pity upon the pig's head with the lemon stuck in its mouth, which he very cleverly extracted from its jaws, and undertook, with great avidity and experienced hand, its further dissection. Just as he was in the act of swallowing the first mouthful of one of the choicest bits, the burgomaster came to him also, with the same exhortation, "Why don't you eat, why don't you drink?" Breitenstein looked at him with astonishment, but his speaking organs had no time to exercise their functions; he however nodded his head, and pointed to the well-polished bone of the haunch of roebuck in his plate. The little man, also, with the cracked voice, though it appeared unnecessary, would not be debarred repeating his friendly exhortation--

"But eat and drink and take your fill,--
Such is our magisterial will."

And thus it was in the good old times. At least no one could complain of being invited to a mere parade dinner. The table soon after assumed a different appearance. The large dishes and plates were removed, and were replaced by spacious bowls and large jugs filled with generous wine. The wine passed freely, and the frequent drinking of healths, at that time very much the custom in Swabia, soon produced its usual effects. Dieterick Spät and his companions sang burlesque songs on Duke Ulerich, and confirmed each oath or bit of coarse wit with a horse laugh or a deep draught. The Franconian knights called for dice, threw for the duke's estates, and drank to the taking of the castle of Tübingen. Ulerich von Hutten and his friends carried on a controversy in Latin with some Italians about a recent attack on the papal chair, which a monk of Wittemberg of no reputation had undertaken. The Nürnbergers, Augsburgers, and some few Ulmers had got together, and disputed upon the merits of their respective republics; in short, the room resounded with the din of laughter, singing, quarrelling, and the clatter of silver and pewter tankards.

But at the upper end of the table a much more becoming and sober hilarity prevailed. George von Fronsberg, old Ludwig Hutten, Waldburg Truchses, Franz von Sickingen, and other elderly grave men occupied seats there.

Hans von Breitenstein, who was a captain of the League, having now fully satisfied his appetite, turned his eyes in that direction, and said to Albert, "The noise about us here is not at all agreeable,--what say you? would you like to be presented to Fronsberg now, as you told me a few days ago you wished so to be?"

Albert, whose desire it had long been to become acquainted with the general, gladly accepted the offer, and getting up, followed his old friend. We will not stay to inquire the reason why his heart beat quicker on this occasion, why his face assumed a higher colour, or why his steps, as he approached him, were slower or less firm. Who has not experienced in his youth similar feelings on being introduced to the notice of a brilliant character, crowned with glory? Whose darling self, "I," has not sunk into utter insignificance before the giant-like idea we have formed of a renowned man! George von Fronsberg was accounted one of the most famous generals of his day. Italy, France, and Germany had witnessed his victories, and his name will go down to posterity in the annuls of the art of war, as the author and founder of a regular system, by which a body of infantry is trained to fight in ranks and companies. Tradition and chronicles have brought down the exploits of this noble personage to our times, and who can help calling to mind the heroes of Homer, when they read the following description of this man:--"He had such strength in his limbs, that with the middle finger of his right hand he could displace the strongest man from his seat, let him hold himself as firm as he might; he could seize the bridle of a horse on the full gallop, and stop him; and he could carry alone, from one place to another, the largest gun and battering ram of the time." Breitenstein conducted the young man to him.

"Who do you bring us now, Hans?" said George von Fronsberg, as he noticed the well-grown youth with interest.

"Look at him well, noble sir," answered Breitenstein, "and you will not fall to recognise the house whence he sprung."

The general regarded him with still greater attention; old Truchses von Waldburg also run his scrutinizing eye over his person. Albert was timid and shy before these great men; but whether it was that the friendly, frank manner of Fronsberg gave him confidence, or whether he felt how important that moment was to his future prospects, he overcame the shame of being put out of countenance by the looks of so many renowned men, and faced them with determination and courage.

"I recognise you at once by that look," said Fronsberg, and gave him his hand: "you are a Sturmfeder."

"Albert von Sturmfeder," answered the young man: "my father was Burkhardt Sturmfeder; he fell by your side in Italy: so it has been told me."

"He was a brave man," said the general, whose eye rested thoughtfully on Albert's features, "he remained faithful by my side in many a warm day of battle, and fell covered with glory and honour in defence of my person. And you," he added, "have you determined to follow his steps? Methinks you have left your nest somewhat early, for you are scarcely fledged."

Waldburg, a weather-beaten, hard featured old soldier, interrupted Fronsberg, and said, with a gruff, surly voice, "I suppose that young bird is seeking a few flocks of wool to repair the dilapidated family nest."

This rude allusion to the ruined castle of his ancestors, called up a crimson blush on the cheek of the young man. He had never been ashamed of his poverty, but these words sounded so full of scorn and insult that he felt himself, for the first time, really poor, as he stood before the more affluent derider of his name. His eye at that moment passing over Truchses Waldburg, fell on that well-known bow window, where, thinking he perceived the person of his love, his usual courage resumed its dominion. "Every struggle has its price. Sir Knight," he replied; "I have proffered head and arm to the League; the motive of this step can be but indifferent to you."

"Well, well," answered the other, "we shall see what the arm can do; but as to the head it cannot be quite so clear, if you take in earnest what was meant as a mere joke."

The offended youth was about to make an angry reply, when Fronsberg, taking him kindly by the hand, said, "Just like your father; dear young man! you will in time become like him, a stinging nettle1 also,--we shall require friends whose hearts are in the right place. You will not be the last thought of, you may rest assured."

These few words, from the lips of a man who had won so high a reputation among his contemporaries by bravery and experience in war, produced such an effect on the mind of Albert, that the unguarded answer which floated on his tongue sank harmless. He withdrew from the table to a window, partly for the sake of not interrupting the conversation of the officers, partly to convince himself with greater certainty, whether the momentary apparition which he had seen was really his beloved.

When Albert left the table, Fronsberg turned to Waldburg; "That is not the way, Herr Truchses, to win over a staunch ally to our cause. I'll wager he has not quitted us with the same zeal he brought with him."

"Do you consider yourself called upon to raise your voice in favour of that hot-headed youth?" said the other; "it is not at all necessary; he must learn to take a joke from his superiors."

"With your permission," interrupted Breitenstein, "it is no joke to be jeer'd on account of unavoidable poverty; but I know you never bore his father any good will."

"And," continued Fronsberg, "you have no controul over him in any way, for he has not yet taken the oath of alliance to the League and is therefore at perfect liberty to go wheresoever he pleases. Should he serve under your colours, I would advise you not to push him too far, as he does not appear much inclined to submit to insult or contumely."

Speechless from rage upon being contradicted, which he never in his life could brook, Truchses first looked at one and then at the other with such fury, that Ludwig von Hutten, fearful of further strife, interposed between them, and said, "Come, an end with these old stories. It is high time to rise from table. It is now getting dark, and the wine is becoming too powerful for our friends lower down there. Dieterick von Spät has already drank twice to Würtemberg's death, and the Franconians have not yet quite settled whether his castles shall be burnt to the ground or divided among them."

"Let them alone," laughed Waldburg, scornfully, "those gentry may do and say what they please to-day; Fronsberg will soon bring them to their senses."

"No," said Ludwig von Hutten, "if any one has a right to talk in such terms, I am the one, the avenger of my son's blood; but until war be declared, intemperate conversation must be restrained. My cousin Ulerich speaks much too violently with the Italians about the monk of Wittemberg, and when he is out of temper, divulges things which ought to be kept secret."

Fronsberg and Sickingen now rose from table, and those about them following their example, the break-up was general.

FOOTNOTE TO CHAPTER III.:

Footnote 1: The same words which Fronsberg made use of in speaking of Götz von Berlichingen.

CHAPTER IV

The eyes with which I gaze on her
Can pierce thro' wood and stone:
They're seated in my heart so true,
That beats for her alone.

Walther von der Vogelweide.

The small distance which separated the table from the window, to which Albert had retired, permitted his hearing every word of the dispute mentioned in the latter part of the last chapter. He rejoiced to perceive the warm interest which Fronsberg took in him, an inexperienced orphan; but, at the same time, he could not conceal from himself that his first step in his military career, had also brought upon him a formidable, bitter enemy.

The unbending pride of Truchses von Waldburg was so well known in the army, that Albert had little reason to hope Hutten's mediatory and conciliatory words would have much effect in soothing the unfavourable impression, which he feared his warmth in upholding the name of his family might have created in the mind of the general. And he was well aware that men of weight and consequence, governed by a violent, imperious temper, such as Waldburg's, do not readily enter into the feelings of those who have excited their anger, nor forgive the ebullition of a generous mind when assailed in its most vulnerable point.

A slight tap on the shoulder interrupted his thoughts, and as he turned round, his friendly neighbour at table, the scribe to the grand council, stood before him.

"I'll bet, you have not looked out for a lodging yet," said Dieterick von Kraft, "and it might be now somewhat difficult to find one, as it is getting dark, and the town is very full."

Albert acknowledged he had not thought about it; he hoped however to find a room in one of the public inns.

"I would not have you be quite so sure of that," answered the other, "and, should you find a corner in one of those houses, you must reckon upon being but badly off. But if my lodging would not appear too small for you, it is very much at your service."

The good secretary of the council pressed Albert with so much cordiality, that he did not hesitate to take advantage of his invitation, though he almost feared lest, when the effects of the wine had passed off, his host might regret his proffered hospitality to him, a perfect stranger. Dieterick von Kraft, however, appeared rejoiced at the readiness with which his proposal was accepted, and taking Albert's arm, with a hearty shake of the hand, led him out of the room.

The square before the town-hall was in the mean time the scene of much bustle and confusion. The days were still short, and the evening having broken in upon the dinner-party, torches were lighted, the glare of which illumined but sparingly the large space, and played on the windows of the opposite houses, and on the polished helmets and cuirasses of the knights. Loud calls for horses and attendants sounding through the town-hall, the clatter of swords, the running here and there of many men, coupled with the barking of dogs, the neighing and pawing of impatient horses, formed a scene, which resembled more the surprise of a military post in the night by an enemy, than the breaking up of a convivial festival.

Albert remained in the hall in a state of amazement at the sight of so many jovial faces and powerful figures, who, having mounted their horses, retired in small groups, singing and springing about in all the hilarity of youth. This nocturnal, fleeting scene, forcibly impressed him with the conviction of the uncertainty and changeableness of all worldly events. These same joyous associates, thought he, would soon be engaged in the dangerous concerns of war, when many of them, even before the spring should be fully advanced, would cover the green grass with their bodies, with no other price offered for their blood than the tear of a comrade, or the short-lived glory of having fallen before the enemy as brave men.

His eye turned instinctively to that quarter where he knew the reward which he hoped would crown the success of his present undertaking awaited him. He there saw many figures at the window, but soon the black smoke of the torches, which suddenly, as a cloud, almost covered the square, veiled the objects so as to give them the appearance of mere shadows. He turned away in disappointment, saying to himself, "Such are my prospects also; at one moment the present indeed looks bright, but in the next, how dark, how uncertain is the prospect of the future!"

His kind friend roused him from this foreboding frame of mind, with the question, "Where are your servants with your horses?" Had the spot where they stood been better lighted, our good Kraft might, perhaps, have discovered a passing blush upon the cheek of his friend at this inquiry.

"A young soldier," answered Albert, quickly recovering his composure, "must learn to look after his own affairs as well as he can, without the assistance and trouble of servants, and therefore I have not brought one with me. I have given Breitenstein's groom charge of my horse."

The scribe of the council applauded the young man for the self-denial which he exercised; but he could not help making the remark, that when once in the field he would not be able to assert his independence so easily. The attention which his companion paid to his own person, his well-combed hair, his neatly curled beard, convinced Albert that he spoke from his heart, and the snug comfortable lodging into which he was introduced did not belie this opinion.

The ménage of Herrn von Kraft was, in fact, a young bachelor's establishment, for his parents died before he attained the age of manhood. He had often thought of looking for a partner to share his comforts with him, but he hesitated to renounce the charm of independence; an advantage he thought not to be despised, flattered as he was by being honored and looked upon by the ladies of Ulm as a desirable match. But ill-natured folks whispered abroad, that it was principally owing to the decided disinclination of his old nurse and housekeeper to have a young mistress in the house, which deterred him from taking so important a step.

Herr Dieterick possessed a large house not far from the cathedral, a pretty garden on St. Michael's Hill, furniture in high preservation, large oak chests full of the finest linen, made of the yarn which the ladies of the house of Kraft, with their female domestics, had for many generations passed their long winter evenings in spinning; and an iron chest in the bed-room, containing a large stock of gold florins. As to his person, he was a good-looking, substantial man, always spruce in his dress, tight-laced, and proud of the fine linen which he wore: his deportment in the council was serious and full of business; he was well conversant in state affairs, as well as in those of his own household; and being sprung from a good old family, it was no wonder that he was respected and looked up to by the whole town, and that any pretty young Ulmer damsel would have thought herself too happy to become mistress of these united advantages.

Upon a nearer inspection, however, the interior of his friend's establishment appeared to Albert any thing but enviable. The only domestic companions of Herr Dieterick were an old grey-headed man-servant, two large cats, and the above-mentioned unsightly fat nurse. These four creatures stared at the new guest with large wondering eyes, which convinced him how little accustomed they were to receive any increase of guests in the establishment. The cats went round him mewing with raised backs; the old woman, in a cross manner, fidgeted her large high round cap, ornamented with gold fringe, out of its accustomed perpendicular position, and asked whether she should prepare supper for two? When she heard her question not only affirmed, but was ordered also (it was not quite clear whether it was an order or a petition) to prepare the corner room on the second floor for the stranger, her patience appeared exhausted; she shot a look of fury at her young master, and left the room rattling a large bunch of keys, which were suspended from her girdle. The hollow sound of her footstep, and the noise of the door, as she, in her ill-humour, slammed it after her, re-echoed through the dead stillness of the spacious corridors.

The old grey-headed servant had in the mean time pushed the table and two ponderous arm-chairs near the immense stove; and having put a black box on the table, with two candlesticks and a tankard of wine, he whispered a few words to his master, and then withdrew. Herr Dieterick invited his guest to take part in his usual evening amusement of playing a game of tric-trac, which the black box contained.

Albert was amused at the proposal of his friend, and particularly when he told him that, since he was twelve years old, he had been in the habit of playing a game with his nurse every evening.

The dead silence which reigned throughout the house was only broken by the occasional snuffing of the candles, the ticking of a large wooden clock in a black case, and the monotonous throw of the dice. Albert would gladly have heard some other symptoms of life, if it were but the grumbling of the old nurse, or her footstep sounding again in the corridors. The game had never possessed any charm for him, and more particularly at the present moment, when his thoughts were otherwise occupied. He was oppressed with a lowness of spirits which he could scarcely control, separated as he now was by a few streets only from his beloved, and anxious to satisfy his longing desire to see her again. The unfeigned pleasure which Herr Dieterick appeared to derive in winning nearly every game, imparted to his good-natured face something so peculiarly agreeable, that it made up in some measure for the loss of time.

When the clock struck eight Dieterick led his guest to supper, which his housekeeper, spite of her ill humour, had prepared in her best manner, for she spared nothing to keep up the dignity and honour of the house of Kraft. The secretary again essayed the powers of his eloquence, with which he sought to season the repast. He talked concerning passing events, of the coming war, and gave Albert to understand that his situation put him in possession of state secrets known only to a select few. But in vain did Albert hope to hear something about his pretty cousins. He attempted to sound him upon a subject so nearly allied to his dearest interests, namely, upon the views of the knight of Lichtenstein in the pending struggle, which he had failed to elicit at the dinner; but the secretary, whether to impress Albert with the importance of his confidential situation in the council, or that he really did not know the intention of Bertha's father, put on a more consequential and mysterious air than usual, and the only information he would impart was, that the knight was then in Ulm with some others of Würtemberg.

This news was at least satisfactory so far as the turn it was likely to give to his fate. His joy was now for the first time complete, in the satisfaction of having joined a party which, except for the great names at the head of it, was otherwise indifferent to him. "And so her father is also among those assembled here!" thought he. "May I not hope to have the good fortune to fight by the side of that good man, and prove myself worthy of my name, and of her I love?" He felt the conviction that Albert von Sturmfeder would not be the last in a battle.

His host, after supper, conducted him to his bed-room, and took his leave with a hearty wish for a good night's rest. Albert examined his room closely, and found it to correspond precisely with the rest of the gloomy house. The round frames of the windows, warped by age, the dark woodwork of the walls and ceiling, the large stove projecting far into the apartment, the enormous bed with a broad canopy and heavy stuff curtains, gave a dull, nay a melancholy, effect to the whole. But still every thing was arranged for his comfort. Clean snow-white sheets invited him within as he threw back the curtains of the bed, the stove threw out an agreeable warmth, a night lamp was placed in a niche in the wall, and even a tankard of spiced hot wine, by way of a nightcap, was not forgotten. He closed the curtains as he got into bed, and scanned over in his mind the passing events of the day. Having taken them in their due order as they had occurred, he had reason to be satisfied with his position; but, when he afterwards fell into the province of dreaming, they were all heaped up in crowded confusion in his mind, far beyond the power of unravelling. One object alone was perfectly clear to him,--it was the portrait of his beloved Bertha.

CHAPTER V

And is it mere illusion? Say--
Or will that one so kind, so true,
To whom my heart and life are due,
Be to my arms restored this day?

F. Haug.

Albert was awoke the next morning by a tap at the door. He threw open the curtains, and perceived that the sun was already high up. The knocking increased, when, shortly after, his kind host entering, inquired how his guest had slept, and explained to him the cause of his early visit. The grand council had determined on the preceding evening to celebrate the arrival of the confederates by a ball, which was to take place that very evening in the town-hall. It was his province, as secretary to the council, to make all the necessary arrangements for this important affair. He had to secure the services of the town musicians, and to invite the first families in the name of the senate. But his first concern would be to hasten to impart this extraordinary piece of good news to his charming cousins.

He related all this to his guest with an air of great importance, and assured him he was so full of business that he scarcely knew where his head was. Albert had only one thought, that of seeing and speaking with Bertha, and he was so overjoyed in the anticipation of such-unlooked for happiness, that he gladly would have embraced the bearer of the good tidings, if prudence had not deterred him from thus exhibiting his secret feelings.

"I can plainly see," said the scribe, "the pleasure this news gives you; the love of dancing brightens up your eyes already. I can promise you a couple of partners, such as you will not find every day. You shall dance with my cousins; for I am their chaperon on such occasions, and I will so arrange the matter that you and no other shall be the first to engage them; they will be enchanted when I promise them the best dancer in the room." With this he left the apartment, wishing his friend good morning, cautioning him when he went out of the house not to forget to notice it, so as to be able to find it again at dinner time.

Herr Kraft being a near relation of the Herrn von Besserer, was entitled to free access to his house, and upon this occasion he made an earlier call than usual.

He found the maidens still at breakfast. Ladies of the present day may perhaps be shocked at the homely meal which our two belles of Ulm, in the year 1519, were partaking of when their cousin Dieterick entered the room. It was not an elegant déjeuné, served up in painted porcelain in the form of beautiful antique vases, or curious-shaped chocolate cups; no, the natural grace of Marie and Bertha was not impaired by the occupation of breakfasting on humble *beer-soup*,1 at six in the morning, served up in the brown-coloured jug of that day. Can this avowal, however, prejudice the attractive qualities of these two beauties? In the eyes of some it perhaps may; but whoever could have seen Marie and Bertha, in their pretty little morning caps and neat clean dresses, would certainly, as cousin Kraft did, have no objection to partake of the breakfast with them.

"I can see at once, cousin," began Marie, after the usual salutations of the morning, "that you would like to partake of our soup, because, I suppose, your old cross nurse has not taken care of you this morning; but don't flatter yourself that you will get any here, for you deserve punishment, and must expect----"

"Oh, we have been waiting for you so long," interrupted Bertha.

"Yes, to be sure we have," said Marie, with her usual quick way; "but don't flatter yourself that we care as much about your society, as to be informed of the news of what is going on, that's all."

The scribe had been long accustomed to be received by Marie in this manner. He determined, therefore, to make himself as agreeable as possible, satisfying her curiosity by giving her all the gossip of the town, in order to pacify the jealous mood, which he thought he had excited. He was about to begin, when Marie interrupted him. "We know," said she, "that you are too fond of a long story, and as we witnessed most of your doings in the town-hall yesterday from the balcony, we'll say nothing touching your drinking bout there, which speaks not much to your credit; but answer me this question."--She placed herself before him in an attitude of comic seriousness, and went on: "Dieterick von Kraft, scribe of the most noble council of state, did you notice among the confederates, at the dinner given yesterday in the town-hall, a remarkably distinguished-looking young knight, with long light-brown hair, a face not so milk-white as your own, but not less handsome; a small beard, not so carefully combed as yours, but much more beautiful; a light blue scarf with silver----!"

"Oh, that is no other than my guest," cried cousin Kraft; "he rode a large brown horse, and wore a blue jacket, slashed at the shoulders, and turned up with light blue."

"Yes, yes, go on; the very one," said Marie; "we have our particular reasons for inquiring all about him."

"Well, that is Albert von Sturmfeder," answered the scribe, "a handsome charming young fellow. It is curious that you should be the first he noticed in coming into the town." Kraft then related all the particulars of what had passed at the dinner, how he was at once struck by the manly figure, the commanding and attractive countenance of the young man, who, by good luck, became his neighbour at table, and that the more he knew of him the more he liked him; so much so, that he had invited him to his house.

Bertha rose from her seat, and went to look for her work-box, turning her back at the same time upon both her cousins, in order to conceal a blush which flew to her forehead, and which proved that not one word of Dieterick's conversation was lost upon her.

"Come, that is very kind of you, cousin," said Marie, as he finished: "I believe it is the first time you have ventured to have a guest in your house. I should like to have seen the face of old Sabina, when master Dieter, as she calls you, brought a stranger home so late at night."

"Oh," said the scribe, "she resembled the dragon attacking St. George; but I gave her to understand pretty clearly, that it was not at all improbable, I might soon bring home one of my pretty cousins----"

"Ah, get away with you, and don't talk nonsense," resumed Marie, as she tried to withdraw her hand, which he had taken, blushing highly at the same time. She had never appeared so pretty in his eyes as at this moment. Bertha's serious face, in proportion as this flirtation increased, lost its attraction in his estimation, the balance of his devotion was all in favour of the animated Marie, who now sat before him in all the bloom of blushing beauty.

Bertha having slipt out of the room, Marie escaped the tender grasp of Dieterick's hand, and profited by this opportunity to turn the subject of the conversation.

"There she goes," she said, as she looked after her cousin; "I would wager she is going to her room to weep again. She cried so violently yesterday, that it has made me also quite melancholy."

"What is the matter with her?" asked Dieterick, with interest.

"I am as ignorant of the cause of her grief as ever," answered Marie; "I have asked her over and over again; but she only shakes her head, as if there was no hope left. 'This unhappy war!' is all she ever gave me for answer."

"And is old Lichtenstein still determined to take her back to his castle?"

"Certainly," answered Marie; "you should have heard how the old man swore yesterday, when the confederates entered! Well, he is devoted to his Duke, heart and soul, so he may go, with all my heart. As soon as war is declared, he intends taking his departure with her."

Herr Dieterick appeared very thoughtful; he rested his head upon his hand, and listened to his cousin in silence.

"And only think," she continued, "yesterday, after the entrance of the leaguists into the town, she wept more than ever. You know she was always serious and melancholy; but as if that circumstance were to decide the fate of the war, she is now quite disconsolate, I don't believe it is the idea of leaving Ulm that affects her; but I suspect," she added, mysteriously, "she has some secret attachment at heart."

"Yes, I have long remarked that," sighed Herr Dieterick; "but how can I help it?"

"You! how can you help it?" laughed Marie, all signs of sorrow on Bertha's account vanishing from her face at these words. "No, indeed, you need not flatter yourself that you are the cause of her suffering. She was in this state long before you ever saw her."

The worthy secretary was very much put out by this assurance. He thought in his heart that a farewell from him was the real cause of Bertha's state, and her care-worn countenance at this moment almost regained the preponderance in his changeable heart. Marie went on to deride his conceitedness, when all of a sudden he recollected the main object of his visit, which he had lost sight of during the conversation. Marie sprang up with a scream of joy, as her cousin imparted to her the news of the ball.

"Bertha, Bertha!" she cried out, at the height of her voice, so that her cousin, startled, and fearing lest some accident had happened, hastened to her assistance. But before she had scarcely had time to enter the room, Marie said again, "Bertha, a ball at the town-hall this evening!"

This news was a happy surprise to her also. "When? are the strangers invited also?" were her rapid questions, whilst a deep red covered her cheeks, and a ray of joy shot from her sorrowful eyes, scarcely able to contain their tears.

Marie and her cousin Kraft were both astonished at Bertha's rapid change from depression of spirits to sudden joy, and Dieterick could not help remarking, that he supposed she must be passionately fond of dancing. But he was equally mistaken in this instance, as he was when he mistook Albert von Sturmfeder for a connoisseur of wine.

Herr Kraft, supposing his cousins would now wish to occupy themselves with the important preparation of dress, rather than listen to anything else he might have to say, took his departure, to fulfil the rest of his weighty duties. He hastened to give the requisite orders, and to invite, in person, the principal guests, and higher families. He was received everywhere as the messenger of good news; for tradition says, that the pleasure of dancing is not the passion of the present day only.

His arrangements were soon accomplished. In those days, in order to be merry and cheerful, it was not absolutely necessary there should be a long suite of apartments, lighted up with flaming chandeliers, and furnished with numerous unmeaning things, which encumber the fashionable apartments of the present age. All was simple. The room in the town-hall was, from its size, well adapted for the purpose, and the humble rude-shaped lamps which hung on the walls, had, up to that time, thrown out light enough to show off the dresses and illumine the pretty faces of the maidens of Ulm.

But not only had the arrangements of the active scribe succeeded in everything he had undertaken on this important occasion; he had also in the course of his visits learned some secret intelligence which had been confided solely to the committee of the council, and the principal officers of the League.

Satisfied with the result of his various avocations, he returned home at noon, when his first step was to inquire after his guest.

Albert had been employed, during the absence of his host, in looking over a beautifully-written book of chronicles, which he found in his room. The neat painted figures which formed the first letter of the chapters, the pictures of fields of battle, and triumphal entries of victorious troops, delineated with a bold outline, and painted with peculiar care and labour, and which were dispersed throughout the volume, had amused him for some time. His mind being full of the warlike figures he had been examining, induced him to think of his own weapons, and of polishing his helmet, armour, and the sword which he had inherited from his father. He accordingly set to work, at the same time singing sometimes a cheerful, sometimes a serious song, to the great annoyance of the unmusical organs of Frau Sabina.

Dieterick heard the sounds of his agreeable voice as he walked up stairs, and he could not resist listening at the door until he had finished his song. It was one of those touching strains, bordering almost on the melancholy, which has been brought down to our times, and is to be heard even now in the mouth of the Swabians. Often and with pleasure have we listened to those strains on the charming banks of the Neckar, struck with the beautiful simplicity and lengthened sound of their harmony.

Albert went on singing:

Swift as thought
All our pleasures come to nought!
The charger yesterday he press'd,
To-day the death-shot pierced his breast,
To-morrow opes the chilly grave.

Such the measure
Of all earthly bliss and pleasure!
In that comely cheek of thine,
The lily and the rose combine;
But rose and lily fade and die.

Then resigned
To God's will, I yield my mind:
Should the trumpet sound a call,
Should it be my fate to fall,
Say "A gallant soldier's gone."

"Really you have a fine voice," said his host, as he entered the apartment; "but why sing such melancholy songs? I prefer a merry and cheerful one, such as a young fellow of twenty-eight ought to sing."

Albert put his sword aside, and gave his hand to his friend. "Every one to his taste," said he, "but I think that to those whose occupation is war, and whose life is in constant jeopardy, a song which carries consolation and encouragement to the heart of the soldier, gives death a milder aspect."

"That's just what I mean, also," said Dieterick; "but what is the use of being melancholy upon a subject which is certainly the lot of all? 'If you paint the devil on the wall, he will surely appear,' says the proverb; however, that saying does not hold good as the case now stands."

"How? is not war decided," asked Albert, with curiosity; "has the Würtemberger accepted conditions?"

"Conditions? none will be made with him," answered the secretary, with an air of contempt; "he has lived his longest day as Duke; it is our turn now to govern. I will let you into a secret," added he, looking big with importance and mystery, "but it must be strictly between us. Your hand! You think the Duke has fourteen thousand Swiss with him? They are scattered to the winds. The messenger we despatched to Zurich and Bern has returned. All the Swiss at Blaubeuren and on the Alb will be obliged to return home immediately."

"Return home?" said Albert, with astonishment, "and for what purpose? Are they at war themselves in their own country?"

"No," was the answer, "they are in profound peace, but have no money. Believe me, before a week passes over our heads, messengers will arrive to order the whole army home."

"But will they go? they came to the Duke's assistance of their own accord; who can order them to leave his colours?"

"That's very easily managed; do you suppose they will disobey the orders of their magistrates at the risk of the loss of their property, and imprisonment? Ulerich has too little money to retain them, and they will not serve him upon mere promises."

"But you cannot call that behaving honourably," remarked Albert, "to deprive the enemy of the arms with which he wishes to meet you in fair contest."

"In politics, as we call it," answered the scribe, thinking to establish his knowledge of state affairs in the mind of the inexperienced young soldier, "in politics, honour at best is assumed but for appearance sake; for example, the Swiss will explain to the Duke, in excuse for deserting him, that it would be against their conscience to allow their troops to serve against the independence of the free towns; but the truth is, that we can fill the pockets of the bears with more gold florins in order to keep them at home, than the Duke can to assist him."

"Well, after all, let the Swiss desert the Duke," said Albert, "Würtemberg will still be able of herself to send forth valiant and ready hearts sufficient to prevent any dog passing the Alb."

"We have thought of an expedient in that case also," replied the scribe, in explanation; "we will address a letter to the states of Würtemberg, and warn them against the insufferable government of their Duke, exhorting them at the same time to cast off their allegiance to him, and join the League in the laudable undertaking of crushing his tyrannous conduct."

"How!" cried Albert, with horror, whose generous mind was as yet unacquainted with the intrigues of politics: "I call that playing the traitor. Would you force the Duke out of his country by such underhand, unworthy means, and corrupt his confiding subjects to induce them to become his bitterest enemies?"

"I believe you have been thinking, all along, that we wish nothing more than that he should restore Reutlingen again to its former rank of a town of the empire? But how then is Hutten, with his forty-two associates, to be remunerated? In what way is Sickingen to satisfy the demands of his thousand cavalry and twelve thousand infantry, if he does not get a good slice of the country to pay them? And the Duke of Bavaria, do you suppose he will not require a share of it also? And we Ulmers, our frontier borders on Würtemberg----"

"But the Princes of Germany," interrupted Albert, impatiently, "do you suppose they will quietly look on and see you parcel out his rightful possession among strangers? The Emperor, surely, will not suffer you to hunt a Duke of the empire out of his country!"

Herr Dieterick had a ready answer to this question also. "There is no doubt," said he, "that Charles succeeds his father the Emperor: we shall then offer to place the country under his protection, and, should Austria throw her mantle over it, who can resist her power? But what makes you look so downcast? if you thirst for war, you will readily find means to gratify your wish. The nobility still hold to the Duke, and many a one will have his head broken before his castle walls. But we shall lose our dinner if we go on talking thus, come soon, and we'll see what old Sabina has provided for us." Upon which the secretary left the room of his guest with a proud step, as if he himself were already installed in the office of protector of Würtemberg.

Albert did not send the most friendly look after his host as he withdrew. He replaced his helmet again in the corner, which he had but an hour ago taken such pleasure in polishing; with sorrow he looked at his sword, that faithful piece of steel, which his father had proved in many a hard conflict, and which he had sent to his orphan son from the field of battle, as his sole legacy. "Fight honourably," was the device engraved on its blade, and he asked himself, could he now draw it in a cause, which bore injustice on its front? Instead of the contest being decided by the military talents of experienced men, and the bravery of individuals, as he had supposed, he now learned that secret intrigue, designated by Herr Dieterick "politics," was to settle the question! Instead of the exhilirating clash of arms, and the prospect of glory, which had induced him to take part in the struggle, he perceived that he was to promote the covetous plans of designing men! Would his honour permit him to assist these low-minded Philistines of townsfolk, in expelling an ancient princely house from its rights, which his ancestors had served with willing arm? No, the thought was intolerable; and to be tutored by this Kraft was still more repugnant to his feelings.

He could not however long entertain any ill-will against his kind-hearted host, when he considered that this plan was not concocted by his own brain, and that men, like this political scribe, when they get hold of a state secret, or some great political scheme, foster it as their own, and as such try to instil it into the minds of their adopted children, as if the wisdom of Minerva had sprung out of their own thick heads.

He therefore met his friend in good humour, when dinner was announced. The conversation between them was dull and common-place. The scribe's thoughts appeared to be occupied with some important project; and Albert taking a review in his mind of the whole state of affairs as they stood, consoled himself with the idea that, as the father of Bertha had sided with the League as he supposed, and such men as Fronsberg had proffered their services in the same cause, there might be less reason to doubt the justice of it than he imagined.

> Youth's ever ready with its word; it seizes
> The first that comes to hand, as 'twould a knife:
> And thus ye cry or "shame," or "nobly done,"
> On every thing--all's either good or bad.

These words of the poet well describe the feelings of Albert at this moment, and the sudden change in his sentiments was also to be attributed to his inexperienced mind in worldly affairs, acting as he did alone, without the aid and advice of any tried friend. Anticipating, therefore, the happy moment of meeting his love at the ball in the evenings where he would be able to speak with her, and from her lips have his doubts cleared up respecting her father's intentions, the gloom with which his mind had been overcast in his conversation with his friend the secretary gave away to the pleasing prospect of seeing her again.

FOOTNOTE TO CHAPTER V.:

Footnote 1: Beer-soup was a mixture of beer, eggs, sugar, cinnamon, and a little milk, with crums of bread, in quantity according to the taste.

CHAPTER VI

"And in the merry dance, she whispers, to impart,
In soft accents, the sorrows of her heart."

L. Uhland.

If we had ransacked all the pawnbrokers' shops, and attended the auction of an antiquary's goods, to find "a pocket-book giving a description of the social pleasures, with the fashionable figure dances, of the year 1519," we could not have been more fortunate than in the fund of information which chance has thrown in our way upon that subject.

Having arrived at that part of the present history which is to treat of a ball so far back as 1519, a difficulty arose of ascertaining what were the figures, and how they were danced in those days.

We might, indeed, have simply said, "they danced;" but how easily might some of our fair readers have made an anachronism, and imagined an old veteran such as George von Fronsberg, booted and spurred, standing up in a cotillon. In this embarrassment a very rare book fell in our way, entitled, "The beginning, origin, and customs of tournaments in the holy Roman Empire. Frankfort, 1564." We found in these precious pages, among other well executed wood-cuts, the representation of a ball in the time of the Emperor Maximilian, which was about a year before the date of this history.

We may, therefore, take it for granted, that the ball in the town-hall of Ulm differed in nothing from the explanations afforded by the above-mentioned drawing, and consequently we shall be able to give a better idea of the amusements of those days, by giving a description of the picture, than by our own delineation.

The foreground is occupied by the spectators; and the musicians, composed of fifers, drummers, and trumpeters, placed in a gallery, "sound a blast," according to the expression in the tournament book. On either side, towards the further end of the room, are arranged those who intend to join in the dance, dressed in rich heavy stuffs. In our days, we see only two standing colours on such occasions, black and white, in which the ladies and gentlemen are divided as night and day. Not so in former times. An extraordinary brilliancy of colours shoot their rays from the picture. The most beautiful red, from fiery scarlet to the deepest purple, accompanied by rich deep blue which surprises us in the paintings of the old masters, form the cheerful colours of their picturesque drapery and dresses. The centre of the apartment is occupied by the actual performers. The dance resembles very much the Polonaise of the present day, in which the gentleman, with his partner, walk around the room in procession. Four trumpeters, bearing heraldic flags suspended to their instruments, open the procession, followed by the first couple. The rank alone of the gentleman entitles him, with his lady, to the honour of leading; and at each change of the dance, the next in precedence takes his place. Then come two torch-bearers, followed by the rest of the dancers in pairs. The ladies walked with modest and reserved demeanour; and the men placed their feet in a singular position, as if they were on the point of making a high leap. Some appear also to stamp with their high heels in time to the music; a custom even now seen in the Swabian village festivals.

Such was the ball in Ulm. The first blast of the trumpets had sounded before Albert von Sturmfeder entered the room. His eye flew through the ranks of the dancers, and soon fell upon his beloved. She was led by a young Franconian knight of his acquaintance; but she did not appear to heed the animated conversation which he addressed to her. Her eyes sought the ground, her look expressed seriousness, bordering on sorrow; very different from the rest of the female part of the company, who, floating in all the pleasures of the ball, gave one ear to the music, the other to their partner; accompanied by inquisitive looks, now to their acquaintances for the purpose of reading approbation in their choice of their cavalier, now towards him, to ascertain if his attention was exclusively taken up with them.

The cornets and trumpets having sounded a finale in lengthened tones, put an end to the first dance. Dieterick von Kraft having remarked the arrival of his guest, came to lead him to his cousins, according to his promise. He whispered to him, that, having himself already engaged Marie for the next dance, he had asked Bertha's hand for him.

Both the girls had been prepared for the appearance of the interesting stranger; nevertheless, upon the recollection of the remark she had made upon him when he passed under her window, Marie's lively features were covered with a deep blush when he was introduced to them. She was unable to account to herself for the embarrassment his presence now produced on her, having only seen him once in her life, and never heard of him before. Whether it was that she had selected him as the most striking cavalier in the procession, or whether, among the young citizens of Ulm, she thought none were to be compared with him in appearance; such was the effect of this sudden attack on her feelings, one to which she had hitherto been a stranger, that she had no little difficulty in endeavouring to conceal her confusion from his observation.

Though Bertha was timid of betraying the secret of her heart before her cousin, she had no such feeling to struggle with in regard to Albert. Their mutual attachment was of long standing and deep-rooted. The first time she had seen him since their separation in Tübingen was in the ranks of the confederates, to whom her father was inveterately opposed. From that moment her peace of mind had vanished. Her soul was troubled with cruel doubts and misgivings; and all her hopes appeared for ever blasted. She nevertheless had sufficient command over herself, and for a moment the weight which oppressed her mind gave way to joy now that he stood before her; and she returned his salutation with the same endearing smile which she was wont to do in the days of their unclouded happiness. And had her cousin not been taken up in concealing her own state of embarrassment, she could not have failed to discover, in the tender glance of Bertha's eye, something which expressed more than common courtesy.

"I bring you Albert von Sturmfeder, my worthy guest," began the scribe to Marie, "who begs to have the pleasure of dancing with you."

"Were I not already engaged to my cousin Kraft for the next," said Marie to the young knight, with recovered self-possession, "I would, with pleasure; but Bertha is disengaged."

"If you are not engaged, may I have that pleasure?" said he, turning to Bertha.

"I am engaged to you," she answered. Then it was that Albert heard again, after so long an absence, that voice which had often called him by the most endearing name; and he dwelt on those eyes which still looked on him with undiminished fidelity.

The trumpets again sounded throughout the room. The second in command of the army of the League, Waldburg Truchses, having the precedence in the coming dance, came forth with his lady: the torch-bearers followed; the couples arranged themselves, and Albert also, taking Bertha's hand, placed himself in the ranks. Her eyes now no longer sought the ground, but were directed solely to him. But in the expression of her countenance, Albert could plainly perceive, there was something hanging on her mind indicative of mental suffering. Joy at meeting him again, which had but a moment before brightened up her features, was now succeeded by an expression of dejection, which he could in no wise account for. So much was he struck by the sudden change in her manner, that he was on the point of upbraiding her, and taxing her unjustly with an alteration of love towards him. Grieved at the pain he appeared to suffer, she gently begged him to wait a fitting moment, and then she would explain every thing. She looked cautiously behind her at Dieterick and Marie, who were the next couple to them, to see if they were near enough to overhear her conversation. Finding they were at some distance, she said, "Ah! Albert, what unlucky star has brought you into this army?"

"You were that star, Bertha," he replied: "I thought your father would be on the side of the League, and I am glad not to find myself mistaken. Can you blame me for having thrown aside the learned books, and taken to the profession of arms? No other inheritance has fallen to my lot than the sword of my father. I will put it to usury; and prove to your father, that he who loves his daughter is not unworthy of her."

"Oh, God! I trust you have not yet sworn allegiance to the League?" she exclaimed, interrupting him.

"Do not frighten yourself so, dearest; I have not yet fully bound myself to it, but I intend to do so in a day or two. Will you not allow your Albert to gain some little fame! What is it that makes you so anxious about me? Your father is old, and still he goes with us."

"Ah! my father, my father!" Bertha said, in a desponding tone, "he is indeed--but stop, Albert, stop, Marie notices us. But I must speak with you to-morrow--I must, should it cost me my happiness. Oh if I but knew how to manage it."

"But what is it that agitates you in this way, beloved?" asked Albert, to whom it was inexplicable how Bertha should only think of the danger that awaited him, instead of being overjoyed at this meeting. "The danger is not so great as you imagine," he whispered to her: "think only of the happiness of being together again, that I can press your hand, and that we can see each other face to face. Enjoy the present moment, and be cheerful."

"Cheerful? Oh, those times are gone by, Albert. Hear me, and be firm;--my father is opposed to the League." She said this in a low subdued tone.

"Good Heavens! what do you say?" cried the young man; and leant towards Bertha, as if he had not distinctly heard the ill-foreboding words. "Oh! tell me; is not your father at present in Ulm?"

The poor girl had thought herself strong enough to withstand the shock she felt at this moment, but it was too powerful; it deprived her of utterance, and she could scarcely contain her tears. She answered only by a slight pressure of her hand; and with downcast eyes went to seek Kraft, led by Albert, in order to gain a little time to combat the grief she experienced. The strong mind of this young maiden at last triumphed over the weakness of her nature; and she whispered to her lover, in a composed tone, "My father is Duke Ulerich's warmest friend; and so soon as war is declared, he will take me back to Lichtenstein."

The noise of the drums at this instant was deafening; the trumpets clanged in their fullest tones as they saluted Truchses, who how passed by the musicians; and, according to the custom of those days, threw them some pieces of silver, which caused the trumpets to redouble their deafening sounds.

The whispered conversation of our two lovers was overpowered by the confounding noise of the instruments; but their eyes had so much the more to say to each other in this apparent shipwreck of their hopes, so that they did not notice the observations, which were passed on them by the surrounding spectators, as being the handsomest couple in the room. Marie's ear was not shut to the passing remarks of the crowd. She was too kind-hearted to be envious of her cousin's praise, and consoled herself with the idea, that, were she in her place, beside the handsome young man, the couple would not be less attractive. But it was the animated conversation which Bertha kept up with her partner, that particularly attracted her attention. Her reserved cousin, who seldom or ever talked long with any man, now appeared to speak with even more earnestness than he did. The music and noise, however, hindered Marie from overhearing the subject of their conversation. This excited her curiosity to such a degree (a feeling- -perhaps, not without justice--attributed specially to young ladies), that she drew her own partner nearer to them, for the purpose of listening; but whether it was by accident or design, that the conversation either dropped or was kept up in a subdued tone, the nearer she approached, she could not catch a word of it.

Marie's interest in the young man increased with these obstacles to her curiosity. Her good cousin Kraft had never appeared so great a bore to her as now, for all the pretty sayings with which he endeavoured to fix her attention, were only so many hindrances to her observing the others more closely. She was therefore glad when the dance was over. She hoped the next would be more agreeable, with the young knight for her partner.

Albert came and engaged her, when she sprang with joy to the hand which he offered; but she deceived herself in finding him the agreeable partner she had anticipated. Indifferent, reserved, sunk in deep thought, giving short answers to her questions, it was too clear he was not the same person who had but a moment before conversed in so animated a manner with her cousin.

"Was this the courteous knight," thought Marie, "who had saluted them in so polite a manner, without ever having seen them before? Was it the same cheerful and merry person whom cousin Kraft had introduced? the same who had spoken with Bertha so earnestly? or could she--yes, it was too evident that Bertha had pleased him better than herself--perhaps, because she was the first to dance with him."

Marie had been little accustomed to see her reserved cousin preferred before her, which this apparent victory seemed to indicate. Her vanity was piqued, she felt herself estranged from Bertha, and conceived herself bound to exert her talents and winning arts to re-establish herself in her lost rights. She therefore, in her usual merry mood, carried on the conversation about the coming war, which she contrived to lengthen out till the end of the dance. "Well," said she, "and how many campaigns have you gone through, Albert von Sturmfeder?"

"This will be my first," he answered, abruptly, for he was annoyed that she kept up the conversation, as he wished so much to speak to Bertha again.

"Your first!" said Marie, in astonishment. "You surely want to deceive me, for I perceive a large scar on your forehead."

"I got that at the university," he replied.

"How? are you a scholar?" asked Marie, her curiosity still more excited. "Well, then, I suppose you have visited distant countries, Padua or Bologna, or perhaps even the heretics in Wittenberg?"

"Not so far as you think," said he, as he turned to Bertha: "I have never been further than Tübingen."

"In Tübingen?" cried Marie, surprised. This single word, like lightning, unravelled in a moment every thing in her mind which before had been obscure. A glance at Bertha, who stood before her with downcast eyes, her cheeks suffused with the blush of confusion, convinced her that, on that word, hung the key to a long list of inferences which had occupied her thoughts. It was now quite clear why the courteous knight saluted them; the cause of Bertha's tears could be no other, than that of finding Albert had joined the opposite party; the earnest conversation between them, and Sturmfeder's reserve to herself, were satisfactorily explained to her mind. There was no question of their having long known each other.

Indignation was the first feeling that ruffled Marie's breast. She blushed for herself, when she felt she had endeavoured to attract the attention of a young man whose heart was fully occupied by another object. Ill humour, on account of Bertha's secrecy, clouded her features. She sought excuse for her own conduct, and found it only in the duplicity of her cousin. If she had but acknowledged, she said to herself, the feeling which existed between her and the young knight, she never would have shown the interest she took in him; he would have been perfectly indifferent to her; she never would have experienced this painful confusion.

Marie did not deign to give the unhappy young man another look during the evening, and he was too much occupied with the painful sensations of his own mind, to be aware of her ill will towards him. He was also so unfortunate as to be scarcely able to say another word alone and unobserved to Bertha. The ball ended, and left him in doubt as to what her future fate, or the intentions of her father were likely to be. She seized, however, a favourable moment to whisper to him on the staircase, when she was going home, begging him to remain in the town on the morrow, in the hope of finding an opportunity to speak with him.

The two girls went home, both ill at ease with each other. Marie gave short, snappish answers to Bertha's questions, who, whether it was that she suspected what was passing in her cousin's mind, or whether she was overwhelmed by grief, became more melancholy and reserved than ever.

But when they entered their room, silent and cold towards each other, then it was that they both felt how painful was the interruption of their hitherto affectionate intercourse. Up to this eventful evening, they had always assisted each other in all those little services, which unite young girls in friendship. How different was it now? Marie had taken the silver pin out of her rich light hair, which fell in long ringlets over her beautiful neck. She attempted to put it up under her cap, but unaccustomed to arrange it without Bertha's help, and too proud to let her enemy, as she now called her cousin in her mind, notice her embarrassment, she threw it away in a corner, and seized a handkerchief to tie it up.

Bertha, unconscious of having offended her cousin, could not fail noticing her change of affection towards her, and felt acutely the apparent sting of her ruffled temper. She quietly picked up the cap, and came to render her cousin her usual assistance.

"Away with you, you false one!" said the angry Marie, as she pushed away the helping hand.

"Dearest Marie, have I deserved this of you?" said Bertha, gently, and with tenderness. "Oh, if you but knew how unhappy I am, you would not be so harsh with me."

"Unhappy, indeed!" loudly laughed the other, "unhappy! because the courteous knight only danced with you once, I suppose."

"You are very hard, Marie," replied Bertha; "you are angry with me, and will not even tell me the cause of your displeasure."

"Really! so you do not know how you have deceived me? but you cannot keep your duplicity a secret any longer, which has subjected me to scorn and confusion. I never could have thought you would have acted so ungenerously, so falsely by me!"

The wounded feeling of being out-done by her cousin, and as she thought, despised by Sturmfeder, was again awakened in Marie's mind; her tears flowed, she laid her heated forehead in her hand, and her rich locks fell over and hid her face.

Tears are the symptoms of gentle suffering, they say: Bertha had experienced it, and continued her conversation with confidence. "Marie! you have accused me of keeping a secret from you. I see you have discovered that, which I never could have divulged. Put yourself in my situation--ah! you yourself, cheerful and frank as you are, would never have confided to me your inmost secret. But I will conceal it no longer--you have guessed what my lips shunned to express. I love him! Yes, and my love is returned. This mutual feeling dates much further back than yesterday. Will you hear me? and I will tell you all."

Marie's tears still flowed on. She made no answer to Bertha's last question, who now related to her the way in which they became acquainted with each other in the house of her good aunt in Tübingen; how she liked him, long before he acknowledged his love of her; and narrated many endearing recollections of the past--the happy moments they had spent together, their oath of fidelity at their separation. "And now," she continued, with a painful smile, "he has been induced to join the League in this unhappy war, because we were in Ulm, thinking, very naturally, that my father was embarked in the same cause. He hopes to render himself worthy of me by the aid of his sword; for he is poor, very poor. Oh! Marie, you know my father--how good he is, but also how stern, when any thing runs counter to his opinion. Would he give his daughter to a man who has drawn his sword against Würtemberg? Certainly not. This is the cause of all the trouble and grief I suffer. Often have I wished to unburden my heart to you, but an uncontrollable feeling closed my lips. But now that you know the whole truth, can you still be angry with me? shall I lose my friend also, as well as my beloved?"

Poor Bertha could contain her tears no longer, and wept aloud. Marie, overpowered by the grief of her friend, embraced her cousin with the warm affection of a tender heart sympathising in her painful situation, and all feeling of enmity was in a moment extinguished in her breast.

"In a few days," said Bertha, after a short silence, "my father will quit Ulm, and I must accompany him. But I must see Albert again, if it were only for a quarter of an hour. Marie, your ingenuity can easily find us an opportunity; only for a very short quarter of an hour!"

"But you do not wish to make him desert the good cause?" asked Marie.

"I know not what you call the good cause," replied Bertha. "The Duke's cause is, perhaps, not less good than yours. You talk thus because you belong to the League. I am a Würtemberger, and my father is faithful to his Duke. But shall we girls decide upon the merits of the war? rather let us think of the means, whereby I may see him again."

Marie had listened with so much interest to the history of her cousin, that she quite forgot having ever entertained any ill-will towards her. Besides which, being naturally fond of any thing involved in mystery, she was glad of an opportunity, such as the present, to exercise her wits. She felt all the importance and honour of being a confidant, and consequently determined to spare no pains in serving the lovers in their critical position.

After a few moments' thought, she said, "I have it; we'll invite him at once into our garden."

"In the garden!" asked Bertha, fearful and incredulous; "and by whom?"

"His host, good cousin Dieterich himself shall bring him," answered Marie. "That's a good thought! and he shall not know anything of the plot; leave that alone to me."

Though Bertha was strong and determined in matters of importance, she trembled for the result of this rash step. But her bold and cheerful little cousin knew how to combat her scruples and fears. With renewed hope, then, in the success of their scheme for the morrow, and their hearts being restored again to their former mutual confidence, the girls embraced each other with tender affection, and retired to rest.

CHAPTER VII

As like a spirit of the air
She hangs upon his neck,
In falt'ring tones the lovely fair
At last essays to speak;
"And wilt thou, then, thy true love leave
For ever?"--thus the fair
Began, when, overcome by grief,
Her words are lost in air.

Schubart.

Albert was sitting in his room, in the forenoon of the day after the ball, thoughtful and dejected. He had paid a visit to his friend Breitenstein, from whom he heard little that was consoling to his hopes. A council of war had been assembled early in the morning, and war was irrevocably decided upon. Twelve pages were despatched through the Goecklinger gate to convey the declarations of defiance of the Duke of Bavaria, the nobility, and assembled states, to the Würtembergers at Blaubeuren. This news was speedily spread from mouth to mouth through the streets, and joy at the prospect of marching at last into the field, was visibly depicted on every countenance. To one alone was the announcement a terrible blow. Grief drove him from the circle of the joyous multitude, who adjourned to the wine shops, to celebrate, by loud carousal, the birthday of the war, and to cast lots for the booty of anticipated victory. Ah! his lot was already cast! A bloody field of battle was spread between him and his beloved; she was lost to him for a length of time, perhaps for ever.

Hurried steps ascending the staircase, roused him out of his melancholy mood. His friend the scribe put his head in at the door, crying out, "Good luck, my boy! the dance is about to commence in good earnest. Have you heard the news? war is announced, and our messengers have been despatched an hour ago, with the declaration to the enemy."

"I know that already," said his gloomy guest.

"Well, and does not your heart jump more freely? Have you also heard--no, you could not," continued Dieterich, as he approached him in confidence--"the Swiss have withdrawn their aid from the Duke."

"How? Have they deserted him?" replied Albert. "Well, then, I suppose that will put an end to the war."

"I would not be quite certain of that," said the scribe, doubtfully. "The Duke of Würtemberg is young and bold, and has many knights and followers at his command. He will not, indeed, run the risk of fighting a battle in the field, but many fortified castles and cities remain faithful to his cause. Höllenstein, defended by Stephen von Lichow, Göppingen, which Philip von Rechberg will not give up at the first shot, Schorndorf, Rothenberg, Arsperg, but, above all, Tübingen, which he has strongly fortified, still hold faithful to him. Many a one will bite the grass before your steed drinks of the water of the Neckar."

"Well, well!" he continued, perceiving this news did not cheer up his silent guest, "if this warlike message does not please you, you will, perhaps, lend a willing ear to a more peaceful commission. Tell me, have you not a cousin somewhere or other?"

"A cousin, yes; but why do you ask?"

"Only think! now I understand the confused conversation I had with Marie a little while ago. As I came out of the town hall, she winked to me from her window to come to her, when she desired me to bring my guest this afternoon into her garden on the Danube. Bertha, who knows your cousin very well, has something of importance to send to her, and hopes you will be so kind as to be the bearer of it. Such secrets and commissions generally consist in mere trifles. I would bet, it is nothing but a little model of a weaver's loom, or a pattern of fine wool, or some mysterious secret in the art of cooking; perhaps a few seeds of some rare flower, for Bertha is a great florist. However, if these girls pleased you yesterday, you will have no objection to accompany me to-day."

In the midst of his painful thoughts, on the hour of separation from his love, Albert could scarce refrain from laughing at the cunning ingenuity of the girls; he proffered his hand heartily to the welcome messenger, and prepared to follow his friend.

The garden was situated on the banks of the Danube, about two thousand paces below the bridge. It was not large, and bore the appearance of being kept with care and attention. The fruit trees were as yet not clothed with foliage, neither were the curiously formed flower beds ornamented with flowers; a long walk of yew trees skirting the bank of the river, and terminating in a large arbour, formed a pleasing picture by their bright green colour, and gave sufficient protection to a white neck and arm, against the piercing rays of a burning sun. The two girls, awaiting the arrival of the young men, were seated on a commodious stone bench in the arbour, and had an extended view, up and down the Danube, through apertures made in the side of it.

Bertha sat there in sorrowful thought, her arm resting on one of the apertures, and her head, weary from grief and weeping, supported on her hand. Her dark glossy hair threw out in strong relief her beautiful white complexion, which sorrow had rendered a deadly pale colour; sleepless nights had robbed her brilliant blue eye of its usual animation, and given to it a languishing--perhaps so much the more interesting--look of melancholy. Beside her sat the rosy Marie, fresh and plump, a perfect specimen of a merry heart. Her golden tresses, animated round face, bright hazel eyes, light and lively movements, were peculiarly striking when compared with the dark locks, oval careworn countenance, and thoughtful look of her dejected cousin.

Marie appeared to have summoned up her most agreeable mood, expressly for the purpose of consoling her cousin, or at least to dissipate her pain. She prattled about indifferent things--she laughed at and mimicked the gestures and peculiarities of many of their acquaintances--she tried a thousand little arts, with which nature had endowed her--but with little success; for only now and then a painful smile spread over Bertha's beautiful features.

As a last resource, she took to her lute, which stood in the corner. Bertha was an accomplished performer on this instrument, and Marie would not have been easily persuaded to play before so expert a mistress on any other occasion; but now, she hoped to be able to elicit a smile, at least, if it were only on account of her bad performance.

"What is Love, I'm ask'd to tell:

Fain we would his nature know;

You who've studied it so well,

Why he pains us, prithee show.

Joy it brings, if love be there;

If pain, of love 't is not the spell;--

Oh, then, I know the name that it should bear."

"Where did you get that old Swabian song?" asked Bertha, who had lent a willing ear to the music and words.

"It is pretty, is it not? but the remainder is still more so; would you like to hear it?" said Marie. "A music master, Hans Sacks, taught it me in Nürnberg. It is not his own composition, but Walther's, the bird-feeder, who lived and loved a good three hundred years ago. But listen:

"How I rightly may divine

Love's enigma, prithee say.

'Tis the charm of pow'r to join

Two hearts, where each must own its sway;

One heart avails not, each must share

Its influence: dear mistress mine,

Say, wilt thou share with me, thou lovely May?

"Well, though you have shared your love equally with the poor young man," said the playful Marie, "I pity you, from my heart, the painful burden of its weight. If such be its chains, cousin Kraft, who would willingly give me a portion of his, must wait awhile, and groan under the load of carrying the whole charge of it on his own shoulders. But I see you are again absorbed in thought," she added, "so I must sing you another of Walther's songs:

"I know not what has chanced, I ween

My sight was never on this wise.

Since in my heart she first was seen,

I see her still without my eyes.

What miracle is this? What pow'r

Enables me, without the aid of sight,

To see her every day and every hour?

"Would you then learn the organs and the art,

By which I see to earth's extremest zone?

They are the thoughts I nourish in my heart;

They penetrate through walls of brick and stone;

And, should these watchers fail, her presence still

Is evermore, as 't were, before my eyes,

Seen by my heart, my spirit, and my will."

Bertha praised the song of Walther the birdfeeder, as being consolatory in separation. Marie agreed with her. "I have one more verse," she added, smiling:

"Though she wander'd in Swabia, far and wide,

Through castles and walls her course he espied.

O'er the Alb unto Lichtenstein had she gone,

His eyes would have follow'd through rock and stone."

Marie was going on with her singing, when the garden door opened. Footsteps were heard in the walk, and the girls rose to receive their expected visitants.

"Albert von Sturmfeder," began Marie, after the usual salutations were over, "you will pardon me for having ventured to invite you into my father's garden; but, as my cousin, Bertha wishes to give you some commissions, for her friend, I have taken the liberty." She then turned to Dieterich von Kraft, and said, "We will not interrupt their conversation; so, come and talk over the ball of last evening." Upon which she took the hand of her cousin, and led him away down the yew-tree walk.

Albert seated himself beside Bertha, who laid her head on his breast, and wept bitterly. His most soothing words were unable to calm her grief. "Bertha," he said, "you were always so stout-hearted; how can you thus give up all hope of a happier destiny?"

"Hope?" she replied, sorrowfully: "to our hope, to our happiness, there is an eternal end."

"But hearken, dearest," replied Albert, who, to cheer up her drooping spirit, endeavoured to inspire her with courage; "let not this slight interruption to our hopes throw its chilling influence over the purity of our love, as if it were to extinguish altogether its bright flame. All will be well yet. Rather let us put our trust in God, and wait his almighty will; for I never can believe that He who knows the secret of our hearts, and has joined them together by the indissoluble tie of faithful attachment, will not, in his own way, make all things to work for our good." These consoling words produced a smile upon her countenance; but it pourtrayed the character of despondency rather than of hope.

She replied, after a short silence, "Listen to me with attention, Albert. I must acquaint you with a profound secret, upon which hangs my father's life. He is as bitter an enemy to the League, as he is the firm friend of the Duke. He is not come here solely for the purpose of fetching his daughter home; no, he is using his utmost endeavour to find out the plans of the enemy, and with money and address to spread distrust and confusion among them. Do you suppose, then, that such a determined adversary to the League, would ever consent to give his daughter to a man who seeks to raise himself by our destruction? to one who has attached himself to a party, whose object is not justice, but plunder?"

"Your zeal, Bertha, for the Duke's cause, carries you too far," the young man interrupted her; "you ought to know that many an honourable man serves in our army."

"And even if this were the case," she replied, with animation, "still they are deceived and led away, as you yourself also are."

"How are you so certain of that?" answered Albert, who, though he suspected she was somewhat right, blushed to find the party he had espoused should be so vilified by his beloved: "might not your father be also equally blinded and deceived? How can he serve with such zeal the cause of that proud ambitious Duke, who murders his nobility, treads his citizens in the dust, squanders the industry of the land in riotous living, and allows his peasantry to starve with hunger?"

"Yes, his enemies represent him in this light," she replied; "this army speaks of him in the same terms; but ask those below, on the banks of the Neckar, if they do not love their hereditary Prince, though his hand may lay heavy on them at times? Ask those faithful men who have rallied around him, whether they are not willing and ready, to shed their blood for the grand-child of Eberhard, rather than allow that proud Duke of Bavaria, that rapacious nobility, those needy townsfolk to tread their land?"

Albert was thoughtfully silent for a time. "But," he asked, "how can his warmest supporters exculpate him from the murder of Hutten?"

"You are very ready to talk of your honour," Bertha answered, "and will not suffer the Duke to defend his own. Hutten did not fall by treachery, as his partisans have given out to the world, but in honourable fight, in which the Duke's life was equally exposed. I do not wish to excuse him for all his actions, but it is but just to remember, that a young man, like him, surrounded by evil advisers, has not the power always to act wisely. But he is really good, and if you knew how mild and humane he can be!"

Albert was piqued that Bertha should speak in such glowing terms of the Duke's virtues, and jealousy for a moment took possession of his soul and ruffled his temper. He replied with a sarcastic and malignant smile, "A little more, and you would call him the handsome Duke; who, for aught I know, if he were aware what an advocate he had in you, might think it worth his trouble to ingratiate himself in your heart, and supplant poor Albert."

"I really did not think you capable of such petty jealousy," Bertha answered, and turned away, with a tear of indignation starting into her eye, from a feeling of wounded dignity. "Cannot you believe it possible for the heart of a young girl to beat warm in the cause of her country?"

"Do not be angry with me," Albert implored, and felt ashamed at the injustice of his remark; "really, I meant it in joke."

"Can you indulge in a joke at this moment, when our life's happiness is at stake! My father leaves Ulm to-morrow, war being declared. It will be long, perhaps very long, before we see each other again--and can you joke now? Ah! could you have witnessed the many nights I have prayed God, with burning tears, to incline your heart to our side, to defend us from the misery and pain of being separated for ever, you certainly would not have trifled so cruelly with my feelings."

"He has not inclined it to happiness," said Albert, looking about him, agitated.

"And is it still impossible," said Bertha, as she took his hand, with the most expressive tenderness, "is it still impossible? Come along with us, Albert; think how happy my father would be to present a young warrior to his Duke? He has often said that one gallant sword is of great price in such times; you will be highly esteemed by him, you will fight by his side, my heart will not then be torn or divided between the conflicting parties, my prayers for prosperity and victory, will not wander in doubtful agitation between the two armies."

"Stop, for heaven's sake, stop!" cried the young man, and covered his eyes with his hands; for the conquest of conviction beamed from her looks, the power of truth was encamped on her sweet lips. "Do you wish to persuade me to become a deserter? I entered but yesterday with the army, war is this day declared, and shall I ride over to the Duke to-morrow? Is my honour so indifferent to you?"

"Honour!" Bertha said, "is such honour dearer to you than your love? How different were his words, when Albert swore eternal fidelity! Well, then, go and be happier with them than with me! But when the Duke of Bavaria creates you a knight on the field of battle, for carrying desolation through our fields, when he decorates the neck of Albert von Sturmfeder with the chain of honour, for having been the foremost in crushing Würtemberg's citizens, may the joy of your thoughts not be troubled then, by having broken the heart of one so true to you--of one who loved you so tenderly!"

"Dearest," answered Albert, whose breast was torn by conflicting feelings, "grief does not permit you, to perceive how unjust you are. But be it so; you conceive that I prefer the glory, which is leading me onwards, to making a sacrifice of it to love. But hear me. I dare not come over to your side. I will give in my resignation to the League. Let those fight and conquer who will; my dream of glory is thus at an end."

Bertha sent a look of gratitude to heaven for this avowal, and rewarded the words of the young man by a sweet acknowledgment. "Oh! believe me," she said, "I know how much this sacrifice must cost you. But do not let me see you look so sad, when you cast your eyes at your sword. The sun will still shine upon our happiness one of these days. I can now bid you farewell with consolation in my heart, for, whichever way the war may end, you can appear unconstrained before my father, who will rejoice to hear of your having made the heavy sacrifice for my sake."

Marie now gave her friends the signal that she was unable to retain the clerk of the council any longer, which roused them from their absorbing conversation. Bertha quickly composed herself, and with Albert quitted the arbour.

"Cousin Kraft wishes to depart," said Marie, "and requires his friend to accompany him."

"I must indeed go with you, if I wish to find my way home," replied the young man, who was too well acquainted with the received customs of his day, not to be aware that he, a stranger, could not remain with the young ladies, without their cousin being of the party, precious as the last moments, before a long separation from his love, might be to him.

They proceeded down the garden, the silence only broken by Dieterick, who expressed his sorrow, in very courteous terms, at the prospect of his cousin leaving Ulm so soon as the morrow. But Marie, thinking she discovered something in the look of Albert's eye, which expressed a wish not yet satisfied, and to the accomplishment of which witnesses might be unwelcome, drew cousin Kraft on one side, and questioned him so closely upon a plant, whose leaves were just bursting, that he had not time to observe what was going on behind his back.

Albert took immediate advantage of the happy moment, and pressed Bertha once more to his heart. The noise occasioned by her heavy silken dress, and the clattering of his sword, drew the scribe's attention from his botanical observations; he looked around, and oh, wonder! he saw his very reserved cousin in the arms of his guest.

"That was a salute for the dear cousin in Franconia, I suppose?" he remarked, after he had recovered from his surprise.

"No, Mr. Secretary," answered Albert, with firmness, "it was a salute for me alone, and from her whom I hope one day to call my own. Have you anything to say against it, my friend?"

"God forbid! I congratulate you with all my heart," answered Dieterick, somewhat subdued by the determined look of the young man. "But, by the powers, I call that an entire case of *veni, vidi, vici.* I have been trying my luck with the beauty for more than a quarter of a year, and I can scarcely boast of one kind look from her during the whole time."

"Forgive the joke, cousin, which we have played upon you," said Marie; "be reasonable, and let me explain the matter." She then gave him to understand, why Albert and he had been invited into the garden, and begged him to be silent upon the subject before Bertha's father. He was softened into compliance by the kind look of Marie, upon condition, that she would submit also to the same ordeal her cousin had just undergone.

Marie gently repelled his unmannerly request, and, by way of teazing him, asked him again at the garden door the natural history of a violet, the first of the season. He was kind enough to give her a long and learned dissertation upon the subject, without allowing himself to be interrupted by the noise of a rustling silk dress or clattering sword. A grateful look from Bertha, a friendly shake of the hand from Marie, rewarded him at parting; and long floated the veils of the pretty cousins over the garden hedge, as their eyes followed the path of the young men.

CHAPTER VIII

"In the still cloister's solitary grove,
A maiden walk'd, and thought upon her love;
The virgin moon, as if in mockery,
Shed forth her splendour on her misery,
And the bright lustre of the beams that fell
Lit up the tears that coursed her cheek so pale."

L. Uhland.

During the following days, Ulm resembled a large camp. Instead of the peaceable peasant, the busy citizens, passing, as in ordinary times, through the streets with sober tranquil step to their several avocations, were now to be seen strange figures, with helmets and caps of iron, carrying lances, cross bows and fire-arms. In lieu of statesmen in their plain black dresses, proud knights clad in steel, and wearing helmets adorned with waving plumes, strode about the squares and market places, accompanied by numerous bands of followers. Still more animated was this warlike scene without the gates of the town. In an open space on the banks of the Danube, Sickingen was exercising his cavalry, whilst, in a large flax-field towards the village of Soeflingen, Fronsberg was occupied in manœuvring his infantry.

One fine morning, about three or four days after Bertha von Lichtenstein had left Ulm with her father, an immense concourse of people were assembled in the above field, to witness Fronsberg's infantry going through their evolutions. They looked upon this man, whose military reputation had long preceded him, with not less interest than we should, perhaps, were we to see the imperial or royal son of Mars performing the part of a field marshal. The state of an army depends in great measure on the character and experience of its leader; and we are more or less interested in the accounts given in history, or the public papers, of battles, according to the renown of the general who fought them. Such might have been the motive, which induced the inhabitants of Ulm on that morning to quit their narrow streets, to see the celebrated man of the day, employed in his military occupations. The dexterity with which he kept his men in solid masses, who before were accustomed to fight in scattered bodies; the celerity with which they moved on all sides at his word, or closed together, producing a formidable array of pikes and fire-arms; his powerful voice, which even rose above the noise of the drums, and his noble warlike figure, formed a sight so novel and attractive, that even the citizen most fond of his ease, was tempted to pass a long forenoon on foot, to enjoy the spectacle.

The general appeared, on this morning, more cheerful and friendly than usual. The warm interest which the good people of Ulm took in him, and which was visibly depicted on every countenance, perhaps produced this feeling; or perhaps he felt himself happier when engaged in military exercises, than confined to the cold narrow streets. Whatever might have been the cause, the crowd took his gay mood in such good part, that each individual thought himself specially noticed and saluted by him as he passed, and the cheer, "A gallant man, a brave knight!" followed his path.

But there was a certain spot, to which his attention appeared to be more particularly drawn; for, every time he rode by it, he was observed to salute some one, either with his sword or hand, and to nod familiarly. Those in the rear of the spectators stood upon tiptoes to find out the object of his friendly nod, those in front looked inquisitively at each other, wondering who the favoured one could be, as none of the assembled citizens thought themselves worthy of the honor. When Fronsberg passed the same spot again, and repeated his salutation, an hundred heads were on the stretch to satisfy their curiosity, and they discovered that it was directed to a tall slim young man, who stood in the front rank of the spectators. His jacket of fine cloth, slashed with silk, the high feather in his cap playing in the morning breeze, his long sword and his scarf or sash, distinguished him as a man of quality from among his surrounding neighbours, who were less adorned than he was, and whose diminutive stature and broad faces did not set them off to the best advantage beside him.

The good townsfolk felt hurt that the young man did not appear flattered by the high favour conferred on him in their very presence. His attitude, also, standing there as he did, with sunken head, and his arms folded across his breast, they thought did not betoken good breeding, so especially noticed as he was by an old warrior. Besides which, the salutation of the general seemed to spread confusion over his countenance, for he returned it by a slight inclination of the head only, and followed it with a gloomy though friendly look.

"That gentleman must be a strange fellow," said the chief of the Ulm weavers to his neighbour, a sturdy armourer; "I would give my Sunday jacket for such a salute from Fronsberg; but he scarcely notices it. Would it not be the inquiry of the whole town, what has Fronsberg done to Master Köhler, that he did not return his salute, for they were lately like two brothers? 'Oh! they are long acquainted,' would be the answer, 'they knew each other from their youth up.' But it vexes me much, that so sensible and superior a man should salute such an apparent coxcomb."

The armourer, a little old fellow, nodded assent to his friend's remark. "May God punish me, but you are right, Master Köhler. There are many other people here, whom he might have noticed. The burgomaster is on the ground, and my godfather Hans von Besserer, who lives in the corner house, stands among the crowd also,--both as good as that youngster! If I were his master, I would soon teach him to bend his head, though he looks to me, as if it would require an emperor to make him do so. He must be a man of some consequence, for the secretary to the council, my neighbour in town, who is otherwise an enemy to receiving guests, has given him a lodging in his own house."

"Kraft?" asked the weaver, astonished; "but stop, there may be something in it. He must be a young nobleman, or, likely enough, the son of the burgomaster of Cologne, who intends to join the army also. Is that not old John, Kraft's servant, standing there?"

"Yes, that's him," said the armourer, whose curiosity was excited by the weaver's inquiry: "it is him; and I will stand confessor to him, in spite of the provost of Elchingen." But though the space between the two citizens and Kraft's servant was small, the smith could not accost him, on account of the density of the crowd. The important bearing, however, of the chief of the weavers among his brother tradesmen, for he was rich, and respected in the town, enabled him to force his way, and he succeeded in getting possession of John, and forthwith conducted him to the armourer. Old John, when questioned, could not give them much information on the subject of their inquiry; all he could say was, that his master's guest was a Herr von Sturmfeder, and that he could not have come from any great distance, as he had only one horse, and no servant. "But my master will get the worst of it," he said, "for our old Sabina is as furious as a dragon, because he has destroyed the economy of the house by inviting a stranger, booted and spurred, without consulting her."

"No offence," interrupted the chief of the weavers, "but your master, John, is a fool! I would have thrown that old witch--God forgive me!--long ago out of the window. The gentleman has already arrived at years of discretion, and why does he allow himself to be treated as if he were still in swaddling clothes?"

"You have spoken well, Master Köhler," answered the old servant, "but you don't understand matters properly. Throw her into the street, indeed! who would take care of the house, then, I should like to know?"

"Who," cried the inflamed weaver, "who? he should take a wife, a housekeeper, as other Christians and citizens do. Why does he remain a bachelor, and run after all the young girls in the town? Did I not catch him, not long ago, saying pretty things to our Katharine? I should like to have thrown my looms, beams and all, at his worship's head; but when I recollected, that his good mother had many a good piece of linen wove by me, I was obliged to take off my cap, and say, 'An humble good evening, and has your honour any commands?' May the----"

"Upon my word," said John, with a displeased look, "I have always thought that a gentleman, like my master, the secretary to the grand council of state, might exchange a word in all honour with your daughter, without the wicked world----"

"Really! exchange a word! and after vesper bell in March! He will not marry her, nevertheless; and do you suppose the reputation of my daughter must not be kept as clean as the white cravat of your master? I should like to know that!" Master Köhler's voice during this conversation was raised to so high a pitch as to draw the attention of the bystanders, and having grasped Old John by the collar, there was no saying what might have been the consequences, had not the master smith dragged the querulous couple away by force, and separated them. He thereby quelled the dispute, but he could not stop the report, which was speedily circulated through the whole town, that Old John, having an intrigue in his old age with Master Köhler's young daughter, had been brought to an account by her angry father, in the open field.

The manœuvres of the infantry were by this time at an end, the crowd separated, and the young man, who had been the original cause of the foregoing conversation, was observed to bend his way also towards the town. His step was slow, and undecided; his face looked paler than usual, his eyes sought the ground, or wandered occasionally, with an expression of silent grief, towards the distant blue mountains, the boundaries of Würtemberg. Albert von Sturmfeder had never felt so unhappy as in these moments. Bertha had left Ulm with her father; she had made him swear again to be faithful to his promise, an act which he unavailingly felt to create a lurking regret in his breast. It had cost him no small struggle at the time, to consent to her wishes, but the overwhelming pain at parting from her, and the grief exhibited by the beloved girl, had mastered every feeling but that of desire to soothe the agony of her mind. His position was now one of extreme difficulty, when he calmly considered his future plans. To crush in the bud all those golden dreams and bright hopes of glory and honour, with which he thought to render himself worthy the hand of the daughter of Lichtenstein, was nothing, he felt, compared with the disgrace and contempt, which he must expect to meet at the hands of men, whose esteem was dear to him, for having deserted their colours, at a moment when the struggle was about to commence. How could he give a reason, or find words sufficiently convincing, to justify his conduct, before that gallant old friend of his father, Breitenstein? How could he appear before the noble Fronsberg? Ah, that friendly salute, with which he appeared to encourage the son of his brave companion in arms, produced a thousand torments. His father had fallen by his side, and he had heard him, in his dying moments, bequeath to his orphan child the renown of his name and a brilliant example, as his sole inheritance. Before this man, who, mindful of his father's bequest, had kindly opened to him a path which would lead to the accomplishment of his parent's wishes, he must now appear in very doubtful light.

Troubled with these gloomy forebodings, he had slowly approached the gate of the town, when he was suddenly seized by the arm, and turning around, a man, to appearance a peasant, stood before him.

"What is your business with me?" asked Albert, rather angrily, annoyed at being disturbed in his musing.

"My answer will depend upon whether you are the person I am looking for," answered the man. "Tell me, what belongs to *Licht* and *Sturm*?"

Albert was astonished at this singular question, and observed him more closely. He was not very tall, but strongly built, broad-chested, and of mean appearance. His face, much tanned by the sun, might have passed as plain and insignificant to a superficial observer, but, upon a narrower inspection, there was a certain expression about the eyes and mouth which, in addition to cunning and acuteness, bespoke daring and audacity. His hair and beard were dark yellow, and smooth; he carried a long dagger or knife in his leathern girdle; in one hand he held an axe, in the other a low round leathern cap, such as the Swabian peasant of the present day wears.

Whilst Albert made these hasty observations, he narrowly watched the expression of his features.

"Perhaps you did not thoroughly understand me, sir knight," continued the other, after a short silence; "so I will explain myself more fully. Let me ask, what should be added to *Sturm* and *Licht*, to form two noble names?"

"*Feder* and *stein*," answered the young man, to whom it was immediately clear, what was to be understood by the question; "but what is your business?"

"So you are Albert von Sturmfeder?" said the other; "and I come from Bertha von----"

"For heaven's sake be silent, friend; mention no names," said Albert; "tell me quickly, have you got any thing for me?"

"A note, sir," said the peasant; when, unbuckling a broad black leather band, wound under his knee, he produced a small strip of parchment.

Albert took the parchment with hasty joy; there were a few words written on it with black shining ink. It appeared to have cost some trouble to the writer, and proved that the young ladies of 1519 were not so ready with their pen, to express their tender feelings, as those of the present day, when every village beauty can write an epistle to her swain as long as her garter. The chronicle whence we have taken this history, has happily preserved every word of the confused traces on the parchment, which Albert's greedy eye now speedily deciphered as follows:

"Remember your oath--fly bytimes. God conduct thee. Your Bertha---- to eternity."

These few words expressed a pious, tender feeling, dictated by a loving heart. No wonder then that Albert was for some moments lost in a state of joyous intoxication. He sent a look of gratitude toward the distant blue mountains in the direction of Lichtenstein, and thanked his love for the consolation these lines afforded him, for truly, never had he stood so much in need of comfort, as at this moment. He was now convinced, that a being, the dearest that existed in the world to him, had not forsaken him. His heart resumed its usual cheerfulness, he proffered his hand to the trusty messenger, thanked him cordially, and asked him how he came by the strip of parchment.

"Did not I know," he answered, "that that little scrap of paper contained no evil enchantment, for the young lady smiled most kindly as she pressed it into my rough hand! I came to Blaubeuren last Wednesday, where our army is encamped. There is a magnificent high altar in the convent church there, over which the history of my patron, John the Baptist, is represented. About seven years ago, when I was in great distress of mind, and upon the point of suffering an ignominious death, I made a vow, to perform a pilgrimage to the spot every year about this time. I have never neglected this duty, having been saved from the hangman's hand, by a miracle performed by my saint. When I have finished my prayers, I always go to the abbot to present my offering of a couple of fine geese or a lamb, or any thing else he may prefer. But, sir, you will be tired with my gossip."

"No, no,--go on," said Albert; "come, sit down on that bench, beside me."

"That would not be proper," answered the messenger; "for a common peasant to place himself beside a gentleman, whom the general took such notice of before all the people this morning, would be out of all character: I would rather stand, with your permission." Albert seated himself on the stone bench by the road side, and the countryman, leaning on his axe, went on with his story. "I had little inclination to prosecute my pilgrimage in these unsettled times, but it is said, an unfulfilled oath is displeasing to the Almighty; so I was obliged to perform my vow. This year, when I rose from my prayer, and, as usual, was going to present my offering to the abbot, one of the priests told me, I could not go to his reverence this time, because many nobles and knights were waiting on him; but I insisted on it, for I knew the abbot to be a kind benevolent man, and he would have been displeased, had I gone away without seeing him. Should you ever visit the convent, don't forget to notice a long and narrow staircase leading from the high altar to the dormitory, through a thick wall, which separates it from the church. There it was that the lady met me. She approached me, a delicate-formed female, descending the stairs, covered with a long veil, with breviary and rosary in her hands. I pressed myself close to the wall, to allow her to pass, but she stood still, and said, 'Well, Hans, whither are you going?'"

"But how did the lady know you?" Albert interrupted him.

"My sister is her nurse, and----"

"How, is old Rosel your sister?" said the young man.

"Do you know her also?" said the messenger, "only think! but let me proceed. I was very happy to see her again, for I visited my sister often in Lichtenstein, and I have known the young lady, ever since she was taught to walk with the help of her father's sword belt. I should scarcely have known her again, she is grown so much, but her rosy cheeks have disappeared, like the snow on the first day of May. I don't know how it was, but I was so much struck by her looks, that I could not help asking her if any thing was the matter with her, and whether I could render her any assistance. She thought for a moment, and then said, 'Yes, Hans, if you can be discreet you may indeed render me a very great service!' I promised, and she appointed a meeting after vespers."

"But how is it, that she is in the convent?" Albert asked; "for formerly no female foot dared cross its threshold."

"The abbot is a friend of her father's, and as there are so many people in Blaubeuren at present, she is in greater safety in the convent than in the town, where strange things come to pass. After vespers, therefore, when all was quiet, I stole softly into the cloister, and met her. I cheered her sunken spirits, as well as we peasants know how to do, when she gave me that strip of parchment, and bid me find you out."

"I thank you heartily, good Hans," said Albert; "but is that all she charged you with?"

"No," answered the messenger; "she moreover commissioned me to tell you, by word of mouth, to be upon your guard, for there was a plot laid against you."

"Against me?" said Albert; "you must have misunderstood her. Who, and what can any one have to say about me?"

"Ah, there you ask me more than I can answer," replied the other; "but, if I dare guess, I believe the League has an eye upon you. The lady added also, that her father had spoken about it. I saw Fronsberg nod to you to-day, and honour you like the Emperor's son, to the astonishment of every one present. Believe me, there is something in the wind, when such a man beckons in so friendly a manner to another."

Albert was surprised at the plain remark of the simple countryman. He recollected, however, that Bertha's father, having pryed deeply into the secrets of the leaders of the League, might have heard something, which more immediately concerned him; but, whichever way he turned his thoughts, he could discover no ground upon which Bertha's mysterious warning could be founded. His mind was torn with doubt and conjecture; and he abruptly asked the messenger, how he had found him out so soon?

"Without Fronsberg's aid, it had not been such an easy matter," said he: "I was desired to inquire for you at Dieterick von Kraft's house. But as I was entering the gate of the town, I saw a large crowd of people in the field. I thought half an hour would make no great difference, so I joined the spectators to see the infantry exercise. Really, Fronsberg has done wonders. Well; it struck me I heard your name mentioned. I looked round, and saw three old men talking about you, and pointing to you. I noticed your figure, and followed your steps; but not certain if I was quite right, I put the enigma of Sturm and Licht to you."

"You have acted cleverly," said Albert, smiling; "but come to my house, and get something to eat. When do you go home again?"

Hans considered a moment; at last, he said, with a cunning smile on his mouth, "No offence, sir; but I have pledged myself to the young lady, not to quit you before you have taken your leave of the League."

"And then?" asked Albert.

"And then I go direct to Lichtenstein, to give her good news from you. How she longs to hear the happy tidings! She stands on the rock of the garden every day, and all day long, to see whether old Hans is coming."

"She shall soon have that pleasure," answered Albert; "I will be off to-morrow, if possible; and will write to her in the mean time."

"But be cautious what you do," said Hans; "the strip of parchment must not be longer than the one I brought you, for I must conceal it also under my knee-band. We cannot be too careful in these times; and no one will look for it there."

"Let it be so, then," answered Albert, as he rose from his seat. "And now adieu for the present; come to me at noon at Dieterick von Kraft's house, it is not far from the cathedral, and any one will shew it you. If they ask you where you come from, say you are a countryman of mine from Franconia, because the Ulmers are not well affected towards the Würtembergers."

"Don't be afraid, sir; you will not have any fault to find with me," replied Hans, as he parted from Albert. He looked back at the slim young man, and thought his sister's foster child, had made no bad choice in the object of her love.

CHAPTER IX

"The world and all I'd sacrifice for thee;
And do it cheerfully--but only flee."

SCHILLER.

Albert felt some uneasiness, at first, as to how his new acquaintance might behave in Kraft's house. It was not without reason, that he feared he might betray himself by his dialect or inconsiderate explanations, which would put him in an awkward position; for, though it was his firm resolution to quit the service of the League in a few days, still he did not wish it to be suspected that he was in correspondence with Würtemberg. Neither could he nor would he betray the secret of Bertha having sent a messenger to him, should he be unfortunately discovered. He thought of turning back, looking for the man, and begging him to leave the town as soon as possible; but when he recollected that, he must have long since left the place where they had held their conversation, and that he might in the mean time have arrived at the house, it appeared to him more advisable to hasten home to put Hans on his guard, and warn him against committing an indiscretion.

There was, however, something so peculiar in the sharp eye and the bold cunning countenance of the man, which gave him reason to hope, that Bertha, in the hasty choice she had made of the means of communicating with him, would not have confided her message to uncertain hands.

Albert had scarcely entered Kraft's house, when, at noon, a countryman from Franconia was announced; and the messenger of his love was shewn in. Can this man now before me be the same who left me but a few moments ago, thought Albert, surprised at his appearance, with his back bent nearly double, his arms hanging lifeless by his body, his eyes devoid of all animation? He could scarcely believe his eyes and ears, when he addressed Kraft, who saluted him in pure Franconian dialect, and answered his many questions with the volubility of a native of that country. Albert with difficulty repressed a smile at the strange metamorphosis of his new acquaintance; and was tempted to believe in the supernatural stories he had heard in his childhood, which described kind magicians, or gracious fairies, devoting themselves under all sorts of forms to the service of true lovers, and carrying them safely through the wiles of fate.

The charm was soon dispelled, when Albert and the messenger were left alone in the room; and the Swabian peasant had assured him of his being the same person. But Albert could not conceal his astonishment at the part he had acted so well.

"I hope you will not think less honourably of me," said the countryman; "we are often put to our wits to get on in the world: such arts hurt no one, but assist him who knows how to practise them."

Albert assured him of his confidence, when the messenger urgently pressed him to think of his immediate departure; and not to forget how ardently the lady longed to hear the news of it. He added, that he dared not return home, before he could bring her the positive intelligence of his having quitted Ulm.

Albert said, he would only wait until the army of the League had marched, and then return home.

"Oh! then you will not have to remain much longer," said the messenger, "for, if they do not march to-morrow, they will do so the day after, as the heart of the country is open before them. I know I can trust you, sir, therefore I tell you this."

"Is it true then, that the Swiss have deserted the Duke; and that he will not fight a battle in the field?" asked Albert.

The peasant threw a searching look around the room, carefully opened the door, to assure himself that no one was listening in the neighbourhood, and said,

"Sir, I was present at a scene, which I shall never forget, if I live ninety years. On my way hither, I met large bodies of Swiss on the Alb, going homewards, recalled by their councils and magistrates. But there were still eight thousand men at Blaubeuren, all good Würtembergers, and not a stranger among them."

"And the Duke," Albert interrupted him, "where was he?"

"The Duke treated with the Swiss for the last time at Kirchheim; but they withdrew from him, because he could not pay them. He then came to Blaubeuren, where his infantry was encamped. Yesterday morning it was made known by beat of drum, that all the people should assemble on the field of the convent by nine o'clock. The assembly was numerous; and but one feeling ran through the whole. Look ye, sir, Duke Ulerich is a severe master; and does not understand the manner of winning over the peasantry. Taxes are oppressive--the injury done to our fields by hunting is ruinous and galling--and the court squanders what is taken from us;--but when such a master, though tyrant he be, is in misfortune, it is quite a different thing. The only feeling now among us is, that he is our legitimate Duke; and, though unfortunate, he is a brave man, whom his enemies would drive from his country. A whisper was no sooner circulated that he wished to fight a battle, than each man grasped his sword firmer, shook his spear fiercely, and vociferated loud curses on the League. The Duke then came forward----"

"Did you see him? do you know him?" said Albert, with impatient curiosity, "Oh! tell me, what is his appearance?"

"Do I know him?" replied the messenger, with a peculiar smile, "truly, I saw him at a time when the sight of me was not welcome to him. He is still a young man, about two and thirty years old. His person is stately and powerful, and it is easy to perceive that he is well skilled in the use of arms. His eyes sparkle like fire," he added, "and few there are who can withstand his piercing glance, or penetrate his thoughts. The Duke stepped into the circle which the armed multitude had formed, and the stillness of death reigned among them. He said, with an audible, firm voice, that, seeing himself deserted by his allies, he knew not where to look for help. Betrayed by those upon whose aid he had relied,--he was become the sport of his enemies,--for, without the Swiss, he dare not risk a battle. An hoary-headed old man then came forward, and said: 'Duke, do you give up all hope before you have tried the strength of our arms? Look, sir, every man of us is ready to bleed for you; I have brought my four boys, each with his spear and knife, and so have many thousands besides. Are you tired of your country, that you disdain our assistance?' These simple but patriotic words touched the Duke's heart; he wiped the tears from his eyes, and gave the old man his hand. 'I don't doubt your courage,' said he, with a loud voice, 'but we are too few,--death, not victory, will be our fate. Go to your homes, my good faithful people, and there remain true to me. I must fly my country, and wander about with bitter misery for my portion; but, with God's assistance, I hope soon to return.' So spake the Duke; our people wept, and, grinding their teeth in anger against his enemies, withdrew in sorrow and despondency."

"And the Duke, what became of him?" asked Albert.

"He rode away from Blaubeuren, it is not known whither. The knights occupy his castles, to defend them, until he can procure succour."

The appearance of old John, the servant, interrupted the messenger, and announced that Albert was ordered to attend the council of war, which was to be held at Fronsberg's quarters at two o'clock. The young man was not a little astonished at this summons. What could they want with him at the council of war, of all places? His conscience acquitted him, indeed, of having given rise to any suspicion of his intentions, but he was fearful lest his friend Fronsberg might have proposed his being employed on some service which would compromise his promise to Bertha, and from which it might be difficult for him to excuse himself honourably--these were the thoughts which flew through his mind.

"Take care of yourself, sir," said the messenger, as soon as old John had left the room, "and think of the promise you gave the young lady. Above all, don't forget what she said to you, namely, to be on your guard against a plot. Allow me to remain in your house as your servant; I can look after your horse, and am ready for any other service you may require."

The offer of the faithful man was accepted with thanks by his new master, and Hans entered at once into his service, by assisting him to put on his sword, and arranging his cap properly. He again reminded him of his oath, and warned him of the plot, on the threshold of the door, as Albert left his abode.

Albert proceeded towards the house pointed out to him, meditating upon the incomprehensible summons to the council of war, and the peculiarly striking warning sent to him by Bertha. When he arrived there, a broad winding staircase was pointed out to him, at the top of which, in the first room on the right, he would find the military commanders assembled. But he was not permitted immediate entrance into this sanctuary, for, just as he was on the point of opening the door, a grey-bearded soldier, asking his business, gave him to understand that he would have to wait at least half an hour before he obtained an audience, and, taking the young man by the hand, led him through a narrow passage into a small room, there to exercise his patience awhile.

Whoever has danced attendance, under the excitement of anxious expectation, in an anteroom, may well imagine the torment Albert experienced during that hour of solitary meditation. His heart beat impatiently to learn the result of his present unexpected position, his mind was on the stretch, and when he heard a distant door creak on its hinges, or footsteps in the passage, or when indistinct voices in an adjoining chamber became plainer, he hoped that rescue was at hand. But in vain did the doors creak, the approaching footsteps receded, and the indistinct voices died away into mere whispering sounds. He endeavoured to beguile time by counting the boards in the floor, and the windows of the neighbouring houses, when the clear tones of a clock reminded him of having passed a tedious half hour. He then paced the confined space of the apartment in nervous agitation, until, his patience being nearly exhausted, he heard a door open again, and heavy footsteps coming towards his room. The door opened, and the same old grey-headed soldier entered, and said, "George von Fronsberg sends you his compliments, and a can of wine for vespers. The council may still last some time, but, as it is uncertain how long, you must remain here in the meanwhile." Saying which, he set the wine on the ledge of the window, for there was no table, and left the apartment.

Albert followed the old warrior with a look of amazement, for he thought such treatment unpardonable. He passed more than an hour in this situation, and still nothing had come to pass. He took a draught of wine, which he found was not indifferent, but it was out of the question enjoying his glass in his present painful solitude.

It is a fault common to young people of Albert's years to conceive themselves of more importance than their station in the world really warrants. An experienced man will bear with patience, or, at least, restrain his displeasure, upon feeling himself slighted, whilst the young man is apt to take fire upon the least hint derogatory to what he imagines a point of honour. No wonder, then, that Albert, when he was called to attend the council, after having been kept waiting two long solitary hours, was not in the best of humours. The old soldier, at length, having returned, conducted Albert to the council, leading the way through a narrow passage, with a silence and precaution observed in cases of a prisoner's presence.

When they came to the door, he turned to Albert, and said, in a friendly way, "Do not despise the advice of an old man, sir, and put aside that fierce sullen look of yours; it will be of no service to you in the presence of the stern men in there."

Around a large unwieldly table sat eight elderly men, who formed the council of war of the League. Some of them were known to Albert. George Truchses, Baron of Waldburg, occupied the upper place at the table; on each side of him sat Fronsberg and Sickingen. He was not acquainted with the rest, excepting old Ludwig von Hutten; but the chronicle whence this tale is taken has faithfully transmitted their names to us. There was Christoph Count of Ortenberg, Alban von Closen, Christoph von Frauenberg, and Diepold von Stein, aged men, and of repute in the army.

Albert paused at the door as he entered, but Fronsberg beckoned to him in a kind way to approach. He went up to the table, and faced the assembly with an open bold look peculiar to him. The members also took a survey of him, and appeared pleased with his appearance and manly bearing, for their eyes rested upon him with kindness, whilst some even encouraged him by a friendly nod.

Truchses von Waldburg at length addressed him. "It has been reported to us that you have been brought up at the high school in Tübingen; is it so?"

"Yes, sir knight," answered Albert.

"Are you well acquainted with the neighbourhood of Tübingen?" continued the other.

Albert blushed when this question was put to him. He thought of his love, who was now at Lichtenstein, only a few hours (*stunden*) distant from the university. But he answered composedly, "I have not hunted much in that neighbourhood; neither have I made many excursions there; but I am generally acquainted with its locality."

"We have determined," said Truchses, "to send a confidential person into that neighbourhood to find out what may be the Duke's intentions upon our approach, and to gain correct information upon the state of the fortifications of the castle of Tübingen, together with the feeling of the people of the surrounding country. Such a person, by prudence and sagacity, may do more harm to the Duke's cause than a hundred horsemen: we have selected you for this service."

"Me!" cried Albert, in horror.

"You, Albert von Sturmfeder: dexterity and experience are no doubt requisite in such undertakings: but you must look to that; whatever is wanting on your part, in the execution of this piece of service, your head will answer for."

The effect which this order produced on the young man was visibly depicted on his features. His face turned pale, his eyes became fixed, his lips firmly pressed together. The warning of Bertha flashed across his mind, and struck him with increased force; but, however favourable this opportunity might be to quit the service of the League, he was too much taken by surprise to be able to decide at that moment.

Truchses fidgeted about in his chair, showing evident symptoms of impatience at the young man's hesitation to give an answer: "Well," he cried, "will it come out soon? what are you thinking about so long?"

"Spare me this commission," said Albert, at length, but not without dread; "I cannot, I dare not undertake it."

The old men looked at each other in astonishment, as if they did not trust their ears. "You dare not, you cannot," Truchses repeated slowly, a deep red at the same time mounting up to his eyes, and colouring his forehead, the forerunner of rising anger.

Albert immediately perceived he had been too hasty in his expression; he recovered himself, and spoke with more composure: "I proffered my services to the League for the glory of honourable fight, not to steal into the enemy's country in the ignominious guise of a spy, to discover by secrecy and treachery what is not to be obtained openly. It is true, I am young and inexperienced; but this much I know, that I am answerable to myself alone for the propriety of my conduct. Who among you, as a father, would advise his son to commence his military career in the dishonourable garb of a spy?"

Truchses contracted his dark eyebrows into a frown, and shot a penetrating glance at the young man, who had ventured to entertain an opinion so different to his own. "What are you thinking about, sir?" he cried, "your opinion has nothing to do here; the question is, not whether your conscience will allow you to execute our orders--it treats of obedience to our commands, which we insist upon, and which you *must* submit to."

"And I will not," replied the young man, with a resolute voice. He felt his courage increase every moment, in proportion as the insulting tone of Waldburg excited his anger. He even hoped Truchses might persist in his offensive manner; for it would strengthen him still more in his resolve, and fully justify his determination to quit their service.

"Yes, yes!" laughed Waldburg, in sarcastic rage, "to ride about alone in the enemy's country is certainly a dangerous undertaking. Ha, ha! These are your fine-spoken gentlemen, proffering head and arm, with high-sounding words and lofty looks; but, when it comes to the point, if any service is required of them which is attended with danger, their hearts fail them. But one generation resembles the other; the apple does not fall far from its stem; and where there is nothing to be gained, the Emperor has lost his rights."

"If those words be meant as a reflection on my father," answered Albert, irritated, "there are witnesses sitting here, who can vouch that he lives in their memory as a brave man. You think to have achieved sufficient renown to warrant your taking the liberty of undervaluing the merits of others."

"Shall such a downy chin prescribe to me what I shall say?" interrupted Waldburg. "But an end to this trash. I want to know, youngster, whether or not you will saddle your horse to-morrow, and follow our orders?"

"Truchses von Waldburg," answered Albert, with more composure than he thought himself master of, "your arrogant language only convinces me how little you know the way to address a gentleman, who has tendered his services to the League with honourable motives, and who is the son of a brave father. You have addressed me in the name of the League, as president of this council, and have insulted me, as if I were its greatest enemy. I have, therefore, no other answer to give, than, in following your orders, to saddle my horse; but I now most decidedly declare, assuredly no longer in your service. My honour forbids my remaining under your colours; I therefore pronounce myself henceforth free and unshackled from you for ever;--farewell."

The young man spoke with vigour and firmness, and turned around to depart.

"Albert," called Fronsbergc, springing from his seat, "son of my friend!--"

"Not so rash, young man," cried the rest, and cast looks of disapprobation at Waldburg; but Albert walked out of the apartment without looking back; the iron latch of the door rang sharply as it fell; heavy oaken pannels lay between him and the recall of the better-intentioned members of the council, and separated Albert von Sturmfeder for ever from the Swabian League.

CHAPTER X

Oh, when, enveloped in a night of grief,
Thy wounded heart can nowhere find relief;
When the sun plunges in the western sea,
Ah, let the star of love not set to thee.

P. Cony.

Albert felt much relieved when he got to his room, and reflected on what had just happened. He rejoiced that the weight which had oppressed his mind ever since he promised to quit the service of the League, was now removed, in a way which could not have been more *à propos*, and which he conceived to be every way honourable to his feelings. He determined, therefore, without delay, to leave Ulm, letting Truchses take all the blame of this step to himself.

How rapidly had everything changed in the last four days! how different were his feelings when he first entered the town, from those which were about to drive him from its walls! At that time, when the thunder of cannon, mingling with the deep tolling of the church bells, celebrated the entrance of the League's troops, and the animating sound of trumpets saluted his ear, seeming to give applause to the part he had taken in the coming straggle; how his heart then beat for the opportunity of proving himself worthy of his love! And when he was first presented to Fronsberg, how elevated and encouraging was the thought of emulating the reputation of his father, and reaping praise under the eye of that great commander! But now, all those bright hopes were blasted. He had learned the intentions of the League. Excited by motives of sordid interest and cupidity, their only object was plunder. He blushed to draw his sword in such a cause:--the brilliancy with which his youthful imagination had coloured his future prospects was gone for ever. And then again, how painful the thought of being opposed to Bertha's father, the faithful friend of the unfortunate Duke, perchance to encounter him in the struggle. It would break his love's heart, which beat so true for him. "No!" said he, looking up to heaven, in gratitude, "all has been ordained for my good. Upon any other who had stood in my situation this day, destruction might have fallen, but I have been saved!" In thankfulness for the mercies apparently vouchsafed to him, he cast away the gloomy forebodings with which his mind had been haunted; his natural cheerfulness returned, and he sang a song as merrily as in his former happy mood.

Herr von Kraft beheld him with astonishment, as he entered the room. "Well, that is curious," said he; "I hastened home to console my guest in his distress, and find him merrier than ever: how do these two things rhyme together?"

"Have you never heard, Herr Dieterich," replied Albert, who thought it advisable to conceal his joy, "have you never heard that one can laugh in anger and sing in pain?"

"I have certainly heard it, but never witnessed it till this moment," answered Kraft.

"Well, and so you have heard of my vexatious affair with the grand council?" asked Albert. "I suppose it has run through all the streets already?"

"Oh no!" answered the secretary to the council; "no one knows any thing of it; for it would not do to trumpet forth your intended secret embassy to Würtemberg. No, thank God! I have my private sources, and learn many things the very hour they are done or spoken. But, don't be offended, if I say that I think you have acted a foolish part."

"Really," answered Albert; "and in what way?"

"Could there have been a better opportunity offered you to distinguish yourself? To whom would the commanders of the League have been under greater obligations than to him who----"

"Out with it at once," interrupted Albert--"than to him, you mean, who would steal into the enemy's country as a spy, worm out their secrets, and then, like other villains, betray them. I only regret that the name and honour of my father had not secured for me a higher and brighter destination."

"Those are scruples which I would not have thought to find in you. Really, if I were as well acquainted as you are with that neighbourhood, they should not have asked me a second time."

"You, perhaps, in this country, possess different principles upon this point from us in Franconia," replied Albert, not without disdain: "Truchses von Waldburg should have thought of that, and appointed an Ulmer to the service."

"You remind me now of another subject; the general of the forces! How could you think of making him your enemy? He will never forgive what has taken place, you may depend upon that."

"That is the least I care about," answered Albert; "but one thing annoys me, which is, that I cannot meet that insolent arrogant fellow at the end of my sword, and prove to him, who has already vilified my father's name upon other occasions, that the arm which he has this day thrust from him, is not quite so despicable as he supposes."

"For God's sake," said Kraft, "don't speak so loud; it might come to his ears. Above all, you must be very cautious what you say, if you intend still to serve in the army under him."

"I intend soon to free Truchses of my hateful person. With God's will, I have seen the sun set for the last time in Ulm!"

"And is it really true what I also heard, but which I cannot believe," asked Kraft, with astonishment, "that Albert von Sturmfeder would quit our good cause on account of this trifle?"

"To wound a man's honour is by no means a trifle," replied Albert, gravely; "at least, according to my mind. But having carefully reconsidered what you call your good cause, I find I should have to draw my sword neither in an honourable nor a just one, but only to satisfy the cupidity of a few unwashed townsfolk."

The unfavourable impression which the last words, in particular, seemed to make on the secretary, did not escape Albert; he went on to say, therefore, in a milder tone, taking his hand at the same time, with a friendly squeeze: "Do not take what I have said amiss, my kind host; God knows, I did not intend to offend you; but from your own mouth I have learnt the object of the different parties in this army. You may, therefore, attribute my actions partly to your own explanations; for you had already taken the bandage off my eyes."

"You are not quite so wrong, after all, good sir; strange things will come to pass when once these gentlemen begin to divide that fine country among themselves. But I have thought, if they go to a certain spot, you might also claim your mite. It is said,--you must not be offended with me,--that your house is somewhat dilapidated; therefore it appeared to me----"

"Nothing more upon that subject," said Albert, hastily, touched by the kind hint of his well-meaning friend. "The house of my ancestors is indeed in ruins, the doors hang on their broken hinges, grass grows upon the drawbridge, and owls inhabit the watch-tower. In fifty years hence a tower or a bit of a wall may still be standing, to remind the wanderer, that once upon a time a knighted race dwelt there. But should the decayed wall fall upon me, and bury the last of my family under its ruin, no one shall ever say of me--He drew his father's sword in an unjust cause."

"Every one to his thinking," answered Dieterick; "all this sounds very fine, but I, for my part, would stretch a point for the sake of re-establishing my house, and making it habitable. But whether you change your determination or not, I hope, at all events, you will remain with me a few days longer."

"I am grateful for your kindness," answered Albert; "but, you see, under existing circumstances, I have nothing more to do in this town. I propose leaving it by daybreak tomorrow."

"Well, then, one may send a remembrance to a friend by you, I suppose?" said the secretary, with a most crafty smile: "of course you ride the direct road to Lichtenstein?"

The young man blushed up to the forehead. Since Bertha's departure she had not been the subject of conversation between him and his host, and therefore his sly question took him so much the more by surprise. "I perceive," said he, "that you do not understand me yet. You believe I have only turned my back on the League for the purpose of joining the enemy? How can you think so ill of me?"

"Ah! away with you," replied the wary scribe; "no one else but my charming cousin has influenced your conduct. You would have shut an eye to every thing the League did, had old Lichtenstein been on our side; but now that you know he belongs to the other party, you think yourself justified in joining it also."

Albert might defend himself as well as he could; the secretary was too firmly rooted in his opinion to allow himself to be talked out of it. Moreover, he thought this step very natural, and saw nothing in it dishonourable or blamable. With a hearty remembrance to his cousin in Lichtenstein, he left the room of his guest. But on the threshold of the door he turned round again, and said, "I had almost forgotten to mention, that I met George von Fronsberg in the street, who begs you will go and see him this evening at his house."

Albert had already determined not to depart without taking leave of Fronsberg, but he felt nervous at appearing before a man whose intentions towards him were kind, but whose plans he had thwarted. He buckled on his sword, thinking upon this painful meeting, and was arranging his cloak, when his attention was drawn to an unusual noise on the stairs. Heavy steps of a party of men approached his door; he thought he heard the clatter of swords and halberts on the stone floor of the ante-room. He stepped quickly towards the door to ascertain the cause of this visit; but before he reached it, it opened, and by the light of a few candles he perceived many armed men about to enter. The same old soldier who had received him when he went to the council of war, stepped forward.

"Albert von Sturmfeder!" said he to the young man, who retreated a step in astonishment, "by order of the grand council of war I make you my prisoner."

"Me--prisoner?" said Albert, with consternation. "Why? what am I guilty of?"

"That 'a not my affair," answered the old man, surlily, "but probably you will not be left long in ignorance. Be so good to deliver up your sword to me, and follow me to the town hall."

"How? give up my sword?" replied the young man in the rage of insulted pride. "Who are you that dares to demand my weapon? The council must send men of a different stamp for that purpose before I submit; I know too well what your profession is."

"For God's sake give up your sword," cried his friend, the secretary, who forced himself through the crowd to his side, "obey the order-- resistance were vain. You have to do with Truchses," he whispered: "he is a fearful enemy; do not force him to extremities."

The old soldier, interrupting the secretary, said, "It is perhaps the first time, sir, you have been arrested; therefore I forgive the hasty language you have made use of against a man who has slept in the same tent with your father. You may, however, retain your sword: I well know its hilt and scabbard, and I have witnessed many a deed of glory achieved with its blade. It is praiseworthy of you to be jealous of its falling into other hands. But you must come with me to the town hall, for it were folly in you to bid defiance to power."

The young man, to whom every thing appeared a dream, submitted quietly to his fate. He whispered to his friend the secretary to go to Fronsberg, and inform him of his arrest, and concealing his person as much as possible under his cloak, to avoid the unpleasant gaze of the crowd in the streets, followed the old leader, surrounded by his party.

CHAPTER XI

The iron door upon its hinges creaks,
A lurid light upon the prison breaks,
The captive, starting at a footstep's sound,
Springs from his lonely couch, to gaze around.

Wieland.

The troop, surrounding their prisoner, moved on in silence towards the town hall. A single torch was their only light on the way, and Albert thanked Heaven that it gave but a feeble glare; for he fancied that every one who met him must suppose he was being led to prison. But this was not the only thought which engrossed his mind. This was the first time in his life he had been in any dilemma, and it was not without dread that he figured to himself all the horrors of a damp dreary dungeon, remembering to have visited the one in his old castle. He was on the point of speaking to his leader on the subject, when it struck him he might be accused of a childish fear, and therefore he proceeded in silence.

He was, however, not a little surprised when he was led into a large handsome room, not very habitable indeed, as its furniture consisted only of a bedstead, and an uncommon large fire-place, but it was a palace compared to what his imagination had conjured up. The old soldier wished his prisoner a good night, and retired with the rest of his party. A little thin old man then made his appearance; a large bunch of keys, which hung by his side, rattling like a chain when he moved, announced him as the gaoler or servant of the town hall. He laid some large logs of wood in the fire-place, and made a blazing fire; a cheering companion on a cold night in March. He then spread an ample woollen covering on the bedstead, and the first word that Albert heard from him was a friendly invitation to make himself comfortable. He thanked the old man for his kind attention, though his place of rest for the night did not offer much to tempt him to repose.

"This apartment is set aside for knights in your situation," said the old gaoler; "the common people are confined under ground, and are not so well off."

"Is it long since any one lodged here?" asked Albert, looking around the room.

"A Herr von Berger was the last; he died on that very bed seven years ago: God be merciful to his soul! He appeared to be fond of this place, for he often rises from his coffin at midnight to visit his old quarters."

"How?" said Albert, smiling, "has he been seen since his death?"

The old man looked fearfully around the room, now faintly lighted by the dying embers of the fire: he put another log on, and murmured, "Ah, many strange stories are about."

"Did he die on that covering?" said Albert, whilst an involuntary shudder came over him.

"Yes, sir," whispered the gaoler, "he breathed his last on that very covering; God grant he may not have descended lower than purgatory! That covering is now called his winding-sheet, and this apartment the knight's death-room!" With this, the old man quietly slipt out of the room, as if he were afraid the slightest noise might awaken the departed knight.

"And so I am to sleep on the winding-sheet in the death-room of the knight," thought Albert, and felt his heart beat quicker, for his nurse and old servants had often related ghost stories to him in his boyhood. He was undecided whether he should lay himself on the bed. There was neither stool nor bench in the room; and the brick paved floor was still colder and harder than the appointed place of repose; but he began to feel ashamed of his fears, and at once rolled himself in the winding-sheet on the death-bed of the knight.

A clear conscience softens a hard bed. Albert said his prayers, and soon fell asleep. But it did not last long, for he was awoke by strange noises, which appeared to be in the room. He thought it was a dream; he took courage--he listened--he listened again: it was no deception--he heard heavy footsteps in his apartment. The fire at this moment blazed up, and threw its light upon a large dark figure. The distance of the fire-place from the bed was not great. The figure moved towards him; he felt the winding-sheet shake; he was unable to control a momentary shudder, when a cold hand, endeavouring to remove the covering, fell on his forehead. He sprang up, and eyeing the figure which stood before him by the light of the fire, he recognised the well-known features of George von Fronsberg.

"Is it you, general?" said Albert, who now breathed more freely, and threw his cloak aside to receive the knight with proper respect.

"Remain, remain where you are," said the other, and gently compelled him to resume his seat; "I will set myself beside you, and have half an hour's talk, for it is only just past nine o'clock, and no one is yet in bed in Ulm, excepting such hot-brained fellows as you, whose heads require cooling on a hard pillow."

"Oh! how can I merit this kind consideration at your hands," said Albert, "after having treated your good intentions towards me with apparent ingratitude?"

"No excuse, my young friend," answered the general, "you are but the counterpart of your father; just like him, precipitate in praise and blame, in decision and speech. That he was an honorable man, I know, and I know also how unhappy his violent temper made him, as well as his obstinacy, which he called firmness."

"But tell me, dear sir," replied Albert, "could I have acted otherwise to-day? Did not the conduct of Truchses push me to extremities?"

"You might have acted otherwise, if you had humoured the ways of that man, who gave you a specimen of his character the other day. You ought to have known also that there were many present who would not have seen you imposed upon. But you threw away the good with the bad, or as the proverb says, 'You threw away the child out of the bathing tub with the water,' and flew out of the room."

"Age and experience will, I trust, cool my blood in due time," replied Albert; "I can put up with harshness and severity, when they do not affect my honour. But premeditated insult, contempt for the misfortunes of my family, is beyond all bearing. What pleasure could a man of his high station find in wounding my feelings?"

"His wrath always manifests itself in that way," Fronsberg informed him; "the more cool and collected he appears outwardly, the more fiercely he burns within. It was his idea alone to send you to Tübingen, partly because he knew of no one else who was so well acquainted with the place, partly because he wished to repair the injustice he had done you. But you have affronted him by your refusal, and lowered him in the eyes of the council of war."

"How!" cried Albert, "Truchses himself proposed me? I thought it was your doing."

"No," answered the General, with a significant smile; "no, I did all I could to prevent it; but to no purpose, for I could not tell him the real state of the case. I knew, before you came before us, that you would decline accepting the office. But do not open your eyes so wide, as if you would pierce through one's leather jacket, and look into my heart. I know enough of the history of my young hot-brain!"

Albert felt confused. "Were not my reasons satisfactory?" said he: "is there any thing more you wish to know, and which you may think mysterious?"

"There is nothing exactly mysterious; but you should have decided upon your line of action beforehand, for if you do not wish to be noticed, you ought not to conduct yourself at balls as if you were afflicted with St. Vitus' dance, nor visit a couple of pretty girls at three o'clock in the afternoon. Yes, yes, my son, I know many things," he added, whilst he good-naturedly threatened with his finger: "I know also that that impetuous heart of yours beats for Würtemberg."

Albert blushed; and would gladly have avoided the piercing look of the knight. "Beats for Würtemberg?" he replied: "you do me wrong; you cannot call that going over to the enemy; upon my honour, I swear----"

"Do not swear," Fronsberg quickly interrupted him: "an oath is an easy thing to take, but not so easy to be absolved from; it is like an oppressive chain which we cannot shake off. I am convinced your honour will not suffer by your actions. Instead of an oath, you must promise one thing to the League, namely, not to draw your sword against us for the next fourteen days; and on these conditions only will you be released from arrest."

"I see you still entertain a false opinion of me," said Albert, agitated: "I could not have thought it! how unnecessary is that promise! To whom else should I offer my services? The Swiss have withdrawn their aid from the Duke, the peasantry have dispersed, the knights guard the fortresses, and will take care not to let the army of the League within their walls; the Duke himself has fled----"

"Fled!" cried Fronsberg: "that's not quite so certain;--where did you hear this? Have you been tampering with any of the members of the council of war? or is it true, as some maintain, that you carry on a suspicious correspondence with Würtemberg?"

"Who dares assert that?" cried Albert.

The piercing eye of Fronsberg darted a searching look at Albert. "You are too young, and I believe too honourable, to be guilty of such a villanous deed," said he; "and should you even have had such an intention, we know you would have scarcely quitted the League, but have remained among us as Würtemberg's spy. This clears you in my mind. Appearances, however, are against you."

"Am I then so evil spoken against? If you have a particle of regard for me, tell me who is the wretch that has thus calumniated me," said Albert, starting up in anger.

"Do not be so violent," replied Fronsberg. "Do you suppose, that if George von Fronsberg had heard such things spoken of in public, or believed the report, he would have come to visit you? But there must be some foundation for the report. A suspicious-looking countryman often came to old Lichtenstein in the town; he was not at first particularly noticed among the many assembled here. But it was hinted to us, that this man, a cunning, crafty fellow, was a confidential messenger from Würtemberg. Lichtenstein took his departure; and the countryman and his mysterious occupation were forgotten. He appeared, however, again this morning, and had a long conversation with you outside the town; and was seen afterwards in your house. Now what is the meaning of this?"

Albert heard his friend with increasing astonishment. "As true as God lives," said he, when Fronsberg had finished, "I am innocent. A countryman came to me this morning----" Albert was silent.

"Well, why are you silent all at once?" asked Fronsberg; "you colour up to the eyes: what have you to do with this messenger?"

"Ah! I feel ashamed of myself; but you have already guessed every thing; he only brought me a--a few words from----, my love." The young man then opened his waistcoat, and produced the strip of parchment which he had concealed on his person. "There; this is all he brought to me," said Albert, as he gave it to Fronsberg.

"And is that really all," laughed Fronsberg, after reading the contents: "poor young fellow! and you know nothing more of that man? Do you not know who he is?"

"No; he is nothing more to my knowledge than our messenger of love--I am certain of it!"

"A pretty love messenger, who at the same time pries into our affairs! Are you not aware that that dangerous man is the fifer of Hardt?"

"The fifer of Hardt?" asked Albert: "this is the first time I have heard that name; what does it mean?"

"Nobody knows exactly; but he was one of the most formidable leaders in the insurrection of Poor Conrad, for which he, however, afterwards obtained pardon; since that time he leads a restless, roving life, and is now a spy of the Duke of Würtemberg."

"Is he arrested?" inquired Albert, for he involuntarily felt a warm interest in his new servant.

"No; it is just that which is so incomprehensible; whatever notice we may have of his being in Ulm, though communicated in the quietest manner possible, becomes known to him immediately; for example, when we heard of his being in your stable, and sent secretly to arrest him, he was not to be found. But I trust to your honour that he comes to you on no other business. You may be assured of this, however, if it be the same man I mean, he does not visit Ulm for your sake alone. Should you ever meet him again, be guarded how you trust such a vagabond. But the watchman now calls ten o'clock. Lay down again, and dream away your confinement. But before I go, give me your word about the fourteen days; and, I can tell you, if you leave Ulm without saying farewell to old Fronsberg----"

"I will not fail to do so!" cried Albert, touched by the pain which he perceived his revered friend felt at parting, and which he tried to smother under a smile. He gave him his hand as a pledge of his promise, according to the desire of the council of war, upon which the knight left the room, with long measured steps.

CHAPTER XII

"Could I but once that face so dear
Behold before we sever;
And once again those accents hear,
Before we part for ever."

C. Grüneisen.

On the following day a horseman, oppressed by the heat of the mid-day sun, was bending his way over that part of the Swabian Alb which leads towards Franconia. He was young, more slim than strong built, and rode a large brown horse; he was well armed with cuirass, dagger, and sword; some parts of his defensive apparel, such as his helmet, and steel plates to cover his limbs, hung to his saddle. The striped light blue and white scarf, which passed across his breast over the right shoulder (the distinguishing prerogative of high rank in those days), shewed the young man to be of noble birth.

He had reached the summit of a hill, which afforded a view into the valley below, and stopping his horse, he turned on one side to enjoy the beautiful prospect. Before him lay an extended plain, bounded on each side by wooded heights, through which flowed the green waters of the Danube; on his right the chain of hills of the Würtemberg Alb; on his left the distant snow-capped Tyrolean Alps. The blue vault of heaven encircled the scene, and its soft colouring brought out in strong relief the dark walls of Ulm, its massive spire, and the whole extent of the town, which lay at the foot of the mountain.

Noon was announced at this moment by the tolling of the bells of the cathedral; their solemn tones resounded throughout the town and its extended plain, until they were lost among the distant mountains.

"The same sounds accompany my departure which greeted my arrival," thought the young man: "but how different did I interpret their brazen voices, when for the first time they reached my ear, and guided me to my love; and now that I depart disconsolate, and without object, the same tones follow me! They celebrated the birth of my hope, and now ring its knell. It is the picture of life!" he added, as he took a last farewell of the town in the valley beneath, and turned his horse away: "it is, indeed, the picture of life! These same sounds float over cradle and coffin; and the bells of the chapel of my house which rang a merry peal at my baptism, will also accompany the last of the Sturmfeders to the grave."

The mountain now became steeper; and Albert, whom the reader will have recognised as the young cavalier, allowed his horse to have his own way. Upon quitting Ulm, he had determined to return to his home in Franconia, and there wait events, or at any rate the expiration of the fourteen days' truce he had promised his friend Fronsberg. His heart naturally would lead him to Lichtenstein, the contrary way to the path he was now pursuing; yet he felt he had chosen the one most honourable to his engagements. The balance, however, between the two was very equally poised, and had he had a friend to decide for him and convince him that he was now a free agent to travel whither he pleased, provided he took no part in the contest for fourteen days, he felt that the bent of his inclinations would turn the scale in favour of the neighbourhood of his love. The comparison between his present situation and the former position which he had held only a few days back, did not tend to cheer his spirits. Sudden changes--violent emotions-- his confinement on the day before--and, above all, the pain of taking leave of men who had his welfare at heart, produced recollections which almost unmanned him.

Dieterick von Kraft, above all, bewailed his departure. From the first moment of their acquaintance in the room of the town hall when they pledged each other in a bumper, to the last hour when they bid adieu in a parting cup, that excellent friend had manifested the same uninterrupted good feeling towards him. And how had he requited his kindness? Occupied solely with self, he had but partially expressed his sense of obligation to him; and to the honest, straightforward Breitenstein, who, as well as Fronsberg, had held him up as their favourite in the army, what return had he made? Truly there is nothing more painful to a noble mind than the thought of being ungrateful where its object is to be esteemed.

Full of these gloomy thoughts, he proceeded some distance on his journey. Feeling the rays of the March sun oppressive, and the mountain path becoming more rugged, he determined to repose himself and horse under the shade of an oak tree. He dismounted, loosened the girths of his saddle, and let his weary beast make the most of the stunted grass in the neighbourhood. He stretched himself under the tree, and though his fatiguing ride and the cool shade invited him to rest, still the unquiet state of the country, so near the theatre of war, the care of his horse and of his weapons, kept him awake until he at last sank into that state between watching and sleep, which the body combats in vain.

V He might have been about half an hour in this situation, when the neighing of his horse roused him; he looked about, and perceived a man with his back towards him, occupying himself with the beast. His first thought was, that taking advantage of his carelessness, the man intended to make away with his steed; he sprang upon his legs, drew his sword, and in a trice was by his side. "Stop, villain! what have you to do with that horse?" he cried, at the same time taking him by the collar rather roughly.

"Have you already discharged me from your service, sir?" said the man, whom Albert immediately recognised as the messenger Bertha had sent to him. The young man was undecided what line of conduct to pursue; for Fronsberg's warning made him distrustful of the man, whilst Bertha's confidence in him recommended him. The countryman continued his conversation, showing him at the same time a handful of hay; "I guessed you would not have provided fodder for your journey; and as there is not much grass to be picked up on the mountains, I brought an armful with me for the brown horse." So spoke the peasant, and continued feeding the beast.

"And where do you now come from?" asked Albert, having recovered from his astonishment.

"Why, you rode away from Ulm in such haste, I was not able to follow you immediately," he answered.

"Don't tell me a falsehood," said the young man, "otherwise I cannot trust you any more. You do not come from that town at present."

"Well, I suppose you will not be angry, if I was a little earlier than you on the road?" said the countryman, and turned away; but the cunning smile on his countenance did not escape Albert.

"Let my horse alone," said Albert, impatiently. "Come, sit down with me under that oak, and tell me, without hesitation, why you left the town so suddenly yesterday evening?"

"It was not with the Ulmers' good will; for they even wanted to induce me to remain longer with them, and to give me board and lodging gratis," replied the man.

"Yes, they would have put you in the lowest cell of the prison, where you would have seen neither sun nor moon, the place appropriated to spies and such like gentry."

"Excuse me, sir," replied the messenger, "though I might have been somewhat lower, we should both have been under the same roof."

"Dog of a spy!" cried Albert, with anger burning on his cheek; "would you place my father's son in the same rank with the fifer of Hardt?"

"What is that you say?" replied the other with menacing tone; "what name is that you mentioned? do you know the fifer of Hardt?" At these words he grasped his axe, though perhaps involuntarily. His compact, broad-chested figure, spite of his low stature, gave him the appearance of an adversary not to be despised: and many a man, single handed, would have been staggered at his determined countenance and fierce eye.

But the young man leaped up, threw back his long hair, and met the dark look of his companion with one full of pride and dignity; he seized his sword, and said calmly, "What do you mean by placing yourself in that threatening position? If I do not mistake, you are the man I mentioned, the mover and leader of those rebellious hounds; away with you or I will show you how such outcasts ought to be treated!"

The countryman struggled with rage; he threw His axe with a powerful swing into the tree, and stood unarmed before Albert. "Allow me," said he, "to give you another piece of advice, namely, never to let your adversary stand between you and your horse, for if I had taken immediate advantage of your order to take myself off, I should have had by far the best of it."

A look at his horse proved the truth of what the man said, and Albert blushed for his inexperience. He quitted the grasp of his sword, and, without replying, seated himself again on the ground. The countryman followed his example, but at a respectable distance, and said, "You are perfectly justified in being suspicious of me, Albert von Sturmfeder; but if you knew the pain that the name you have just mentioned gives me, you would pardon my violent conduct. Yes, I am he who goes by that name; but I have an abhorrence to be called by it: my friends call me Hans--my enemies the fifer of Hardt, which they know I so much detest."

"What has that name to do with you?" asked Albert; "why are you called by it? and why do you dislike it?"

"Why do people call me so?" answered the other: "I came from a village of the name of Hardt; it lies in the low country, not far from Nürtingen. I follow the profession of music, and play at fairs and wakes, and when young people want to dance. For this reason I go by the appellation of the fifer of Hardt; but as this name was stained with crime and blood in an evil moment, I have dropped it, and cannot bear the sound of it any longer."

Albert measured him with a searching look, and said, "I know very well the evil moment to which you allude: when you peasants rebelled against your Duke, you were one of the worst among them. Is it not true?"

"I see you are acquainted with the history of an unfortunate man," said the countryman, with penitent downcast looks: "but you must not believe that I am still the same person; the Holy One saved me and changed my way of thinking, so that I may now say, I am an honest man."

"Oh! tell me," interrupted Albert, "what was the cause of the insurrection? How were you saved? and how is it that you now serve the Duke?"

"I will spare you this information for a more fitting occasion," he replied, "for I trust this will not be the last time we meet; allow me to ask you instead, where does this road lead to? It does not lead to Lichtenstein!"

"I am not going there," said Albert, dejected; "this way leads to Franconia, to my old uncle; you can tell the lady my plans, when you go to Lichtenstein."

"And what are you going to do at your old uncle's? To hunt? you can do so elsewhere; or perhaps to kill time? you can do that cheap enough all over the world. Take my advice in a few words," he added, with a good-humoured smile; "turn your horse's head the other way, and take a ride with me for a couple of days about Würtemberg. I know the country well enough to keep you out of harm's way, and though war is declared, the roads are tolerably safe yet."

The fifer gave him this assurance, in order to encourage him to bend his steps towards Lichtenstein, which he knew would gratify the wishes of the lady who had entrusted him with her message of love. He was fully aware of the possibility there was of falling in with the patroles of the League, which were scattered over the country; but he had, at the same time, sufficient confidence in his knowledge of the unfrequented paths among the mountains, to be able to escape their vigilance.

"I have given the League my word, not to serve against it for fourteen days; how can I remain, therefore, in Würtemberg?"

"Do you call that fighting for Würtemberg, if you only travel peaceably on the roads? In fourteen days, did you say? Do they think the war will be over in fourteen days? Many a head will be broken against the walls of Tübingen long after that time. Come with me; it is not against your oath."

"And what shall I do in Würtemberg?" cried Albert: "shall I go and see my old companions in arms reaping glory under the walls of the fortresses? shall I go and meet the colours of the League again, to which I have bid an eternal farewell? No; I will return to my home in Franconia, and bury myself among its walls, and dream how happy I might have been."

"That is a fine determination for a young man of your spirit and determination? Have you no other interest in Würtemberg than to wish to storm the tottering castles of the Duke? Well, go, in God's name!" continued the countryman, looking at Albert with a cunning smile; "but just try for once whether the ancient castle of Lichtenstein may not be taken by storm?"

The young man blushed deeply; and said, half angrily, half smiling, "I don't like your joke."

"I had no intention to joke with my young master," answered his companion; "I am serious when I wish to persuade you to go there."

"And what to do?"

"Why, to win over the old gentleman, to be sure, and dry the tears of the young lady, who weeps day and night on your account."

"But how can I go to Lichtenstein? Bertha's father does not know me; how shall I make his acquaintance?"

"Are you the first knight who has ever demanded free quarters in a castle, according to the custom of our forefathers? If you will leave that to me, I will promise to satisfy your scruples."

The young man pondered over his friend's proposal for some time; he carefully weighed all the reasons for and against it; he considered whether it was not against his honour, to be in the neighbourhood where the war would in all probability be carried on, instead of retiring from the theatre of it. But when he reflected upon the mild manner in which the commanders of the League had received his retreat from their cause, and the easy conditions which they had laid on him; but above all, when he called to his memory the unhappy position of his beloved Bertha, his inclination to proceed to Würtemberg turned the scale.

"I will see and speak with her once more," thought he to himself.---- "Well, then," he called to the countryman, "if you will promise never to say a word to me about joining the Würtemberg cause, and assure me that I shall not be looked upon as a partizan of your Duke, but merely a guest of Lichtenstein, I will follow you."

"As far as lies in me, I can safely promise you," said his companion; "but it is impossible for me to answer for what the knight of Lichtenstein might propose. He is the Duke's warmest friend, and it is not unlikely he may endeavour to persuade you to join his cause."

"I already know the terms you are upon with him, that you often visited him in Ulm, and brought him secret intelligence of all kinds. He has confidence in you, and therefore I wish to put you on your guard, not to acquaint him with the state of my affairs; for I have my reasons to keep them as yet unknown to him."

The fifer of Hardt eyed the young man some time with a look of astonishment. "Where did you learn that I had been the bearer of secret intelligence to the knight of Lichtenstein? But it signifies little to me what my persecutors may have told you. I have a debt to pay, and until it is fully discharged, I call not my life my own. My death, I hope, will absolve me from my creditor." With these portending words, he promised to follow Albert's wishes to the letter, and added, "Now mount your horse, whilst I lead on, and you shall be welcome in the castle of Lichtenstein."

CHAPTER XIII

The herdsman says, "If you will trust in me
And follow boldly, I will bring you free;--
A secret path there is, to man unknown,
And trodden by the mountain goat alone."

                                                            L. Uhland.

There were two ways from the spot where Albert had decided upon following his mysterious guide, leading to the neighbourhood of Reutlingen, in which the castle of Lichtenstein was situated. One was the high road from Ulm to Tübingen. It went through the beautiful Blauthal, or blue valley; when, reaching the town of Blaubeuren, at the foot of the Alb, it crossed immediately over that mountain, passing the fortress of Hohen Urach, near the villages of St. John and Pfullingen. This was the usual and most convenient road for travellers on horseback, in litters, or carriages; but at the time of our story, when Albert and the fifer of Hardt had to cross the country, it was not advisable to choose this route. The troops of the League already occupied Blaubeuren, their advanced posts stretched as far as Urach, and any one whom they found on the road, that did not belong to the army, or acknowledge their party, were rudely handled and otherwise ill-treated. Albert, therefore, had good reason to avoid this road; and his companion was too mindful of his own safety to dissuade him from it.

The other, a mere footpath, and known only to the inhabitants of the country, passed through thick woods, and deep ravines, where but a few single detached houses were to be met with, scattered over a distance of twelve hours (stunden), or between thirty to forty miles. Here and there the track made a circuit to avoid the high road, and for this reason possessed the greater advantage of security. It was very fatiguing, and, indeed, in many places scarcely passable for horses.

The fifer of Hardt chose this route, which his young master joyfully acceded to, as being the least likely to fall in with the League's troops. They set forward accordingly, the countryman walking on Albert's side: in the difficult parts of the path, he carefully led the horse by the bridle, and showed so much attention generally, for both man and horse, that Albert by degrees began to lose sight of Fronsberg's warning, and to look upon his companion as a trustworthy servant.

They conversed upon different subjects, when the peasant reasoned and argued in so clear-sighted a manner, upon many things which in general do not come within the compass of a common countryman's mind, that his master could not at times control an involuntary smile. He had stories to relate of every tower and castle they saw in the distance, through the break of the forest; and the clearness and liveliness with which he described them, proved that he had been present as musician at many a marriage feast and village dance; but as often as Albert endeavoured to turn the conversation to the subject of his own life, and particularly to that period when the fifer of Hardt played so prominent a part in the insurrection of Poor Conrad, he either cut it short or turned it to some other channel, with a facility which bespoke a man of discernment.

In this way they proceeded on their journey, without stopping, except to refresh man and beast. Hans was well acquainted with the places where they would find accommodation. He was known everywhere, and received in a friendly manner, though, as it appeared to Albert, his appearance excited astonishment at times. He generally had a quarter of an hour's whisper with the host, during the time that the bustling hostess would wait on the young knight with bread, butter, and pure home-made cider; whilst the little boys and girls were lost in admiration at the tall figure of the guest, with his fine clothes, his brilliant scarf, and the waving plumes of his cap. After the frugal meal was finished, the whole family accompanied the travellers to the door; but, strange to say, the young cavalier could never induce the good people, upon any account, to accept a remuneration for their hospitality. When he asked his conductor to solve this riddle, his answer, "that when they visit Hardt, they always come to my house," appeared a mere parry to the question.

They passed the night in one of those solitary houses, where the hostess, with equal readiness, prepared a bed for her distinguished guest, and sacrificed, in honour of him, a couple of pigeons for his supper, served up with a dish of oatmeal.

They pursued their journey the following day in the same manner, excepting that it struck Albert, his leader appeared more cautious than on the day before: for, when they came within five hundred paces of a dwelling, he bid his master stop, whilst he approached it warily; and not till after he was perfectly satisfied that all was right, did he make him a sign to follow. In vain did Albert question him, whether the road was now more dangerous, or whether the troops of the League were in the neighbourhood? He could not elicit a direct answer.

Towards noon, as the country became more open, and the path descended into the plain, their route consequently was attended with more danger. The musician of Hardt, thinking it no longer prudent to approach any habitation, had provided himself at the last place with a sack of fodder for the horse, and a sufficient supply of provisions for his master and himself; he sought the most unfrequented paths, and it appeared to Albert that they did not follow the first direction, but had turned sharp to the right.

They halted on the skirt of a shady beechwood, by the side of a clear stream with fresh grass on its banks, which invited them to repose. Albert dismounted, whilst his provident guide produced the contents of his wallet, and set before him a good dinner. After he had looked to the horse, he placed himself at the feet of the young knight, and set to eating, with a hearty appetite.

Albert having satisfied his hunger, surveyed the neighbourhood with an attentive eye. He looked down upon a beautiful broad valley, at the bottom of which flowed a small rapid rivulet; the surrounding fields, with inclosed orchards here and there, appeared in high state of cultivation, a cheerful village reared its head on a hill at the further end of the valley, and the whole country was of a more pleasing description than that over which they had passed on the crest of the mountain.

"We have now quitted the district of the Alb, it seems," said the young man, as he turned to his companion; "this valley and those hills greet the eye with much more cheerful effect than the rugged rocks and deserted meadows we traversed yesterday. The air also feels milder and warmer here than higher up on the hills, where the wind was so piercing."

"You have spoken rightly, sir," said Hans, as he carefully put the remains of their meal into the wallet; "these vallies form part of the lowland, and that rivulet which you see yonder flows into the Neckar."

"But how comes it that we have gone so much out of the way?" Albert asked. "I noticed that circumstance when we were on the mountain, but you would not listen to me then. As far as I know about the situation of Lichtenstein, this road will take us much too far to the right."

"Well, now I'll tell you the reason," answered the countryman, "why we have made this circuit. I did not wish to create an unnecessary anxiety in your mind when we were on the Alb, but at present, with God's will, we are in safety; for, let the worst come to the worst, we are scarcely four hours distant from Hardt, where no harm can happen to us."

"In safety," Albert interrupted him in astonishment, "what have we to fear?"

"The Leaguists, to be sure," replied the musician; "their cavalry overrun the Alb, and some of them were not a thousand paces from us at times. For my part, I would not like to fall into their hands, for, as you well know, they bear me no good will; and perhaps it would not be quite so pleasant for you to be brought prisoner before old Truchses."

"God defend me from Truchses!" cried Albert. "I would rather allow myself to be shot on the spot than undergo such disgrace. But what are they doing here? There is no fortress of Würtemberg in this neighbourhood, and yet you say they scour the country hereabouts; what is their object?"

"Look ye, sir! Wicked men are to be found everywhere; a true Würtemberger would rather let himself be flayed alive than betray the Duke, after whom the League is now on the search. But Truchses has secretly offered a bribe of a heap of gold to any one who takes him; and for this purpose has sent his cavalry out all over the country; the report is, that many peasants, instigated by money, willingly assist these bloodhounds in searching all the caverns and holes of the rocks after their prey."

"Searching after the Duke? I thought he had already fled the country, or, as others say, has shut himself up in Tübingen with forty knights!"

"Yes, the forty nobles are there, true enough," answered the countryman, with a knowing look; "the Duke's young son, Christoph, is also with them; that's as it should be; but where the Duke himself is, no one can tell. Between you and I, sir, knowing him as well as I do, nothing but dire necessity will compel him to seek shelter in a fortress; he is a bold restless man, and prefers the freedom of woods and mountains to other resources, even if there is danger attending it."

"So they are searching after him? is it possible he can be in this neighbourhood?"

"Where he is at present, I know not," answered the fifer of Hardt; "and I would bet that no one but God alone knows; but where he will be," he added, and appeared to Albert as if he were inspired with the idea, "I know where he will be should fate push him to extremities; I know the spot where his faithful friends will find him in case of need, where many a true breast will be assembled and form a wall of defence to protect their lord against his enemies. For though he may be a severe master, he is still a Würtemberger, and his heavy hand is dearer to us than the slippery words of Bavaria or Austria."

"And should they happen to fall in with the unfortunate prince, would they be able to recognise him? Has he not disguised his person? You described his appearance to me once, particularly his brilliant commanding eye, so that I almost fancy I see him now before me? Can you describe his figure to me?"

"As I told you then, he may be eight years older than you," replied the other; "not quite so tall, but your figures resemble each other so much, particularly when you are on horseback, that when I look at you from behind, I say to myself, 'there goes the Duke himself.'"

Albert got up to look after his horse; the conversation of the countryman had made him anxious for his own safety; and he now thought, for the first time, that he had acted foolishly in stealing about the country occupied by an enemy. It would have been particularly unpleasant to be taken prisoner at this moment; for though there was certainly nothing against his oath in travelling as he did, provided he took no active part against the League: still he felt the disadvantageous light into which he would be thrown were he found in this neighbourhood, and in company with a man of whom the officers of the League were suspicious, and indeed were afraid of. To retrace his steps would, he thought, be imprudent, as it was almost certain the road would be occupied by the enemy's patroles; the safest way, therefore, appeared to be to hurry on as fast as possible, and get beyond reach of their advanced posts.

Albert, to his great dismay, when he came to examine his horse, found him somewhat lame.

His companion remarked the distress of the young man. After having looked at his feet, he thought the beast only wanted rest, and therefore proposed remaining in their present situation for some time longer, and travel part of the night; for, to Albert's consolation, he assured him he was sufficiently acquainted with their route to find it in the dark.

CHAPTER XIII

Sent by the Suabian League,
The hunters do not tarry;
But range the plain, and seek
To strike a princely quarry.

G. Schwab.

The youth resigned himself to his fate, and sought to dissipate time in the enjoyment of the beautiful prospect which, in proportion as the countryman led him higher up from the place where they had made their mid-day meal, presented itself to his view on a much more extended scale. They stood upon the crest of a rock commanding a large circuit of the Swabian Alb. An extended panorama spread itself before the spectators, to Albert's delight, who was so enraptured with the diversified colouring which the evening gradually threw over the whole, that he was for a time lost in ecstasy. And, in truth, whoever possesses a mind sufficiently pure for the enjoyment of the beauties of nature as existing in the peaceful landscape, the quiet valley, and lonely dell, such as are to be found in the Rhinegau, let him but mount the Swabian Alb, and he will be gratified by the sight of scenery which he will long cherish as among the most charming images in his remembrance. A range of mountains, so distant as scarcely to be reached by the eye, skirted the horizon, graduated with soft grey tints and different shades of blue, whilst a foreground of dark green hills completed the picture. On the summit of the extended ridge innumerable castles and towers were conspicuous, placed like watchmen as it were on these heights to overlook the country. Their remains are now in ruins, their stately gates and approaches no longer exist, the moats are filled with rubbish and overgrown with moss, and their halls, once the scenes of jovial mirth, now tell their tale in mournful silence. At the moment, however, when Albert and his companion stood on the rock of Beuren, many of them were to be seen in all the pride of solid and substantial defence, ranging themselves in array like an unbroken band of powerful men.

"This Würtemberg is a beautiful country," cried Albert, his eye wandering from hill to hill; "how bold, how sublime the summit and declivities of those mountains, how picturesque those rocks and castles!

And when the eye turns to the valley of the Neckar, how truly charming are those soft hills interspersed with orchards and vineyards, and watered by gentle streams and rivulets; the whole being blessed by a mild climate and a good race of people!"

"Yes, indeed," said the countryman, "this is a fine country; but it is not to be compared to the neighbourhood of Stuttgardt, the true lowland! There it is a real pleasure to wander about in summer or spring, on the banks of the Neckar; nature is prolific in all her bounties of cultivation; the vine grows to a large size and plentiful on the hills; the boats and rafts on the river float up and down in cheerful activity; the people are gay and happy at their work; and the girls sing like larks!"

"Those vallies, on the Rems and Neckar, may indeed possess their beauties," replied Albert; "but this one at our feet, and those heights about us, possess also a peculiarly peaceful charm: what is the name of that tower on the hill yonder? and tell me how are those distant mountains called?"

The countryman scanned the neighbourhood, and pointed to the most distant ridge of mountains, which, on account of the mist, was scarcely visible. "That, between the east and south, is the Rossberg mountain; in the same direction,' but nearer towards us, those many-pointed rocks which you see are the heights of Urack: more to the westward, is the Achalm; not far from which, but you cannot see it from hence, lies the rock of Lichtenstein."

"There it is," thought Albert to himself, "there, where that small cloud hovers amidst the evening tints; in that direction, a true heart beats for me; at this very moment she, perhaps, stands on the pinnacle of the rock, and looks this way, among that world of mountains. Oh, that the evening breeze might waft her my remembrance, and that rosy cloud acquaint her with my vicinity!"

"You see that sharp corner, further in the distance, that is the castle of Teck; our dukes call themselves Dukes of Teck: it is a strong fortress. Look to the right, that high steep mountain was once the residence of a renowned Emperor; and is called Hohenstaufen."

"But what is the name of that castle, near us, which appears to rear its head out of the deep mist?" asked the young man. "Only observe how the sun plays on its white walls; how the golden mist seems to rest about its battlements; and how beautifully the red light illumines its towers!"

"That is Neuffen, sir; also a strong castle, which the League would be glad to get possession of."

The sun was fast going down during this conversation. The shades of evening threw a dark veil from the mountains over the vallies, and obscured the distant objects. The moon rose pale, and surveyed her nightly province. The high walls and towers of Neuffen only were lighted up by the last rays of the sun; and with its departure, Neuffen was enveloped in darkness; the night air began to whisper through the trees of the surrounding wood mysterious salutations to the rays of the rising moon.

"This is the proper time for robbers and travellers fearful of the light of day, such as we are," said the countryman, as he bridled the horse; "in an hour hence, the night will, I hope, be dark as coal; and then, before the sun rises again, no Leaguist dog of a horseman shall come upon our scent."

"If there is any likelihood of our being attacked," said Albert, "we had better prepare for the worst; for I am resolved not to allow myself to be taken for a mere trifle." And taking his cap off, he was preparing to substitute in its place his helmet, which hung by his saddle.

"You had better keep on your cap, sir," said the countryman, smiling; "it will be warmer in the night breeze than your helmet; they will scarcely look for the Duke in this neighbourhood, and should we meet them, we two are a match for any four of them."

The young man thought he had betrayed a want of courage; and a feeling of shame rose in his breast, when he noticed the unconcern of his conductor, on foot, who had nothing but a thin leathern cap on his head, and armed only with an axe and knife. He mounted his horse, and his guide, taking the bridle, led him down the hill.

"You believe, therefore," asked Albert, after a pause, "that the Leaguist cavalry do not venture thus far?"

"It is not very likely," answered the fifer of Hardt; "because Neuffen is a strong fort, and contains a good garrison; the Leaguists will, however, soon besiege it; but vagabonds, such as Truchses' cavalry, will not venture in small bodies so near an enemy's position."

"Look how clear and beautiful the moon shines!" cried the young man, whose mind, still dwelling on the sight of the mountains they had left, admired the fantastic shades of the wood, and the brilliant shining rocks; "look how the windows in Neuffen glimmer in the moonlight."

"I would much rather she did not shine this night," replied the countryman, who at times looked anxiously about him; "a dark night would have suited us better; the moon has betrayed many a brave man. She now stands directly over the Reissenstein, where a giant once lived; it will not be long, however, before she goes down."

"What is that you say of a giant, who lived on the Reissenstein?"

"Yes," said Hans, "tradition says that many years back a giant lived on that spot; there, just where the moon shines on the mountain, stands his castle, called Reissenstein, or Achalm; it belongs now to the Helfensteiners; it is built on the declivity of the rock, high up in the air; and has no nearer neighbours than the clouds, and the moon. Just opposite the castle, on another eminence, upon which now stands Heimenstein, is a cavern, in which a giant formerly lived. He possessed an enormous treasure of gold, and could have lived nobly and in luxury, had there been other giants and giantesses besides him to keep him company. He was determined to build a castle, such as other knights possessed on the Alb. The rock opposite appeared to him the most convenient spot. He however was a bad architect; he dug out rocks of the height of a house from the Alb, with his nails, and placed them one upon another; but, as they always fell, he found his labour was in vain. He then mounted on the top of the Beuren rock, and cried out in the valley below for workmen; carpenters, masons, stone-cutters, blacksmiths, any one who would come and help him should be well paid. His voice was heard all over Swabia; from Kocher to the lake of Constance; from the Necker to the Danube; the call brought masters and workmen from all parts, who came to assist the giant build his castle.----Keep in the shade here, out of the moonshine, sir," he added, "your armour shines like silver, and could easily be seen by some of those bloodhounds.

"Well, to go on with the giant's history; it was curious to see him sitting in his cavern, in the sunshine, overlooking the progress of the workmen in building his castle on the top of the rock; masters and workmen worked merrily, and had their jokes with the giant, who understood nothing of their art. At last the castle was finished, and the giant took possession of it; when viewing the valley below from the uppermost window, where the master and his men were assembled, he angrily remarked, 'that one nail was wanting in the outside of the building, and that they had deceived him in reporting it complete.' The master blacksmith excused himself, and said: 'no one would venture to perch himself outside the window, to drive the nail in.' The giant would hear of no excuse; and refused to pay the reckoning until the nail was in its place. They all returned again to the castle; the most daring among them swore it was not a feat worth talking of to drive the nail in; but when they came to look out of the window, and beheld the great depth of the valley below, with its perpendicular rocks, they shook their heads, and retired in shame. The master offered a ten-fold reward to him who would venture on the perilous undertaking; but a long time elapsed before one bold enough could be found. There was a smart young fellow among the rest, who loved the master's daughter, and she loved him; but as he was poor and the master a hard man, he could not gain his consent to marry her. Taking courage, and thinking this a good opportunity to be able either to merit his love or to die in the attempt; for life without her was a burden to him: he went to his master, her father, and said, 'Will you give me your daughter if I drive the nail in?' The other thought this a good chance to get rid of him should he fall into the valley, and answered 'Yes.'

"The youth took the nail and hammer, said a prayer, and prepared to get outside the window and drive in the nail for the sake of his beloved. A burst of joy broke from the bystanders, which awoke the giant out of his sleep, when he asked what was the matter; and, when he heard that a volunteer was found to drive the nail in, he looked at the young locksmith for some time, and said: 'You are a fine fellow, and have more courage than all your milk-hearted companions; come, and I'll assist you.' He then took him by the nape of the neck, almost crushing him to atoms, lifted him out of the window in the air, and said, 'drive in, now--you shall not fall.'

"When the young lover was suspended in the air over the immense depth below, though held by the iron grasp of the giant's hand, fear came over him, his sight became dim, giddiness seized his brain, and, thinking he was on the point of being hurled into the abyss beneath, he would have cried out 'Ach Allmächtig!' (Oh, Almighty!) but had only time enough to pronounce, 'Ach Allm,' when the giant secured him from his perilous situation, and landed him again in safety. From that moment the mountain has retained the name of the Achalm.

"The lad drove the nail in firmly,--the giant kissed him for his fortitude,--and a tender hug which he gave him almost cost him his life,--he then led him to the master, and said: 'Give your daughter to the brave lad.' He afterwards went to his cavern, took out his money bag, and paid each his due. But when he came to the bold young blacksmith, he said, 'Go home, my daring young fellow, fetch your master's daughter, and take possession of the castle, for it belongs to you now.'

"His companions all rejoiced at his good fortune; the young blacksmith went home, and----"

"Hark! did not you hear the neighing of horses?" said Albert, not feeling quite at his ease, as they were passing through a deep ravine. The moon still shone bright, the shadows of the trees waved with the breeze, there was a rustling among the bushes, and he often fancied he saw dark figures passing in the wood.

The fifer of Hardt stopt, vexed that his companion had interrupted him in his story, and answered, "I thought so, likewise, just now, but it is nothing but the noise of the wind among the trees. If we were but on the other side of the meadow, which is open and as clear as day, we should regain the wood, and be free from all anxiety, for there it is dark enough. Give your horse the spur, and trot on; I'll run by your side."

"But why do you want to get on faster now? do you think there is anything to be apprehended? Own it, did you not see some figures in the wood sneaking along not far from us? Do you think they belong to the League?"

"Well, yes," whispered the countryman, looking round, "it struck me as if some one was watching us; hurry on, therefore, and let's get out of this cursed hollow path: a good round trot across the valley will carry us clear of danger, and then we may bid defiance to it."

Albert looked to his sword, and held the reins firmer in his hand. They descended in silence the gorge through which the path led, and, by the light of the moon, he could perceive each motion of his guide, and saw him raise his axe to his shoulder, and, taking out a knife, which he had concealed under his jacket, stick it into his girdle.

Just as they were entering the open valley from the hollow way, a voice was heard in the bush: "That's the fifer of Hardt--seize him! he on the horse must be the right one."

"Fly, sir, fly," cried the faithful guide, and placed himself in a position of defence with his axe. Albert drew his sword, and, in a moment, was attacked by five men, whilst his companion was engaged with three others hand to hand.

The confined spot where this rencontre took place prevented Albert profiting by the advantage he otherwise would have had over his opponents. One of them seized his bridle, but, in the same moment, Albert's blade fell with such force on his head that he sank to the ground without a groan; the others, furious at the loss of their companion, pressed him with increased vigour, calling out to him to surrender; but, though Albert began to bleed copiously from many wounds he had already received in his arms and legs, he answered only by fresh blows.

"Dead or alive," cried one of the combatants, "if the Duke will have it so, let him take the consequences!" and with these words a heavy blow on the head, brought Albert von Sturmfeder from his horse to the ground. His eyes closed in a state of fainting stupor, but he still was sufficiently conscious, to feel himself raised and carried away, amidst the sarcastic jeers of his opponents, who appeared to triumph and rejoice over their royal captive, as they supposed him to be.

He was placed on the ground shortly after, when a horseman galloped up, dismounted, and spoke to the men who carried him. Albert, having somewhat recovered from the violence of the stunning blow he had received, opened his eyes and surveyed the surrounding group. An unknown figure bent over him, as if to examine his features. "Who have we here?" said this man: "this is not him we are looking for--leave him to his fate; we must hurry away without loss of time--alarm is already spread in Neuffen, and the garrison is on the alert." Falling again into a state of stupor from excessive weakness, Albert closed his eyes a second time, his ear only was alive to the confused sound of indistinct voices, which soon were hushed into dead silence, and he was left alone. The damp ground of the meadow chilled his limbs, but a sweet slumber coming to his aid, he sank under it, his beloved Bertha occupying his last thought.

CHAPTER XIV

The Swabian League displays her mighty power,
Her warriors people many a castle wall,
Her banners wave from many an ancient tower,
And every city answers to her call.
Alone, will Tübingen no homage proffer,
But stand apart, and grim resistance offer.

G. Schwab.

The forces of the Swabian League had advanced in large numbers into Würtemberg. Uninterrupted success crowned all their undertakings,--its army became daily more formidable. Hollenstein and the strong castle of Heidenheim were the first that fell into their hands after a long and brave defence. The latter was defended by Stephan von Lichow; but with only a couple of culverins and a handful of men at his command, he could not hold out against the thousands of the League and the military experience of a Fronsberg. Göppingen soon after experienced the same fate. Not less brave than Lichow, Philip von Rechberg distinguished himself there, and obtained an honourable retreat for himself and garrison; but his gallant conduct was not able to turn the fate of the country. Teck, at that time a strong fortified position, was lost through the imprudence of the garrison. Möckmukh held out the longest; it possessed a man within its walls, who would have been a match for twenty of the besiegers, and whose determined resistance was equalled only by the power of his iron hand. Its walls were, however, demolished, and Götz von Berlichingen was also reckoned among the prisoners. Schorndorf could not withstand Fronsberg's cannon; it was reckoned, of all places, one of the strongest holds, and with it the rest of the low country belonging to Duke Ulerich fell into the hands of the League.

The whole of Würtemberg, as far as the neighbourhood of Kirchheim, being now in the power of the League, the Duke of Bavaria broke up his camp, for the purpose of besieging Stuttgardt in person. An embassy from the town met him, however, at Denkendorf, to beg for mercy. The ambassadors did not attempt to make any excuse before the bitter enemies of their Duke, nor to shelter themselves under the allegiance they owed to their hereditary Prince; they merely asserted, that as he, the cause of the war, was no longer within their walls, they craved exemption for their town being occupied by the troops of the League. But this petition found no grace in the stern mind of Wilhelm of Bavaria and the covetous desires of the other members of the League. The only answer they received was, that Ulerich's conduct had merited punishment, and that, as the country had supported him, Stuttgardt therefore must also open its gates unconditionally.

The townsfolk of the capital being unable to defend themselves against the powerful forces of the League, were obliged to submit to these hard terms, and admit a garrison within their walls.

The conquest of the country was, however, far from being complete with the capture of the capital. The greatest part of the hill country still held for the Duke, and, judging from the spirit of its inhabitants, they were not likely to submit to the first summons. This elevated district was commanded by two fortified places, Urach and Tübingen;--and so long as they remained firm to the Duke, the surrounding neighbourhood also determined not to desert his cause. In Urach, however, the citizens, fearful of the power of the League, wished to come to terms, whilst the garrison held faithful to their master. The two parties at last came to blows, in which the brave commander was killed, and the garrison was then obliged to surrender.

By the middle of April Tübingen, which had been strongly fortified, was the only place left to the Duke. Ulerich confided the defence of the castle, with the care of his family and the treasure of his house, to forty gallant and experienced knights, having under them two hundred of the bravest of his countrymen. The position of this fortress was strong, and being well supplied with ammunition and provisions, all eyes in Germany looked to its fate with anxiety; for, Tübingen being a town of great repute in those days, it was thought that if it could but hold out until the Duke relieved it, he might then be able to re-conquer the country. The League, to frustrate their enemy's last hope, now marched against it with their whole force. The heavy steps of armed bodies of men sounded through the forests in their march towards the place; the vallies of the Neckar trembled under the tread of cavalry; the artillery, with the baggage and ammunition waggons, and all the apparatus for a long siege, which was brought with the army, left deep ruts in the fields as a witness of the coming event.

Albert von Sturmfeder knew nothing of the progress of the war. A deep but sweet slumber, like a powerful enchantment, suspended the operations of his faculties for a long time. He suffered no inconvenience in this state of stupor, but resembled a child who, sleeping on the breast of its mother, occasionally opens its eyes to gaze at a world it knows not, and closes them again for a time. Pleasing dreams of better days soothed his situation, a placid smile often played upon his pale countenance, and comforted those who nursed him with tender solicitude.

We will now introduce the reader to the humble cottage, which had received him with hospitality, and treated him with tender care the day after he had been wounded.

The morning sun of this day threw its enlivening rays on the round frame of a small window, and illumined the largest room of a needy peasant's house. Though the furniture bespoke poverty, cleanliness and order reigned throughout. A large oaken table stood in one corner of the room, on two sides of which were placed wooden benches. A carved chest, painted with bright colours, contained, as was generally the case in such habitations, the Sunday wardrobe of the inhabitants, and fine linen spun by themselves; around the dark wainscot of the walls was a shelf, upon which were ranged well polished cans, goblets, and smoothing irons, earthen utensils with mottos in verse painted on them, and all kinds of musical instruments, such as cymbals, hautboys, and a guitar, hung on the walls. At the further end of the room stood a bedstead, with cotton curtains, of a coarse texture, ornamented with figures of large flowers. It was partly concealed from view by a range of clean linen hanging to air around an earthenware stove, which projected far into the apartment.

A young girl, of about sixteen or seventeen years of age, sat beside the bed. She was dressed in that picturesque costume which, with little difference, has been handed down to our days among our Swabian peasantry. Her golden hair was uncovered, and fell in two long tresses plaited with different coloured ribands, over her back. Her cheerful face was somewhat tanned by the sun, but not so much as to obscure the lovely youthful colour of her cheeks; a lively blue eye sparkled from beneath a long eyelash. Plaited full sleeves of white linen covered her arm down to the hand; a scarlet bodice, laced with a silver chain, and trimmed with fancy-worked linen, of a finer texture than the sleeves, sat close to her shape; a short black petticoat fell scarcely below the knee. This ornamental dress, together with a clean white apron and high clocked stockings of the same colour, fastened up with pretty garters, did not appear quite in keeping with the humble furniture of the room, nor with the week-day costume of a peasant's daughter.

The young girl was busily employed spinning fine thread; at times she opened the curtains of the bed, and peeped in. But, as if she had been caught in the act, she quickly closed them again, and smoothed the folds, so that no one might remark what she had been about.

The door opened, when a little plump elderly woman entered, dressed much in the same way as the girl, but not so smart. She brought a basin of hot soup for breakfast, and then arranged the plates on the table. When she saw her daughter (for such she was) sitting beside the bed, she was so startled at her appearance, that a little more and she would have dropped the jug of cider which she also held in her hand.

"For God's sake, what are you thinking about, Barbelle," said she, as she placed the jug on the table and approached the maiden; "what are you thinking about, to sit and spin there with your new bodice on? And she has got her new petticoat on, too, and the silver chain, I declare, and has taken a clean apron and stockings out of the chest! What a piece of vanity, you foolish thing! Don't you know that we are poor folks, and that you are the child of an unfortunate man?"

The daughter patiently allowed her bustling mother to expend her astonishment; she cast her eyes down, it is true, but there was a roguish smile on her face, which proved that the lecture did not sink very deep. "Ah! what's the use of being angry?" she answered; "what harm can it do to my dress, if I wear it once on a week day? The silver chain will not suffer, and I can easily wash the apron."

"So! as if we had not washing and cleaning enough? But tell me, what has put it into your head to make yourself so smart to-day?"

"Ah! don't you know, mother," said the blushing Swabian child, "that to-day is the eighth day? Did not my father say the gentleman would awake on the eighth day, if his medicines had their desired effect? And so I thought----"

"Yes, this is about the time," replied the mother, kindly; "you are quite right, child: if he awakes and sees everything about him slovenly and dirty, we shall get into trouble with the father. And I am not fit to be seen! Go, Barbelle, and fetch me my black jacket and red bodice, and a clean apron."

"But, mother," said the young one, "you had better go and dress yourself, while I remain here, for perhaps the gentleman may awake when you are putting your things on."

"You are right again, girl," replied the mother, and, leaving the breakfast on the table, retired to adorn her person. Her daughter opened the window to the fresh morning air, for the purpose, according to her usual practice, of feeding her pigeons, which were assembled before the house waiting for their accustomed meal; larks and other little birds saluting her in full chirping chorus, partook also of her bounty, which the young girl enjoyed with innocent pleasure.

At this moment the curtains of the bed were opened, when the head of a handsome young man looked out; we need not say it was Albert von Sturmfeder.

A slight colour, the first messenger of returning health, played on his cheeks; his look was as brilliant as ever, and his arm felt as powerful. He surveyed his situation in astonishment; the room, with its furniture, were strangers to him; everything about him was a riddle. Who had bandaged his head? who had put him in this bed? His position appeared to him like that of one who had passed a jovial night with his companions, and, having lost his senses, awoke in some out-of-the-way place.

He observed the girl at the window for some time. He could not keep his eyes off her, as she was the first object he had seen; for the purpose of drawing her attention, he made a rustling noise with the curtains as he threw them further back.

She' started when she heard the noise, and looking round, exhibited, to Albert's astonishment and delight, the beauty of her countenance, now slightly tinged with a blush. His sudden apparition appeared for a moment to deprive her pretty smiling mouth of the power of finding words to welcome the invalid to returning life. She soon collected herself, however, and hastened to the bedside, but immediately after checked her steps, as if she were not quite certain of her patient being really awake, or whether it were proper to be in the room when he returned to his senses.

The young man, observing the embarrassment of this beautiful maiden, was the first to break silence.

"Tell me, where am I? how came I here?" asked Albert. "To whom belongs this house, in which, it appears, I awake out of a long sleep?"

"Are you really in your senses again?" cried she, clasping her hands for joy. "Ah! thank God, who would ever have thought it? But you look at one as if it were true, though you have been so long ill as to make us very fearful and anxious about you."

"Have I been ill?" inquired Albert, who scarcely understood the dialect of the Swabian girl. "I have only been a few hours without consciousness?"

"Eh! what are you thinking about," giggled the girl, and bit the end of the tress, to suppress a rising laugh; "a few hours, did you say? This night will just be the ninth that I have been watching you."

The young man could not comprehend what he heard. Nine days, and not arrived at Lichtenstein, to see Bertha? And with this thought his recollection of the past returned in full force to his mind; he remembered having renounced the service of the League,--that he had determined to visit Lichtenstein,--that he had crossed the Alb by unfrequented paths, and that he and his leader had been attacked. But now, when he looked about him, fearful doubts oppressed his mind. Am I a prisoner, he thought to himself; and immediately put the same question to his pretty attendant.

She had noticed, with increasing anxiety, the placid countenance of the young knight, as it became ruffled, and the wild look his features had suddenly assumed. Fearful he might relapse again into his former situation, which the languid tone of his voice seemed to indicate, she hesitated what to do, whether to remain in the room, or call in the assistance of her mother.

She did not return an answer, and retired towards the door. Her heart was touched at the distress which appeared to oppress her patient; and Albert, judging by her silence and the anxious expression of her countenance, which he construed into an affirmation to his question, that he was now in the hands of his enemies, exclaimed, "I am a prisoner then, separated from her without hope, without consolation, without the possibility of hearing from her perhaps for a long time!" The shock was too great for his weak state of body to withstand; a tear stole from his eye.

The girl observed the tear: her anxiety was changed into pity, she approached nearer, and seating herself again by the bed-side, ventured to take the hand of the young man. "You must not give way to grief," she said, "your honour is well again, and----you can very soon proceed on your journey," she added, with a cheerful smile.

"Proceed on my journey?" asked Albert, "then I am not a prisoner?"

"Prisoner? no, certainly not; you might have been so, indeed, once or twice, for the patroles of the League often came to our house, but we always concealed you, because my father told us not to let any one see you."

"Your father!" cried the young man, "who is your father? Where am I?"

"Where are you?" answered Barbelle, "why, in Hardt, to be sure."

"In Hardt?" a glance at the walls adorned with musical instruments convinced him that he was indebted to the man for his life and liberty, who had been sent to him from Bertha as a guardian angel. "So I am in Hardt? and your father is the fifer of Hardt, is he not?"

"He does not like to be called by that name," said the girl; "he is certainly a musician, but he prefers being known by the name of Hans."

"But how did I come here?" inquired Albert.

"Don't you recollect anything about it?" smiled the young girl, and played with her hair again. She then related, in Swabian dialect, that after her father had been absent many weeks, he suddenly arrived nine days ago, in the night, and knocked at the door some time before it awoke her. Having recognised his voice, she hurried down to let him in. He was accompanied by four men, carrying a wounded man, covered with his cloak, whom they brought into the house. When her father withdrew the cloak from the sick man, and desired her to bring a light, she was terribly frightened at seeing a person bleeding, and apparently half dead. He then ordered her to heat the stove immediately, and they brought the wounded man into the room, and laid him on the bed. His dress was that of a person of distinction. "My father," added she, "applied some herbs to his wounds, he also prepared a cordial for him, for he understands the art of medicine both for man and beast. The young man was for two days very restless and violent, which caused us all great anxiety. But after my father had given him a third dose of medicine he became easy and quiet, and then he said that, on the eighth morning, the invalid would be himself again, and his prediction has actually come to pass."

Albert listened to the story of the young girl with much interest; he was obliged occasionally to interrupt her in her narration, when he did not exactly understand the expressions she made use of in her Swabian dialect, or when she described more minutely the herbs with which the fifer of Hardt had prepared his medicines.

"And where is your father?" he asked.

"How can we know where he is?" she answered, as if she wished to avoid the question; but, recollecting herself, she added, "I think I may tell you, because you must be a good friend of his; he is gone to Lichtenstein."

"To Lichtenstein?" cried Albert, and blushed deeply; "and when will he come back again?"

"He ought to have been here two days ago, as he told us, if nothing happened to detain him. Folks say the cavalry of the League are on the look-out for him."

The mere mention of Lichtenstein seemed to invigorate his weak frame with renewed strength. He fancied himself strong enough to mount his horse immediately, and, by the rapidity of his movements, make up for the time he had lost on the bed of sickness.

His next and most important question, therefore, was to inquire after his horse; and when he heard it was quite well in the cow-house, he thought he would be able to set out without further loss of time. He thanked his kind little nurse for the care she had taken of him, and asked for his jacket and cloak. She had long since cleaned his clothes, and carefully washed out all spots of blood; and taking them out of the carved painted chest, where they had been placed among her Sunday's attire, spread them out one by one before him, and appeared pleased with the grateful acknowledgements which he expressed for her attention. She then hurried out of the room to acquaint her mother with the joyful news of the young knight's restoration to health and vigour.

We know not whether she told her mother that she had had half an hour's gossip with the handsome gentleman; we have reason however to doubt it, for that good lady had learnt from the experience of her youthful days, and thought it necessary to repeat the warning constantly to her daughter, that "she should take good care not to speak to a smart young fellow longer than it would take to repeat an 'Ave Maria.'"

VOL. II

CHAPTER XV

Art thou troubled, maiden? Tell me what,--
Thou speak'st of matters which beseem thee not.

Schiller.

Barbelle went up stairs to her mother, who was still occupied in adorning her little plump person, to appear before her guest in proper attire. They then descended together to the kitchen on the ground floor, which adjoined the apartment of Albert. The attention of the good matron was more excited by getting a peep at him through a small window looking into his room, than in preparing a mess of oatmeal porridge for his mid-day meal. Barbelle was also determined to satisfy her curiosity in like manner, and standing upon tiptoes, looked over her mother's shoulders.

She beheld the young man with wondering eyes, and her heart beat violently for the first time in seventeen years at the sight of his fine figure. She had been often moved to tears as he lay on the bed of sickness, insensible, almost lifeless; deeply affected at the pallid appearance of his fine manly features struggling with death, as she imagined, she had watched him with the tender anxiety of a pious mind; but now she felt he was quite a different object to behold. His eye was reanimated by a beautiful expression, and it struck Barbelle, young though she was, that she had never seen the like before. His hair fell no longer in wild disorder over his forehead; it now hung down his neck arranged with care and combed into neat curls. The colour had returned to his cheeks, and his lips were as fresh as cherries on the festivals of Peter and Paul; and how well did his embroidered silk jacket become him, and the broad white collar which he had put on over his dress! But the little girl could not comprehend why he was so much occupied with a certain white and blue silk scarf; she even thought that he pressed it to his heart and raised it to his lips, full of the devotion which is paid to some esteemed relic.

The elderly matron had, in the meantime, satisfied her curiosity in the examination of her guest, and returned to her culinary occupations. "The gentleman looks like a prince," she said, as she gave the mess of oatmeal porridge a stir, "what a jacket he has! no Stuttgardt beau can boast of a finer one. But what is he always doing with that band he holds in his hand? He never ceases to look at it. Perhaps there is a spot of blood on it which he cannot get out?"

"No, that's not it!" said Barbelle, who could now look into the room with greater ease. "But do you know, mother, what I think? he looks at it with such ardent eyes, that it must certainly be something from his love."

The matron could scarcely help smiling at the supposition of her child, but she soon recover her dignity, and replied, "Ah, what do you know about love! Such a child as you must not think of the like. Get away from the window, and fetch me a napkin. The gentleman has been accustomed to good living, so I must put more melted butter in the porridge." Barbelle left the window rather in a pet. She knew that she dare not disobey her mother, but nevertheless thought that she was in the present instance decidedly in the wrong. For, had she not been in the habit of joining the other girls of the village for a whole year past, when they talked and sang of their loves and favourites? Had not some of her companions, who were only a few weeks older than herself their appropriate sweethearts? and should she alone be debarred from even speaking on the subject,--not even to know anything about it? No, it was too bad of her mother; who now forbad her knowing anything about such affairs, when but a moment before she had not objected to her standing upon tiptoes to look over her shoulder. But, as it often happens that prohibition excites transgression, so Barbelle was determined not to rest satisfied until she had discovered why the young knight regarded his scarf with such enraptured eyes.

The breakfast of the young man was, in the meantime, ready, wanting only a can of wine to complete it; this was also soon provided; for, though the fifer of Hardt was a man of low condition, he was not so poor that his cellar could not produce a bottle or two upon extraordinary occasions. The girl carried the wine and bread, whilst her mother, dressed in her complete Sunday's attire, preceded her daughter into the room, bearing the dish of oatmeal porridge in both hands.

Albert had some difficulty to dispense with the ceremonious respect, which the fifer's wife thought was due to such a distinguished guest. She had once served in the castle of Neuffen, and knew what good manners were, and therefore remained on the threshold of the door, with the smoking hot dish in her hands, until the young man positively ordered her to approach. Her daughter stood blushing behind the round plump matron, and her confused countenance was only occasionally visible to Albert when her mother curtsied very low. She also followed her mother through the number of requisite ceremonies, but felt, perhaps, less embarrassment now than she might have done, had she not had half an hour's previous conversation with their guest.

Barbelle covered the table with a clean cloth, and put the porridge and wine before Albert, who was to sit on the end of the bench under the crucifix, which hung on the wall. She then stuck a curiously carved wooden spoon into it, which, standing unassisted upright, was a proof that the meal was of the best cooking. When the young man had seated himself, the mother and daughter also took their places at the table to partake of the breakfast, but placed themselves at a respectful distance, not forgetting to put the salt between them and their distinguished guest, for such was the custom in the good old times.

During the time that each was occupied with their repast, Albert had sufficient opportunity to make a few passing observations upon his companions. In the appearance of the stately personage who filled the situation of honour in the fifer of Hardt's house, self importance and dignity seemed pre-eminent whilst much kindliness of expression was marked on her features. Had not her better half been a man of determined character, and positive in maintaining the upper hand in the essentials of domestic government, there was something in the bearing of his wife which indicated, that one less bold might easily have been brought under her dominion.

In her daughter's countenance, the combined charms of simple unaffected goodness and innocence beamed forth in all their glory. The purity of her heart, and kindliness of her feelings, were delineated in the delicate lines of her features, and the soft modest expression of her eye bespoke unconsciousness of nature's best gifts. Such was this child of nature, bred and born in the lonely cottage of a restless intriguing peasant; Albert could not behold her without admiration, and owned to himself that, had his heart not been already fully occupied with another, and the distance between the heir to the name of Sturmfeder and the lower born daughter of the fifer of Hardt been immeasurably great, she might have won no insignificant place in it. His eye rested with peculiar pleasure and interest upon her innocent face, and, had not her mother been so much occupied with her porridge, she could not have avoided noticing the blushes of her child, when a stolen look at the young knight by chance met his glance.

"Now that the platter is empty, is the time to gossip," is a true saying; which was put in practice as soon as the table cloth was taken away. Albert had two things particularly at heart. He wished to know for certain, when the fifer of Hardt would return from Lichtenstein, because he only awaited intelligence from Bertha to hasten immediately to her; and, secondly, it was highly necessary for him to learn where the army of the League was at the present moment. To the first question he could not expect any further information, than that which the maiden had already given him, namely, that her father had been absent about six days, but, having promised to be back on the fifth, she now looked for his arrival every hour. The good matron shed tears as she bewailed to her guest how her husband, since the commencement of the war, had been but a few hours at home; how he had always had the reputation of being a restless character; and how people rumoured all sorts of stories about him, which would certainly bring his wife and child into misfortune and trouble by his dangerous mode of life.

Albert tried all means to console her and stop her tears; and so far succeeded, as to enable her to answer his questions respecting the army of the League.

"Ah! sir," she said, "terror and misery are our portion now-a-days! it is just as if a wild huntsman were riding on the clouds, driving over the country with his ghost hounds. They have overrun all the low country, and now the whole force is gone to attack Tübingen."

"So all the fortresses are in their hands?" said Albert, astonished: "Höllenstein, Schorndorf, Göppingen, Teck, Urach--are they all taken?"

"All of them, I believe; a man from Schorndorf told me that the confederates were in Höllenstein, Schorndorf, and Göppingen. But I can tell you for certain about Teck and Urach, as we are only three or four hours' distance from them." She then related that, on the 3rd of April, the League's army advanced to Teck; one part of the infantry was posted before one of the gates of the town, and had a parley with the garrison about surrendering. Every one flocked to the spot to hear the summons, and in the meantime the enemy scaled the other gate. But, in the castle of Urach, there were four hundred ducal infantry, which the citizens would not admit into the town when the enemy advanced. A battle took place between them, in which the soldiers were forced into the market place, where the commander was wounded by a ball, and afterwards run through the body by a halbert; the town then surrendered to the League. "It is no wonder," said the fifer of Hardt's wife, as she concluded her narration, "that they take all the towns and castles; for they have long falconets and bombarding pieces which shoot balls as large as my head, breaking down walls and upsetting towers."

Albert could easily foresee from this information, that the journey from Hardt to Lichtenstein would not be less dangerous, than that which he had already performed over the Alb, for he knew that he would be obliged to pass directly between Urach and Tübingen. But, as the army of the

League had been withdrawn from Urach several days back, and the siege of Tübingen necessarily required a large force, he might hope there was no post of any importance occupied by the enemy, in the country through which he would have to travel. He therefore awaited the arrival of his guide with impatience.

The wound on his head was quite healed; though the blow had been severe enough to deprive him of his senses for many days, it was not deep, owing to the feathers of his cap and the thickness of his hair having blunted the sharpness of the cut. He had recovered also of the wounds on his legs and arms, and the only inconvenience he suffered from the result of that unfortunate night, was a debility arising from the loss of blood, and lying so long upon the bed of sickness. But his constitution hourly gained strength, his natural buoyancy of spirit resumed its sway, and his only thought was to proceed onwards to his destination.

He was, however, compelled to summon up all his spirits, to make the tedious hours he was still doomed to pass in his present quarters at all bearable. The daughter of the fifer, perceiving how the prolonged absence of her father distressed him, did her best to beguile the time by amusing him with her cheerful conversation. The delay was nevertheless not without its advantages, for he became acquainted with the character and life of the Swabian peasant. Their manners and dialect were quite new to him. His countrymen, the Franconians, although bordering so near on this part of Würtemberg, were to his mind a race more subtle and crafty,--in many respects less polished,--than these. But the kind-hearted honesty of the Swabians, which their looks, address, and actions bespoke,--their cheerful industry, their cleanliness and order, giving to poverty a respectable, indeed a substantial, appearance; in short, everything he saw induced him to think they possessed more intrinsic good qualities than their shrewder neighbours.

He was very much taken with the unaffected simplicity of the young girl's talk. Her mother might scold as much as she liked, and remind her continually of the high rank of the knight, she was not to be deterred from entertaining him, and she was particularly bent upon not giving up her secret plan to ascertain whether she or her mother were right in their views respecting the white and blue scarf. Upon this subject she had her own thoughts, arising out of the following circumstance:

One night when Albert was very ill, she had remained up late to keep her father company, who was watching by his bed-side. But having fallen asleep over her work, she was aroused, it might have been about ten o'clock, by a noise in the room. She saw a man in earnest conversation with her father, whose features did not escape her notice, although he tried to conceal them under a large cap. She thought she recognised in the stranger a servant of the knight of Lichtenstein, who had often been in the habit of coming in a mysterious way to the fifer of Hardt, upon which occasion she was always obliged to leave the apartment.

Bent upon knowing what this man had to communicate to her father, she feigned to be asleep thinking he would not disturb her. She was right in her conjecture; and heard the stranger speak of a young lady, who was inconsolable, on account of a certain young man. She had commissioned him to go to Hardt to ascertain the truth of the report which had given her great concern, and had determined to acknowledge every thing to her father respecting her acquaintance with the invalid, and in case he returned to her with unsatisfactory intelligence, she would immediately proceed to nurse him herself.

The messenger from Lichtenstein spoke in an under tone, as if afraid of being overheard; and her father, lamenting the case of the lady, represented the state of the patient as being likely soon to be ameliorated, and promised that, when he was decidedly better, he would immediately convey the consoling news to her himself. The stranger then cut off a lock of the sick man's hair, folded it up carefully in a cloth, which he carried under his jacket, and being led out of the room by her father, took his departure.

The many occupations of the following days, had driven the conversation of the stranger from the recollection of the fifer's daughter; but when she witnessed the scene from the kitchen window, it came back in full force to her mind. She knew that the knight of Lichtenstein had a daughter, because her aunt had been her nurse, and now was her attendant. It could be no other than this very lady, who had sent the servant to inquire about the sick man, and intended to come herself to nurse him.

All the stories she had ever heard as she sat at the spinning-wheel on a long winter's evening,--and there were many terrible ones, of king's daughters in love, of gallant knights sick in prison, saved by the hands of noble ladies,--came to her remembrance. She did not exactly know what people of quality thought of love, but she supposed that sensation must be much the same kind of thing, which girls of her village felt, when they surrendered their hearts to handsome young fellows of their own rank in life. With this idea strong in her mind, she thought how painful must be the situation of the noble lady, living in the high and distant castle, not to know whether her treasure were dead or alive, nor to be able to come to him, to see him, and to watch over him.

These reflections brought tears into her eye, generally so animated and cheerful. Her heart was touched at the idea of the narrow escape the lady had run of losing her lover; and supposing her to be the daughter of a noble, rich knight, she necessarily must be very beautiful, her imagination led her to fancy her situation to be doubly inconsolable. But was not the young man to be equally pitied, if not more so? thought she. Her father had surely ere this imparted to the lady the gratifying news of her lover's recovery; whilst he, poor man, had not heard one word from her for many days! Has he not been deprived of his senses during nine whole days; and since their return been left in anxious suspense on her account? These circumstances, therefore, left no doubt upon her mind, of the reason why he cherished the scarf with such tender regard, and convinced her from whose hands it came, at the same time that it satisfied her why he constantly pressed it to his heart and lips. Thinking to give him comfort, she determined to relate to him what had passed on that night, when she overheard the conversation between her father and the stranger.

Whilst Barbelle was occupied at her spinning wheel, Albert remarked that she was not so cheerful as usual, that there was a cast of seriousness on her countenance, which he had never observed before. Her mind appeared occupied with a thought that distressed her; nay, he even perceived a tear in her eye. He was so much struck by the change, as to wish to know the cause of it. "What have you at heart, girl?" he asked, just after her mother had left the room. "What makes you all at once so silent and serious? you even moisten your thread with tears!"

"And can you be gay, sir?" asked Barbelle, and looked at him inquisitively in the face. "I think I saw something once fall from your eye also, which moistened that scarf. I am sure it was given you by your love; and I was just thinking how much I grieved that you were not by her side."

Albert was taken by surprise at this remark of his young friend, and blushed deeply, which satisfied her she had made a better guess about the mysteries of the scarf than her mother had. "You are not far wrong," he answered, smiling; "but I am not uneasy on that account, as I hope to see her again very shortly."

"Ah! what joy there will be at Lichtenstein when that happy event comes to pass," said Barbelle, whose countenance had now resumed its wonted gaiety.

What could be the meaning of this, thought Albert? could her father have made known to her the secret of his love? "In Lichtenstein, did you say? what do you know about me and Lichtenstein?"

"Ah! I rejoice to think of the happiness the noble lady will have when she sees you again. I have heard how miserable she was when you were ill."

"Miserable, did you say?" cried Albert, springing upon his feet, and approaching her; "was she aware of my state? O speak! what do you know of Bertha? Are you acquainted with her? What has your father said of her?"

"My father has not said a single word to me; and I should not have known there was such a person as a lady of Lichtenstein, if my aunt was not her nurse. But you must not be offended at me, sir, if I listened a little; look ye, this is the way I know it." She then related how she became acquainted with the secret; and that her father was probably gone to Lichtenstein to give the lady comforting intelligence of his recovery.

Albert was painfully affected at this news. He had all along cherished the hope that Bertha would have heard of his misfortune and recovery at the same time, and have been spared much anxiety on his account. He well knew how the cruel uncertainty of his being safe from the vigilance of the enemy's patroles, even had his health been restored, would wear upon her spirits; perhaps affect her health also. Truly his own misfortune appeared nothing, when he compared it to the distress of that dear girl. How much had she not gone through in Ulm! how painful the separation from him! and now scarcely had she enjoyed the thought of his having quitted the colours of the League, scarcely had she been able to look forward to a more cheerful futurity, when she was terrified by the news of his being almost mortally wounded. And all this she was obliged to suffer in secret, to conceal it from the looks of her father--without possessing one single soul as a friend, to whose sympathy she could confide the secret of her heart--and from whom she might seek consolation. He now felt more than ever how necessary it became to hasten his departure for Lichtenstein; and his impatience was inflamed into anger, that the fifer of Hardt, otherwise a cautious and clever man, should just at this moment remain so long absent.

The maiden guessed his thoughts: "I plainly see you long to be away-- oh, were but my father here to shew you the way to Lichtenstein! It would be imprudent in you to go alone, for there would be no difficulty in detecting your not being a Würtemberger by your speech. Do you know what? I'll run to meet my father, and hurry him home."

"You go to meet him?" said, Albert touched by the proposal of the good-hearted girl; "do you know whether he be in the neighbourhood? he may be still some distance from home; and it will be dark in an hour."

"And were it so dark, that I should be obliged to grope my way blindfolded to Lichtenstein, I'll wager you could not go faster to your----."

Blushing, she cast her eyes down; for although her good heart induced her to proffer her services as a messenger of love, she felt confused when she touched upon the tender subject, which had been made so clear to her this day, and which confirmed her in her former suspicions.

"But if you volunteer to go to Lichtenstein out of regard for me, there is no reason why I should not accompany you, rather than remain behind, to await the arrival of your father. I'll saddle my horse immediately, and ride by your side; you can shew me the way until I am far enough not to mistake the rest of it."

The girl of Hardt scarcely knew which way to look, when Albert made this proposal; and playing with the ends of her long plaits of hair, said, almost in a whisper, "But it will be so soon dark."

"Well, what does that signify? So much the better, because I shall then be able to arrive in Lichtenstein by cock-crow," answered Albert; "you yourself proposed finding the way through the darkness."

"Yes, to be sure, so I could," replied Barbelle, without looking up; "but you are not strong enough yet to undertake the journey; and he who has just risen from a sick bed, must not think of travelling six hours in the night."

"I cannot pay any more attention to that," said Albert; "my wounds are all healed, and I feel as well as ever I was; so get ready, my good girl, we will start immediately; I'll go and saddle my horse." He took the bridle, which hung on a nail on the wall, and went to the door.

"But, sir! hear me, good sir!" cried the girl, in a beseeching tone, after him: "pray do not think of going now. It would not be proper for me to travel alone with you in the dark. The people in Hardt are very censorious, and they would certainly say some ill-natured thing of me if----; better stay till to-morrow morning, when I will willingly go as far as Pfullingen with you."

The young man respected her reasons, and replaced in silence the bridle on the nail. It would certainly have been much more agreeable to him, if the folks of Hardt had been less inclined to think evil of their neighbours; but he could not do otherwise than meet the well-meant scruples of Barbelle in their proper light. He therefore determined to remain the night waiting the arrival of the fifer of Hardt; should he not then come, he would mount his horse by daybreak, and set out for Lichtenstein, under the conduct of his young friend.

CHAPTER XVI

The whispering breezes fan the day,
And gently blow around;
With fragrance passing sweet they play,
And break with dulcet sound.
Now, my poor heart, be not oppress'd by fear,
Those breezes will a better fortune bear.

L. Uhland.

But the fifer of Hardt did not return home that night; and as Albert could no longer restrain his desire to prosecute his journey, he saddled his horse at break of day. His good hostess, after no small struggle, allowed her daughter to accompany him. She was afraid lest such an extraordinary event should furnish conversation, perhaps not to the credit of her child, for many an evening's gossip in the spinning occupations of her neighbours, and therefore reluctantly gave her consent. Upon the consideration, however, of the interest her husband must have taken in the welfare of the young knight, having treated him like a son in concealing him in his house, she thought she could not well refuse him this last piece of service. She accordingly permitted her daughter to go as his guide, upon the sole condition, that she was to proceed a quarter of an hour's distance in advance, and wait for him at a certain milestone.

Albert was affected in taking leave of the kind-hearted matron, who, out of respect for him, had decked herself out in her best Sunday's attire. He had placed a gold ducat in the carved chest, as a mark of gratitude for the attention he had received from her; a considerable present in those days, and a large sum out of the travelling purse of Albert von Sturmfeder. It would appear that the fifer of Hardt never knew a word about this deposit whether it was, that his wife did not find the piece of gold, or that she did not like to inform him of it, fearing lest he might return the present to the donor, and thereby affront him. But so much is certain, that the musician's wife was shortly after seen in church dressed in a new gown, to the astonishment and envy of all the women of the neighbourhood, and her daughter Barbelle wore a beautiful bodice of the finest cloth, trimmed with gold, which had never been seen before, at the next feast, kept in commemoration of the dedication of the church. She was always seen to blush, also, whenever any of her companions felt the texture of the new bodice and congratulated her upon the acquisition of it. Such was the effect which a single piece of gold produced in the village of Hardt, in those good old times!

Albert found his conductor sitting on the appointed milestone. She jumped up as soon as he arrived, and walked with a quick pace beside his horse. The girl appeared much more cheerful than the day before. The fresh air of an April morning had given her cheeks a high colour, and her eyes sparkled with kindness. Her costume was well adapted for a long walk, for her short petticoats did not impede her progress. A basket hung on her arm, as if she were going to market. But neither vegetables nor fruit were contained in it, which was generally the case on such occasions; she only carried a large shawl, as a precaution against April showers. The young man thought to himself, as his companion walked by his side, what a housekeeper she would make for some country swain, who should be fortunate enough to possess her for a wife!

She had inherited much of the vivacity of her father's character. For in the same way that he beguiled the time of his companion on their journey over the Alb, by relating stories and pointing out the principal features of the country, did she draw his attention to the most beautiful points of view of the surrounding vallies and mountains; or imparted to him, unsolicited, the popular anecdotes of castles, or other striking objects.

Choosing the most unfrequented paths, she led her guest only through two or three villages, and rested awhile after every two hours' walk. At last, after having made four such stations, a town was seen about a short half-hour's walk from them; the road parted at the spot of their last halt, and a foot-path to the left conducted to a village. At this point of separation, the girl said: "That is Pfullingen which you see yonder, from whence any child will show you the road to Lichtenstein."

"How! are you going to leave me already?" asked Albert, who was so much charmed with the cheerful conversation of his companion, that the thought of parting from her took him by surprise. "Will you not come at least as far as Pfullingen, where you can rest yourself, and have some refreshment? You don't intend to return home immediately?"

The girl endeavoured to look merry and unconcerned; but she could not conceal an expression about her mouth and eye, which betrayed the pain she felt at parting from her guest, whose presence might have been much dearer to her than she was, perhaps, altogether aware of. "I must leave you here, sir," she said, "much as I would willingly go on with you;

but my mother will have it so; I have a cousin in that village on the hill, where I will remain to-day, and return to Hardt to-morrow. And now may God and the Holy Virgin protect you, and all the Saints take you under their care! Remember me to my father, should you meet him; and," she added with a smile, as she quickly dried a tear, "give my respects to the lady also whom you love."

"Thanks, many thanks, Barbelle," replied Albert, as he took her hand to wish her goodbye; "I can never repay your faithful care of me; but when you get home, look into the carved chest, where you will find something which will, perhaps, provide you with a new bodice or petticoat for Sunday. And when you put it on for the first time, and your true love kisses you, then think of Albert von Sturmfeder."

The young man gave his horse the spur, and trotted across the green plain towards the town. When he had gone about two hundred paces, he turned around to have one more look at his young guide. There she stood on the same spot where he had left her, watching him as he increased his distance from her, with her hands up to her eyes; but whether to guard them from the rays of the sun, as she followed him with her look, or whether to wipe away the tear which stood on the brink of her eyelid as they parted, Albert could not precisely tell.

He was soon at the gate of the town, and, feeling tired and thirsty, inquired where the best inn was? He was shown a small gloomy-looking house, having the sign of a Golden Stag, and a spear and shield, over the door. A little bare-footed boy led his horse to the stable, whilst he was received at the entrance by a young, good-natured looking woman, who conducted him into the room common to all. This was a large dark apartment, around the walls of which were placed heavy oak tables and benches. The number of well-polished cans and jugs, placed in regular order upon shelves, proved that the Stag was much frequented. As it was, there were already many men seated, drinking wine, although it was only just mid-day. They scrutinized the distinguished-looking knight very closely, as he passed their table to the place of honour which was situated at the top of the room, in a kind of bow window of the shape of a lantern, with six glass sides; but their conversation was in no wise interrupted by the appearance of the stranger, for they went on talking of peace and war, battles and sieges, in the way which independent citizens were wont to do, Anno Domini 1519.

The hostess appeared pleased with the bearing of her new guest. She peered at him with a smiling look as she passed him, and when she brought him a can of old Heppacher wine, and set a silver tankard before him for his use, her mouth, which was somewhat large, expressed friendly intentions.

She promised to roast a chicken, and prepare a table for him, if he would wait patiently a little while; in the mean time, she hoped the wine was to his taste. The bow window, in which Albert had taken his seat, was a couple of steps higher than the floor of the room, so that he could easily look down upon and examine the company. Though he was not accustomed to pass much time in inns and drinking rooms, he had a peculiar tact in judging of the characters of men, and from the circumstance of his being more a man of observation than of talk, he now had an opportunity of putting this talent into practice.

The party which was sitting around one of the large oak tables, consisted of ten or twelve men. There did not appear to be much difference in point of circumstances among them, at the first glance; large beards, short hair, round caps, dark jackets, were common to them all; but, upon a closer inspection, three of them were to be particularised from the rest. One, sitting nearest to Albert, was a short, fat, good-humoured looking man; his hair, which fell over his neck, was longer and more carefully combed than his neighbours'; his dark beard appeared also to be the peculiar object of his attention. His cloak of fine black cloth, and a felt hat with a pointed crown and broad brim, which hung on a nail behind him, denoted him to be a man of some consequence, perhaps holding the rank of counsellor. He appeared also to drink a better sort of wine than the rest, for he sipped it with the air of a connoisseur, and when he made a sign that his jug was empty, by putting on the cover, a fashion peculiar to those days, he did it with a certain grace and in more polished manner than the others. He listened to everything that was said with a cunning look, like one who knew more than he would deign to express upon the present occasion. He enjoyed also the privilege of patting the waiting maid on the cheek, or stroking her round plump arm, when she replenished his can.

Another man, who sat at the opposite end of the table, was not less distinguished than his fat neighbour, from the rest of the group; every thing belonging to him was lengthy and gaunt. His face from the forehead to a long pointed chin, measured at least a good span; his fingers, with which he was beating time to a song he hummed to himself, closely resembled the limbs of the spider tribe; and as Albert happened to bend himself, he discovered two long lanky legs, belonging to the same personage, stretched under the table. There was something about the twist of his nose also that expressed self-sufficiency, evidently a prominent feature of his character, for he invariably contradicted the rest of the party, whenever they spoke. His manner altogether was that of one who pretends to unrestrained intimacy with persons of higher rank in life than himself, but who never feels at ease in their society. Albert thought it not likely that he belonged to the town of

Pfullingen, for he occasionally inquired of the hostess after his horse, and forming his opinion upon the whole bearing of this extraordinary looking person, he supposed him to be a travelling doctor, who in those days rode about the country, dispatching people professionally.

The third person who attracted Albert's observation was ill-conditioned, and raggedly clothed; but there was something quick and cunning in his appearance, that distinguished him from the good-humour and tranquillity of his companions, particularly the fat man. He wore a large plaister over one of his eyes, whilst the look of the other was bold and sharp. A large walking stick, with an iron spike at the end, lay beside him, and a well-worn leather back to his coat, upon which he probably carried a basket or box, prompted the idea of his being either a messenger, or more likely a travelling pedlar, one who visits fairs and festivals, bringing wonderful news from distant lands, remedies for women against mad animals, and all sorts of coloured ribands and silks for girls.

These three men led the conversation, which only now and then was interrupted by an expression of astonishment from the rest of the worthy burghers, or by the noise of the covers of their wine cans.

One subject, among others, appeared the principal point of discussion between them, and drew the attention of Albert. They spoke of the undertakings of the League in the low land of Würtemberg. The pedlar with the leather back related the storming of Möckmühl by the League, where Götz von Berlichingen had shut himself up with many brave followers, and where that iron-fisted man was made prisoner.

The counsellor smiled knowingly at this piece of news, and took a long draught of wine; Raw-bones did not permit the leather back man to finish his story, but beating time with renewed force with his long fingers, said, with sepulchral voice, "That's a rank lie, friend! it is impossible, d' ye see; because Berlichingen understands the art of war, and is a determined man; I ought to know that; and besides, he alone, with his iron hand, has in many a battle killed two hundred men as dead as mice; do you suppose then that such a man would allow himself to be taken?"

"With your permission," interrupted the fat gentleman, "you are wrong in what you say, because I know that Götz is, in fact, a prisoner, and is now confined in Heilbron. He did not surrender himself, however; neither was his castle of Möckmühl stormed; but when he was marching out of the gate, the League having promised him and his followers a free retreat, they fell on him, took him prisoner, and killed many of his men. That was not fair, and he has been infamously treated."

"I must beg of you, sir," said the thin man, "not to speak of the League in such terms; I am acquainted with many of the officers, for example, Herr Truchses von Waldburg is my most intimate friend."

The fat man looked big, and appeared as if he wished to make a reply, but, upon second thoughts, washed the words which were upon the tip of his tongue, down his throat with a draught of wine. The other burghers, however, broke out in a murmur of astonishment at the mention of such a high acquaintance, and raised their caps out of respect.

"Well, if you are so well acquainted with the movements of the League, as you pretend to be," said the pedlar, with something of a haughty mien, "you will be able to give us the last intelligence respecting the state of Tübingen."

"It whistles out of its last hole," answered the rawbone man; "I was there but a short time ago, and saw most formidable preparations for the siege."

"Eh!--what?" whispered the inquisitive burghers among themselves, and drew nearer, expecting to hear some important news.

The thin man leaned back on his chair, grasped the handle of his sword with his long fingers, stretched out his legs a yard further, and said, with an air of triumph, "Yes, yes, my friends, it looks very bad there; the surrounding places in the neighbourhood have suffered; all the fruit trees have been cut down, the town and castle furiously bombarded, the former having already surrendered. Forty knights, indeed, still defend the castle; but they cannot hold out their tottering walls much longer!"

"What tottering walls do you talk of?" cried the fat man; "whoever has seen the castle of Tübingen, must not talk of tottering walls. Are there not two deep ditches on the side towards the mountains, which no ladder of the League can scale, and walls twelve feet thick, with high towers, whence the falconets keep up no insignificant fire, I can tell you?"

"Battered down, battered down!" cried the thin man, with such a fearful hollow voice, as made the astonished burghers think they heard the falling of the towers of Tübingen about their ears: "the new tower, which Ulerich lately built, was battered down by Fronsberg, as if it had never stood there."

"But everything is not lost with that," answered the pedlar; "the knights make sallies from the castle, and many a one has found his bed in the Neckar. Old Fronsberg had his hat shot from his head, which makes his ears tingle to this day, I'll be bound."

"There you are wrong again," said the thin man, carelessly; "sallies, indeed! the besiegers have light cavalry enough, who fight like devils; they are Greeks; but whether they come from the Ganges or Epirus, I know not, and are called Stratiots, commanded by George Samares, who does not allow a dog of them to sally out of their holes."1

"He also has been made to bite the grass," replied the pedlar, with a scornful side glance: "the dogs, as you call them, did make a sally, in spite of the Greeks, and made their leader prisoner, and----"

"Samares prisoner?" cried the rawbone man, startled out of his tranquillity; "you are not right again, friend!"

"No?" answered the other, quietly; "I heard the bells toll, as he was buried in the church of Saint George."

The burghers looked attentively at the thin stranger, to notice the impression this news would make on him. His thick eyebrows fell so low that his eyes were scarcely visible; he twisted his long thin mustachios, and striking the table with his bony hand, said: "And if they have cut him and his Greeks into a hundred pieces, the besieged can't help themselves! the castle must fall; and when Tübingen is ours, good night to Würtemburg! Ulerich is out of the country, and my noble friends and benefactors will be the masters."

"How do you know that he will not come back again? and then----" said the cautious fat man, and clapped on the cover of his goblet.

"What! come back again?" cried the other: "the beggar! who says he will come back again? Who dares say it?"

"What does it signify to us?" murmured the guests; "we are peaceable citizens; and it is all the same to us who is lord of the land, provided the taxes are lowered. In a public house a man has a right to say what he pleases."

The thin man appeared satisfied that none of the company dared return an angry answer. He eyed each of them with a searching look, when, assuming a kinder manner, he said, "It was only to put you in mind, that we do not want the Duke any longer as our master that I speak as I do; upon my soul, he is rank poison to me; so I'll sing you a *paternoster*, which a friend wrote upon him, and which pleases me much." The honest burghers, by their looks, did not appear very curious to hear a burlesque song upon their unfortunate Duke. The other, however, having cleared his throat with a good draught, began a few words of a burlesque parody on the Lord's Prayer, in a disagreeable hoarse tone of voice--a vulgar song, apparently familiar to the ears of his audience--for no sooner had he commenced, than the good taste of the burghers manifested itself by a whisper of disapprobation; some shrugging their shoulders, others winking at each other; symptoms sufficiently evident to the thin man, that the burden of his song was not welcome to their ears. He therefore stopt short, looking around for encouragement; but, finding none, he threw himself back in his chair, with a scowl of contempt on his features.

"I know that song well," said the pedlar; "and shame be to him who would offend the ears of honest men with it. With your permission," he added, addressing the company, "I'll give you one I think more to your taste." Encouraged by the rest of the burghers, excepting the thin man, who squinted at him with scorn, he began:

> Mourn, Würtemberg! thy fallen state,
>
> Thy drooping pride, thy luckless fate!
>
> A Quack, whom even dogs despise,
>
> Presumes to make thy fortunes rise.

Noisy applause and laughter, mingled with the hisses of the thin man, interrupted the singer. The burghers reached across the table, shook the pedlar by the hand, praised his song, and begged him to proceed. The raw bone man said not a word, but looked furiously at the company. He knew not whether to envy the applause which the songster received, or to feel offended at the subject of his song. The fat man put on an air of greater wisdom than usual, and joined in approbation with the rest. The leather-backed pedlar was going on, encouraged by his audience:

> Of Nurenberg he, a knife-grinder by trade;
>
> His friend was a weaver, a man of low grade--

when the thin man, upon hearing these words, and not able to contain his indignation, flew into a violent rage, and vociferated: "May the cuckoo stick in your throat, you ragged dog! I know very well who you mean by the weaver,--my best friend, Herr von Fugger. That such a vagabond as you should calumniate him!" expressing his anger by a frightful distortion of his countenance.

But his opponent was in no wise to be daunted, and held his muscular fist before him, saying, "Vagabond yourself, Mr. Calmus, I know who you are; and if you don't keep silence, I'll twist those pot-ladle arms of yours off your half-starved body."

The crest-fallen guest rose immediately, and pronounced his regret to have fallen into such low company; he paid for his wine, and walked out of the room with the strut of a man of quality.

FOOTNOTE TO CHAPTER XVI.:

Footnote 1: The appearance of these Greeks at the siege of Tübingen was an extraordinary event; they were called Stratiots, and were commanded by George Samares, from Corona, in Albania. He was buried in the collegiate church of Tübingen. Crusius says, he was famous for wielding the lance.

CHAPTER XVII

Hope, faith, and confidence are there,
For all that I esteem are near;
And yet suspicion finds its way,
And makes my hopeless mind its prey.

Schiller.

When the offensive man left the room, the guests looked at each other with astonishment; they were in a state of mind similar to that of one who sees a heavy storm arise, and expects it to burst and overwhelm him; when, behold, it produces little more than a flash in the pan. They thanked the man with the leather back for having driven away the odious stranger, and inquired what he knew of him?

"I know him well," he answered; "he is a worthless, idle fellow, a travelling doctor, who sells pills to cure the plague; extracts the worm from dogs, and crops their ears; eases young women of thick necks; and gives the old ones eyewater, which, instead of healing, makes them blind. His proper name is Kahlmaüser, or baldmouse; pretending to be a learned man, he calls himself doctor Calmus. He fastens himself upon the great, and should one of them call him ass, he fawns upon him as his best friend."

"But he cannot be upon good terms with the Duke," remarked the cunning-looking man; "for he abused him in no measured terms."

"Yes, he certainly is not happy with him; and for this reason--the Duke had a beautiful Danish sporting dog, which had run a thorn deep into its foot. It was a great favourite of the Duke, who inquired after an experienced man to cure it; and it so happened that this Kahlmaüser was on the spot, and tendered his services, with a look full of consequence. The wretch was fed every day with the best of food in the castle of Stuttgardt, and the fare was so palatable that he remained more than a quarter of a-year, doctoring the dog's foot. The Duke one day called for both doctor and dog, to know and see what had been done. The quack, it appears, talked a great deal of learned stuff, to which the Duke paid no attention; but, upon examining the wound himself, he found the dog's foot worse than ever. He laid hold of the doctor, tall as he was, led him to the top of the long flight of steps, so contrived that a horse can mount up to the second story, and threw him headlong down. He was half dead when he arrived at the bottom, so you may imagine that since that time, Doctor Calmus does not speak well of the Duke. He is also said to have been a spy between Hutten and Frau Sabina, and only undertook the care of the dog for the purpose of remaining in the castle to carry on intrigues."

"Really! was he in correspondence with Hutten?" said one of the burghers; "if we had but known that, he should not have come off so cheaply, the vagabond doctor; for Hutten's amorous intrigue is the cause of this unhappy war; and it appears that this Kahlmaüser assisted him in it!"

"*De mortuis nil nisi bonum,*--we ought to spare the dead, say the Latins," replied the fat man; "the poor devil has paid his crime dear enough with his life."

"It served him right," cried the other burgher, angrily; "had I been in the Duke's place I would have done the same; every one must protect his domestic rights."

"Do not you ride sometimes hunting with the bailiff?" asked the fat man, with a peculiar crafty smile: "you surely have the best opportunity to assert your rights; you possess a sword, and could easily find an oak tree to hang a corpse upon."

A loud laugh from the burghers of Pfullingen apprised the stranger in the balcony, that the jealous upholder of domestic rights was not so well able to administer justice in his own house. He coloured up, and murmured some unintelligible words as he put his can to his mouth.

The pedlar, however, who, as a stranger, thought it not courteous to join in the laugh, took his part: "Yes, indeed, the Duke was quite in the right, for he had the power of hanging Hutten upon the spot, without giving him a chance of his life in fair honourable fight. Is he not president of the Westphalian chair, and of the secret tribunal, which gives him the power of dispatching villanous fellows without further ceremony? Had he not the best proof of his treachery before his eyes? Have you ever heard a pretty little song upon that subject? I'll sing a couple of verses, if you like:

"In the forest he turn'd him to Hutten, to know,
What't was on his hand that glittered so?"
"Lord Duke, it is this little ring you see,
This ring which my sweet love gave to me."
"Hey, Hans, by my troth thou art nobly drest,
A chain of gold, too, lies on thy breast."

The Banished | 139

"That, too, my true love gave so free,

A pledge that she would remember me."

"And then it goes on:

"Oh! Hutten, away! nor spare the goad,

The Duke's eye rolls with fury wode;

Away, whilst there is yet time to fly,

The scabbard is voided, his sword is on high."

The fat man put on a serious face, and said, "I would not advise you to go on; such songs in public houses, in these times, are dangerous; they cannot serve the Duke's cause at present. The confederates being round about us, some one of them might easily overhear it," he added, as he cast a scrutinizing glance at Albert, "and then Pfullingen might have to pay another hundred ducats contribution."

"God knows, you are in the right," said the pedlar; "it is no longer the case, as it used to be, when one could freely speak his mind, and sing a song over his glass; but now a man must always be on the look out, to see that a partizan of the Duke's does not sit on one side, or a Leaguist on the other; but, in spite of Bavarian or Swabian, I'll sing the last verse:

"There stands an oak in Schönbuch wood,

It shoots aloft and it spreads abroad;

And centuries hence recorded shall be,

That the Duke hang'd Hutten on that very tree."

When he had finished, the conversation among the burghers sunk into a whisper, which made Albert suspect they were making comments upon him. The good-natured hostess also appeared curious to know who she entertained in the balcony. When she had spread a clean table-cloth over the round-table, and placed the repast she had prepared before him, she took her seat on the opposite side, and questioned him, but with respect and deference, whence he came, and whither he was going?

The young man was not inclined to give her positive information as to the real object of his journey. The conversation to which he had listened at the long table, made him cautious in giving an answer to her leading question, for he felt that in times of civil strife, it was not less indiscreet than dangerous to declare, in a place like a public inn, to what party he belonged. Albert's peculiar circumstances at this moment required him to exercise more than ordinary prudence, and he merely said, "that he came from Franconia, and was going further into the country, in the neighbourhood of Zollern." With this general answer to the question, he cut short any other upon the same subject. But being now in the neighbourhood of Lichtenstein, he thought he might be able to learn something of the family from the loquacious landlady of the Golden Stag. Putting a few questions to her respecting the different surrounding castles and their inhabitants, in the hope of gaining his point, she very soon related to him reports which deeply affected his future prospects; for upon the truth or falsehood of them seemed, to his ardent mind, to depend his future happiness or misery.

The hostess, fond of a gossip, in less than a quarter of an hour gave him the history of five or six castles about the country, and among them of Lichtenstein. The young man drew a deep breath at the sound of that name, and pushed away the plate from before him, to devote his whole attention to what she said:

"Well, the owners of Lichtenstein are not poor; on the contrary, they possess fields and woods in plenty, and not an acre of land is mortgaged; rather than do so, the old gentleman would allow his beard to be shaved off, for believe me he prizes it much, and takes a pride in smoothing it down when people speak to him. He is a severe stern man, and what he has once determined upon must be done; as the saying is, should the bow not bend, it must break. He is also one of those who have continued faithful to the Duke, for which the League will make him pay dear."

"How is his----, I mean--you said he had a daughter?"

"No," answered the hostess, whilst her cheerful face became clouded of a sudden, "I certainly said nothing about her, that I am aware of. But he has a daughter, the good old man; and it had been much better for him that he went childless to the grave, rather than depart in sorrow on account of his only child."

Albert could scarcely believe his ears at these words: what reason could the landlady have to throw out this allusion? "What has happened to the young lady?" he asked, whilst he in vain sought to appear indifferent: "you have excited my curiosity; or is it a secret you dare not divulge?"

The woman of the Golden Stag mysteriously looked around on all sides, to see that no one was listening; the burghers were quietly taken up with their own conversation, and paid no attention to them, and there was no one else in the room who could overhear them. "You, I perceive, are a stranger," she said, after her scrutiny; "you are travelling further, and have nothing to do in this neighbourhood, so that I can communicate to you what I would not confide to every one. The lady who lives there on the Lichtenstein rock, is a----, a----yes; what the citizens with us would call, a wicked girl, a----"

"Landlady!" cried Albert.

"Don't speak so loud, worthy sir; the people will notice it. Do you suppose I would venture to say what I do not know to be certain truth? Only think, every night as the clock strikes eleven, she lets her lover into the castle. Is not that wicked enough for a well-bred young lady?"

"Mind what you say! Her lover?"

"Yes, alas! at eleven o'clock in the night, her lover. Is it not a shame, a disgrace! He is a tall man, and comes to the gate enveloped in a grey cloak. She has so well arranged it, that all the servants are out of the way at that hour except the old porter of the gate, who has assisted her in all her wicked tricks from her childhood. When the clock strikes eleven in the village, she always comes herself down into the court, cold as it may be, and brings the keys of the drawbridge, which she beforehand steals from her father's bed; the old sinner, the porter, then opens the lock, lets down the bridge, when the man in the grey cloak hastens to the presence of the young lady."

"And then?" asked Albert, who scarcely had any more breath in his breast, scarcely any more blood in his cheeks,--"and then?"

"Then she brings food, bread and wine: so much is certain, that the nightly lover must have an uncommon appetite, for many nights running he has demolished half a haunch of roebuck, and drank three or four pints of wine; what else they do, I know not; I guess nothing, I say nothing; but I suppose," she added, with an upward look to heaven, "they don't pray."

Albert was angry with himself, after a moment's reflection, for having doubted for an instant the falsehood of this narration, spun from some gossiping head; or, should there be any truth in it, it was impossible that Bertha could act with dishonour to herself. We are told that, though the passion of love in the young men of the good old times was not less ardent than in our days, it bore more the character of idolized respect. It was the custom, in those days, for the lady wooed to think herself not only not upon an equality, but far superior to her suitor.

If we look to the romantic tales and love stories in old chronicles, we shall find many descriptions of enamoured knights allowing themselves to be cut to pieces on the spot, rather than doubt the faith and purity of their mistresses. Judging therefore from this fact, it is not surprising that Albert von Sturmfeder could not bring his mind to think ill of Bertha, and however puzzling these nocturnal visits appeared to him, he clearly perceived it had not been proved that her father was ignorant of the transaction, or that the mysterious man was her lover. He mentioned these doubts to his hostess.

"Really! you suppose that her father is acquainted with it?" said she; "not at all--I know it for a certainty, because old Rosel, the young lady's nurse----"

"Old Rosel said so?" cried Albert, involuntarily: the nurse, being the sister of the fifer of Hardt, was well known to him. If she had really said so, the case was no longer to be doubted, for he knew that she was a pious woman, and devoted to her charge.

"Do you know old Rosel?" she asked, wondering at the warmth with which her guest inquired after that woman.

"I know her? you forget that I come for the first time to-day in your neighbourhood; it was only the name of Rosel which struck me."

Albert parried this question, being desirous the woman should not suspect he was acquainted with the Knight of Lichtenstein or his family.

"Don't they call her so in your country? Rosel means Rosina with us, and the old nurse in Lichtenstein goes by that name. But observe, she is a particular friend of mine, and comes now and then to see me, when I give her a glass of hot sweet wine, which she loves dearly, and out of gratitude tells me all the news. What I have told you comes from her mouth. Old Lichtenstein knows nothing of the nocturnal visits, because he goes to bed regularly at eight o'clock; and his daughter sends her nurse every evening at eight o'clock also to her apartment. It struck the good Rosel, however, a few nights ago, that there must be some mysterious cause for this conduct. She pretended to go to bed,--and only think what happened? Scarcely was everything quiet in the castle, when the young lady, who otherwise never touches a chip of wood, laid heavy logs on the hearth with her own delicate hands, made a fire, cooked and roasted the best way she could, got wine out of the cellar, and bread out of the cupboard, and spread the table in the dining room. She then opened the window and looked out in the cold dark night, when, just as the village clock struck eleven, the drawbridge rattled down on its chains, the nocturnal visitor entered, and went into the dining room with the young lady. Rosel has often listened in vain to hear the conversation between them, but the oak doors are very thick, and she peeped also once through the keyhole, but could only perceive the head of the stranger."

"Well, is he an old man? What does he look like?"

"Old, indeed? what are you thinking about? She does not look like one who would put up with an old lover. Rosel told me he was young and handsome, with a dark beard on his chin and lip, beautiful smooth hair on his head, and looked very kind and gracious."

"May Satan pluck hair for hair out of his beard!" muttered Albert, as he passed his hand over his own chin, which was tolerably smooth. "Woman! are you sure you have really heard all this from old Rosel? Have you not added more than she told you?"

"God forbid that I should calumniate any one! You don't know me, sir knight! Rosel told me every word of it, and she suspects a great deal more, and whispered in my ear things which it does not become a respectable woman to relate to a young man. And only think how very wicked the young lady must be; she has had also another lover, to whom she is unfaithful."

"Another?" asked Albert, to whom the narration appeared to gain more and more the semblance of truth.

"Yes, another; who according to Rosel's account must be a charming nice young man. She was with her young mistress in Tübingen, and there was a Herr von ---- von ----, I believe he was called Sturmfittich; he studied at the University; they became acquainted with each other there; and the old nurse declares such a handsome couple was not to be found in all Swabia. She was over head and ears in love with him, that's true; and was very unhappy when she parted with him in Tübingen; but now her false heart is unfaithful to the poor youth, and Rosel really weeps when she thinks of him; he is handsomer, much handsomer, than her present lover."

The hostess, who had quite forgotten her household duties in her zeal to relate the gossip of the neighbourhood, was now called by the fat man in the drinking room: "Landlady," said he, "how long must I knock here, before I get another can of wine."

"Coming, coming, sir!" she answered, and flew to the bar to satisfy the importunate man, and from thence she went to the cellar, and then to the kitchen, and was all of a sudden so full of business, that her guest in the bow had sufficient time to ponder over all he had just heard. He sat there, his hand supporting his head, looking with fixed eyes into the bottom of his silver tankard; he remained in that position from the afternoon till the evening; night advanced, and still he sat at the round table, dead to all the world about him, giving signs of life only by an occasional deep sigh. The landlady did not know what to make of him. She had placed herself at least a dozen times near him, had tried to speak with him, but he only looked at her with a staring eye, and answered nothing. She at last got very uneasy, for just in the same way had her good husband of blessed memory gazed at her when he died, and left her in possession of the Golden Stag.

She consulted the fat man, and he with the leather back gave his opinion also. The landlady maintained that he must be either over head and ears in love, or that some one must have bewitched him. She strengthened her supposition by a terrible history of a young knight, whom she had seen, and whose whole body became quite stiff from sheer love, which caused his death.

The pedlar was of a different opinion; he thought that some misfortune must have happened to the stranger, a circumstance which often befals those engaged in war, and that, therefore, he was in deep distress. But the fat man, winking, asked, with a countenance full of cunning conjecture, what was the growth and age of the wine the gentleman had been drinking?

"He has had old Heppacher of the year 1480," said the landlady: "it is the best that the Golden Stag furnishes."

"There we have it," said the wise fat man; "I know the Heppacher of the year eighty, and such a young fellow cannot stand it; it has got into his head. Let him alone, with his heavy head upon his hand; I'll bet that before the clock strikes eight he will have slept his wine out, and be as fresh as a fish in water."

The pedlar shook his head and said nothing; but the hostess praised the acknowledged sagacity of the fat man, and thought his supposition the most probable.

It was now nine o'clock; the daily visitors of the drinking room had all left it, and the landlady was also on the point of retiring to rest, as the stranger awoke out of his reverie. He started up, made a few hasty steps about the room, and at last stood before the hostess. His look was clouded and disturbed, and the short time which had elapsed between mid-day and the present moment had so far altered the features of his otherwise kind, open countenance, as to impart to them an expression of deep melancholy.

The kind-hearted woman was grieved at his appearance; and calling to mind the sagacious supposition which the fat man had pronounced as to the cause of his agitation, she proposed cooking a comfortable supper and preparing a bed for him; but her kind offices were altogether unavailing, as he appeared bent upon a rougher pastime for the night.

"When did you say," he inquired with a altering voice, "when did you say the nocturnal guest went to Lichtenstein? and at what hour did he depart?"

"He enters at eleven o'clock, dear sir," she replied; "and at the first cock crow he retires over the drawbridge."

"Order my horse to be saddled immediately, and let me have a guide to Lichtenstein."

"At this hour of night!" cried the landlady, and clasped her hands together in astonishment; "you would not start now: you surely cannot be in earnest."

"Yes, good woman, I am in real earnest; so make haste, for I am in a hurry."

"You have not been so all day long," she replied, "and you now would rush over head and ears into the dark. The fresh air, indeed, may do invalids such as you some good; but don't suppose I'll let your horse out of the stable this night; you might fall off, or a hundred accidents might happen to you, and then it would be said, 'where was the head of the landlady of the Golden Stag, to let people leave her house in such a state, and at such an hour.'"

The young man did not heed her conversation, having relapsed into the same melancholy mood as before; but when she finished, and paused to get an answer, he roused up again, and wondered that she had not yet put his orders into execution.

While she still hesitated to meet his wishes, and saw he was on the point of going himself to look after his steed, she thought that, as her good intentions were unavailable to retain him in her house, it would be more advisable to let him have his own way. "Bring the gentleman's horse out," she called to her servant, "and let Andres get ready immediately, to accompany him part of the way. He is in the right to take some one with him," she said to herself, "who may be of use to him in case of need. How much do you owe me, did you say, sir knight? why, you have had a measure of wine, which makes twelve kreuzers; and the dinner,--as to that it's not worth talking about, for you ate so little; indeed you scarcely looked at my fowl. If you give me two more kreuzers for the feed of your horse, you shall receive the thanks of the poor widow of the Golden Stag."

Having paid his reckoning in the small current money of the times, Albert took his leave of his kind landlady, who though her opinion of him was somewhat changed since he first entered her house, proceeding from an air of mystery about his character which she could not account for, still she could not conceal from herself, when he threw himself into the saddle by the light of a torch, that she had seldom seen a handsomer youth. She therefore impressed upon the lad who accompanied him to be very careful, and keep an especial look out upon the gentleman, "who," she added, "did not appear to be quite right in his head." Having reached the outer gate of Pfullingen, the guide asked his new master where he wished to go? and upon his answer, "to Lichtenstein," took a road to the right, leading to the mountains. Albert rode on in profound silence; he looked not to the right nor to the left, neither at the stars over head nor in the distant horizon; his eye only sought the ground. His mind now was in much the same state as at that moment when a blow from the hand of an enemy laid him senseless on the ground. His thoughts stood still, hope no longer animated him, he had ceased to love and to wish. But at that time, when he sank, exhausted, on nature's cool carpet, his last thoughts were cheered with the endearing recollection of his beloved, and his benumbed lips were still able to pronounce once more her idolized name.

But that light seemed to be extinguished which had hitherto guided his steps. It appeared as if he had but a short distance still to go in the dark, in order to seek his peace of mind in a light different to that he had fondly hoped to find on the Lichtenstein rock. His right hand went occasionally to his sword, as if to assure himself that at least this companion was faithful to him, for he now trusted to it alone, as the important key by which he might open the door that would lead from darkness to light.

The travellers had long since reached the wood; the path became steeper, and the horse with difficulty ascended the hill with his rider, who was, however, unconscious of all surrounding objects. The night air blew cool, and played with the flowing locks of the young man,--he felt not its effects; the moon rose and lighted up the road, which ascended amidst huge masses of rock and tall oaks, under which he passed,--he noticed them not; time flowed on unobserved by him; hour followed hour in rapid succession, unheeded by his troubled mind.

It was past midnight when they arrived at the summit of the highest hill, and having reached the skirts of the wood, they beheld the castle of Lichtenstein before them, situated upon an insulated perpendicular rock, rising as if by magic from the depths of darkness, and separated by a broad chasm from the surrounding country. Its white walls, its indented rocks, glimmered in the moonlight; it seemed as if the castle slumbered in the profound tranquillity of solitude, cut off from the rest of the world.

Albert cast a troubled glance towards it, and sprang from his horse, which he fastened to a tree, and sat down on a stone covered with moss directly opposite the castle. The guide stood waiting for further orders, and asked several times in vain, whether his services were required any longer.

"How long is it to the first crow of cock?" inquired Albert at last.

"Two hours, sir," was the answer of the lad.

He then gave him a handsome reward for his conduct, and made signs to him to depart. The boy hesitated to obey him, as if afraid of leaving the young man in his present state of mind; but, upon his repeating the sign with impatience, he withdrew with a slow step. He looked back once before he regained the wood, and observed his silent master still seated upon the same stone, under an oak, with his hand supporting his head.

CHAPTER XVIII

This hollow path must be his way,
It doth to Küssnacht lead,
So here I will his coming stay,
And here I'll do the deed.

Schiller.

Much has been said and written in all ages upon the folly of jealousy, but since the days of Uriah the world has nevertheless not grown wiser upon the subject.

The news which Albert von Sturmfeder had heard from the hostess of the Golden Stag respecting the nocturnal visits of the stranger to the castle of Lichtenstein, had created a feeling in his breast to which it had hitherto been a perfect stranger, and he did not possess sufficient coolness of blood, to exercise his judgment with calmness and moderation, upon a subject of such vital importance to his future prospects. Though he was of an age in which an open generous disposition places implicit reliance in the honour of others, yet taken by surprise, as his unsuspicious heart now was, in its dearest affections, the consequences were likely to become fatal to his happiness. The anguish attendant upon plighted faith broken, burnt within him; he could scarcely control the feeling of wounded pride, at being made the dupe of misplaced confidence; that calm judgment which teaches us to discriminate between right and wrong forsook his mind, and the truth was veiled from his sight in an atmosphere of gloomy foreboding. The fiendish associates, contempt, rage, and revenge, which, with many others, compose the steps of the ladder of feeling between love and hatred, now assailed him, and rendered even jealousy a secondary passion in his breast.

Brooding over these tormenting sensations, he sat upon the moss-covered stone, insensible to the chill of the night air, and his only thought was, to meet the nocturnal visitor, and demand an explanation.

When the clock struck two in a village beyond the wood, he observed lights moving in the windows of the castle. His heart beat in full expectation; he grasped the hilt of his sword. A few moments after the lights were visible behind the trellis of the gate, and dogs began to bark. Albert sprang upon his feet, and threw his cloak aside. He heard a deep voice very distinctly say, "Good night." The creaking drawbridge was lowered over the abyss which separates the rock of Lichtenstein from the country; the gate opened, when a man, his hat falling deep over his face, and enveloped in a dark cloak, came over the bridge, directly towards the spot where Albert was standing.

When he had arrived at a few paces from him, the young man called out in a threatening tone, "Draw, traitor, and defend your life!" and advanced on him. The man in the cloak stepped back, drawing his sword; in a moment the two blades met.

"You shall not have me alive," cried the other; "at least I'll sell my life dear!" and with these words the stranger attacked him vigorously, proving himself by the rapid and heavy blows which he dealt to be an experienced swordsman, and no despicable opponent. This was not the first time Albert had crossed blades in anger; for at the university of Tübingen he had fought many an honourable duel with success; but now he had found his match. His adversary pushed him hard, and his attack was maintained with so masterly a hand, that Albert was compelled to confine himself solely to his own defence, when, in a last attempt to settle the affair by one powerful thrust, his arm was suddenly seized by a strong hand from behind, and in the same moment his sword was wrested from his grasp. A loud voice, from the person who now held him fast in both his arms, cried, "Run him through, sir; such assassins don't deserve a moment's time to say their paternoster."

"You do it, Hans," said the stranger; "I am not the one to take the life of a defenceless man; run him through with his own sword, and be quick about it."

"Let me rather do it myself, sir," said Albert, with a firm voice; "you have robbed me of my love,--what further need have I of life?"

"What is that I hear?" said the stranger, and approached nearer.

"What voice is that?" said the other stranger, who still kept a firm hold of Albert; "I ought to know its sound." He turned the young man in his arms, and, as if struck by lightning, he let go his hold. "What on earth do I see! we might have made a pretty business of it!--but what unlucky star has brought you to this spot, sir? How could my people think of letting you depart without my knowledge?"

It was the fifer of Hardt who addressed Albert, and now offered him his hand. He was not, however, much inclined to return the friendly salute of a man who but a moment before was going to perform the part of executioner. Burning with fury, he looked at the man in the cloak, and then at the fifer: "Do you mean to say," said he, addressing himself to the latter, "that I ought to have allowed myself to remain a prisoner in your house, for the purpose of not witnessing your traitorous designs? Miserable impostor! And you, sir," turning to the other, "as you value your honour, defend yourself singly, and not fall two upon one. If you wish to know my name, I am Albert von Sturmfeder, come here for the express purpose of measuring swords with you, to uphold my previous claim to the Lady of Lichtenstein, which pretension, perhaps, may not be unknown to you. I demand my sword back again, having been wrenched from my hand by an act of treacherous cowardice, and let each make good his pretensions in honourable fight. With my life alone will I cease to assert my right."

"Albert von Sturmfeder!" replied his opponent in surprise, but in a friendly manner. "It appears you must be labouring under some mistake. Believe me, that, instead of being your enemy I am much interested in you, and have long wished to see you. Accept my friendship, upon the word of honour of a man; and do not imagine I visit the castle with the sinister views you attribute to me."

He stretched out his hand from under his cloak, and offered it to the astonished youth, who hesitated, however, to take it. The skill with which he wielded his sword, and the heavy blows he dealt out, strengthened Albert in his opinion, that his opponent was accustomed to the use of his weapon; and that he was a man of honourable and generous character, seemed satisfactorily proved in the frank and unreserved manner he proffered his hand when he became acquainted with his name. Under these circumstances therefore he could scarcely forbear trusting to his word. Still his mind could not in an instant shake off doubts of being deceived under the specious dealings of the stranger, which made him undecided to accept, without further reserve, the proffered friendship of a man whom but the moment before he had looked upon as his bitterest enemy.

"Who is it that offers me his hand?" demanded Albert; "I have given you my name, it is but just you tell me yours."

The stranger threw his cloak back, and raising his hat, discovered to Albert, by the light of the moon, a noble countenance, with a brilliant sparkling eye, bearing the expression of commanding dignity. "Ask not my name," said he, whilst a ray of sorrow played about his mouth; "that I am a man of honour, is sufficient for you to know. I once, indeed, bore a name which was upon a level with the most honourable in the world; I once wore the golden spurs, and carried the waving plume of feathers in my helmet, and, at the sound of my bugle, could assemble hundreds of my people around me--but now all is lost. One thing alone remains to me," he added, with indescribable dignity, taking the hand of the young man with a firm grasp, "I am a man, and carry a sword,--

'Si fractus illabatur orbis

Impavidam ferient ruinæ.'"

With these words he drew his hat again over his face, and throwing his cloak over his person, withdrew, and was soon lost in the wood.

Albert von Sturmfeder stood in dumb astonishment, resting on his sword. The commanding look of the stranger, his winning benevolent features, his brave and generous conduct, filled his soul with admiration and respect. Revenge, which had agitated his breast before he crossed swords with him, no longer ruffled it, but gave way to the contemplation of the virtues which his opponent had displayed in his unexpected rencontre with one, whose life he might have taken in the just defence of his own person. But what conduced above all to raise this man higher in Albert's estimation, was the frank and honest manner in which he had disavowed any clandestine acquaintance with Bertha, having confirmed it by a gallant defence of his honour, which he seemed as capable of asserting as he did of wielding his weapon. Such was the result of this adventure upon the mind of Albert, that he felt it relieved of a mountain's weight of trouble and anxiety, with which, but a few moments back, it had been oppressed. The malicious reports of the hostess of the Golden Stag, which he had too readily given credit to, now stung him with shame and remorse. He would willingly have risked every thing at that moment to have gained admittance to the castle, and thrown himself at the feet of his beloved, to implore her forgiveness for having given place to a doubt of her faithful attachment.

When we consider the weight and respect which physical qualities carried with them in those times,--how bravery, even in an enemy, was prized and admired,--and that the word of a gallant man was held as sacred as an oath on the altar;--and, if we further recollect how imposing is the effect of a pleasing outward appearance upon a young, generous mind, it is not to be wondered that the change in Albert's feelings was as decided as it was rapid.

"Who is that man?" he asked the fifer, who still stood by him.

"You heard from his own lips that he has no name, and neither do I know what to call him."

"You don't know who he is," replied Albert, "and still you were present when we fought? Away with you; you deceive me."

"Indeed not, sir," answered the fifer: "it is true, God knows! that in these times he has no name. But, if you must know what he is, I can tell you. He has been driven from his castle by the League, and now wanders in banishment: he was once a powerful knight in Swabia."

"Poor man! for this reason he conceals his person? Well might he, indeed, have taken me for an assassin. I recollect his having said he would sell his life dearly."

"Don't be offended, worthy sir," said the countryman, "that I also took you for one of those who are lurking about to take his life; I came therefore to his assistance, and, had I not heard your voice, who knows how much longer you would have breathed? But what brought you hither at this hour of the night? and what mishap threw you into the path of the banished man? Truly, you may think yourself fortunate that he did not cut you in two, for there are few who can stand before his sword. Some one, I suspect, has been playing this cruel game with you."

Albert related to his former guide the news he had heard in the Golden Stag of Pfullingen. He pointed out particularly the evidence of the nurse, the fifer's sister, which gave it an air of so much probability.

"I thought it would come to that," replied the fifer: "Love has played many worse tricks, and I don't know what it might not have done to me in such a case, when I was young. No one is in fault but old Rosel, the gossip! What business had she to make the hostess of the Golden Stag her confidant, who cannot keep a secret for a moment?"

"But there must be some truth in the affair," said Albert, whose former suspicions were again awakened; "for Rosel could never have said it without some foundation."

"Yes, there is indeed much truth in the report. Everything is as true as she has related. The servants are sent to bed, and the old spy also. At eleven o'clock the man appears at the castle,--the drawbridge is let down,--the doors open,--the young lady receives him and leads him into the saloon----"

"Well, don't you see?" cried Albert, impatiently, "if all be as you say, how could that man swear that he had nothing to do with----"

"That he had nothing of any kind to do with the lady, you would say?" answered the fifer, "without hesitation he can swear to that; but there is one essential difference in the story, which that old goose Rosel certainly never knew; namely, that the knight of Lichtenstein always receives his guest in the saloon, and, as soon as his daughter has placed before him the refreshments which she has prepared, she withdraws. The old gentleman remains with the banished man till the first crow of the cock, when, after having well satisfied his hunger and thirst, and warmed his weary limbs at the fire, he leaves the castle in the same way that he entered it."

"Oh, fool that I was not to have thought of all this before! The truth was close at hand, and I pushed it from me! But cursed be the curiosity and slanderous spirit of those women, who always fancy they can divine something extraordinary in the most trifling circumstance, and whose greatest charm consists in conjecturing improbabilities. But tell me," said Albert, after a moment's thought, "it strikes me very odd, that this banished man should visit the castle every night exactly as the clock strikes eleven-- in what inhospitable neighbourhood does he reside, which obliges him to seek subsistence here at that unseasonable hour? Now, mind, I am not to be trifled with!"

The eye of the fifer rested upon Albert with an expression almost amounting to disdain: "Such gentlemen as you," he answered, "certainly know little of the pain of banishment; you never experienced the horror of being obliged to conceal yourself from the hand of the assassin, shivering in damp caves, living in inhospitable caverns, among the society of owls, deprived of a warm meal and a cheering glass! But come with me, if you have an inclination,--the day does not break yet, and you cannot go to Lichtenstein by night,--and I will lead you to the habitation of the banished knight. You will not ask me again why he visits the castle at midnight."

The appearance of the stranger had excited Albert's curiosity to such a degree, that he willingly accepted the offer of the fifer of Hardt, more particularly as he then would have the best opportunity of finding out the truth or falsehood of his assertions. His guide took the bridle of his horse, and led him down a narrow pathway in the wood. Albert followed, after he had taken a farewell look at the windows of Lichtenstein. They moved on in silence, which the young man made no attempt to break, his thoughts being wholly taken up with the person whom he was about to visit, and the strange occurrence which had just taken place. He recollected to have heard somewhere or other that many staunch partisans of the Duke had been driven from their possessions by the fury of the League, and he thought that it must have been in the inn at Pfullingen, where mention had been made of a knight of the name of Maxx Stumpf von Schweinsberg, whom the confederates were in search of. The bravery and extraordinary strength of this man was the common talk of all Swabia and Franconia; and when Albert recalled to his mind the powerful figure, the commanding countenance of his late heroic opponent, he thought it could not possibly be any other than this knight, one of Duke Ulerich's most faithful followers. The idea of having had an affair with such a man, and to have measured swords with him in fair fight, was particularly flattering to the *amour propre* of the young man, although the result had been left undecided.

So thought Albert von Sturmfeder on that night. And after a lapse of many years, when his noble antagonist had been long reinstated in his rights, and by sound of bugle could as formerly assemble his followers in hundreds, he reckoned it among his best feat of arms to have stood his ground before the brave and powerful stranger.

They were now arrived at a small open meadow in the wood, which terminated in a thick hedge of thorns and briars. The fifer having secured the horse to a tree off the path, made a gap through the entangled branches, and gave a sign to Albert to follow. It was not without difficulty and some danger that he obeyed his leader's directions, who in many places was obliged to assist him with his hand, as they proceeded down a narrow footpath into a deep ravine. When they had descended about eighty feet they came to even ground again, where the young man expected to find the dwelling of the banished man; but he was disappointed. His companion then went to a tree of great circumference, and which was hollow from age, and brought forth two large torches of pine wood, and striking fire by means of a steel and flint, and a small bit of sulphur, ignited them.

Albert observed, by the brilliant light of the torches, that they stood before a large opening which nature had formed in the wall of the rock. This must be, he thought, the entrance to the habitation of the stranger, who, as the fifer had expressed himself, had his lodgings among owls. The man of Hardt took one of the torches, and giving the other to his companion, said, "The path is dark, and here and there difficult to trace." With this warning he went on in front, leading through the dark entrance.

Albert, whose imagination was on the stretch, had expected to be introduced to a low cavern, short and narrow, like the dwelling of wild beasts, such as he had seen about the forests of his own country; but what was his astonishment, when he entered an immense natural cavern, resembling the lofty halls of a subterranean palace! He had heard in his boyhood, from a man-servant whose great-grandfather had been prisoner in Palestine, a story, which had been handed down from generation to generation in his family, of a boy who had been enticed by the arts of a wicked magician into a palace under ground, which surpassed everything in magnificence he had ever seen above it, and displayed to his view whatever the bold imagination of the east could fancy of splendour. Golden pillars surmounted by crystal capitals, arched cupolas studded with emeralds and sapphires, walls of diamonds dazzling the eye by their numerous refracting rays, were united in this subterranean habitation of the genii. This story, which had made a deep impression on his youthful imagination, now came to his recollection, and appeared to be realised in what he saw before him. He stopped every moment in fresh surprise, and holding the torch high up, viewed in amazement and wonder the lofty and majestic vaulted arches which continued the whole length of the cavern, sparkling and glittering like thousands of crystals and diamonds. But his astonishment was still more excited when his leader, turning to the left, conducted him into a spacious grotto, which fancy might figure to itself the magnificent saloon of the subterranean palace.

The fifer could not help remarking the powerful impression which this wonder of nature made on the mind of the young man. He took his torch from him, and mounting a high jutting rock, illumined more effectually the greatest part of the grotto.

Brilliant white rocks composed its walls. The bold arched cupola, formed of innumerable stalactites, from the ends of which hung millions of small drops of water, reflected the light in all the colours of the rainbow. The surrounding rocks were thrown together in such happy confusion, as to give the imagination full scope to fancy it could discover in their grotesque shapes, here a chapel, having its high altarpiece ornamented with flowing drapery; there its corresponding pulpit of rich gothic architecture. An organ even was not wanting to complete the idea of a subterranean church, and the changing shadows thrown on the walls by the light of the torches, resembled the solemn figures of martyrs and holy men placed in niches.

The guide came down again from his position on the rock, after having, as he thought, sufficiently satisfied the curiosity of his companion. "This is called the Nebelhöhle, or the Misty Hollow," said he; "it is little known in the country, excepting to huntsmen and shepherds, and few venture to enter it, as all kinds of fearful stories are abroad of ghosts inhabiting its chambers. I would not advise any one who is not minutely acquainted with its locality to venture down, for there are deep cavities and subterranean waters, whence no one would see the light again, if once entangled amidst their intricacies. There are also secret passages and compartments known only to five individuals now alive."

"But the banished knight," asked Albert, "where is he?"

"Take the torch, and follow me," replied the other, and led the way though a side passage. They had proceeded about twenty paces, when Albert thought he heard the deep tones resembling those of an organ. He drew the attention of his leader to it.

"That is some one singing," the fifer answered, "the voice sounds particularly beautiful and full in these caverns. When two or three men join their voices together, it resembles the full chorus of monks chanting the *Ora*." The music became still plainer; and as they approached the spot, the expressive feeling of a beautiful melody was distinctly heard. They were obliged to bend themselves under the corner of a rock, as they proceeded, when the voice of the songster sounded from above, and broke in repeated echo on the indentations of the wall of rock, until it was lost in the mingled noises of dripping water from the moist stones, and the murmur of a subterranean waterfall.

"That is the place," said the guide; "above there, in the side of the rock, is the habitation of the unhappy man. Hearken to his voice! We'll wait and listen till he has finished, for he never was accustomed to be interrupted, even when he lived above ground." It was with great difficulty that they could catch the following words on account of the great echo and the murmur of falling and rushing water.

> The tow'r from whence my childhood gazed
> Upon the subject fields so fair,
> Now bears a stranger's banner, raised
> Where erst my father's fann'd the air.
>
> To ruin sink my father's halls,
> The portion of my ancestry;
> O'erthrown and unavenged, the walls
> In earth's deep bosom buried lie.
>
> O'er fields, where once in happier tide
> My jocund bugle horn I blew,
> The savage foemen fiercely ride:
> A noble quarry they pursue.
>
> I am their game, the quarry chased;
> The slot-hound follows where he flies,
> Athirst the stag's warm blood to taste,

Whose antlers1 are the hunter's prize.

The murderers have bent their bow,
They ransack forest, hill, and plain;
Whilst clad in rags I nightly go
A beggar on my own domain.

Where once I rode in lordly state,
Whilst greeting vassals bow'd the head;
I fear to tap the cotter's gate,
And beg in pity's name for bread.

From my own doors ye thrust me out;
Yet will I knock while knock I can:
All is not lost, if heart be stout:
I bear a sword, I am a man.

I quail not: tho' my heart should break,
I will endure unto the end;
And thus my foes of me shall speak,
"This was a man, and ne'er would bend."

A deep sigh, which followed the conclusion of the song, gave the hearers reason to suppose, that the burden of it had not afforded the unfortunate exile much consolation. A large tear had rolled down the tanned cheek of the man of Hardt as they stood listening; and Albert perceived the inward struggle which this good peasant seemed to contend with in order to compose his mind, and appear before the inhabitant of the cavern with a cheerful countenance. He requested the young man to hold his torch awhile; and clambered up the smooth, slippery rock which led to the grotto whence the sounds they had just heard had issued. Albert supposed he had gone to acquaint the stranger of his arrival, but his guide returned with a strong rope in his hand. He descended half way down the rock again, threw one end of the rope to him, and desiring him to tie the torches on to it, he pulled them up, and placed them in a secure corner in the rock. He then assisted his young master to mount to the spot where he was standing, which he would not have been well able to accomplish alone. Once up there, they were only a few paces from the inhospitable abode of the exile.

We have attempted to describe this remarkable cavern according to its natural formation. Some further observations may be interesting to the reader. The entrance is about 150 feet in circumference; two paths, which form two natural excavations, one of 100 feet long, the other 82, lead from thence, and, taking different directions, meet again in the interior at the distance of about 200 feet. The place where they join forms a grotto, whence, on the right towards the north, higher up in the rock, is another smaller one, the spot to which we have led the reader, to the dwelling of the exile. The whole length of the cavern, from the entrance to the innermost point, is about 577 feet.

FOOTNOTES TO CHAPTER XVIII.:

Footnote 1: Referring, probably, to the arms of Würtemberg.]

CHAPTER XIX

The rugged rocks fantastic forms assume,
Seen in the darkling of the midnight gloom;
And the wild evergreens so dimly bright,
Seem to reflect a kind of lurid light;
This sight so strange may well our knight amaze,
He stops, upon the witchery to gaze.

Wieland.

The spot to which they had arrived in this large cavern, possessed one great advantage, that of being perfectly dry. The ground was covered with rushes and straw; a lamp hung on the side of the rock, which threw sufficient light on the breadth, and a great part of the length, of the grotto. Opposite the entrance sat the stranger upon a large bear skin, and near him stood his sword and a bugle horn; an old hat, and a grey cloak lay on the ground. A jacket of dark brown leather, and trowsers of coarse blue cloth, covered his person; an unseemly costume, but which did not the less set off the powerful shape of his body, and the noble features of his countenance. He was about thirty-four years old, and his face might be called still handsome and pleasing, although the first bloom of youth was worn off by hardship and fatigue, and his beard having grown wild upon his chin, imparted to his look an air of severity. Albert made these fleeting remarks as he stopped at the entrance of the grotto.

"Welcome to my palace, Albert von Sturmfeder," said its inhabitant, whilst he rose from his bear skin, and offering him his hand, begged him to take a seat beside him on a deer skin: "you are heartily welcome," he repeated. "It was no bad thought of our friend the musician, to introduce you into these lower regions, and bring me such agreeable society. Hans, thou faithful soul! thou hast been our major domo and chancellor up to this moment, from henceforth we nominate thee our head-master of the cellar and purveyor-general. Look behind that pillar, and thou'lt find the remains of a bottle of good old wine. Take my beech-wood hunting-cup, the only utensil left us, and fill it up to the brim, to the honour of our worthy guest."

Albert beheld the exiled man in astonishment; though he might have expected to find the energies of his mind unsubdued by the storms of life, still he was prepared to see him brooding over his misfortunes in sullen melancholy, driven by hard fate to seek shelter in these inhospitable regions. What, therefore, was his surprise to find him, on the contrary, cheerful and unconcerned, joking about his situation, just as if he had been merely overtaken by a storm in hunting, and had sought shelter from its violence in the grotto! It was a storm, indeed, more terrible than the fury of the elements which had driven him from the castle of his ancestors, for he was the prey that had taken shelter here from the shots of his murderous huntsmen.

"You look at me and my abode with astonishment, my worthy guest," said the knight: "you, perhaps, expected to hear me bewailing my hard fate--but of what use would that be? As no one can retrieve my misfortune in this moment, I think it the wisest plan to put a bold face upon what I cannot alter. But tell me, am not I as well lodged here as many princes in their palaces? Have you noticed the halls and saloons of this my palace? do not the walls shine like silver, and the vaulted ceilings sparkle as if they were set in pearls and diamonds? and the pillars, do they not glitter with emeralds, rubies, and all sorts of precious stones? But here comes Hans, my purveyor, with the wine. Say, my trusty subject, does that cup contain the whole of our cellar?"

"Your habitation can boast of water, as clear as crystal," answered the fifer, who well understood the cheerful mood of his companion; "the remainder of the wine in the cellar will fill more than three cups, and--as we have another guest to-day--we may indulge a little. Luckily, I brought a jug full of good old Uhlbacker from the castle to-night."

"You have done well," said the exiled knight, whilst a ray of joy flashed from his brilliant eye; "you must not think, Albert von Sturmfeder, that I am a wine-bibber; but good wine is a noble thing, and I love to see the full glass circulate in friendly society. Put the jug down here, worthy master of the cellar, we'll enjoy ourselves, as in the best days of our prosperity. Here's to you, and the former splendour of the house of Sturmfeder!"

Albert thanked the knight, and drank. "I wish I could return the honour, in drinking to your name," he said; "but, as you have already hesitated to give it me, I will not ask it now, sir knight. But here's to you, and may you return victorious to the castles of your fathers, and may your family live and nourish there for ever--huzza!" He pronounced the last word with a loud voice, and just as he set his cup down, he was astonished to hear it repeated by many sounds, which appeared to be voices, coming from the whole length of the grotto: "What is that?" he said, "are not we alone?"

"Those are my vassals,--spirits," answered the knight, smiling; "or, if you prefer it, the echo, which responds to your kind wish. I have often heard," he added, in a more serious tone, "in the days of my prosperity, the success of my house cheered by hundreds of voices; but I have never been more pleased, or more affected, than to have it drank to, by my only guest, and re-echoed among the rocks of these lower regions. Fill the cup, Hans, and drink, and if you can give us a good toast, let's have it."

The fifer of Hardt filled the cup, and glanced a significant look at Albert: "Here's to you, sir, and something which will please you more,--the Lady of Lichtenstein!"

"Hollo, right so, right so! drink, sir, drink!" cried the exile, and laughed so heartily, that the cavern appeared to tremble under it. "Drink out every drop! long may she live, and bloom for you! Well done, Hans! only look how the blood mounts up in the cheeks of our guest; how his eyes sparkle, as if he actually kissed her beautiful lips. You need not be bashful! I also have loved and wooed, and know the state of a light merry heart of four-and-twenty, on such an occasion!"

"Poor man!" said Albert, touched by a sigh of deep feeling which accompanied these last words.--"Have you loved and wooed also? and perhaps been obliged to leave a beloved wife and children to lament and bewail your present misfortunes!" As he said this he felt his cloak pulled from behind, when turning around, the countryman winked to him, as a sign, that it was a subject of all others the most painful to the knight to hear. Albert immediately saw the effect it produced on his features; and regretted having been the cause of giving him pain.

With a look of wild despair, and evidently trying to combat his feeling, he merely said, "Frost in September destroys the beautiful flower which blossoms in May, and we scarcely know how to account for it. My children are left in the hands of rough but faithful nurses, who will, with God's help, take care good of them till their father returns home again." He was so much affected when he spoke these words, that it required no small effort to enable him to resume his good humour. "Hans is witness," he said, after a pause, "how often I have wished to see you, Albert von Sturmfeder; he told me of your being wounded, on that occasion when you were surprised by a party of the League, who probably took you for one of us outcasts; but happily gave you an opportunity to escape."

"Yes, I had a narrow escape," answered Albert. "I almost believe they took me for the Duke, for they were on the look out for him at that time. I would willingly have suffered much greater loss, to be the instrument of saving him."

"Well, that is saying a good deal; are you aware, that the cut which was made at you might have cost you your life?"

"He who takes the field," replied Albert, "must settle all his accounts with the world beforehand. I would certainly prefer falling before the enemy in the field of battle, surrounded by friends and comrades, that I might receive from their hands the last offices of regard and love. But still, to parry the murderer's hand from the Duke, I would have sacrificed my life, at any time, had it been necessary."

The exile regarded the young man with emotion, and pressed his hand. "You appear to take great interest in the Duke," he said; "I should hardly have supposed it; because they say, your heart is with the League."

"As I know you are a partisan of the Duke," answered Albert; "I trust you will excuse me if I speak my mind freely. Well, then, I must tell you, I think the Duke has acted, in many respects, not becoming his high station; for example, he ought not to have meddled in the affair of Hutten in the manner he did, whatever might have been his reasons; and then, the treatment of his wife was excited by violence and an overbearing spirit; and you must admit, that it was rage and revenge, and not a just ground for attack, which moved him to take forcible possession of Reutlingen."

He paused, expecting to hear a remark from the knight, upon what he had just said; but as he remained silent, Albert continued: "Upon these reports I formed the idea of the Duke's character when I joined the ranks of the confederates, among whom he was vilified in still stronger terms; but, on the other hand, he had a warm advocate in the Lady of Lichtenstein, who was better acquainted with his virtues than his enemies, and who you may perhaps have already heard was the principal cause of my quitting their service. I will not, therefore, say more upon the subject further than she opened my eyes to the true state of existing circumstances. In consequence of her information, I gave myself some trouble to penetrate the ulterior views of the League, and found they were directed, not only to the dispossessing him of his dominions and banishing him his country, but, in order to gratify the real object of their views, they grasped at the partition of his sovereignty among themselves. With the impression of the injustice of their intentions strong in my mind, I viewed the Duke's cause in a light totally different to what I had hitherto done. His character was raised still higher in my estimation, when I also learnt, that though urged by the patriotism and love of his people to venture a battle in defence of his rights, he would not risk the blood of his faithful Würtembergers in such a hazardous game. And though possessing the power of extorting money from his subjects to subsidize the

Swiss, he rather preferred exile for the good of his country. These are my reasons for befriending the ill-used Prince."

The knight, whose eyes had been fixed on the ground, now raised them upon Albert, and he seemed overpowered with the kind expressions which he had used towards the Duke. "Truly," he said, "your feelings are pure and generous, my young friend! I know the Duke as well as I do myself, and I may venture to say with you, that he rises superior to his misfortunes, and merits a far better name than report gives of him. Ah! if he had a hundred hearts such as yours, not a rag of the League's ensigns would ever float over the castles of Würtemberg;--could I but persuade you to join his cause! Far be it from me, however, to invite you to share his misery; it is enough that your sword, and an arm such as yours, do not belong to his enemies. May your days be happier than his! may heaven reward your good opinion of an unfortunate man!"

The spirit which breathed throughout the words of the exile, struck many a corresponding chord in the heart of Albert. He was flattered and encouraged to hear his own actions thus acknowledged.

The similarity which appeared to exist between the fate of his unknown friend and the impoverished fortunes of his own house, together with the prompting of the noble desire to espouse the weakest but honest cause in the pending struggle, in preference to taking the side of victorious injustice, were so many irresistible inducements to the manly mind of Albert to stand by the exile in his present deep distress.

Inspired by this feeling, he took his hand, and said, "Let no one henceforth talk to me of the imprudence,--let it not be called folly,-- of sharing the misfortunes of the persecuted! May others partake of the division of the Duke's fine country, and carouse in the spoils of the unhappy man's property,--I feel courage enough to suffer with him in his sufferings; and, when he draws his sword to re-conquer his lost possessions, I will be the first by his side. Take my hand, sir knight, as my pledge: let what may happen, I am the Duke's friend from henceforth, for ever."

A tear of gratitude started in the eye of the exile as he returned the shake of his hand. "You risk much, but you lose nothing by becoming Ulerich's friend. The country, beyond these inhospitable regions, is now in the possession of tyrants and robbers; but here below faithful hearts still beat true to Würtemberg. Forget for a moment that I am a poor knight and an exiled man, and figure me to yourself the Prince of the country, as I am lord of this cavern, with his knight and citizen standing before him. Ah! as long as these three estates hold firm together, be they concealed ever so deep in the lap of the earth, Würtemberg still exists. Fill the cup, Hans, and join your rough hand to ours; we'll seal the alliance in a bumper!"

Hans replenished the jug and filled the cup, "Drink, noble sirs, drink," said he; "you cannot pledge yourselves in a more noble wine than in this Uhlbacher."

The knight having emptied the cup by a long draught, ordered it to be filled again, and presented it to Albert. "Does not this wine," asked Albert, "grow about the castle whence Würtemberg's royal blood sprang? I think the heights about it are called Uhlbacher?"

"You are right," answered the exile; "the hill is generally called the Rothenberg, at the foot of which the vine grows; the castle stands upon its summit, built by Würtemberg's ancestors. Oh! the beautiful vallies of the Neckar, the luxuriant hills of fruit and wine! Gone, gone for ever!" He uttered these words with a voice which bespoke a heart almost broken by suffering and grief; he could scarcely conceal the anguish of his soul, which his inflexible mind had hitherto veiled under the mask of a forced hilarity.

The countryman knelt beside him, took his hand, and to rouse him from a state of painful wandering, in which he was lost for some moments, said, "Be of good cheer, sir; you will return to your country again happier than you left it."

"You will behold the vallies of your home again," said Albert. "When the Duke regains his lost rights, and reoccupies the castles of his ancestors, the vallies of the Neckar, and its richly clothed hills of vineyards, will echo with the rejoicings of his people, and you also will be able to join in the jubilee. Banish gloomy thoughts from your mind, *nunc vino pellite curas;* drink, and let us hope for better times. I pledge you in this Würtemberg wine,--'to the Duke's happy return with his faithful followers!'"

These words seemed to reanimate the sunken spirits of the knight, and like a ray of sunshine shed a smile over his features. "Yes!" he cried, "sweet is the word which sends comfort to the broken-hearted; it is like a drop of cold water to refresh the weary wanderer in the desert. Forget my weakness, my friend; pardon it in a man who otherwise never gives place to grief.

"But if you had ever looked down from the summit of the Rothenberg, shaded by its green woods, into the heart of Würtemberg, and beheld the gentle stream of the Neckar winding its course along its richly cultivated banks; with its fields of high standing corn waving in the breeze; the red roofs of its villages peeping out from a forest of fruit trees, with their industrious inhabitants, consisting of strong men and beautiful women, busily employed in their gardens or dressing their vines on the heights; had you surveyed all this, and with my eyes, and then been compelled to take refuge from the bloodthirsty hands of ruffians in these inhospitable regions, surrounded by the benumbing chill of these walls, outlawed, condemned, banished.--Oh! the thought is terrible! too overwhelming for man's heart to bear!"

Albert, fearful lest the recollection of his past days, and the keen sense of his present situation, might a second time have too powerful an effect upon the mind of the exile, sought by changing the subject of conversation, to divert his mind and calm his thoughts.

"As I suppose you have been often with the Duke," he said, "pray tell me, now that I am his declared friend, what is his disposition? what is his appearance? is it true, as is reported, that he is of a very changeable and capricious temper?"

"No more upon that subject at present, if you please," answered the exile; "you will soon have an opportunity to judge for yourself when you see him. We have already spoken enough upon these matters, but you have said nothing about your own affairs; not a word about the object of your travels, nor of the beautiful lady of Lichtenstein? You are silent and look confused when that delicate subject is mentioned. Do not suppose I wish to be curious when I ask that question; no, it is solely because I think I can be of use to you."

"From what has passed between us this night," replied Albert, "I have nothing to conceal from you; secrecy is no longer necessary. It strikes me, that you must have long known I love Bertha, and that she likewise is faithful to me?"

The exile answered, smiling, "O yes, there was no mistaking the symptoms of her feelings, for when you were mentioned her confused look bespoke the secret of her heart, and the blush which accompanied it was an evident witness of the truth of it. When she named you it was with a peculiar tone of voice, as if the strings of her heart sounded in full accord to that key-note."

"This observation of yours will encourage me to go to Lichtenstein without further delay. It was my original intention, after I had quitted the service of the League, to go direct to my home; but as the Alb is about half way between Franconia and this place, and the desire I had to see my love once more was uppermost in my thoughts, I determined to endeavour to accomplish it. This man Hans conducted me over the Alb; you know the cause which delayed me eight days on my journey. To-morrow, at day-break, I purpose announcing myself at the castle, and I trust I shall now appear before the old knight in a more welcome light than I should otherwise have done, had I not performed my promise to the League of remaining neutral fourteen days, and now joined his colours."

"You may be assured of his welcome," said the knight, "particularly if you go as the friend of the Duke, for he is his faithful and most devoted adherent. But, may be, he would not trust your word, unsupported by some introduction, being, so it is said, rather incredulous, and shy of strangers. You know upon what terms I am with him. He is the kind-hearted Samaritan to me; and when I creep out of my hole at night, he nourishes my body with warm food, and my heart with still warmer consolation for the future. A couple of lines from me will be better received by him than a passport from the Emperor. Take this ring, which he and many others know and respect, and wear it in remembrance of the time we have passed together; it will announce you as a friend of Würtemberg's good cause." With these words, he took a broad gold ring from his finger. A large red stone was set in the middle, upon which was engraved, in the armorial helmet, the three stag horns,1 with the bugle, which Albert recognised as the arms of Würtemberg. Around the ring were the letters, U.D.O.W.A.T. in relievo, the meaning of which he could not comprehend.

"Udowat? what does that name signify?" he asked. "Is it a parole for the followers of the Duke?"

"No, my young friend," said the exile. "The Duke has worn this ring long on his finger; he valued it much; but as I have many other souvenirs from him, I can best spare it, and could not place it in worthier hands. The letters mean, Ulerich, Duke of Würtemberg and Teck."

"I shall value it as long as I live," replied Albert, "as a relic of the unfortunate Prince whose name it bears, and as a pleasing remembrance of you, sir knight, and the night we passed together in this cavern."

"When you come to the drawbridge of Lichtenstein," continued the knight, "deliver a note which I will write, and this ring, to the first servant you see, and desire them to be conveyed to the lord of the castle, when he will certainly receive you as the Duke's own son. But for the lady, you must use your own passport, for my charm does not extend to her: a tender squeeze of the hand, or the mysterious language of the eyes, or perhaps still better, a sweet kiss on her rosy lips, will serve the purpose. But in order to appear before her as she would wish to see you, you need some rest, for if you pass the whole night without sleep, your eyes will be heavy. Therefore follow my example, stretch yourself on the deer skin, and make a pillow of your cloak. And you, worthy major domo, grand chamberlain and purveyor, Hans, faithful companion in misfortune, give this Paladin another glass for his nightcap, it will soften his deer-skin, and enchant this rocky grotto into a bed-room. And then may the god of dreams visit him with his choicest gifts!"

The men drank a good night to each other, and laid themselves to rest, Hans taking up his position as a faithful dog, at the entrance of the rocky chamber. Morpheus soon came with light steps to the aid of the young man, and as he was dropping off to sleep he heard, in a half doze, the exile saying his evening prayer, and, with pious confidence in the Disposer of events, imploring him to shower down his almighty protection on him and his unhappy country.

FOOTNOTES TO CHAPTER XIX.:

Footnote 1: Three stag horns, the two upper ones having four ends and the lower one three, were the ancient arms of Würtemberg.

CHAPTER XX

See that arrowy crag so tapering rise,
From the depths of that valley so sweet;
There Lichtenstein's fort rears her head to the skies,
And smiles on the world at her feet.

Schwab.

When the fifer of Hardt awakened Albert in the morning, the youth was at first puzzled to recollect where he was, and to recognize the objects about him; but he soon came to his senses, and the remembrance of the last evening's occurrences. He returned the hearty shake of the hand with which the exile saluted him, who said, "Although it would give me great pleasure to detain you some few days with me, yet I would rather advise you to proceed at once to Lichtenstein, if you wish to have a hot breakfast. I cannot, alas! prepare such in my cavern, for we never dare make a fire, lest the smoke betray our position."

Albert consented to his proposal, and thanked him for his night's lodging. "I may truly say," he answered, "that I never passed a night more to my satisfaction, than I have done in this place. A deep-felt, though melancholy, charm would seem to hallow the society of friends in such a situation as this, and I would not have exchanged my abode among these rocky walls, for the most splendid apartment of a ducal palace."

"Yes, indeed, secure from persecution, and among friends, when the glass circulates freely, banishment has its charms," replied the exile; "but when I sit here, day after day, in solitude, brooding over my calamities, my heart yearning for liberty, and my eye wearied with the sameness of these subterranean splendours, then it is I drink the full cup of misery. And then again, my ear is deafened with the unceasing monotonous murmur of these waters, dripping drop after drop from the rocks! Jealous of their freedom, my imagination follows their course through the depths below, whence they escape to swell the running stream, whose gentle ripple, with the note of the cheerful lark, would seem to join chorus in the universal praise."

"My poor friend, I pity thee! yes, indeed, this solitary life must be terrible," said Albert.

"Nevertheless," continued the other, raising himself up, "I reckon myself happy to have found this asylum, with the help of a few trusty friends. Rather than fall into the hands of my enemies, to be their sport and laughing-stock, I would descend a hundred fathoms lower, where the vital air scarce sustains life. And before I would surrender my liberty, these hands should dig my way into the heart of the earth, until I reached its centre; there to invoke the curses of heaven upon my oppressors as a just punishment of the wrongs I endure from the persecutions of their revengeful designs."

The exile having worked himself up into a state of fury, Albert involuntarily retreated a pace or two. His figure appeared to gain in height--all the muscles of his body were on the stretch--his cheeks glowed with rage--his eyes shot fire, as if they sought an enemy upon whom to revenge his sufferings; and the loud and violent tone of his voice; echoed among the rocks the maledictions which issued from his mouth.

Albert could not but sympathise with the man in giving vent to his feelings in such a burst of passion; he who was so cruelly persecuted by his enemies, for his faithful attachment to his lord. "I admire your strength of mind," said he to the knight; and, as if a sudden thought had crossed his mind, continued, "will you pardon me for asking you one question, which perhaps you may deem indiscreet; but since you have admitted me to your friendship and confidence, I will venture to do so. Tell me, are you not the celebrated Maxx Stumpf von Schweinsberg?"

There must have been something particularly strange in this question; because the gravity which had shaded the knight's countenance disappeared at once, at the mere mention of this name. He first smiled; but not able to contain himself, broke out into a loud laugh, in which Hans considered himself permitted to join.

Albert was unable to comprehend the meaning of the sudden burst of merriment which his question had occasioned. He felt confused, and looked for an explanation of it, first at one, then at the other; but his embarrassment only excited their merry mood still more.

At length the exile said, "Pardon me, worthy guest, for having violated in an unmannerly way the rights of hospitality; for I ought rather to have bitten off the end of my tongue than have given you cause to suppose I had thought you said anything ridiculous; but how comes it that you take me for Maxx Stumpf? Do you know him?"

"No, I never saw him; but I know him to be a brave knight, whom the League has expelled from his country, on account of his faithful adherence to the Duke, and that they are now endeavouring to apprehend him. Is not yours a similar case?"

"I thank you for comparing me to such a man; but I would not advise you to fall in his way in the night, upon the same terms as when we met; for Stumpf, without further to do, would soon have cut you up into slices fit for cooking. Schweinsberg being a little thick-set fellow, and a head shorter than me, it was the comparison which made me laugh so irresistibly. He is, however, an honourable man, and one of the few to be depended upon who will not desert his master in misfortune."

"So you are not Schweinsberg?" replied Albert; "then I must leave you without knowing who my friend is."

"Young man!" said the exile, with dignity, "you have found a friend in me, by your gallant, honourable behaviour; which your open, frank countenance has confirmed. Let it suffice for you, to have gained this friend; ask no further questions, one word might perhaps interrupt this confidential intimacy between us, which is so gratifying to me. Farewell; think on the banished man without a name, and be assured that, before two days are over, you shall both hear from me, and know my name."

In spite of his unseemly dress, the whole demeanour of this man appeared to Albert to be more that of a Prince dismissing a subject from his presence, than an unfortunate exile, parting from a friend who had participated in his afflictions.

During the last conversation, the fifer of Hardt had lighted the torches, and stood waiting at the entrance of the grotto; the knight pressed a salute on the lips of the young man, and waved him to go. He departed, unable to account why a man so familiar and friendly in his address, should, at the same time, inspire him with the idea of being so much his superior in rank; he had never felt, until this moment, how an individual, devoid of all the external marks of distinction, exhibiting outward signs of poverty, rather than the contrary, could possess a personal influence sufficiently great to subdue vanity and self-love. Occupied with these thoughts, he retraced his steps through the cavern. The beauties of nature, which had surprised him and fixed his attention when he first entered it, had lost their charm to his eye, and his wonder was no longer excited at the grandeur of the surrounding objects. His mind was exclusively taken up with the contemplation of a subject more imposing and instructive than these rocks, however magnificent they might be. The human mind, rising superior to the frowns of this world, exemplified so well in the character of his unknown friend, filled him with admiration, and proved to him that the dignity of man's nature will force its way through the garb of poverty and the suffering of persecution, and remain unsullied amidst the frowns of fate.

A bright day greeted Albert and the fifer of Hardt, as they issued from the darkness of the cavern into the light of heaven. Albert breathed more freely in the freshness of the morning air, than he had done amidst the damp exhalations which streamed from the galleries and grottos of the subterranean vaults, from which they derive the name of the misty caverns. He found his horse in the same place, fastened to the tree, where he had left him the night before, as fresh and lively as ever; the military weapons attached to the saddle not having suffered from the night dew, which Albert was fearful might have been the case. But Hans had had the precaution to cover the beast with a large coarse cloth, in order to guard against bad weather. The young man arranged his dress as well as he was able, after such a night's lodging, whilst the countryman gave his horse a feed of fresh hay. They then set forward on their journey, and having gone but a few paces, the tolling of a church bell from the valley below saluted their ears, and broke the solemn stillness of the morning. Shortly afterwards, another bell answered, and then three or four more followed, when the number, increasing to at least twelve, spread their melodious tones over the heights and vallies. The young man stopt his horse, surprised at this early chorus of bells: "What means this salutation?" he asked, "is it a signal that there is a fire in the neighbourhood? or may be to-day is a holiday? God knows that, since my illness, I have quite lost all knowledge of time, and can only distinguish Sunday from the other days of the week by the peasant girls being clad in their best dresses and clean aprons."

"That is not an uncommon case with many a military man," replied Hans; "I myself have often been obliged to guess what day it was, when I had other things in my head, which I regret to say I deemed more important than hearing mass. But now it is different," he added, with a serious countenance, and crossed himself, "to-day is Good Friday."

"That reminds me," said the young man, "that this is the first time in my life that I have not celebrated this day as becomes a Christian; it also brings with it many happy hours of my youth to my recollection. My father was then alive; I possessed a tender, good mother, and a dear young sister. We two children always rejoiced upon the anniversary of Good Friday, and, though we did not know exactly what it meant, we remembered that it was only two days from Easter, a season when our mother invariably gave us some token of her affection. *Requiescant in pace!*" he added, turning away to conceal a tear; "they are all three gone."

These last words, which he pronounced in remembrance of his departed parents, the spontaneous effusion of his affectionate heart, did not escape the fifer's observation, who raised his cap in respect to the feelings of his companion. Such had been the restless life of this extraordinary man from his infancy, that he might have been thought to be void of all sense of religion; but since his escape from the hand of the executioner, which he had hinted at in a former conversation with Albert, and professed to have become a better man, serious thoughts at times occupied his mind.

Albert having alluded to his own case of receiving a present from his mother at Easter, the fifer took occasion to say, with a good-natured smile, "that the time was coming, when he hoped he would also be able to perform the same office to his own children." But the young man was offended at this familiarity, and showed symptoms of his displeasure.

"No offence, sir," he replied, and drew his attention to the castle before them. "Do you see the tower peeping out among the trees?" he added: "another short quarter of an hour, and we are there."

"From what I could remark yesterday in the dark," said the young man, "the castle appeared to be erected upon a solitary, steep rock. By heavens! a bold thought, whoever built it; for no one could attempt to scale its walls unless he were in league with the devil, and had the power of flying. It might be bombarded, however, from this spot with heavy artillery."

"Do you think so? I can tell you, that they have four good match-guns in the hall, which would return an answer too sharp to any one who should attempt it. Had you made a careful survey, you must have observed, that the rock is separated from the mountain by a broad deep valley, which surrounds it, so that much damage could not be done to the castle. The only weak side is that nearest the mountain, upon which the drawbridge is placed. Let but an enemy attempt to plant guns there, and he would soon see old Lichtenstein's battery hurl them down in the abyss below, before they had even touched a pane of glass in his windows. But the great difficulty would be to get guns up this declivity, and transport them over these cavities, without exposing men to more danger than that nest is worth."

"You are right," Albert answered; "I should like to know who ever thought of building a castle upon that rock."

"I'll tell you," replied Hans, who was well acquainted with all the legends of his country: "once upon a time there lived a fair lady, who suffered much persecution from her suitors, and did not know how to escape them. She came to this rock, and saw a large eagle with its family perched upon the top of it, secure from all interruption. Having determined to expel the eagle, she built the castle on its nest; and when everything was complete, drew up the drawbridge, and from the summit of the tower proclaimed aloud, 'I henceforth devote myself to God, and forswear the world.' From that day forth no one was able to annoy her;--but we are arrived. Farewell; perhaps I may see you again tonight. I am now going about the country, to endeavour to ascertain what is going on, and will return to the exile in the cavern with what news I can gather as to the state of the Duke's affairs. Don't forget, when you come on the bridge, to send the ring and letter to the lord of the castle; and take care you do not break the seal yourself."

"Don't fear! I thank you for your conduct; salute my kind host of the cavern for me," said Albert; and, pushing his horse forward, in a few minutes stood before the fortress of Lichtenstein.

A guard at the gate demanded his business, and called a servant to deliver the letter and ring to his master. Albert had in the meantime an opportunity to examine minutely the castle and its environs. Having only seen it the night before by the dim light of the moon, and too much occupied with other important subjects to fix his exclusive attention to its structure, he had not been able to imagine even what he now viewed with rapture. A perpendicular isolated rock, like the colossal tower of a cathedral, rising from the valley of the Alb, stood before him in bold independence. Its position impressed him with the idea, that it might have been cleft from the surrounding hills by some violent convulsion of nature, either by an earthquake, or by a deluge in ancient times, which had washed away the softer materials of the earth, leaving the solid mass of rock untouched. Even on the south-west side, where he now stood, the deep ravine which separated the rock from the nearest part of the adjoining country, was too broad for the boldest shamoy to venture a spring across, though not so distant as to baffle the art of man to throw a bridge over. The castle stood on its summit, like the nest of a bird, perched upon the highest branch of an oak, or the pinnacle of a lofty tower. Except the tower, which peered above all, the only apparent habitation was a small fortified apartment surrounded by many round windows. The numerous loop-holes in the lower part of the buildings, and several larger embrasures, out of which peeped the muzzles of guns of the heavy calibre of the time, proved that it was well guarded, and that, spite of its insignificant size, it was no contemptible fortress. The enormous foundation walls and buttresses, which appeared to form part of the rock, and had assumed by age and weather the same yellowish-brown colour of the mass of stone upon which they stood, might well convince the beholder of the solidity of the structure, and its capability to bid defiance to the power of man and the storms of the elements. A beautiful view presented itself before Albert, and he thought how much more extended it must be from the top of the watch-tower.

These observations obtruded themselves upon Albert, as he stood waiting at the outer gate, which was strongly palisadoed towards the ravine, and covered the approach to the bridge. He now heard steps approaching; the gate was thrown open, and the master of the castle appeared himself to receive his guest. It was the same stern elderly man whom he had seen several times in Ulm, whose countenance he could not easily forget; for his dark fiery eye, his pale but noble features, his likeness to his daughter, had made a lasting impression upon his mind.

"Welcome to Lichtenstein," said the old man, offering his hand, the grave features of his face giving place to a more kindly expression. "What are you standing gaping about there, you idle vagabonds?" he said to his servants, after the first salutation to his visitor; "do you suppose the gentleman is to lead his horse up into the room? Take him away to the stable, and bring his weapons into the saloon. I beg pardon, worthy sir, that these carles should have kept you so long waiting; but there is no beating sense into their thick heads. Will you follow me?"

He led on over the bridge, followed by Albert, whose heart beat in full expectation and longing desire to see and surprise his beloved. But recollecting the adventures of the preceding night, and the feeling which first prompted him to come to this spot, he blushed in shame for having suspected her fidelity. His eye sought all the windows in the hopes of seeing her; his ear was sharpened to catch if possible the sound of her voice: but in vain did his eye search the windows; in vain did his ear listen.

They had now reached the inner gate. It was strongly built, according to the ancient manner, with a portcullis, and openings above, to throw down boiling oil and water; and provided with all the other means of defence made use of in the olden times to repel a besieging enemy, should he have made himself master of the bridge. But it was not to the massive walls and fortifications alone which surrounded the castle that Lichtenstein was indebted for its security; nature claimed her share also in it. The rock itself formed a principal part of the habitation, having large roomy stables, and apartments which served as cellars, hewn out of it. A winding staircase led to the upper part of the castle, where military defences were likewise not less thought of than elsewhere. On the landing place, leading to the different rooms, and generally appropriated in similar habitations to the purposes of keeping the household utensils, were now to be seen match-guns, large chests containing shot, and divers other warlike weapons.1 The old knight's eye rested with a peculiar expression of pride upon this singular species of household furniture; and it is a fact that, in those days, the possessor of heavy artillery was accounted a man of opulence and wealth, for it was not every one who could afford to defend his castle with four or six such pieces as were possessed by the lord of the castle.

Another staircase led to the second story, upon which the knight of Lichtenstein showed his guest into a fine large saloon, lighted by several windows. He gave a sign to a servant who had followed them up, to withdraw.

FOOTNOTE TO CHAPTER XX.:

Footnote 1: There is a description, in an old chronicle, of Lichtenstein, as it existed at the end of the sixteenth century, about sixty years after 1519. It is stated therein, "In the upper story, there is a remarkable handsome room, surrounded on all sides by windows, from which may be seen the Asperg. The banished Duke Ulerich of Würtemberg, who often visited it, came every night to the castle, and saying, 'The man is here!' was immediately received." A gamekeeper's house is now built upon the ruins of the old castle, which still retains its name, and serves on Whitsunday as a place of rendezvous for the peasantry of the surrounding country, who assemble in their gayest dresses for dancing and carousal.

CHAPTER XXI

The noble spirit of the victim brave
Affects the knight, he feels that he must save;
The dews of friendship o'er his eyelids steal,
His heart no longer can resist th' appeal.

P. Conz.

When the two men were left alone in the saloon of Lichtenstein, the old knight gazed at Albert full in the face, with a scrutinizing eye, as if to satisfy himself of the honesty of his looks. The noble features of his visitor convinced him of the purity of his heart, and animated the old man's eye with a ray of joy. The air of melancholy which habitually sat on his brow had vanished, he became cheerful, he received Albert as a father would a son, who had returned from a long journey. A tear at length stole from his brilliant eye; but it was a tear of joy, for he pressed the astonished youth to his heart.

"It is not often that I am betrayed into this weakness," he said to Albert, "but in moments such as these nature gives way, because they happen seldom. Dare I indeed trust my old eyes? Do the contents of this letter deceive me? Is the seal really his? and can I believe it? but why do I doubt! has not nature stampt the impression of her noblest gifts upon your open forehead? Oh, yes, honesty is too visibly depicted on your countenance; you cannot deceive me; the cause of my unfortunate master has gained another friend!"

"If you allude to the cause of the banished Duke, you are not mistaken; it has found a warm partisan in me. Report has long since reached my ear of the knight of Lichtenstein being a faithful friend of his, and with this assurance I should perhaps have presented myself to you ere this, of my own accord, without the introduction of the unfortunate man in the cavern."

"Sit down beside me, my young friend," said the old man, who continued to regard Albert with a look of benevolence, "seat yourself, and listen to what I say: generally speaking, I am not an admirer of persons who change their minds. The experience of a long life has taught me to respect the opinion of others, and to assert that a man who entertains pure and honest views of a subject, is not therefore to be prejudged by another, who may think differently. But when a person changes his colours from real disinterested motives, as you appear to have done, Albert von Sturmfeder, and turns his back upon prosperity, for the noble purpose of allying himself to, and aiding the oppressed, in a just cause, then it is that his virtuous intentions justify his conduct, and carry along with them the stamp of a noble act."

Albert blushed for himself, when he heard old Lichtenstein praising his disinterested motives. Was it not for the sake of the beautiful daughter of the knight, that he had principally been induced to join his colours? and would he not sink in the esteem of this man, when, sooner or later, his real motive for embracing his party came to light? "You are too good," he answered; "the views of a man are often buried deeper than we at first sight think. But be assured, that though the step I have taken was dictated partly by a feeling which revolts at the idea of unjust oppression; I would not have you think too well of me, because it would give me very great pain, were you afterwards to be obliged to pronounce an unfavourable opinion upon my actions."

"I love you still more for your frankness," replied the lord of the castle, and squeezed the hand of his guest: "I can trust to my knowledge of physiognomy, and maintain, from what I see in yours, that, though other views may have influenced you, besides the feeling of justice, you never will be found wanting in honour. Whoever is led by evil intentions is a coward, and no coward would dare to run his head against Truchses, the Duke of Bavaria, and the whole Swabian League, and rise superior to the danger, as you have done."

"What do you know of me," said Albert, with joyful surprise; "have you ever heard of me before this moment?"

A servant, who opened the door at these words, interrupted the answer of the old man. He set a breakfast of game and a can full of wine before Albert, and prepared to wait on the guest; but a hint from his master made him withdraw. "Don't spare this morning's meal," said he to the young man; "the first glass, indeed, ought to be drank to the lady of the house, according to courteous habits; but mine has long departed this life, and my only daughter, Bertha, who acts in her place, is gone down to the village church, to hear the sermon and mass on this holiday. Well, you asked me if I have ever heard of you before? As you now belong to our party, I may venture to acquaint you with what I otherwise should have kept secret.

When you entered Ulm, I was also in the town, not only for the purpose of taking my daughter home, who was residing there, but principally to learn many things, which were important for the Duke to know. Gold opened all the doors," he added with a smile, "and unbolted those also of the grand council; by which means I became acquainted with everything the commanders of the League had determined upon. When war was declared, I was obliged to leave the place, but I left faithful men behind me in the town, who informed me of every circumstance, even the most secret."

"Was not the fifer of Hardt one of them," asked Albert, "whom I found with the exile?"

"Yes; the same who conducted you over the Alb." Albert started. "I had daily intelligence of the most secret affairs. Among other things, I learnt that they had determined to send a trusty spy into the neighbourhood of Tübingen, to gain intelligence and advertise the League of our movements. I heard you were selected for that service. I must tell you honestly, that, though you and your name were indifferent to me, for I did not know you personally, still I regretted that your young blood should be employed on that service, for, as sure as you live, the moment you had passed the Alb in the degrading character of a spy, so soon would you have been cut to pieces without grace or mercy. So much more surprising then was the information to me, when I learned further, that you had refused the service, and had spoken boldly before your employers. The fact also of your having renounced their party, and sworn to keep in a state of neutrality for fourteen days, was also made known to me. How much I rejoice then that you have become our friend also, I leave you to imagine!"

Nothing could have been more gratifying to Albert's feelings than the eulogium passed on his conduct by the knight of Lichtenstein. This moment removed all obstacles which had hitherto interrupted the tie between him and Bertha. The only wish of his heart, which he at times thought would never be realised, and had almost given up in despair, he now might hope would be accomplished, for he unknowingly had gained the good will of her father. "Yes, I renounced their service," he answered, "because their intentions outraged my feelings; I became your friend with heart and soul. When I was seated beside the exiled man in the cavern, and heard the disgraceful manner in which the lord of the land and the nobles were treated, I felt the force of his language strengthen my resolutions. In that moment all doubts and difficulties were removed from my mind, every thing was as clear as day, my only desire was, to draw my sword in this cause! And do you think we shall be called into action soon? How stand the Duke's affairs? You must not suppose I am come to you to set with my hands across."

"I can well imagine your anxiety to be in the field," said the old knight; "forty years ago I possessed the same ardour. You are aware, perhaps, in what state our affairs are at present; more upon the decline, I fear, than prosperous. The enemy is in possession of the whole tract of the low country as far up as Urach. Our fate depends upon one solitary circumstance,----if Tübingen holds out, victory is ours!"

"The honour of forty knights will, I think, answer for its safety," replied Albert, with animation; "the castle is strong, I have never seen a stronger; the garrison is sufficient for its defence, and forty men of noble blood will not surrender for a trifle. They cannot--they dare not. Have they not the children of the duke, and the treasures of his house, under their protection?--they *must* hold out."

"It were well if they were all like-minded with you," said the old man. "Tübingen holds a great stake in her hands. If the Duke can bring succour to its relief, he will then have a starting point, whence he will be able to reconquer his country. The place contains large supplies of munitions of war; and most of the nobility are assembled within its walls. So long as they remain faithful to his cause, so long will the feeling of Würtemberg be for the Duke, were he only to possess the spot upon which he stands; but I fear, I fear for the result."

"How? do you think it likely the knights will surrender? Impossible!"

"You have had but little experience in the ways of the world," replied the old man; "you are not aware of the many allurements and snares at work, which may make many a man waver in his allegiance. It is on this account, that the Duke, being doubtful of the fidelity of some of them in Tübingen, has sent Maxx Stumpf von Schweinsberg with a letter to the garrison written in strong terms, not only urging them to hold the castle to the last, but to afford him the means of entering therein himself, being ready to sacrifice his life in its defence, if God should so ordain it."

"Poor man," said Albert, moved by the consideration of the Duke's hard fate; "I cannot believe the nobility of the land will act in a manner unworthy of their rank. His presence among them will encourage their desponding hopes, sorties will be made, the besiegers will be beaten in spite of Bavaria and Fronsberg. We'll join them sword in hand, and drive these Leaguists out of the country."

"Maxx Stumpf is not yet returned," replied the knight of Lichtenstein, with a look of anxiety; "and the firing has ceased since yesterday. We hear every shot here on the Lichtenstein; but during the last twenty-four hours all is as quiet as the grave."

"Perhaps they have ceased firing on account of the holidays; you'll see that, to-morrow, or Easter Monday, they will re-commence with redoubled vigour, and make your rocks echo again."

"What is it you say?" replied the other, "on account of the holidays? To serve the Duke faithfully is a pious undertaking; and the saints in Heaven would perhaps rather hear the thunder of cannon in a just cause than that the knights should remain idle. Idleness is the parent of all vice! But, I trust, when Maxx arrives in the castle, he will rouse them out of their slumbers."

"Do you mean that the Duke had sent the knight of Schweinsberg to Tübingen, and that he intended to follow him, because the garrison has shewn symptoms of surrender? Has he not flown to Mömpelgard, as the people say? or is he still in the neighbourhood? Oh, that I could see him, and accompany him!"

A peculiar smile passed rapidly over the stern countenance of the old man. "You will sec him at the proper moment," he said; "he will be happy to see you also, for he loves you already. And, if fortune favours us, you shall also go with him to his castle, I give you my word. But for the present I must beg you will remain patiently alone for a short time; some business calls me, but it will be soon finished. I leave you in the company of some good old wine; make yourself at home in my house; were it not Good Friday, I would invite you to go out hunting." The old man pressed Albert's hand once more, and left the room; and soon after he saw him ride out of the castle towards the wood.

When the young man found himself alone, he commenced putting his dress in order, which in consequence of his recent adventures, required some attention. Whoever has been in the vicinity of the lady of his love, under Albert's circumstances, will not blame him for taking advantage of a piece of polished metal, which served as a looking-glass, hanging on the wall, to arrange his beard and hair. Having brushed his jacket, and removed all traces of having passed the night underground, he went into the large saloon, and sought among the many windows which surrounded it, the one which would give him the best view of the path leading up to the castle from the church of the village in the valley below, whither Bertha had gone to hear mass.

Cheering thoughts passed through his mind, in rapid succession, like bright vapours flying under the blue vault of heaven. He was now on the spot which had long been the object of his ardent desire to visit; he viewed the mountains and rocks which Bertha had often spoke about; he felt a charm in being in the same house which had been the dwelling of her childhood, and in which she had grown up to woman's estate.

Albert went into the small spot of ground within the walls of the castle, adorned with flowers, and which assumed the name of garden. Again his imagination wandered, in the pleasing supposition that it had been created by her orders; the flowers appeared to speak to him in her name--he was in the act of bending under a tree to pluck a violet, when he heard footsteps at the gate. He turned around to observe who it might be, it was indeed Bertha herself--she stood there wrapt in surprise and motionless, scarcely trusting her eyes. He flew to her, and pressed her to his heart; her astonishment at the unexpected apparition gave way to the conviction that it was really her lover, and not his spirit that embraced her. They had more to ask each other than they knew well how to answer in the first transport of joy, for they could with difficulty convince themselves that it was not a dream, thus to find themselves in each other's presence without fear or interruption. Having returned to the house, Bertha said,

"How much have I suffered on your account, dearest Albert; and with what a heavy heart did I leave Ulm! You had, indeed, sworn to quit the service of the League; but I had no hopes of seeing you so soon. And then, when Hans informed me, that, on your journey with him to Lichtenstein, you had been surprised by the enemy on the road, and dangerously wounded, my heart was almost broken, at the thought that I could not go to you and nurse you."

Stung with remorse for having given place to the jealousy which the story of the hostess of the Golden Stag at Pfullingen had created in his breast, he sunk in his own estimation before the tender love of Bertha. He sought to conceal his confusion, and related to her, amidst the interruption of her numerous questions, all that had happened to him since their separation; the cause which had favoured his quitting the service of the League with honour; the particulars of his perilous escape from the enemy's patrole; the kind care which the fifer's wife and daughter had taken of him, by which he was enabled to prosecute his journey to Lichtenstein.

Albert's conscience was too honest not to feel embarrassed at some of Bertha's scrutinising questions; and when she wished to have her curiosity satisfied upon the subject of his coming to Lichtenstein at so strange an hour of the night he scarcely knew what to answer. Her beautiful eye rested upon him with such an expression of inquisitive penetration, that, though he would gladly have escaped the reproach of harbouring a momentary idea of her want of fidelity, he would not for all the world tell her an untruth.

"I will own," he said, with a confused look, "that I was infatuated by the hostess at Pfullingen; she told me something about you, which I could not hear with indifference."

"The hostess? about me?" cried Bertha, smiling; "well, but what brought you, at that late hour of the night, to this place?"

"Never mind, dearest; we'll not think of it any more. I know I acted like a fool. The exiled knight has quite convinced me how wrong I was."

"No, no," she replied, earnestly, "I am not going to let you escape so cheap; what had that chatterbox to say about me? tell me immediately----"

"Well, then, I give you leave to laugh at me as much as you please: she told me you had another lover, who came to visit you every night, whilst your father slept."

Bertha blushed; indignation, and the inclination to smile at a ridiculous story, contended for the mastery on her expressive features. "Well, I hope," she replied, "you repelled the calumny with proper contempt, and left her house immediately. That was the reason, I suppose, of your arriving here so late, with the intention of passing the night under our roof."

"I honestly avow, I had no such thought. You know I was not quite convalescent, so excuse my weakness. I really did not believe her at first; but when she brought your nurse, old Rosel, to substantiate what she said, and who moreover lamented that I had been deceived, I----oh, do not turn away from me, Bertha; do not be angry! I threw myself on my horse, and rode direct to the castle, for the purpose of exchanging a word with him who dared to love you."

"And could you believe that?" she answered, with tears starting into her eyes: "I cannot think that Rosel said any thing of the kind, though she is fond of a gossip; I am not angry with the hostess, for she does not know better; but that you, you Albert, should give credit to so foul a falsehood, and think it necessary to convince yourself, that----" The tears of the faithful girl flowed in abundance; and the feeling of mortification choked her further utterance.

Her lover was overcome by the sense of his egregious folly; but he also felt the consolation, that though he was to be blamed his suspicions arose purely out of the intensity of his love. "Pardon me this once, dearest; let me assure you, that the jealousy which tormented me, unfounded as it was, would never have been inflamed into reality, did not my whole existence depend upon you."

"He who really loves can never harbour a spark of jealousy, founded upon such reports," said Bertha, in displeasure; "you hinted something of the same kind once before in Ulm, which you know hurt me very deeply. But if you had known me, and loved me with the same unalterable attachment that I love you, you never could have entertained such thoughts."

"No, truly, but you must not be unjust," he replied, and took her hand; "how can you reproach me with not returning your love with the same ardent sincerity? Was it impossible that one more worthy than Albert von Sturmfeder might appear, and supplant him in your heart by some infernal enchantment? Every thing is possible in this world."

"Possible!" interrupted Bertha; and a certain pride, which Albert had often remarked in the daughter of Lichtenstein, appeared now to animate her; "possible? if you ever could have entertained such an opinion of me,--I repeat it, Albert von Sturmfeder,--you have never loved me. A man must not allow himself to be blown about like a reed; he ought to stand firm to his opinion; and if he loves, he must have faith also."

"I have not merited such a reproach, from you at least," said the young man, starting up in great excitement; "I have been, indeed, as you say, a reed shaken about in the wind, and many a man will despise me----"

"That may be!" she whispered to herself, but not so lightly as to escape his ear, and cause his displeasure to blaze up into rage.

"Can you upbraid me thus," said he, "you, who are the sole cause of my vaccilating conduct? Did I not seek you among the friends of the League; and when I found you, was I not overjoyed? You entreated me to quit their colours,--I did so; and still more, I came over to your party, and, though it nearly cost me my life, I held firm to my determination. I visited your father, who received me as a son; and rejoiced that I had bound myself to the Duke's cause. But his daughter compares me to a reed moved by every blast of wind! but once more I will----for the last time, allow myself to be moved by you; I'll leave you, as you requite my love thus; in an hour hence, I wish you farewell." With these last words he girded on his sword; and, taking his cap, turned to depart.

"Albert," cried Bertha, with the sweetest accent, at the same time springing up and seizing his hand; her pride, her displeasure, every trace of ill-will vanished in a moment, and entreating love only beamed from her eyes, "for God's sake, Albert! I did not mean to speak so angrily; remain, I will forget every thing; I am ashamed of myself for having betrayed so unkind a spirit."

But the anger of the young man was not to be appeased in a moment. He turned away, lest her looks should master his resolution of leaving the castle. "No!" he cried, "you shall not turn the reed back again; but you may tell your father the cause which has driven his guest from his house." The windows trembled with the sound of his voice; he looked about him with wildness; he tore his hand away from Bertha's grasp; and, followed by her, he hastily opened the door to fly from her presence, when an apparition arrested his attention on the threshold which we shall describe in the next chapter.

CHAPTER XXII

Prince's favour, April's sky,
Woman's love, the rose's dye,
Cards, dice, and weathercocks are still
Chang'd about, believe't who will.

Old Proverb.

The apparition which so opportunely arrested the attention of Albert on opening the door, was no other than the old nurse, Rosel, hastily rising from a bent position she had taken up at the keyhole. She was one of those old servants, who, having been brought up in the family from her youth, was firmly rooted in it, and now formed one of its principal branches. Since the death of the Lady of Lichtenstein, Bertha's mother, she had shewn her attachment to the family in the assiduous care she had taken in bringing up her charge. Having passed through the different gradations, from nursery-maid to nurse, from nurse to housekeeper, she now occupied the more important post of governess and confidant to her foster-child. Greatly jealous of others, and ambitious to secure all authority in her own hands, she filled for many years the different important domestic situations of the castle, making herself universally necessary in all its concerns. Having gained an ascendancy over her master, who never found fault with her, at least before others, she gave out that she was essential in the management of the domestic affairs of the family, that without her superintendence, things could not go on right.

Of late, she had not lived on the best terms with her young mistress. In the days of her childhood and first youth, she had possessed her whole confidence. Even in Tübingen she was partly in the secret of Bertha's love; and old Rosel took such an interest in every thing that related to her child, as she always called her, as to speak in the first person plural, "*We* love Albert von Sturmfeder most tenderly,"--or "*Our* heart is ready to break in parting from him."

Two circumstances, however, tended to weaken this confidence. The young lady remarked, that her nurse was too fond of gossiping, that she had been even watching her movements, and had been twattling with others about her intimacy with Albert; she, therefore, grew more reserved towards the old woman, who very soon guessed the cause of it. But when the journey to Ulm was undertaken, and she had provided herself with a new woollen-stuff gown, and a superb brocade cap, upon the occasion, her disappointment knew no bounds upon being ordered to remain at Lichtenstein. This widened the breach between her and Bertha, for she attributed the cause of her not accompanying the family to her mistress.

Confidence between them was not restored after the knight of Lichtenstein returned with his daughter to the castle from Ulm. Old Rosel, who always preferred the society of her superiors to that of the domestics, endeavoured to obtain some information from Bertha about Albert, hoping thus to re-establish herself in her good graces; but Bertha, whose heart was then full of the late painful occurrences at the meeting with her lover, and still suspicious of the discretion of her nurse, would not satisfy her curiosity. When, therefore, the exile visited the castle at stated hours every night, and her young lady secretly prepared his meal, and, as her nurse thought, remained alone with him for a length of time, she gratified her pique towards her mistress by opening her heart to the hostess of the Golden Stag at Pfullingen upon the subject. No wonder, then, that Albert was led to believe every word he heard; because, having only known the nurse as the confidant of his love, he was not aware that the intimacy between her and Bertha had suffered interruption.

She had accompanied her mistress the morning of Albert's arrival, in her best Sunday's attire, to her pilgrimage to the church. Having confessed her sins, among which "curiosity" preponderated above the rest, and received absolution, she returned to Lichtenstein with a lighter heart and clearer conscience than she had when she left the castle, sighing under the weight of them. But the words of the father confessor had not probed so deep in her soul as to root out effectually her besetting sin, for when she got into her apartment and was occupied in putting by her rosary and Sunday dress, she heard her young lady and a man's deep voice in angry conversation together, and she even thought her mistress was crying.

"Can the nocturnal visitor have come up here in the day time, and taken advantage of the old man's absence?" she muttered to herself. A natural feeling of curiosity and sympathy drew her eye and ear involuntarily to the keyhole, when she overheard the dispute of which we have already been witnesses.

The young man opened the door so suddenly that she had no time to retreat, scarcely sufficient to recover her upright figure from her bending position. But she did not lose her presence of mind in this awkward predicament, for stopping Albert, and before either of them could speak, seizing his hands, poured upon him a torrent of words.

"Ay, upon my veracity! Could I ever have thought that my old eyes would have beheld Albert von Sturmfeder again! And I verily believe you have grown handsomer and taller than when I last saw you! Who could have thought it? Look, he stands like a stick at the door! Well, but who is it that dares speak thus to my dear young lady? It is not my master, nor any of his servants! Ay! what does one live to see? Young Albert, it is you who have been upbraiding my child!"

During this rapid flow of exclamations, Albert in vain sought to escape from the old woman, and though he determined, in the heat of the moment, to leave the castle, he felt it unseemly to let her suppose he had been quarrelling with Bertha. He shook off the grasp which the nurse had of him, and, in spite of her reproachful smile, took the hand of Bertha, at the same time pressing it to his heart. A glance from her eye calmed the tumult of his feelings. But a fresh conflict, a new embarrassment agitated him. His anger indeed subsided, he felt convinced that Bertha could not entertain that unkindness towards him which his heated imagination had conjured up--but how to reconcile it with his honour, to submit to the shame of being subdued by a squeeze of the hand, or a glance of the eye, before a witness, was a difficulty in which pride had its share. He blushed for his weakness, in standing self-convicted before the old woman; and we have often heard that the feeling of shame, and the embarrassment of getting out of a scrape, such as Albert's precipitation had drawn him into, without committing our honour, is apt often to convert a trifling quarrel into a lasting one, and dissolve ties founded on the basis of tender affection.

Old Rosel perceived with some degree of pleasure the anxiety and sorrow of her young lady, and would perhaps have gladly taken advantage of her distress, by way of punishing her for the withdrawal of her confidence, had not her natural kindness of heart resumed its sway over the malicious joy which she had given way too. She looked at the young man full in the face, and said, "You surely don't intend to leave us so soon, since it is but an hour ago that you arrived at Lichtenstein? Before you have had your mid-day meal, we will not allow you to depart, for that would be quite against the custom of the castle; and besides which, you have probably not yet seen my master?"

It was a great point gained for Bertha's cause to hear Albert speak again: "I have already spoken to him," he said; "as a proof of it, look at the two goblets we have emptied together."

"Well," continued the old woman, "but you would not leave his house without wishing him farewell?"

"No, I ought not certainly, as he desired me to wait for him in the castle," replied the young man.

"Aye, why would you go away in such a hurry, then?" she said, and forced him back into the room; "do you call that manners? My master would wonder, indeed, to think what kind of guest he had entertained. Whoever comes here by day," she added, with a searching look at Bertha, "whoever comes by broad daylight, possesses a clear conscience, and need not *slip away like a thief in the night.*"

Bertha blushed, and pressed the hand of her lover, who could not refrain from smiling, when he thought of the old woman's mistaken notion respecting the nocturnal visitor, and remarked the reproachful glance which she threw at her child.

"Yes, yes, as I said," she continued, "you have no occasion to steal away like a thief in the night. It had been better, perhaps, had you come sooner. The proverb says, 'judge for yourself, to doubt is dangerous, and he who seeks peace and quiet, let him remain with his cow!'--but I say nothing."

"Well, then," said Bertha, "you see he remains here; your proverbs are misplaced. You know, yourself, they do not always agree with the subject."

"Really? but they sometimes hit the right nail upon the head, however disagreeable it may be to the hearer. But repentance and good advice come too late after the evil has happened. I know well enough, that ingratitude is the wages of the world, and I can be silent! he who seeks peace and quiet, let him keep his eyes open, listen, and be silent."

"Come then, be silent," said Bertha, somewhat displeased; "at any rate it will be wise of you not to let my father remark that you know Albert von Sturmfeder; it were not unlikely he might suppose he is come to Lichtenstein for our sakes alone."

Good and ill humour strove for the mastery in old Rosel's breast. She was, on the one hand, flattered to be admitted again into her lady's confidence, by being requested to keep silence before her master, but, on the other, she still felt annoyed that her young mistress confided so little of her heart to her. She kept muttering a few indistinct words to herself, as she put the chairs in their places against the wall, and took the goblets off the table, wiping the marks which the wine had left on the slate slab with which the table was inlaid. Albert had retired to one of the windows, and though he did not feel quite reconciled to his love, yet he could not mistake a sign she gave him. He was particularly anxious her father should, as yet, know nothing of their mutual feeling, for he feared he might attribute to it the principal motive which had induced him to join Würtemburg's cause, and thereby lose the favourable opinion he had formed of him. Thinking it the wisest plan to pacify the old woman, he approached her, and tapping her gently on the shoulder, said, in a kind manner, "Miss Rosalie, you have a very pretty cap on, but the riband does not match it properly, it looks old and faded."

"Eh! what?" she answered in a pet, expecting to be addressed with more respect: "don't trouble yourself about my cap; every one has enough to do to sweep before his own door. Look first to yourself and your own affairs, and then find fault with me and mine. I am a poor woman, and can't dress like a countess. If all the world were alike, and all rich, and all sat at the same table together, who would you find to serve up the eatables and drinkables?"

"I did not mean to affront you," said Albert, and by way of soothing her, took a silver coin out of his purse, adding, "but Rosalie will do me a favour by changing her riband: and that my request may not sound unreasonable, she will not, I hope, refuse to accept a broad piece!"

Who has not seen the sun disperse the mists of a day of October? In like manner was old Rosel's ill-humour dispelled. The polite manner of the young knight, who had touched her weak point, by calling her Rosalie, her favourite name, instead of the familiar one of old Rosel, and presenting her with a dollar, having the bust of the Duke on one side, and the arms of Teck on the reverse, were charms too potent for her to withstand. "Ah, I see you are still the same good friendly gentleman," she said; whilst, stooping down, she glided the dollar into a large leather pocket which hung to her side, and carried the hem of Albert's cloak to her lips: "just so used you to do in Tübingen. When I stood at the fountain of St. George, or went from the hill down to the market place, I was sure to hear you call to me,--'Good morning, Rosalie; and how is your young lady?' And did you not often give me presents? why at least two thirds of the gown I wear comes from the bounty and kindness of your honour!"

"Never mind that now, good woman," said Albert, interrupting the old chatterbox; "But about your master,--you will not----"

"What do you mean?" she replied, half shutting her eyes: "I can pretend never to have seen you in my life. You may rest assured of that. That which does not burn I will not inflame!"

With these words she left the room and went down to the first floor, to attend to her affairs in the kitchen.

Grateful and full of joy, she took the dollar out of her leather pocket, and looked at it over and over again on both sides. She praised the liberality of the youth, and regretted that his love had been so ill requited, for that her young lady was unfaithful to him was a clear case in her eyes. She stood in the kitchen for some time wrapt in thought. She doubted within herself whether to let the thing take its course, or whether it would not be better to give a hint to the young knight, to apprise him of the nocturnal visitor. "But," she said, "in time of need comes help; perhaps he will see it himself, and does not want my advice. Besides, a meddler between two lovers is likely to burn his own fingers. It will be better to wait and look on, for heat in counsel and rashness in action engender nothing but harm. Who seeks peace and quiet, let him keep his eyes open, listen, and be silent!"

Such were the thoughts of the old philosopher in the kitchen. The lovers had in the mean time made up their differences. Albert was unable to withstand the entreaties of Bertha, and when she asked him, in the most tender tone, whether he was still angry with her, he could not bring his heart to say, yes. Peace was therefore re-established between them, and, which is seldom the case, in a shorter time than that which had been taken up in producing the dispute. She listened to the continuation of his adventures with great interest. It required, nevertheless, the conviction of his stedfast faith in her love, and in the word of the exiled man, to restrain his jealousy within due limits; for when he described his first encounter with his opponent, he observed a blush on her countenance, which raised a doubt in his mind whether it expressed joy for his escape from so formidable and experienced an adversary, or whether it was not occasioned by a lurking interest she took in the stranger. In relating further his visit to the exile in the dreary regions of his retreat, and all the circumstances connected with it, his admiration of the knight's noble mind, his greatness of soul amidst privations and miseries, tears started into her eyes, she looked up to Heaven as if in the act of imploring God's protection upon the unhappy man.

The conversation also which he had had with him, and particularly that part of it in which the exile addressed him as his friend, extolling his magnanimity for having pledged his faith to serve Würtemberg,--the cause of the oppressed and banished,--lighted up the glance of Bertha's eyes with unusual brilliancy. She gazed on her lover for some time in silent admiration. The sufferings she had endured since she last saw him were now effaced by the joy she felt in having him by her side as the staunch ally of her father. Albert was ashamed to feel his heart beat quicker at the interest Bertha appeared to take in everything relating to his new acquaintance. But he had command enough over himself to conceal his uneasiness from her, whilst his conscience upbraided him for harbouring the slightest suspicion of her fidelity.

"Albert," she said, "some time hence many a one will envy you this night's adventure. You may think yourself highly honoured, for it is not every one that Hans would venture to conduct to the exile."

"You know him, then?" replied the young man, eager to hear from her what he had failed to elicit from the fifer. "Oh, tell me who he is! I have seldom seen a man whose features, whose whole bearing, have acquired such an ascendancy over me? He told me he would at present be called by no other name than 'the man;' but his arm, whose strength I have felt, his penetrating look, convince me his name must be renowned in the world."

"He had a name, indeed, once," she answered, "which could vie with the most noble in the land. But if he did not tell it you himself, neither dare I pronounce it, because it would be against my word to do so. You must exercise your patience a little longer," she added, smiling, "difficult as it may be to restrain your curiosity."

"But why cannot you tell me," he interrupted her, "are not we one? Ought we to withhold anything from each other? Come, tell me, who is the man in the cavern?"

"Do not be angry. Look ye, if it were my secret only, you know I would not conceal it from you a moment, and you might with justice demand it of me; but, though I know it would be safe in your keeping, I dare not tell it,--I cannot break my word."

Though frankness beamed in her countenance, and not a spark of guile reigned in her heart, her refusal to satisfy Albert's wish irritated him, and he was on the point of taxing her with duplicity, when the door burst open, and an immense dog sprang into the room. Albert gave an involuntary start, having never seen so powerful a beast. The dog took up a position opposite to him, eyed him with a fierce look, and began to growl. His voice bore an ominous sound, whilst a row of white teeth, which he every now and then showed, might have startled the courage of the bravest man; one word from Bertha was sufficient to quiet and make it lay down at her feet. She stroked his beautiful head, from which his sharp eye first glanced inquisitively at her and then at the stranger. "It does everything but speak," she said, smiling; "it comes to warn me not to betray my friend."

"I have never seen so beautiful an animal! How proudly it carries his head, as if he belonged to an emperor or a king."

"It belongs to him, the banished," replied Bertha; "it came to stop my mouth."

"But why does not the knight keep him with him? Truly, such an arm as his, supported by a dog of this kind, might defy a host of enemies."

"It is a watchful beast," she answered, "and savage; if he kept it in the cavern, he would, indeed, be a certain protection. The cavern is so extensive that a man may remain concealed in its interior without fear of molestation. But if by chance any one entered it, a dog might easily betray him, for as soon as it heard a footstep no one could control it; he would begin to growl and bark, and attract the notice of his master's enemies; he therefore ordered it to remain here. The dog understands his duty, and I take care of him. It pines for his master, and you should see his joy when night comes; he knows then that his lord will soon visit the castle; and, when the drawbridge falls, and footsteps are heard in the court, it is impossible to hold him any longer, he would break a dozen chains to get to his side."

"A beautiful specimen of fidelity!" said her lover; "but exemplified by the man to whom this dog belongs in a still higher degree. Faithful to his lord, he prefers banishment and misery rather than betray his cause. It is a folly in me," Albert added; "I am aware that curiosity is not seemly in a man, but I long to know who he is."

"Have patience till the night," said the maiden; "when he comes I will ask him if I may tell you. I doubt not but that he will permit me."

"It is a long time to wait," said Albert; "and really I cannot drive his image out of my head. If you will not tell me, I'll ask the dog; perhaps he will be kinder than you."

"Well, try him," said Bertha, laughing; "if he can speak, I'll allow him to satisfy your curiosity."

"Hearken, you enormous beast," said Albert, turning to the dog, who looked at him attentively; "tell me, what is your master's name?"

The dog raised himself proudly up, opened his broad jaws, and roared out, in terrifying tones, "U--U--U!"

Bertha coloured: "Let's have no more of this nonsense," she said, and called the dog to her; "who would talk to a dog when in Christian society?"

Albert appeared not to heed her remark. "He said 'U,' good dog; I'll wager he has been trained to it! It is not the first time he has been asked what his master's name was?"

Scarcely had he pronounced the last words than the dog repeated his U--U--U! in a still harsher tone. Bertha coloured again, she made it come and lay down at her feet, scolding him in displeasure.

"Well, we have it now," said Albert, in triumph; "his master's name is U!" He recollected that the curious word on the ring which the exile had given him began with an U. It is extraordinary, thought he. "Is your master's name, perhaps, Uffenheim? or Uxhüll? or Ulm? or, by the bye,----"

"Nonsense! the dog has no other note than U. How can you plague yourself in trying to find out a meaning to it? But here comes my father. If you wish to conceal our love from him, do not commit yourself. I'll leave you now, as it would not be right to be found together."

Albert promised to be discreet, and once more embraced Bertha, an indulgence which was likely to be the last for some time, should the presence of her father render it impossible to see her again alone. The dog appeared to watch the movements of the loving couple with astonishment, as if he were really gifted with human sense. The first sound of the horse's feet on the drawbridge was the signal for separation, when Bertha left the room accompanied by the faithful animal.

CHAPTER XXIII

The Duke, so sad, can find no rest,
And dark reflections fill his breast;
"How far, alas! from me removed,
How much is sunk, the land I loved."

G. Schwab.

Good Friday and Easter Sunday passed away, and Albert von Sturmfeder still remained at Lichtenstein. The knight of the castle had invited him to continue his visit until the war should take some decided turn, which would afford him an opportunity to render the Duke important service. We may well suppose how willingly the young man accepted the invitation.

To be under the same roof with his beloved, always near her, occasionally to pass a few moments with her alone, and to be loved of her father, were privileges his fondest dreams had never anticipated. One circumstance only clouded these delights, and that was, a certain gloomy anxiety of expression which at times hung about the brow of Bertha's father. It appeared that he was not satisfied with the news which he received from the Duke and the theatre of war. Messengers came to the castle at different times of day, but they arrived and departed without the knight imparting to his guest the contents of their despatches. Sometimes Albert thought he even saw the fifer of Hardt in the dusk of the evening gliding across the bridge. Hoping to get some information from him, he once hurried down to meet him; but by the time he reached the bridge, no trace of him was to be found.

Feeling somewhat hurt by being left in total ignorance of the state of affairs, which he conceived he had a right to be informed of, after the decided part he had taken, he could not help saying to Bertha, "I have tendered my services unreservedly to the Duke's friends, in spite of their cause not being very prosperous. The man in the cavern and the knight of Lichtenstein have both shewn me much friendship and confidence, but only up to a certain point. Why should I not know what is going on at Tübingen? Why should I not be made acquainted with the Duke's operations? Am I only kept here as a forlorn hope? Why do they disdain my advice?"

Bertha endeavoured to console him, and succeeded at times by mild persuasion to drive such thoughts from his mind; but there were moments when they returned with double force, and particularly when he saw her father absorbed in the consideration of the state of affairs.

At length, on the evening of Easter day, he could contain himself no longer, and put a direct question to the old knight, asking him if their affairs were in danger, what was the state of the Duke's plans, and whether his services would not be called into action soon? But his patron, taking him kindly by the hand, answered, "I have long remarked, that your heart is ready to burst with impatience in consequence of your being denied a share in our labours and cares; but only have a little more patience; perhaps one day longer may decide many important subjects. What is the use of tormenting you with the uncertain intelligence which our messengers have lately brought? Your ardent young mind is not fitted to unmask intrigue, or to counteract artifice. When the crisis approaches upon which we can base our plans with safety, believe me you shall be a welcome member in council and action. All you need know at present is, that our circumstances are neither good nor bad, but that we shall soon be obliged to act with increased decision."

Albert gave the old man due credit for his reserve, but still he was anything but satisfied with his answer. He could not even learn the name of the exile, of whom Bertha had inquired the night preceding, when he came to the castle as usual, if he would allow her to make him known to their guest, but the only answer he gave was, "The proper moment is not yet arrived."

There was still another circumstance which offended Albert's *amour propre*. He had often made known to the knight of Lichtenstein the intense interest he took in the welfare of the exile, and what heartfelt pleasure it would give him to cultivate his further acquaintance; nevertheless, he had never once been invited to join the nocturnal visit of the mysterious guest. He was too proud to press the subject; he waited night after night in the expectation of being called in to speak to the man, but he waited in vain. He resolved therefore to see the stranger some night without an invitation, and for this purpose he sought a fitting opportunity. His room, which he was obliged to enter every night regularly at eight o'clock, overlooked the valley below, and was situated immediately opposite to the side on which the bridge was placed. It was therefore out of the question to see him coming from this position. The large room on the second floor, which was not far from his own, was locked every night, and consequently debarred him from satisfying his curiosity from thence. On the landing place, to which the doors of the different rooms led, there were indeed two windows looking towards the bridge, but as they were grated and stood high, the view from them was confined to the distant country, and there was no possibility of obtaining a sight of the desired spot. Nothing was left for him, therefore, than to conceal himself somewhere in order to gratify his curiosity. On the first floor the plan was impossible, because the many people living there would subject him to discovery. But when he examined the gateway and the stables, which were hewn out of the solid rock, he discovered a niche near the drawbridge, concealed behind the wings of the gate, which were only shut when an enemy was before the castle. This was the spot which appeared best suited to secure him from discovery, and which afforded room enough to enable him to observe what was going on. On the left of the niche the drawbridge joined on to the gate, the stairs which led up to the dwelling rooms were on the right, in front was the entrance passage, which every one must pass who came into the castle. Albert determined to slip into this position on the coming night.

At eight o'clock a page brought him his night lamp, and led him, as usual, to his apartment. The lord of the castle and his daughter kindly wished him good night. He entered his room, and dismissing his servant, who generally assisted him to undress, threw himself on his bed in his clothes. He listened attentively to each hour of the clock as it struck in the village, and whose sounds were wafted towards him by the night-breeze. He often closed his eyes, and at times fell into that state when it requires painful exertion to combat the power of sleep. His present object was sufficiently important to keep him on the alert, and prevent him losing the opportunity of satisfying his curiosity. Ten o'clock had long struck; all was as still as death in the castle. He jumped up, took off his heavy boots and spurs, threw his cloak over him, and cautiously opened the door of his room. He held his breath, fearing to make the least noise; the hinges of the door creaked--he stopped to listen whether any one had heard the treacherous sound. Every thing remained quiet; the moon threw a dim light on the landing place, and Albert thought himself fortunate she had not betrayed him a second time. He glided softly towards the winding stairs, and stopped again to listen if all was quiet; he heard nothing but the whistling of the wind, and the rustling of the oak trees on the further side of the bridge. He stepped carefully down the stairs. The least noise sounds louder in the depth and quiet of night than at other times; attention is awakened at the slightest movement, which would not be noticed in the day time. If his foot stepped upon a grain of sand, its grating sound went up the winding stairs, and startled him into the supposition that the whole house was on the alert. Having arrived at the first floor, he listened again, and heard nothing but the faint cracking of the dying embers on the hearth of the kitchen. At last he got to his destination, an expedition upon which he had expended a whole quarter of an hour's time, which otherwise was an affair but of a moment. He placed himself in the niche, and drew the wing of the gate closer to him, so that it fully covered his position. A fissure in the door was large enough to enable him to see distinctly every thing that passed. Nothing appeared to move in the castle, though he thought he heard light footsteps above him, which he supposed might be those of Bertha.

After waiting a tedious long quarter of an hour, the village clock struck eleven. This being the appointed time of the nocturnal visit, Albert directed all his attention to hear the stranger's approach. A few minutes after he heard the dog bark, when at the same time a deep voice from the other side of the ditch hailed, and said, "Lichtenstein!"

"Who comes there?" was answered from the castle.

"The man is there," replied the other voice, which sounded familiar to his ear as being the one he had heard in the cavern.

The watchman, an old man, came forth from a casemate hewn out of the rock, and opened the lock of the drawbridge with a large curiously wrought key. Whilst he was thus employed the dog came bounding down the stairs, whining and wagging his tail, and jumped upon the old man, as if to assist him in letting fall the bridge for his master to enter. Bertha shortly after descended with a lantern, and assisted him with her light, for it appeared he had some difficulty in opening the lock.

"Make haste, Balthaser," she whispered to the old watchman, "he has been waiting some time, it is cold outside, and the wind blows keen."

"I have now only to unfasten the chain, worthy lady," he answered; "you shall soon see how well my bridge falls. I have oiled the hinges, as you ordered me, so that they do not creek any more, and disturb Mrs. Rosel out of her slumbers."

The chains rattled in their ascent, the bridge sunk gradually into its place, and the banished man, enveloped in his coarse cloak, came across. Though his bearing was deeply engraven on Albert's mind, yet his strikingly bold features, his commanding eye, his open forehead, and the agile movements of his limbs, filled the young man anew with admiration.

The nocturnal guest assisted Balthaser, the doorkeeper, to draw up the bridge, with a power which appeared almost superhuman. When the old man had withdrawn to his sleeping place, Albert overheard the following conversation between the visitor and Bertha.

"Is there any news from Tübingen? Has Maxx Stumpf returned? I read bad news in your countenance."

"No, sir, he has not yet returned," she replied; "my father expected him this very night."

"Oh, that the devil would give him heels! I must remain here till he comes, if it be for a whole day. Ha! a cold night, lady," said the exile; "the screech owls will be frozen in the cavern, for I left them crying in most pitiable tones."

"Yes, it is indeed cold," she answered; "I would not go down there, upon any account; and how dreadful must it be to hear those cries; I shudder to think of it."

"If young Albert accompanied you, you would have no objections to go," answered the other smiling, and chucking the blushing girl under the chin; "is it not so? You would not hesitate to follow him there, much as you appear to dread it now."

"Ah! sir," she replied, "how can you talk in that way? Do you know, I'll not come down again to let you in if you take such liberties."

"Well, but I merely spoke in jest," said the knight, and gently pinched her glowing cheek; "you know how little opportunity I have in my dwelling to enjoy a joke. What will you give me to say a good word to your father, to induce him to make the youth your husband? You are aware the old gentleman does every thing I ask him; and if I recommend a son-in-law to him, he would accept him at all hazards."

Bertha opened wide her beautiful eyes, and cast a grateful look at him. "Dear sir," she answered, "I will not forbid your saying a kind word for Albert, particularly as my father is well inclined towards him."

"But I shall expect some reward for my trouble. Everything has its price; so what will you give?"

Bertha cast her eyes to the ground. "A heartfelt thank-ye," she replied; "but come, sir, my father has been waiting for us a long time."

She was in the act of leading on, when the knight, taking her by the hand, detained her. Albert's heart beat so hard as almost to be heard; he broke out into a violent heat, and then became ice-cold; he laid hold of the handle of the door, and was on the point of sallying forth to forbid the promise of a fixed price being given upon any pretext.

"Why are you in such haste?" he heard the man of the cavern say. "Well, for one kiss only, and I will persuade your father to send for the priest on the spot, to perform the holy ceremony." He bent his head towards the offended, blushing girl. Albert saw every thing swimming before his eyes, and was again on the point of bursting from his place of concealment, but the determined reply of his lady love checked him from taking the rash step. She beheld the man with a forbidding look. "It is impossible your Grace can be in earnest," she said; "otherwise you now see me for the last time."

"If you knew how much this scornful air becomes you," he answered, with unaltered kindness, "you would never cease to be in anger. At any rate I admire your fidelity; for when the heart is deeply engaged with one object, none other need hope for such a favour. But on your marriage day I will demand the favour, with the permission of your bridegroom, and then we'll see who is right."

"That you may do," said Bertha, smiling, whilst she withdrew her hand from his, and led the way with the light in her hand; "but you had better prepare yourself for a refusal, for he is not fond of trifling on this point."

"He is uncommonly jealous," replied the knight, as they proceeded up stairs. "I could tell you something upon that subject, which took place between him and me; but I promised silence----"

The sound of their voices died away gradually, and at last became indistinct to Albert's ear. He breathed freely again. He listened and remained in his position until he satisfied himself thoroughly that no one was on the stairs or in the passages, and, taking advantage of the opportunity, slipped up into his own room much quicker than he had descended from it. The last words of Bertha and the exile still resounded in his ears. He blushed to think of his unfounded jealousy, which had again tormented him this night. Bertha had, unknown to herself, given him evident proofs of the purity of her heart and faithful attachment to him; and it was only when he laid his head on his pillow and fell to sleep, that his mind was eased of the pain of having unjustly suspected her.

When he left his room the next morning at seven o'clock, the hour which the family generally assembled at breakfast, Bertha met him on the landing place with the appearance of having been weeping. She took him on one side, and whispered, "Tread softly, Albert; the knight of the cavern is still with us; he has been asleep about an hour; we must not disturb him."

"The exile!" asked Albert in astonishment, "does he dare remain here during the day? what has happened? is he unwell?"

"No!" answered Bertha, whilst a fresh tear hung on her eyelid, "no! he expects a messenger from Tübingen about this time, and is determined to await him. We begged and prayed him to depart before daybreak, but he would not listen to our warning, so firm is his resolution to remain at all hazards."

"But could not the messenger have gone to him in the cavern?" said Albert; "he runs too great a risk unnecessarily."

"Ah! you don't know him; it is his bane when he once gets a thing into his head to be obstinately immoveable; and then he is so distrustful of others, even of his best friends. It was quite impossible for us to persuade him to leave the castle this morning, because he might have thought, perhaps, we wished to get rid of him for our own safety. His principal reason for remaining is, I believe, to consult with my father, when the messenger arrives."

During this conversation they remained stationary on the landing place, but Bertha now opened the door of her father's apartment as gently as possible, and they entered together.

This room, or what would be called in a modern establishment the gentlemen's room, was distinguished from the saloon on the second floor from being somewhat smaller. It had a view of the surrounding country on three sides, through small round windows, now pierced by the sun's morning rays. The ceiling and walls were wainscoted with dark brown wood, fancifully inlaid with other coloured woods. A few portraits of the ancestors of Lichtenstein graced the side of the wall opposite to the windows, and the tables and furniture shewed that the present occupier of the castle was a friend of old customs and times, and that his property would descend to his daughter in the same unaltered state it had been left by his great-grandfather.

The old knight was seated at a large table in the middle of the room when they entered. Supporting his long-bearded chin in his hand, he sat gloomy and motionless, with his eyes fixed on a large goblet which stood before him. It was not quite evident to Albert whether he had been sitting up all night over his glass, or whether he was taking a draught at this early hour of the morning to recruit his strength and spirits.

He saluted the young man as he approached the table by a slight inclination of the head, whilst a scarcely visible smile played about his mouth. He pointed to a goblet on the table and a stool by his side. Bertha understanding the hint, filled it with wine, and presented it to her lover, with that grace which marked every thing she did. Albert seated himself beside the old man, and drank.

The latter drew his chair near to him, and said in a low tone of voice, "I fear our affairs are in a bad way!"

"Have you had any intelligence?" asked Albert, in the same low tone.

"A peasant told me this morning, that Tübingen had treated with the League last evening."

"Good heavens!" said Albert, involuntarily.

"Keep quiet, and do not wake him! he will learn it soon enough," replied the old man, pointing to the other side of the room.

The young man looked that way. At one of the side windows, looking towards the deep ravine, sat the exile asleep; his arm, resting on the ledge of the window, supported his careworn brow. His grey cloak had partly fallen off his shoulder, and discovered a worn-out leather jerkin, in which his powerful frame was encased. His curly hair hung down over his temples in disorder, and a few tufts of his smooth beard were visible from under his hand. The large dog lay at his feet, his head resting on his master's foot, looking up at him with faithful eyes and watching every motion of his features.

"He sleeps," said the old man, and repressed a starting tear. "He breathes light; oh! that his dreams may be comforting. The reality of life to him is melancholy indeed! Who can help wishing he may remain unconscious of it awhile?"

"His is a hard fate!" replied Albert, casting his eye at the sleeping man. "Driven from house and home--an outcast--a price offered to any villain who chooses to level his gun at him--under the earth by day, and by night wandering about like a thief! Truly, it is hard; and all this because he is faithful to his lord!"

"That man has suffered much in his lifetime," said Lichtenstein, with a serious look. "I have known him from the days of his childhood, and I can vouch for his having always wished to do what is right and just. The means indeed he applied to attain his object were at times not fitted to further his purpose; on other occasions his intentions were misunderstood, and he too often allowed himself to be carried away by the violence of passion--but where lives the man of which this might not be said? Truly, he has wofully repented himself." He stopt short, fearing he had said more than he ought before Albert, who asked in vain to hear something further of his character. The old man sank into silence and deep thought.

The sun having risen over the mountains and dispersed the mist which hung about the vallies, invited Albert to the window to enjoy the splendid view. A lovely valley, surrounded by wooded heights, with three smiling villages scattered over its surface, and a rapid stream running through it, lay at the foot of the rock of Lichtenstein. It was like beholding the earth from a point in the heavens. Leaving the valley and looking to the wooded heights, his eye rested with delight upon picturesque groups of rocks and the mountain of the Alb, behind which rises the castle of Achalm, and forms the boundary of the immediate surrounding country. Beyond the walls of Achalm, the distant hills were visible to the right and left. The rock of Lichtenstein, reaching, as it were, into the clouds, commands an extensive view of Würtemberg, free and unbroken, into the far lowland. The morning sun throwing its oblique rays across the landscape, Albert was transported with the beauty of its scenery.

The fertile fields spread before him, surrounded by the wooded hills, he compared to variegated carpets, edged, as it were, with borders of dark green and brown, deriving their different shades and colours from the tints thrown over them by the dawning day. And then turning to the country between Lichtenstein and the distant Asperg, he exclaimed, "What charms for the lover of the picturesque! No continuous uninterrupted plain to weary the beholder, the eye ranges from hill to mountain in pleasing variety, and rests on the luxuriant valley, with its meandering stream gently rippling along in its course."

Albert stood wrapt in delight. He strained his eyes more and more to see and distinguish each castle and village in the far distance. Bertha stood beside him, and though she had enjoyed the same view from her childhood, she now shared his pleasure; she pointed out every place, and named all the different towers to him. "Where is there another spot in all Germany which can be compared to this!" said Albert; "I have seen vast plains, and mounted heights which command perhaps a more extended view, but such a rich combination of the picturesque and the sublime it would be difficult to find elsewhere. Look at the rich corn fields, the woods of fruit trees, and a little lower down there, where the hill assumes a blueish tinge, that garden of vines! I have never yet envied a prince; but to stand here, and look over those hills, and say this is mine, would be the height of my ambition!"

A deep sigh close to them, started the young couple from their observations. They turned round, and perceived the exile standing at the window a few paces from them. He appeared to view the country with a wild look, which made Albert uncertain whether the conversation he had just had with Bertha, or the thought of his own forlorn state, had troubled his mind.

He saluted the young man, and offered him his hand, and turning to the lord of the castle, asked him, "If a messenger had arrived?" "Schweinsberg is not yet returned," he answered.

The exile retired again to the window in silence. Bertha filled him a goblet of wine. "Be of good courage," she said, "and don't look in so disconsolate a manner over the country. Drink this wine, it is good old Würtemberger, and grows under that blue mountain."

"We cannot remain long melancholy," he answered, and turned to Albert with a forced smile, "when the sun shines so cheerfully over Würtemberg, and Heaven's mildness beams in the eye of one of her fairest maidens? Is it not so, young man? what is the sight of these hills and vallies, compared to the gleam of such eyes and the fidelity of true hearts? take your glass, and let us drink to them! Nothing is irrevocably lost so long as we possess such treasures: here's to 'Good Würtemberg for ever!'"

"Good Würtemberg for ever," replied Albert, and touched glasses. The exile was going to say something more, when the old watchman entered with a face full of importance. "There are two pedlars before the castle, and demand admittance," he announced.

"It's them! it's them!" cried the exile and old Lichtenstein in the same breath, and added, "shew them up."

The servant withdrew. An anxious moment followed the announcement. No one said a word. The knight of Lichtenstein looked as if he could pierce the door with the eye of impatience. The exile endeavoured to conceal his anxiety, but the rapid changes on his expressive features indicated clearly that his whole being was in a state of excitement. At length footsteps were heard on the stairs approaching the apartment. The exile, strong as he was, trembled so much that he was obliged to hold by the table, his body was bent forward, his eye was fixed on the door, as if he would read his fate on the countenance of the messengers--the door opened and they entered.

CHAPTER XXIV

Deserted as thou art, by all forsaken,
Thy fortunes ruin'd and thy power gone,
Thou still shalt find fidelity unshaken,
Although you find it in myself alone.
Thy humble vassal, 'till the hour of death,
I'll hail my sovereign with my latest breath.

L. Uhland.

Albert's expectation was also raised to the highest pitch. His eye examined the two men as they entered, and he at once recognised the fifer of Hardt as one, and the pedlar he had met at the Golden Stag of Pfullingen as the other. The latter disburthened himself of a pack which he carried on his back, tore a plaister from his eye, erected himself from a bent position, which he had assumed for the purpose of disguise, and stood before the assembled group, the short-set, strong-built man, with open bold features, which the exile had already described in the cavern.

"Maxx Stumpf!" cried the exile in a trembling tone of voice, "what means that gloomy countenance? You bring us good news, don't you? they will open the gates to us, and with us hold out to the last man?"

Maxx Stumpf von Schweinsberg looked about him in confusion. "Prepare for the worst, sir!" he said, "the intelligence I bring you is not good."

"How?" answered the other, whilst the blush of rage flew into his cheeks, and the veins of his forehead began to swell, "how, do you mean they hesitate, they waver? It is impossible! be not precipitate in what you say, recollect it is of the nobles of the land of whom you speak."

"And still I will say it," Schweinsberg answered, making a step forward. "In the face of the Emperor and the Empire, I will say they are traitors."

"Thou liest!" cried the exile with a terrible voice. "Traitors, did you say? Thou liest! Dost thou dare to rob forty knights of their honour? Ha! own it, that you lie."

"Would to God I were a knight without honour--a dog that betrays his master! But the whole forty have broken their oaths--you have lost your country. My Lord Duke, Tübingen is gone!"

The man, whom these words more immediately concerned, sank in a chair at the window: he covered his face with his hands, his agitated breast appeared to seek in vain for breath, his whole frame trembled.

The eyes of all were directed to him, expressive of commiseration and pain, particularly Albert's, who now for the first time learnt the name of "the man"--it was him, Duke Ulerich of Würtemberg! Recollections of the first moment he had met him, of his first visit to the cavern, of the conversation they had had, and the way which his whole bearing had surprised him and bound him to his cause, crossed his mind in *one* rapid flight. It was quite incomprehensible to him, that he had not long ago made the discovery.

No one dared to break the silence for some time. The heavy breathing of the Duke only was heard, and his faithful dog, who appeared to partake of his master's misery, added his pitiable whining to the distressing scene. Old Lichtenstein at length giving a sign to the knight of Schweinsberg, they both approached the Duke, and touched his cloak, in order to rouse him, but he remained immoveable and silent. Bertha had stood aloof, with tears in her eyes. She now drew near with hesitating step, put her hand on his shoulder, and, beholding him with a look of tender compassion, at last took courage to say, "My Lord Duke! it is still good Würtemberg for ever!"

A deep sigh escaping from his breast, was the only notice he took of the kind girl's solicitude. Albert then approached him. The expression which the exile had made use of, when they first met, flashed across his mind, and he ventured to address the same words now to his afflicted friend. "Man without a name," said he, "why so downhearted? Si fractus illabatur orbis, impavidum ferient ruinæ!"[1]

These words acted like a charm upon Ulerich. Whether he had adopted them as his motto, or whether it was that combination of greatness of soul, and obstinate contempt of misfortune, which formed his character, and acquired for him the name of the "Undaunted," he was reanimated, as if by an electric spark, when he heard them repeated, and from that moment rose worthy of his name.

"Those are the true words, my young friend," he said at length with a firm voice, proudly raising his head, his eyes sparkling with their usual animation, "those are the words. I thank you for bringing them to my mind. Stand forward, Maxx Stumpf, knight of Schweinsberg, relate the result of your mission. But first of all, give me another glass, Bertha!"

"It was last Thursday, when I left you," began the knight: "Hans disguised me in this garb, and instructed me how to comport myself. I went to the Golden Stag at Pfullingen, just to try if any one would recognise me in it, but the hostess brought me a can of wine with all the indifference she would have done to a perfect stranger she had never seen before. And a city counsellor, with whom I had exchanged angry words not a week before in the same room, drank with me, supposing I had followed the vocation of pedlar from my childhood. That young man," pointing to Albert, "was also in the room."

The Duke appeared to recover his spirits, and was more cheerful. He asked Albert whether he had noticed the knight in his garb of pedlar, and whether he looked the character?

He replied, smiling, "I think he played his part to perfection."

"From Pfullingen I went the same evening to Reutlingen. I entered the public room of an inn, where I met a tribe of Leaguists, consisting of citizens, from all parts, who were exulting with the Reutlingeners, for having torn down the stag horns, the emblems of your house, from their city gates. Though they abused you and sang burlesque songs at your expense, still they appeared to fear your name. On Good Friday I proceeded towards Tübingen. My heart beat high when I descended through the wood near the castle, and saw the beautiful valley of the Neckar before me, with the fortified towers and steeples of that place peering above the hill."

The Duke compressed his lips, turned away, and looked at the distant country. Schweinsberg paused, sympathising in his master's pain, who beckoned to him, however, to proceed.

"Descending into the plain, I wandered onward towards Tübingen. The town had been already occupied by the League some days, the castle still held out, and only a few troops remained in the camp, which was pitched on the hill overlooking the valley of Ammer. I determined to slip into the town, for the purpose of finding out how affairs stood in the castle. You know the little inn in the upper town, not far from the church of St. George? I went there, and called for wine. On my way I learned that the knights of the League often assembled in the same house, and therefore I considered it the best place to attain my object."

"You risked a good deal," interrupted the knight of Lichtenstein: "it was very possible some one might have wished to buy some of your wares, and then the pedlar in disguise would have been discovered."

"You forget it was a holiday," replied the other, "so that I had a good excuse not to open my pack, and recommend my goods for sale, according to the custom of pedlars. But I had sufficient proof of the security of my disguise, for I sold a box of healing plaster to George von Fronsberg, God knows, I would gladly have come to blows with him, and given him an opportunity on the spot to make use of it. They were still at high mass in the church, and no one in the inn; but I learned from the master of the house, that the knights in the castle had agreed to a truce till Easter Monday. When church service was over, many knights and other men came, as I expected, into the room where I was, for their morning's potation. I seated myself in a corner on the bench near the stove, the proper place for people of my condition in the presence of their superiors."

"Who did you see there?" inquired the Duke.

"I knew some of them by sight, and guessed who others were from their conversation. There was Fronsberg, Alban von Closen, the Huttens, Sickingen, and many others. Truchses von Waldburg came in shortly after. When I saw him enter, I drew my cap deep over my face, for he cannot have forgotten the whirl I gave him from his horse some fifteen years ago by a thrust of my lance."

"Did you see Hans von Breitenstein among the rest?" asked Albert.

"Breitenstein?--not that I know; ah! yes, that's his name who will eat a leg of mutton at a sitting. Well, they began to talk of the siege and the truce, and some of them whispered to each other, but as I have very good ears, I heard just what of all things was most essential to know. Truchses related that he shot an arrow into the castle, with a note attached to it, addressed to Ludwig von Stadion. It appears that he must often have practised the same device, for the knights were not astonished, when he added, that he had received an answer the same day by similar means."

The Duke's countenance became clouded. "Ludwig von Stadion!" he cried in agony; "I would have staked castles upon his fidelity! I loved him so, that I satisfied all his desires, and he is the first to betray me!"

"The answer said, that he, Stadion, with many others, being tired of the contest, were more than half inclined to surrender; George von Hewen, however, threatened to denounce them as traitors."

"I have not merited such friendship from Hewen," said Ulerich. "I was once offended with him, for having complained that I had not acted according to his wishes. But how easily are we deceived in the characters of men! Had any one asked me which of these two I had most faith in, I would have named Stadion as my trusty friend, and George von Hewen the doubtful one."

Schweinsberg continued. "The answer also said, that your Grace would probably attempt to relieve the castle; but if that were impossible, you would repair to it in person by some secret way. The Leaguists spoke much upon that subject. They all, however, agreed that it was essential to bring the garrison to terms without delay, before you brought relief, or got into the castle; for if you succeeded in the latter case, they feared the siege might last much longer. After hearing all this, I did not think it advisable to proceed immediately to the castle by the secret path, known only to a few, and shew myself to the garrison, because if Stadion had already gained the upper hand, I should have been lost. I resolved, therefore, to remain the day in the town; and if before Saturday morning I heard nothing to alarm me respecting the spirit of the garrison, then to proceed to my destination, and send your Grace immediate intelligence. I wandered about the town and the camp unmolested until noon, seeking as much as possible always to be near some of the superior officers to assure myself of my disguise."

"That was on the Friday, the holiday?" Lichtenstein asked.

"Yes; on holy Friday. At three o'clock in the afternoon, George von Fronsberg, with many other of the principal officers, rode to the city gate of the castle; and hailed the besieged, inquiring whether they were building a fortification. I was standing among them; and saw Stadion come on the wall, and answer, 'No, that were against the terms of the truce; but I see,' he added, 'you are erecting a fort in the field.' George von Fronsberg cried, 'If it is so, it is without my orders. Who are you?' He in the castle answered, 'I am Ludwig von Stadion;' upon which the Leaguists smiled, and stroked their beards. Having satisfied the besieged, by overturning a few baskets filled with earth, which had been placed in the entrenchments to screen their works, that he had no knowledge of its having been done, Fronsberg then called to Stadion, and invited him, with other of his party, to come down and drink together."

"Did they go?" cried the Duke, impatiently, "and forget their honour?"

"There is an open space on the castle hill beyond the ditch, whence the spectator, having a distant view of the country, can survey the valley of the Neckar, the Steinlach on the height above, the Alb in the distance, with many castles and villages, which complete the scenery. On this spot they placed a table and benches; and the commanders of the League sat down to drink. The gate of Upper Tübingen was then opened, the bridge fell over the ditch; when Ludwig von Stadion, with six others, came forth, bringing with them your Grace's silver covered jugs, golden goblets, and best wine; and having saluted your enemies with a shake of the hand, seated themselves to talk over the state of affairs over a cool tankard."

"May the devil bless them all!" interrupted the old knight of Lichtenstein, and threw his wine away; but the Duke smiled, and nodded to Maxx Stumpf to proceed.

"They caroused together till after dusk; and staggered about with heated heads. I kept near them, so that not one of their traitorous words escaped my ears. When they broke up, Trachses took Stadion by the hand, 'Brother,' said he, 'you have good wine in your cellar; let us in soon, that we may help you to drink it out.' The other laughed, shook him by the hand, and said, 'Time will teach us what to do.' When I saw how affairs stood, I determined, with God's help, at the risk of my life, to get into the castle: I therefore left them, and went to the spot where the secret subterranean way commences. Having succeeded in entering it unnoticed, and reached the middle, I found the portcullis down, with a sentry placed there. He levelled his gun at me, when he heard me coming in the dark, and demanded the parole. I gave, as you desired me, 'Atempto,' the watch-word of your brave ancestor, Eberhard with the beard. The fellow opened his eyes wide, drew up the portcullis, and let me pass. With rapid steps I reached a vault, where I was obliged to remain a few moments to take a breath of fresh air, for the narrow passage is close and damp."

"Faithful Maxx! clear your throat with a draught of wine," said Ulerich; the knight followed his advice, and continued his story with renewed vigour.

"I heard the sound of many voices in the vault, apparently in contention, and following its direction, I saw a number of the garrison sitting round a large cask drinking. There were some of Stadion's party, with Hewen, and many of his friends. The light of a lamp illumined their position, and the large goblets which were placed before them. It was an imposing scene, and put me in mind of a sitting of the secret tribunal. Having concealed myself behind a cask, I listened to their conversation. George von Hewen spoke stirring words, and represented to them the crime of their infidelity; he said there was no reason why they should surrender; that they were well provided with provisions for a long siege; that your Grace was assembling an army for their relief; and that the besiegers were worse off than themselves."

"Ha! brave Hewen! and what gave they for answer?" said the Duke.

"They only laughed and drank. 'It will be long before he can get an army together. Where will he find money, unless he plunders?' said one of the party. Hewen continued: 'But if the Duke cannot succeed so soon as he expected, we are nevertheless bound by our oath to hold to the last, or else be held as traitors to our lord and master.' They laughed and drank again, saying, 'Who dares come forward and call us traitors?' I then called out from behind my cask, 'I will! You are traitors--false to your oaths, to the Duke, and your country!' They were terrified and thunder-struck; Stadion let fall his goblet; when, stepping forward, having first taken off my disguise, I stood before them, and drew your letter from under my jerkin: here is a writing from your Duke, said I; he commands you at your peril to surrender; he is coming himself to conquer or die under the walls."

"Oh, Tübingen!" said the Duke, with a sigh, "fool that I was to leave you in such hands. I would give two of my left fingers for your sake! what did I say, two fingers? I would willingly lose my right hand could I purchase you with the sacrifice, and with my left lead the way to the heart of my enemies. And what was the answer to my words--did they not give any?"

"The false ones eyed me with sullen looks, and appeared not to know what to do. Hewen, however, repeated his warning to them. Stadion at last said, You come too late. Twenty-eight knights have determined to withdraw from the contest, and leave the Duke to settle his affairs alone with the League. If he returns to the country with an army they will faithfully stand by him, but they cannot continue to carry on the war any longer in a state of uncertainty as to the result, seeing that their opposition to the League has only subjected their houses and estates to damage and heavy contributions. I then requested to be led to the hall of the knights, where I would try to discover whether there were not still left honourable men sufficient to defend the castle. I reckoned upon the fidelity of the two Berlichingens, and many others, whose names are familiar to your Grace, as having sworn allegiance to your colours. But Hewen shook his head, and said I was mistaken in most of them."

"But Stammheim, Thierberg, Westerstetten, in whose faith I would have staked my existence--did you see them?" asked the Duke.

"Oh, yes! they were in the cellar with Stadion, and assisted to drink your wine. They would not allow me to go up into the castle. Even Hewen, with Freiberg and Heideck, who were with him, dissuaded me from it, because, they said, the two parties were already much inflamed against each other, Stadion having the majority of knights, and of the soldiers also, on his side. 'If I went up,' they added, 'and it should come to blows in the court of the castle, and in the hall of the knights, there would be nothing left for them, as the weakest party, than to fight for life and death. Willingly as they would shed their last drop of blood for you, they would rather fall before the enemy in the field of battle than be cut to pieces by their own countrymen and brothers in arms. Being foiled in every thing, I asked them, as a last petition, to protect your son, the young Prince Christoph, and your darling daughter, and preserve the castle to them, when they surrendered. Some of them consented, others remained silent, and shrugged up their shoulders. Exasperated, I denounced them as traitors, and giving them my curses as a Christian knight, challenged any five of them to fight with me for life and death when the war should be ended. Upon which I left them, and returned the same way out of the castle that I entered it."

"Würtemberg's honour is gone! could I have thought it possible!" cried Lichtenstein. "Forty-two knights, two hundred soldiers, thus to betray a fortified castle! Our good name is defamed,--futurity will brand with scorn our nobility, who deserted their Duke's banners. The saying 'faithful and honourable as a Würtemberger' is become a term of reproach."

"We could, indeed, once boast of the truth of the saying, 'faithful as a Würtemberger,'" said Duke Ulerich, whilst a tear fell on his beard. "When my ancestor Eberhard once upon a time rode towards Worms, and sat at table with the electors, counts and lords, each prided himself upon the pre-eminence of his own country. One boasted of his wine,--another spoke of his fruits,--a third of his game,--whilst a fourth talked of the metals which his mountains produced,--but, when it came to Eberhard with the Beard to speak, he said, 'I know nothing of your treasures, but this I know, that if I seek shelter in a humble peasant's cot, in the most secluded spot, tired and oppressed with fatigue, I am sure to find a faithful Würtemberger at hand, upon whose lap I can lay my head in safety and sleep in peace.' They all wondered in astonishment, and said, 'Count Eberhard is right, and long live the faithful Würtemberger!' But in these times behold, when the Duke traverses a wood, they lie in wait to kill him; and, if he places his faith in his nobles for the defence of his castles, scarcely does he turn his back but they treat with the enemy. May the cuckoo take such faith! But go on, Maxx, I am the man to drink the dregs of the cup without the fear of seeing the bottom of it."

"Well, it's soon said. I remained in Tübingen until I had convinced myself of its surrender. Yesterday, being Easter Monday, they came to terms; they drew up the articles in writing, and proclaimed throughout the streets by a herald, that, at five o'clock in the evening, the garrison would march out. Prince Christoph, your young son, retains the castle and administration of Tübingen, but in the service and under the guardianship of the League; and as for the rest of the country, it is said, that it will be divided among the knights. I have experienced many misfortunes in life,--I killed a friend at a tilting bout,--I have lost a dear child, and had my house burnt,--but, as true as God and his saints are gracious to me, I never felt so much pain as at that moment when I saw the banner of the League hoisted in lieu of your Grace's, and their red cross cover Würtemberg's stag horns, and bugle."

So spake Maxx Stumpf von Schweinsberg. The sun had risen, during his narration, high above the mountains, having dispelled the mists, leaving only a slight vapour on the heights of the Asperg. It hung upon the horizon like a thin veil, and heightened the beauty of the scenery in its immediate neighbourhood. Drest in the soft verdure of spring, combined with the darker foliage of the woods, ornamented with cheerful villages and stately castles, Würtemberg lay spread before the eye of the beholder, in all the glory of the opening day. The unhappy Prince surveyed the scene with dejected looks. Nature had blessed him with a constancy of courage, and a heart which even grief and misery were unable to subdue; he possessed such control over his feelings that few were able to discern his inward suffering; and when calamity overtook him, then it was that the energies of his vigorous mind were most fertile in resources, and prompted him to immediate action.

In this truly heart-rending moment, when his last hope fell with the loss of his sole remaining castle, he concealed from his friends around him the painful conflict with which he was struggling. His feeling might be compared to the repentant son standing by the death-bed of a beloved mother, whose solicitude and anxiety for his welfare through life he had slighted, whose tender care of him in infancy he had forgotten, and the sacrifices she had imposed on herself to satisfy all his selfish wishes, even to the straitening of her own circumstances to meet the demands of his riotous living, he had treated with ingratitude, deeming them nothing more than his due. But now that her endearing eye no longer beholds him,--now that the ear is closed which was wont to listen to his wishes and complaints,--now that those hands no longer feel his last pressure,--then it is that repentance assails his heart,--then it is that his guilty conscience upbraids him with the bitter reproach of ingratitude and neglect of God's commandment,--to love, honour, and cherish father and mother.

Such was the anguish of self-condemnation which at this moment oppressed the breast of Ulerich of Würtemberg as he viewed his country, now to all appearance lost to him for ever. His noble nature, which he had too often abused in the blandishments of a brilliant court, and whose finer feelings had been deadened by the poisonous flattery of false friends, now upbraided him; not so much for being the author of his own personal misfortunes as for entailing on his country the distress attendant upon the occupation of it by his enemies.

Having stood for some time at the window, his mind harassed with these thoughts, he turned to his friends, who noticed in pleasing astonishment the calm expression of his countenance. They had dreaded his first burst of rage and violence, which they expected he would vent upon the treacherous conduct of his nobility. Instead of which, though he could not conceal the intensity of suffering he was struggling with, he was composed and resigned, and his features exhibited a mildness and resignation which they had scarcely ever seen before.

"Maxx," said he, "how have they acted towards the people of the country?"

"Like robbers," he answered: "they wantonly desolate the vineyards, cut down the fruit trees, and burn them at the guard houses; Sickingen's cavalry ride through the corn fields and tread down what they cannot consume; they ill treat the women, and extort money from the men. The people every where begin to murmur; and should the present drought continue, followed by a failing harvest, a time when the poor people will be called upon to pay the heavy expenses of the war which the league's administration will exact, misery and poverty will then be at its height."

"Oh, what villains!" cried the Duke, "they who boasted, with high sounding words, that they came to free Würtemberg of her tyrant, and to liberate her people from oppression now commit abominations even worse than Turks. But I vow that if God will assist me, and his holy saints be merciful to my soul, I will return to the wasted vallies of the Neckar and its vineless banks, with the scythe of vengeance, cut down their ranks like sheaves of corn, and, as a revengeful vine dresser, tread and crush them under foot. I will avenge myself of all the calamities they have brought on me and my country, so help me God!"

"Amen!" responded the knight of Lichtenstein. "But before you venture to the rescue of your country, you must first withdraw from it, for a season. No time is to be lost, if you would escape unmolested."

The Duke considered awhile, and then answered, "You are right, I will go to Mömpelgard, where I shall be able to make arrangements, and, I trust, collect men sufficient to venture to make a blow. Come here, thou faithful dog, thou wilt follow me into the misery of banishment. Thou knowest not what it is to break an oath or forfeit thy faith."

"Here stands another, who also knows nothing of treachery," said Schweinsberg, and approached the Duke. "I will accompany you to Mömpelgard, if you do not disdain my services."

The knight of Lichtenstein, animated by the same generous feeling, next said:. "Take me also with you, Duke! my feeble arm indeed is not worth much in the field, but my voice in council may still be heard."

Bertha's eyes lighted up more brilliantly than ever, as she beheld her lover, whose cheeks glowed with the ardour of youth, and whose looks bespoke the fire of his noble spirit.

"My Lord Duke," said he, "I proffered hand and arm in your service, when we met in the cavern, when I knew not who you were, and you did not refuse them. I aspire not to have a voice in council--but as you value a heart which beats faithful to you, an eye that will watch over you when you sleep, or an arm that will stand between you and your enemies, take me with you, and let me follow your fortune."

The noble feelings which had at first attached the young man to the "man without a name," now animated his breast, and the consideration of the Duke's misfortune, which he bore with such dignified magnanimity, added to the encouraging glance of his beloved, fed the flame of enthusiasm and devotion to the Duke's cause, and irresistibly threw him at his feet.

The old knight of Lichtenstein looked at his young guest with the joyous pride of a father; the Duke beheld him with emotion, and taking his hand, raised him from his knee and kissed his forehead.

"Where such hearts beat for us," said he, "we have still fortresses and walls to shelter us, and cannot bewail our poverty. You possess my love and esteem, Albert von Sturmfeder; you shall accompany me; I accept your faithful service with joy. Maxx Stumpf von Schweinsberg, I shall require your aid in more important business than to protect my body; I have a commission for you to execute in Hohentwiel and Switzerland. I cannot accept your company, good and faithful Lichtenstein. I honour you as a father, for your kindness to me has been such. You opened your door to me every night. I will repay it. When I return to my country, with God's help and will, your voice shall be the first in council."

The Duke's eye fell upon the fifer of Hardt, who stood aloof in humble retirement. "Come here, thou faithful man!" he called to him, and gave him his right hand, "you once were guilty of a great crime, but you have repented of it sincerely, and by faithful service regained my confidence."

"To attempt another's life is not so soon expiated," said the peasant, with downcast looks: "I am still in your grace's debt, but I will requite it when the time comes."

"Go to your home--such is my will--follow your occupations as heretofore. Perhaps you may be able to collect some faithful hearts in our cause by the time we return to our country. And you, lady! how can I reward your kindnesses? You deprived yourself many a night of rest, to open the door for me and shelter me against treachery! Do not blush so, as if you had some great sin to confess, this being the moment to act. Venerable father," said he, turning to the knight of Lichtenstein, "I appear before you as the intercessor of a couple of loving hearts. You will not disdain the son-in-law whom I propose to you?"

"I do not understand you, gracious Lord," said the knight, looking with astonishment at his daughter.

The Duke took Albert's hand, and led him to the old man. "This young man loves your daughter, and she is not indifferent to him,--what think you of making them a happy couple? But what means that frown of displeasure? Is he not high born, a gallant antagonist, the strength of whose arm I have already experienced, and now become my support in the hour of need?"

Bertha cast her eyes down, her face was suffused with blushes, she trembled for the reply of her father, who looked sternly at the young man. "Albert," said he, "I have had a high opinion of you since the first moment I saw you; it had been, perhaps, not so favourable, had I been aware of the object which brought you to my house."

The youth was about to make an answer, but the Duke interrupted him. "You forget that it was I who sent him to you with my seal and letter--he came not of his own accord. But what are you thinking of so long? I will adopt him as my son, and reward him with a property which will make you proud to call him your son-in-law."

"Do not trouble yourself further upon this point, my Lord Duke," said Albert, indignantly, when he noticed the indecision of the knight of Lichtenstein. "It shall never be said of me, that the heir of the Sturmfeders begged for a wife, and obtruded his importunity to gain the consent of a father against his free will. My name is too dear to me to resort to such means." He was about to leave the room in displeasure, but the old knight held him by the hand: "Hot-headed youth," he cried, "restrain your impetuosity? there, take her, she is yours, but--you must not think of leading her home, so long as an enemy's banner floats over the towers of Stuttgardt. Be faithful to the Duke, help him to return to his country, and if you continue true to his cause, the day that you enter the gates of the capital, when Würtemberg shall see her ensigns floating again over the pinnacles of her castles, my daughter from that moment shall be yours, and you shall then become my cherished son-in-law."

"And on that day," spoke the Duke, "the bride will blush more beautifully than ever, when the merry bells peal from the towers, and the marriage procession moves to the church. I will then approach the bridegroom, and demand the reward to which I claim a right. But now, my good friend, give her the bridal kiss, which is probably not the first, embrace her once more, and then you belong to me, until that happy day when we enter Stuttgardt. Let's drink, my friends, to the health of the happy couple."

A smile mingled with the tears of Bertha, which gleamed in her beautiful eyes. She filled the goblet to the brim, and having tasted the wine, a custom in those days done by the cup-bearers at courts, presented it first to the Duke, with a look so full of gratitude and lovely grace, that he thought Albert the happiest man in the world, and that many a one would not have hesitated to risk his life in order to gain a gem of her worth.

The men took each their goblet, waiting for a toast, which the Duke should give after his fashion. But Ulerich von Würtemberg, casting a long farewell look at his country, which he was about to quit, felt a tear start in his eye, which forced him to tear himself away from the painful view. "I now turn my back," said he, "upon objects which are dear to me, but, please God! I'll see them again in better days. Do not bewail my fate, but be of good cheer: as long as the Duke and his trusty friends are united, our good cause is not lost. 'Here's to good Würtemberg for ever!'"

FOOTNOTE TO CHAPTER XXIV.:

Footnote 1: If a crushed world should fall in upon him, the ruins would strike him undismayed.

CHAPTER XXV

In Swabia did thy princely father reign
Beloved, and all did glad allegiance yield;
And of the people, many now remain
Who fought beneath thy banners in the field.
Sure memory cannot be in Swabia dead.
Towards Swabia let us then our footsteps turn,
And as we the Black Forest's mazes tread,
Reviving hopes will in our bosoms burn.

L. Uhland.

So hot a summer as that of the year 1519, had scarcely ever been known in Würtemberg. The whole country had submitted to the power of the League, and its inhabitants now hoped their troubles were at an end. But the original intentions of its chiefs only began now to be fully developed, and it was evident that the mere reoccupation of Reutlingen was not the sole object for which they had coalesced. They were still to be indemnified for their expenses, and to be requited for their services. Some were for dividing Würtemberg equally among themselves, others proposed to sell it to Austria, whilst a third party insisted upon keeping it under the administration of Ulerich's children, subject to their own guardianship. They quarrelled about the possession of the country, to which none of them could found the slightest claims. Disunion and party spirit spread their baneful effects among them, now that they had satisfied their revenge in driving the legitimate lord from his dominions. The expenses of the war were to be met, and there was no one who could or would pay. The knights held this a favourable opportunity to declare themselves independent. Citizens and peasants were drained of their money by continual forced contributions, their fields were desolated and trodden under foot, and they saw no prospect of recovering their losses. Neither would the clergy contribute to the expenses of the war; so that the result of it was only dispute and violence. Many a heart felt how cruelly their legitimate prince had been persecuted, and bitterly repented having driven him into banishment, far from the land of his fathers. And when they compared his system of government with that of their present rulers, they found they had not bettered themselves by the change; on the contrary, they were much worse off than before. But they were too much under subjection to venture to publish their grievances.

The discontent of the people did not escape the government of the League. Their ears were not shut to "much strange and wicked talk," as we read in old official documents. They tried to gain adherents to their cause by rigorous measures. They spread lies concerning the Duke; one of which was, that he had cut a boy of noble blood in halves, of the name of Wilhelm von Janowitz. It made a great noise at the time, but when he was pointed out some time afterwards to a Swiss, as the man of whom the enemies of Ulerich had spread the report, he gave for answer, "He must indeed have been a good carpenter who put the boy so well together again." The priests were ordered to announce from the pulpit, that whoever spoke favourably of the Duke was to be put in prison, and those who supported or assisted him were to lose their eyes, and perhaps their heads.

Ulerich had many faithful friends among the country people, who secretly gave him intelligence how things were going on in Würtemberg. He remained in Mömpelgard with the men who had followed him in his misfortune, waiting a favourable moment to return to his country. He wrote to many Princes, imploring their assistance, but none would bestir themselves in his behalf. He petitioned also the Electors, assembled for the purpose of electing a new Emperor. The only aid they rendered him was to oblige the new Emperor to add an additional clause to his contract, favourable to Würtemberg and the Duke,--but he paid no attention to it. Though he felt himself thus deserted by all the world, he did not give way to despondency, but set all his energies at work to recover his lost country by the resources of his own mind. Many circumstances appeared to favour his project: the League, having satisfied themselves that no one would dare shelter the exile in the country, disbanded most of their troops, composed chiefly of lansquenet, retaining only weak garrisons in the towns and castles; and in Stuttgardt itself, the capital, there remained but few infantry under their banners.

These measures of the League, however, were the cause of creating a formidable enemy to themselves, in a quarter they did not suspect, but which very soon contributed essentially to produce a change in the Duke's favour. This enemy were the common foot soldiers, or the lansquenet. This body of men, collected together from all ends and corners of the empire, and composed of all nations, generally offered their services to those who paid them best. The cause for which they were to fight was perfectly indifferent to them. Being a licentious set, and difficult to be restrained even by severity of discipline, they indemnified themselves by robbery, murder, plunder, and forcibly exacting contributions, if they were not regularly paid. George von Fronsberg had been the first to keep them in some measure in subordination, and by the renown of his name, by daily exercise, and unbending severity, succeeded in forming them into something like an army. He divided them into regular companies and brigades, appointed special officers to each, and taught them to move and fight in columns and masses. These men now shewed that they came from a good school, for when the League disbanded them they did not, as formerly, separate and spread over the country, seeking service individually, but confederating together, formed twelve companies, chose their own commanders from among themselves, and appointed their general in the person of a man who went by the name of *Long Peter*. Being exasperated against the League, and living upon plunder and forced contributions, they became the dread of the whole country. Anarchy had spread its baneful spirit throughout Würtemberg to such a degree, that no one was able to resist their depredations. The party of the League was enfeebled by continual disunion, and was too much employed with its own affairs to think of freeing the impoverished land of this formidable band. The knights, being at variance with each other, remained shut up in their castles, looking on with indifference at the state of affairs. The garrisons of the towns were weak, and not able to repel them by force. The citizens and peasantry, when they were not hard pressed by these marauders, treated them civilly, being equally averse to the government of the League, whom no one now favoured; it was even said they were not disinclined to reinstate the Duke, by the assistance of the same arms that had dethroned him.

On a fine morning of the month of August this body was assembled, and encamped in a meadow of a valley touching the boundary of Baden. Tall black firs and pines encompassed the spot on three sides, and formed part of the Black Forest, with the rivulet called the Würm running through it. Partly under the shade of the wood, partly stretched out among the bushes of the meadow, the little army was distributed about in different groups, taking their rest. At the distance of about two hundred paces were to be seen advanced posts of armed men on the look-out, whose shining lances and lighted matches inspired dread and awe to the by-passer. In the middle of the valley, under the shade of a large oak tree, sat five men, round an out-spread cloak, which served them for a table, where they were playing at a game of cards, called to this day lansquenet. These men were distinguished from the rest of their companions by a broad red scarf, hanging down over the shoulder and breast; but their dress had otherwise much the same ragged worn-out appearance with the others. Some of them wore helmets, others large felt hats, bound with iron, and all of them leather jerkins, of every possible shade and colour, which long service in rain, dust, and bivouacing had imparted to them. Upon a closer inspection, there were two things which particularly distinguished them from the rest of their comrades. They had neither gun nor pike, which were the ordinary weapons of the lansquenet, but wore rapiers of uncommon length and breadth. They also carried in their hats and helmets, in fashion with the nobility and leaders of armies of those days, cock's tail feathers of various colours, assuming to themselves the rank of superiority.

These five men, particularly one who was seated with his back to the tree, appeared much interested in the game which they were playing. He wore a hat with a brim of the breadth of a good sized millstone, trimmed with dingy gold lace, and ornamented in front with a gilt portrait of Saint Peter, out of which sprang two enormous red cock's feathers. His language was a compound of French, Italian, and Hungarian, put together in such strange mixture, that he was scarcely intelligible to those to whom he addressed himself. No one knew what country gave him birth; but he commanded a certain respect among his comrades from the fact of his having served in most of the armies of Europe, and been in nearly all the campaigns of his day; and as he generally prefaced most of his phrases with oaths which he had picked up in the countries he had passed through, and which he pronounced after his own fashion, he thought to render himself thereby of more consequence among those over whom he had assumed the title of general. His beard was dressed in the Hungarian fashion, for being twisted up with pitch, it stuck out on both sides from under his nose a whole span's breadth in the air, much like two iron spikes.

"*Canto cacramento!*" cried this man, with a threatening bass voice, "the little knave is mine; I'll cut him with the king of spades!"

"It's mine, with your permission," cried his neighbour, "and the king into the bargain; there's the queen of spades!"

"Morbleu!" vociferated the other, in a rage; "do you want to take the trick from your commander, Captain Löffler? For shame, for shame! he is a rebel who dares do that. May my soul be punished, but you want to take the command away from me." The general, for such he was, frowned furiously, pushed his hat off his ears, and discovered a large red scar on his forehead, which heightened the savage appearance of his look.

"There is no military discipline at play," General Peter, "answered the other. You may order us captains to blockade a town, and raise contributions, but at play one man is as good as another."

"You are mutinous, a rebel against the authorities! Thunder and lightning! were it not against my honour, I would cut you into a hundred pieces;--but play on."

"There's an ace," said one. "Here's a quart," said another. "I cut with the ten," exclaimed a third. "And here's the knave,--who can take him?" said the fourth player.

"I can," cried the large man; "there's the king,--Morbleu! the trick is mine."

"Where did you get the king?" said a little thin man, with a cunning face, small searching eyes, and shrill voice, "didn't I see it at the bottom of the pack when you dealt. He has cheated! Long Peter has cheated, by all the saints!"

"Muckerle, captain of the eighth company! I advise you to hold your tongue," said the general; "*Bassa manelka!* I don't take a joke,--the mouse should not play with the lion."

"And I say it again,--where did you get the king? I'll prove you false before the pope and the king of France, thou foul player."

"Muckerle," replied the general, drawing his sword deliberately out of its scabbard, "pray another Ave Maria and a Gratias, for as soon as the game is over you are a dead man."

The other three men were roused from a state of indifference at these angry words. They sided with the little captain, and gave the general to understand clearly that they thought he was capable of the imputed meanness. He, however, looked big, and full of importance, and swore he had not cheated. "If the holy Peter, my gracious patron, who I carry on my hat, could speak, he would bear me witness, as true as I am a Christian lansquenet, that I have not played false!"

"He played fair," said a strange voice, which appeared to issue from the tree. The men crossed themselves to defend them from an evil spirit, the gallant general even turned pale, and let drop his cards; when a peasant stept forward from behind the tree, armed with a dagger, and having a guitar slung over his shoulder with a leathern strap. He beheld the group with an undaunted eye, and said, "That gentleman did not cheat; I saw all the cards that were dealt to him."

"Ah! you are a fine fellow," said the general, much pleased; "as I am an honest lansquenet, what you say is all right."

"But how is this?" said the little captain, with a sharp look, "how did this peasant get here without being announced by the piquet? He is a spy, and deserves to be hung."

"Don't be astonished, Muckerle, he is no spy; come and sit down by me, my friend, you are a musician, I see, by your instrument hanging over your shoulder, like a Spaniard going to serenade his love."

"Yes, sir! I am a poor musician; your guard allowed me to pass when I came through the wood. I saw you playing, and I ventured to look on."

The commanders of this free corps not being accustomed to hear themselves addressed in such polite terms, took a liking to the peasant, and invited him courteously to seat himself among them; for they had learned in the military service of foreign countries that kings and princes often went about in the guise of minstrels.

The general filled a cup of wine out of a pewter bottle, offered it to the little captain, and said, with a good-natured smile, "Muckerle, what I drink shall be my death, if I don't forget everything that has passed between us! an end to strife and quarrel. We won't play any more, gentlemen: I love a song and the sound of the guitar--what say you to some music?"

The men agreed, and threw the cards aside. The peasant tuned his instrument, and asked what he should sing.

"Give us a song upon card-playing!" cried one of the party.

The musician considered awhile, and sung the following upon the game of lansquenet, which they had just been playing.

"Cinque, quatre, and ace
Bring many a man to disgrace;
Quatre, and cinque, and tré
Make many to cry well-a-day;
An ace, a seize, and a deuce
Make many an empty house;
A quatre, a trois, and cinque
Cause many pure water to drink;
A cinque, a trois, and quatre
Make parents' and children's eyes water;
From cinque, and quatre, and seize,
Miss Catherine and Miss Elize
Must long unmarried remain,
Unless from your play you refrain."

Long Peter and his associates praised his singing, and reached him the flask with their thanks. "May God bless you!" said the singer, as he returned the bottle; "I wish you luck in your campaign. If I don't mistake, you are the commanders of the League, and are on your march to the enemy. May I ask who you are going against?"

The men looked and smiled at each other, but the general answered him: "you are quite in the wrong. We did, indeed, serve the League formerly, but we are now free and our own masters, ready to assist any one who wants us."

"This will be a good year for the Swiss, for it is said the Duke will return to his country with their assistance," said the peasant.

"May the Swiss be hunted by wolves," said the general, "for having treated him so ill! The good Duke set all his hopes upon them, and, *diavolo maledetto!* did they not desert him in Blaubeuren?"

"Yes, it was too bad," said Captain Muckerle; "but when one looks at the circumstance in its proper light, it served him half right, because he should have known them better. May the devil take them all!"

"They were the Duke's last resource," replied the musician; "but if he had trusted to such men as you, the League would still be at Ulm."

"You have spoken a true word there, my hearty friend!" said the captain. "He ought to have preferred the lansquenets before those Swiss dogs. And if he trusts to them now, I know what will happen. I say it again: he should take lansquenets. Is it not so, Magdeburger?"

"That's my opinion also," said the Magdeburger: "no other than lansquenets can seat the Duke upon his chair again. The Swiss only know how to use their long halberds; that's all their art. But you ought to see us load our guns, how we lay them in the fork, and fire them with a match. No one can come near us in that manœuvre. The Swiss take half an hour to fire their guns, but we only half of a quarter."

"With all respect, gentlemen of this noble corps," said the peasant, raising his cap respectfully, "the Duke should certainly have thrown himself upon your bounty. But the League rewarded you too well for the poor Duke to be able to crave your assistance."

"Rewarded, did you say?" cried the captain of the fifth company, and laughed; "yes, those Swabian dogs would have melted gold out of lead if they could! But I say they paid us ill, and if his grace the Duke will take me, my services are at his command."

"You are right, Staberl," said the general, and stroked his beard. "*Morbleu!* the cat likes to have his back stroked:--if the Duke pays well, the whole corps will join him."

"Well, you shall soon see that," said the peasant, with a cunning smile; "have you had an answer to your message to the Duke?"

The general's whole countenance became as red as fire at this question. "*Mordelement!* Who are you, child of man, who knows my secret? Who told you I had sent to the Duke?"

"Did you, Peter, send to him? What secret have you between each other that we should not know? Tell us immediately," said the Magdeburger.

"Well, I thought it was my duty to think for you all again, as I always have done, and sent a man to the Duke in our name, and with our compliments, to know if he required our services? Our terms were, half a broad piece a man per month, and for us generals and captains a gold florin, with four measures of old wine."

"Those are no bad terms: a gold florin a month! none of us will object to them. Have you had an answer from the Duke?" said the Magdeburger.

"Not yet," said the general. "But, *bassa manelka!* tell me, how do you come to know my secret, peasant, or I'll cut off your ear, and pin it to my hat? Tell me immediately, or off it comes."

"Long Peter," cried the little captain Muckerle, "let him go in peace, for God's sake! he is a resolute man, and possesses the art of witchcraft. I recollect his face as well as if it was but to-day, when we had orders to arrest him in Ulm, and were sent to look for him at the stable of Herrn von Kraft, the clerk of the council, where he resided. He was a spy, and was able to make himself smaller and smaller, not bigger than a sparrow, and flew away from us."

"What!" cried the gallant general, and edged away from the peasant; "is this the man? Why did not the magistrates of Ulm order all the sparrows to be shot, because a Würtemberger spy had turned himself into one?"

"That's him," whispered Muckerle; "that's the fifer of Hardt; I knew him as soon as I saw him."

The general and his companions did not recover their astonishment for some time. They beheld the man of whom many wonderful stories had been related with mingled curiosity and apprehension. Hans was clever enough, however, to understand what they whispered to each other, without the appearance of remarking the state of surprise he had created among them. At length, Long Peter, the official organ of the rest, took heart, twisted his whiskers, and, taking off his enormous hat, thus addressed the fifer of Hardt: "Pardon us, worthy companion, and highly respected fifer of Hardt, that we have treated you with so little ceremony; but how could we know who it was we had among us? be many times welcome; I have long wished to see so renowned a man as the fifer of Hardt, who had the power of flying away from Ulm like a sparrow in the middle of the day."

"Let's have done with those old stories," interrupted the fifer, hastily. "I heard this day from the Duke, who desired me to find you out, to know if you were still inclined to join him upon the terms he has proposed."

"*Canto cacramento!* he is a good man! a gold ducat a month and four measures of wine daily! Long may he live!" cried the general.

"When will he come?" asked captain Löffler. "Where shall we meet him?"

"This very day, if no ill luck attends him. He was to advance upon Heimsheim this morning, where the garrison is weak, and, when he has taken it, he will come on this way."

"Look! there rides a man in armour, to all appearance a knight!" The men looked towards the end of the valley, and remarked a helmet and armour shining in the sun, with a horse occasionally visible. The fifer of Hardt jumped up and climbed the oak, whence he could overlook the valley with greater ease. The horseman was too distant from him to be able to recognise his features, but he thought he knew the scarf which he wore, and that it was the person he had been expecting to appear.

"What do you see?" said the men; "is it one riding by chance through the wood, or do you think he comes from the Duke?"

"That's him with the white and blue scarf," said the fifer; "that's his long hair, and his seat on horseback. Oh, precious youth, welcome back to Würtemberg! He observes your advanced post, and rides towards it; only look how the fellows present their lances and spread out their legs!"

"Yes, yes, the lansquenet knows the arts of war; no one dare pass the spot where the commanders are, without knowing his business," said the general.

"Stop! they are calling to him; he speaks to them; they point this way; he comes!" cried the fifer, who came down from the tree with a joyful countenance.

"*Diavolo maledetto! bassam terendete!* They won't let him ride alone, I hope? Ah! I see one of them has hold of his bridle 1 How? It is really a knight that comes!

"A nobleman as good as any in the empire," answered the fifer; "the friend and favourite of the Duke." Upon hearing this they all stood up, for, though they fancied themselves men of importance and rank, they were aware of their being only lansquenets, and bound to pay proper respect to their superiors. The general seated himself again, with an air of gravity, at the foot of the oak--stroked his beard to make it shine--arranged his hat with the cock's feathers properly--supported his hand on his enormous sword-- and in this manner awaited the arrival of the stranger.

VOL. III

CHAPTER XXVI

The Duke at length is coming,
The battle field's not far;
For vanquish'd is the foeman,
. And he brings the spoils of war.

G. Schwab.

A knight in armour, his horse being led between two of the lansquenet from the outpost, now approached the place where Long Peter, their general, and the other men, were assembled. Though he had drawn the vizor of his shining helmet over his face, the fifer of Hardt thought he recognised him as the man he expected, by the plates and cuish of steel which encased his muscular limbs, the plumes which waved high in the breeze, and the well known scarf which crossed over his coat of mail. And he was not mistaken, for one of the men who led his horse advanced to the General, and acquainted him that the noble "Knight of Sturmfeder" wished to speak to the leaders of the lansquenet.

Long Peter answered in the name of the rest, "tell him he is welcome, and that Peter Hunzinger the General, Staberl of Vienna, Conrad the Magdeburger, Balthaser Löffler, and the brave Muckerle, all well appointed Captains, are ready to receive and hear him. May my soul be punished, but he has a beautiful suit of armour, and an helmet fit for King Francis; and as to his steed, I have never seen a finer--*Morbleu*, how well he stands on his four legs!"

The men kept at a respectful distance from the stranger, who now approached, but shewed no inclination to dismount. Raising his vizor, he spoke to one of the men, and discovered his handsome friendly countenance. "Is not that Hans, the musician?" said he, to the men. "I have a word to say to him first."

The general made a sign to the fifer to approach the young knight, who immediately dismounted from his horse. "Welcome in Würtemberg, noble sir," said the man of Hardt, and returned a hearty shake of Albert von Sturmfeder's hand: "what news do you bring? The Duke's cause prospers, if I can judge from the expression of your countenance."

"Come on one side," he replied, in anxious haste. "How fares it in Lichtenstein? Have you a letter or a couple of lines for me? O give it quickly!"

The fifer smiled at the impatience of the lovesick youth; "I have neither letter nor line. The lady is well, and the old knight also; that is all I know."

"How!" replied the other, "nothing, not even a message? I am sure she did not let you depart without something for me!"

"When I took my leave of the lady the day before yesterday, she said, 'Tell him to hasten the entrance into Stuttgardt;' and when she spoke, became as red in the face as you are at present."

"We'll soon be there, with God's will!" he answered. "But how has she passed the long summer? I have only heard from her three times since we parted. Were you often in Lichtenstein, Hans?"

"Dear sir," answered the fifer, "have patience, and I will relate every thing, in length and breadth, on the march: for the present, be satisfied with the assurance, that so soon as the old knight hears you are advancing to Stuttgardt, he will set out from Lichtenstein with your bride, for he does not doubt of your overpowering the garrison. Have you succeeded in taking Heimsheim?"

"We have: I rode through the gates with twelve horsemen, before they were aware of our coming. Though the garrison were somewhat stronger than us, they were dispirited and dissatisfied. I treated with them in the Duke's name, and made them believe that he was coming up with a large body of troops, upon which they surrendered: thus far are we in Würtemberg. But in what state is the road before us?"

"Open, into the heart of the country, open. I have important news for the Duke from the knight of Lichtenstein, namely, that the men in power are out of the land, do you know----"

"Is it the meeting they now hold at Nördlingen you mean?" interrupted Albert. "Oh! yes, we know it, for it was that news which determined the Duke to commence operations."

"Well, when the cats are away, the mice will play," said the fifer; "the garrisons are every where careless. None of the League think any more of the Duke, their attention being wholly taken up with the meeting at Nördlingen, where it will be decided, whether Austria, or Bavaria, or Prince

Christoph, or the Leaguist towns Augsburg and Aalen, Nürnberg, and Bopfinger, will reign over us."

"What long faces they will make," exclaimed Albert, smiling, "when they hear that the chair about which they are quarrelling is already possessed:

'The frog jumps into the muddy pool,
Tho' he may set upon a golden stool!'

says the proverb; they may shoulder their guns and give up governing now. And the Würtembergers, what are their feelings towards the Duke at present? Do you believe many will come to his assistance?"

"He may reckon upon the citizens and peasantry," replied the fifer. "How it stands with the knights, I don't know; for when I asked the old man of Lichtenstein, he shrugged up his shoulders and muttered a couple of curses: I fear that matter is not so well as it should be. But citizens and peasants hold to a man for their Prince. Many extraordinary signs have appeared, which encourage the people. Lately in the valley of the Rems a stone fell from the sky, on one side of which a stag's horn and the following words were engraved, 'Here's to good Würtemberg for ever,' and on the reverse, in Latin, 'Long live Duke Ulerich.'"

"Did you say it fell from the sky?"

"So it was said. The peasantry were overjoyed at it, but the officers of the League put the magistrate of the place where it had fallen into prison, and wanted to extort from him the name of the person who had engraved the letters. And when it was proclaimed, upon pain of severe punishment, that no one was to speak of the Duke, the men only laughed, and said, 'We dream of him now.' They all wish him back again, and would rather be oppressed by their legitimate Lord than be flayed by strangers."

"That's as it should be," said Albert. "The Duke and his cavalry may be here in a few hours. His intention is, to cut his way straight through the country to Stuttgardt. The capital once ours, the rest will soon follow. But how is it with these lansquenets--will they join us?"

"I had almost forgotten them," said Hans, "we had better go to them; else they will become impatient if we keep them waiting. You must be cautious how you treat them, for they are proud fellows, and have no small idea of their own importance. By winning these five to our interests, the whole twelve companies are sure to follow. With their General, Long Peter, mind and be very civil and courteous."

"Which is Long Peter?"

"The big man, sitting under the oak; he with the stiff mustachios and hat of distinction on his head. He is the commander in chief."

"I will talk to him, and follow your advice," Albert answered, and proceeded towards them. The long conversation which they had held had somewhat displeased the men, and little Muckerle in particular eyed the ambassador of the Duke with a penetrating glance. But when the young knight appeared among them his noble demeanour disconcerted them, they became shy and embarrassed before him, so much so, that the courteous words which he addressed to them soon had the desired effect of bringing them over to the Duke's cause. They listened to him in respectful silence.

"Most experienced general and brave commanders of the assembled lansquenet," said Albert, "the Duke of Würtemberg having approached the boundary of his country, and captured Heimsheim, is determined in the same way to recover his whole dukedom."

"May my soul be punished, but he is right!" said Long Peter; "I would do the same."

"He has already experienced the courage and military science of the lansquenet, when they fought on the side of his enemies, and he trusts they will manifest the same bravery in his cause, promising upon his princely word, faithfully to fulfil the engagements he has proposed."

"A pious man," murmured the commanders among themselves, with approving nods; "a gold florin a month, and, *morbleu!* four measures of wine a day for the superior officers."

The general rose from his seat, saluted him by uncovering his bald head, and said, though often interrupted by many coughs of embarrassment, "We thank you, most noble sir; we agree--we'll join you. We'll give back to the Swabian League what they gave us, that we will--hard usage. The very best and most courageous, as well as the most excellent of men, have they dismissed, as if they did not value our services. There stands, for example, Captain Löffler: if there is a braver lansquenet in all Christendom, I'll allow my skin to be peeled off and walk about in my bones the rest of my life! Look at Staberl of Vienna: the sun and moon have never shone upon his equal! And the Magdeburger there, no Turk ever fought like him; and as for little Muckerle, though he does not look it, he is the best shot in the world, and can hit the bull's eye in the target at forty paces. I won't say anything of myself; self praise does not sound well. But, *bassa manelka!* I have served in Spain and Holland--and, *canto cacramento*--also in Italy and Germany! *Morbleu!* Long Peter is known in every army. May my soul be punished, when I and the others get behind the Swabian dogs, *diavolo maledetto,* they'll take to their hareskin, and be off as fast as their heels can carry them!"

This was the longest speech Long Peter had ever made; and when many years after he sealed the renown of the German lansquenet with his death before Pavia, his companions, in relating to their young comrades the events of his life, always mentioned this moment as the most glorious of his career. He was described as standing before his audience, leaning upon his long sword, his large hat with the red feathers cocked over his ear, the right hand resting upon his side, and his legs spread out, wanting nothing to complete his pretensions to a regular general than a better jerkin and the chain of honour.

The commanders, after the flattering speech of their general, invited their new guest to pass their army in review. The hollow sound of enormous drums soon roused the men from their rest. They appeared still to be under the influence of Fronsberg's military genius and strict discipline, by the activity they displayed in forming themselves, in a few moments, into three great circles, each composed of four companies. To an eye accustomed, as in our times, to the rapid but steady movements of regiments, and the beautiful appearance of their uniformity of dress, the sight of this heterogeneous multitude would cause surprise if not ridicule. Though the lansquenets were generally clothed according to their own taste, there was still a semblance of an attempt to uniformity after the fashion of those days. For the most part they wore jerkins of leather setting tight to the body, or leather waistcoats with arms of coarse cloth, and enormous wide trousers tied under the knee, and falling by their own weight a little below it. The legs were covered with coarse stockings of a light colour, and the feet with shoes of untanned leather. A hat, leather or metal cap, probably articles of plunder rather than of purchase, covered the head; and the bearded faces of these men, many of whom had served twenty years in all the armies and under every climate in Europe, gave them a very bold and martial appearance. They were armed with a dagger and halberd, and some with guns, which were fired with a match.

Standing with outstretched legs, and foot to foot meeting, they presented a bold front; and Albert's military spirit rejoiced at the sight of these experienced warriors, who, however, were well aware, that in single combat they had no confidence, but formed in mass they were formidable even to a more numerous enemy.

The commanders had carefully retained all the manœuvres and words of command of their former leader. They walked into the middle of one of the circles, followed by their new acquaintance, when the deep and loud-toned voice of Long Peter gave the word "Attention! face about."

The celerity with which the order was obeyed by turning around facing inwards, proved they had not forgotten their lesson. They listened to the proposals of the Duke of Würtemberg which the commanders addressed to them, and manifested by a murmur which ran through the ranks, that they were satisfied with the terms, and would serve his cause with the same zeal as they had not long since served against it. They were then put through several manœuvres, which they performed with an address that astonished Albert, who thought the art of war of his day would never be surpassed as long as the world existed. But he deceived himself. His error of judgment was, however, pardonable, for in the same way did our grandfathers hold the heroes of Frederick the Great in estimation, as the *ne plus ultra* of military discipline, and did not anticipate the ridicule of their descendants on the subject of perruques and long gaiters. And may not the time come, when the *good old times* of 1839 will also have their share of ridicule? Certainly such elegant laced-up figures as are seen now-a-days among military men, were not the fashion among the lansquenet and their commanders, A. D. 1519.

About an hour after, it was announced from the advanced posts, that they had perceived at the further end of the valley, in the neighbourhood of the road leading from Heimsheim, the glittering of arms, and when they put their ears close to the ground, they heard distinctly the trampling of many horses.

"That's the Duke," cried Albert; "bring me my horse; I will ride and meet him."

The young man galloped away through the wood, to the admiration of the bystanders, who were astonished at the activity he displayed in throwing himself upon his steed, encumbered as he was with his heavy armour. Helmets with high plumes and shining lances were shortly after seen moving among the bushes of the valley. As they approached, the cavalry issued from the wood, seen first breast high among the underwood, and then their whole figures were visible on a small height, where the whole body assembled. The joy of the fifer of Hardt was indescribable when he got a sight of the gallant band, headed by the Duke. He took the general by the hand, and pointed to them with an air of triumphant satisfaction.

"Which is the Duke?" asked Long Peter; "is that him on the black piebald horse?"

"No, that is the noble knight Von Hewen: the banner-bearer of Würtemberg:--but, no, am I mistaken? I declare Albert von Sturmfeder carries it!"

"That's a great honour! *Morbleu*, he is only five-and-twenty, and carries the flag! In France the only man who is entitled to that privilege is the constable, the next man to the king in honour. In that country it is called the standard, and is made all of gold. But which is Duke Ulerich?"

"Do you see that man in a green cloak, with the black and red feathers in his helmet? he that rides next to the banner, mounted on a black horse, and is speaking to the young knight. He points this way. That's the Duke."

The body of cavalry was composed of about forty men, mostly noblemen and their servants, who the Duke, in his banishment, had assembled together, or appointed to meet him on the boundary of his country, when his plans were ripe for an invasion. They were all well mounted and armed. Albert von Sturmfeder carried Würtemberg's banner; next to him rode the Duke in complete armour. When they came within about two hundred paces of the lansquenet, Long Peter, in a loud voice, said to his people, "Attention, my people. When his Grace is near enough, and I raise my hat off my head, let every one cry, 'Vivat Ulericus!' lower the colours, and you, drummers, rattle upon your sheep-skins like thunder and lightning! Give us the animating flourish of the drum as at the storming of a fortress! *Bassa manelka*, beat away till the drumsticks break--that's the way the brave lansquenet salute a prince."

This short speech had the desired effect. The Duke's praises were murmured through the warlike band; they shook their halberds, stamped their fire-arms clattering on the ground, the drummers prepared their drums and sticks to obey their general's orders in full vigour; and when Albert von Sturmfeder, the standard-bearer of Würtemberg, sprang forward, followed by Duke Ulerich, majestic as in the best days of his power, with bold dignified countenance, Long Peter uncovered his head in respectful submission, the preconcerted signal was instantly obeyed, the drummers executed their military music, the colours were lowered in salute, and the whole body of the lansquenet vociferated a loud and cheering "Vivat Ulericus!"

The peasant of Hardt remained at a distance, not heeding the salute, for his whole soul appeared concentred in his eye, which was fixed on his lord in the intoxication of joy. The Duke stopped his horse, and looked about him in the dead silence which afterwards succeeded. The fifer then came forward, knelt down, holding his stirrup for him to dismount, and said, "Here's to good Würtemberg for ever!"

"Ha! are you there, Hans, my trusty companion in misfortune, the first to salute me in Würtemberg? I expected my nobles would have been the foremost to greet my arrival in my country, my chancellor and my council--where are the dogs? Where are the representatives of my estates? will they not welcome me to my home? Is no one here to hold my stirrup but this peasant?"

The followers of the Duke hastened around him in surprise when they heard these cutting words. They scarcely knew whether he was in earnest, or whether it was a mere sarcastic joke over his own misfortunes. His mouth, appeared to smile, but his eye bespoke anger, and his voice sounded stern and commanding. They looked at each other in doubtful apprehension as to the meaning of this burst of passion, when the fifer of Hardt replied,

"For this once a peasant only assists your Grace on Würtemberg ground; but despise not a true heart and a willing hand. The others will soon come, when they hear the Duke treads his native land again."

"Do you think so?" said Ulerich, with a bitter smile, as he swung himself from his horse; "do you think they'll come? Hitherto we have little reason to flatter ourselves; but I'll knock at their doors, and let them know that the old gentleman is there, and will have admittance to his house! Are these the lansquenets who have agreed to serve me?" he continued, attentively observing the little army; "they appear well armed, and in good condition. How many men are there?"

"Twelve companies, your Grace," answered Peter the general, who still stood without his hat, in a state of embarrassment, twisting his mustachios occasionally. "Nothing but well-trained men. May my soul be punished--pardon my oath--but the king of France has no better soldiers!"

"Who are you?" asked the Duke, looking with astonishment at the large heavy figure of the general, with his immense sword and red face.

"I am a lansquenet of my own order, and am called Long Peter, but now the well-appointed general of the assembled----"

"What, general! this folly must have an end. You may be a very brave man, but you are not made to command. I will be your general henceforth," said the Duke, "and my knights will be named as your captains."

"*Bassa manelka!*--I am sorry I swore, but permit an old soldier to say a word to your Grace. What you propose would be against our terms of a gold florin a month, and four measures of wine a-day. There stands, for example, Staberl of Vienna, not a braver man under the sun----"

"Very good, very good, old man! we'll not talk of the gold florin and wine now," replied the Duke. "The captains shall retain their present commands, but I command you. Have you any ammunition?"

"Yes, to be sure," said the Magdeburger; "we have plenty, which belonged to your Grace, and which we brought away from Tübingen. Each man has eighty rounds."

"Very well," answered the Duke; "George von Hewen and Philip von Rechberg, do you divide the men, and each take six companies. Let their captains remain with their men, and assist their commanders. Ludwig von Gemmingen, I appoint you to command all the infantry. And now we'll march direct for Leonberg. Rejoice, my faithful standard bearer," said the Duke, as he mounted, "with God's assistance we'll be in Stuttgardt tomorrow."

The troop of cavalry, with the Duke at their head, led the way. Long Peter stood fixed in the same place, with his hat and its cock's feathers in his hand, observing the horsemen.

"That is a Prince, indeed!" he said to the other commanders who stood beside him. "What a powerful voice he has; and when he rolls his eyes about it makes one quake for fear! I thought he would have swallowed me, head and all, when he asked me who I was."

"I felt much in the same state as if hot water had been poured over me," said the Magdeburger. "This man is more to be dreaded than the Emperor in Vienna."

"Our reign has been but a short one," said Captain Muckerle; "our dignity has not lasted long."

"Fool! so much the better. Dignity only brings cares, says the proverb; our people don't submit readily to our orders--*diavolo!*--for one of them laughed at me in my face only this day. Things will go much better when the knights lead us: and we shall receive a gold florin and four measures of wine; that's our principal business." So said Peter.

"I think so too," said the Magdeburger; "and we have to thank Long Peter for our good fortune. Long may he live!"

"Thank you," said the general; "but I tell you, the Duke will set the League in flames again, *morbleu!* and when he draws his sword, he alone will hunt them out of the country. And did you hear how he cursed his council, chancellor, and nobles? I would not like to be in their skins."

The conversation of the veterans was now interrupted by the rolling of the drums, which no longer sounded at their command. Long Peter had been so often accustomed, during his many campaigns, to the vicissitudes of fortune, by being raised and lowered suddenly in rank, that he was not disconcerted by his present loss of command. He very quietly deprived his large hat of its ornamental cock's feather; he laid aside his red scarf and long sword, the emblems of his dignity, and shouldered his halberd. "May my soul be punished, but mine is a hard case, who but yesterday was in supreme command, and am now obliged to go back into the ranks," said he, as he took his place among his comrades. "But by Saint Peter, my holy patron and brother lansquenet, every thing is for the best in this world." His companions shook him by the hand, and agreed with him in his sentiments. It did his brave heart good to hear them approve of his conduct, the short time he had wielded the command over them. The three knights, their newly appointed leaders, mounted and put themselves at the head of their brigades; the lansquenets arranged themselves in the common order of march, and, Ludwig von Gemmingen ordering the drums to beat the advance, the little army broke up their camp, and set forward.

CHAPTER XXVII

The summit of the wall is gain'd
All in the silent night,
And now the fortress is attain'd!
We do not fear the light.
Now, let us sound the battle cry,
And be it "Death or victory!"

Schiller.

Duke Ulerich appeared before the gate of Stuttgardt, called the Red Hill Gate, on the night previous to the holiday of the Assumption of the Virgin Mary. Having captured the little town of Leonberg on his way, he prosecuted his march on the capital without further interruption. The news of his being in the country spread through the land like wild-fire, and judging by the numbers that joined his colours, as well as by the joy with which he was everywhere received, he had reason to suppose the people would rejoice to see their legitimate Prince re-established in his rights, and the hateful government of the League abolished.

The intelligence of his advance had reached Stuttgardt, and had caused much difference of feeling amongst its inhabitants. The nobility scarcely knew what they had to expect from the Duke; the shameful surrender of Tübingen being an event of too recent a date to leave them wholly without fear of his wrath. But the recollection of the brilliant court of Ulerich von Würtemberg and the merry days they had formerly passed under his sway, compared to the oppressions the League had inflicted on them, led them to incline to submission. Not a few, however, among them had reason to dread his return. The citizens could scarcely restrain their joy; and, quitting their houses, assembled in groups about the streets, talking over coming events. They cursed the League in strong terms, but silently, clenching their fists in their pockets, and were beyond measure patriotically inclined, and full of pugnacious propensities. Calling to mind the illustrious ancestors of their exiled Prince, whose name of Würtemberg they themselves bore; they reckoned up the many noble lords sprung from the same family, under whom they and their fathers had lived happily, and whose glorious deeds had spread their country's fame abroad. But the most important topic of their conversation was, that upon them depended, in a great measure, the decision of the struggle between the League and the Duke, as the whole country would now look upon the Stuttgardters as the fuglemen in the contest. They were, however, no way inclined of themselves to create an insurrection against the garrison of the League, whom they still feared, but they whispered to each other: "Brother, wait a little, and we'll soon have an opportunity to show those Leaguists what we Stuttgardters are made of."

The insurrectionary spirit of the burghers did not escape the notice of Christoph Schwarzenberg, the Leaguist governor. He perceived, but too late, the mistake that had been committed in disbanding the army. He applied to the representatives of his party assembled at Nördlingen for assistance, but gave them no hope of holding Stuttgardt unless they sent immediate relief. Scarcely had he time to make some feeble preparations for defence, when the rapid advance of the Duke checked his ardour. Perceiving he could not trust the citizens, that the nobles would not stand by him, and aware that the garrison was not strong enough even to ensure the safety of the gates of the city, he absconded in the night with the state council to Esslingen. Their flight was so sudden and secret, that their families even were ignorant of it, and no one in the town suspected the intentions of the governor and his senate. The partisans of the League, therefore, never dreaming of the desertion of their chiefs, treated the news of the approach of the Duke with indifference, for they did not believe the report of his being in the immediate neighbourhood.

The market-place in those days stood in the heart of the city. But even then two considerable suburbs, the Saint Leonhard and the field of tournament, were built around the town, provided with outer ditches, walls, and strong gates, which gave them also the appearance of fortified cities. They were separated from the old town which possessed its own walls and gates, and its inhabitants looked down with contempt on those of the suburbs. The market-place was the spot where the burghers were accustomed to assemble, according to the fashion of olden times when any extraordinary occurrence took place; and therefore, on the eventful evening before the day of the Assumption of the Virgin, the citizens streamed in crowds to this central point. Though every man in those days carried arms with impunity, which gave to an assembled multitude a fearful appearance, still the honest burghers of Stuttgardt would not have dared to utter, in the day-time, what they now ventured to do in the dusk. Had many of them been asked their opinion of the Duke in the forenoon, they would have answered, "What do I care about him? I am a peaceable citizen:" but upon this occasion, they raised their voices, I and cried, "We'll open the gates to the Duke! away with the Leaguists! Würtemberg for ever!"

The moon shone bright on the assembled crowd, which waved to and fro in restless motion, whilst a confused murmur seemed to indicate indecision as to what was to be done, perhaps because no one was bold enough to put himself forward on the occasion. Many heads looked out of the windows of the gable-ended houses which surrounded the market-place; they were the wives and families of the congregated citizens, listening with intense anxiety to what was going on: for it must be observed that the Stuttgardt ladies were in those days equally given to curiosity as they now are, and in their hearts pitied the Duke.

The hum of voices became louder and louder, whilst the feeling which ran through the crowd became more distinct. The cry "let's drive; the soldiers from the gates, and open them to the Duke," passed from mouth to mouth, when a tall, meagre-looking man was seen to spring up on a stone bank which surrounded the fountain, whence he overlooked the assemblage of burghers. He flourished his long arms about in the air, opened his large mouth, and hallooed with all his might to obtain a hearing. The noise about him having partially subsided, a few detached words and sentences were heard by the immediate bystanders. "What! do the honourable burghers of Stuttgardt intend to break the oath which they have sworn to the League? To whom do you want to open the gates--to the Duke? He can't have a very strong force with him, for he has no money to pay them, and he will make you open your purses. If you surrender to him, you will have ten thousand florins to pay. Do you hear? ten thousand florins, I say!"

"Who is that lanky fellow?" the citizens asked one another. "He's right," said one of them, "we shall have to pay handsomely."--"Is he a citizen, that man up there?"--"Who are you?" said one of the boldest; "how do you know we shall have to pay?"

"I am the renowned Doctor Calmus," said the speaker, with solemn voice, "and am quite sure of it. And who do you want to drive away? The Emperor, the Empire, the League? Will you run your heads against so many rich lords? and why? for Duke Utz, who only throws dust in your eyes! Do you forget his oppressive game laws, the least part of his tyranny? He has no more money left; he is a beggar, and has squandered everything in Mömpelgard----"

"Make him keep silence!" cried the burghers: "What is that to you? you are not one of our citizens; away with the bald-headed mouse,--kill him,--throw him into the fountain to feed the fish!--Long live the Duke!"

Doctor Calmus raised his voice again, but was overpowered by the loud shouts of the bystanders.

At this moment another troop of burghers arrived in great haste from the suburbs. "The Duke is before the Red Hill gate," they cried, "with cavalry and infantry. Where is the governor and his council? He will fire into the town if the gates be not instantly opened! Away with the Leaguists!--Who is a good Würtemberger?"

The tumult increased. Perceiving the crowd still undecided, another speaker mounted the bank: he was a comely-looking man, who, for a moment, imposed on the crowd by his outward appearance. "Consider, honourable men," he cried: "what will the illustrious council of the League say if you----"

"Out with the illustrious council!" they answered, "away with him, tear him down, him with the rose-coloured cloak and smooth hair, he is an Ulmer--at him, he is an Ulmer!"

But before they could put their threats into execution, a powerful man stept up between the two orators, knocked the Doctor over with his right hand, and the Ulmer with his left, waving his cap in the air to obtain a hearing. "Silence! that is Hartman," whispered the burghers, "he understands the world; listen to what he says!"

"Hear me!" said he: "the governor and his council are nowhere to be found, they have fled, and left us in the lurch; we'll therefore seize these two, and keep them as hostages. And now to the Red Hill gate; our true Duke stands before it: it is better to open the gate of our own accord than that he should use force to do so. Who's a good Würtemberger, let him follow me."

He descended from his position, and was joyfully received by the crowd. The two advocates of the League were bound and led away before they had time to look about them. The stream of burghers now flowed from the marketplace through the upper gate and over the broad ditch of the old town leading to the field of tournament, and, passing the fortification, arrived at the Red Hill gate. The Leaguist troops, who occupied it, were soon overpowered, the gate was opened, the drawbridge fell, and laid over the town ditch.

The leader of the Duke's infantry had, during these occurrences in the town, stationed his best troops at this gate, as it was doubtful what steps the League would take at the approach of the Duke. Ulerich himself had examined the post. In vain did Albert von Sturmfeder endeavour to persuade him that the garrison of Stuttgardt was too weak to make any formidable resistance, in vain did he represent to him the desire the burghers had to see him again, and would willingly open the gates, the Duke looked darker than the night, pressed his lips together, and gnashed his teeth in anger.

"You don't understand these things," he muttered to the young man; "you don't know the world; they are all false; never trust any one but yourself. They accommodate themselves to every change of wind. But I have them this once under my thumb. Do you suppose I have been obliged to turn my back upon my country to no purpose?"

Albert was unable to comprehend the Duke's meaning. He had seen him firm in misfortune, yea even mild and gentle, and in speaking of the many beneficent plans for the good of his people, which he intended to put into execution when he returned to his country, he had seldom manifested any violent fits of passion in talking of his enemies, and scarcely ever betrayed any ill will towards his subjects, who had deserted him. But whether it was the sight of his country that awakened the feeling of vexation stronger in him than usual, whether he was irritated that the nobility and representatives of his estates had not come forward to welcome his arrival after he had passed the boundary of Würtemberg; whatever was the cause, his spirits were no longer cheerful and buoyant. His look appeared as if troubled by a thirst for revenge, and a certain severity and harshness in giving his opinion, struck those about him as indications of alteration in his temper. Albert von Sturmfeder, in particular, could not account for this new turn in Ulerich's manner.

The town had been summoned more than half an hour. The time which had been given was nearly expired, and still no answer had arrived. The hum of voices was heard in the town, and a restless moving about the streets, shewing that the besieged were doubtful whether their terms would be accepted or not.

The Duke rode up to the lansquenets, who were resting on their halberds and match guns, headed by their leaders, who were each occupied in preserving discipline among their men. Albert remarked the countenance of the Duke by the light of the moon. The veins of his of his forehead were swollen beyond their common size, his cheeks being deeply flushed, and his eyes sparkled like fire.

"Hewen! get the scaling ladders ready," said the Duke with a stern voice. "Thunder and lightning! I stand before my own house, and they will not let me in. The trumpets shall sound once more, when, if they don't open the gates instantly, I'll fire the town and burn it to the ground."

"*Bassa manelka!* that's what I like," said Long Peter to his comrade, who stood in the front rank near the Duke. "The ladders are going to be brought, we'll climb up like cats, and drive those fellows from the walls, and then the musqueteers will pepper them properly, *canto cacramento!*"

"Ah! yes," said the Magdeburger, "and then we'll sally into the town, set fire to all corners--plunder--burst open the doors--that's the fun for us lansquenets!"

"For God's sake, my Lord Duke," said Albert, who had heard his last words, and had observed the rapacious spirit which animated the soldiers, "only wait a short quarter of an hour longer; recollect it is your own capital. They are most likely still deliberating."

"What have they got to consult so long about?" replied Ulerich with ill humour: "their rightful lord stands before his own gate, and demands admittance. My patience is already exhausted. Spread my banner to the light of the moon, Albert; let the trumpets sound; summon the town once more for the last time; and if the gates are not opened by the time I have counted thirty after the last word, by the holy Hubertus, I'll storm the walls. Be quick! Albert."

"O sir! consider your town, your best town! Having lived so long in it, would you now give it to the flames? Give them a little more time."

"Ha!" laughed the Duke in anger, and struck the armour of his breast with his steel glove, which sounded through the stillness of the night, "I see you are not inclined to enter Stuttgardt, and merit your wife thereby. But no more words now, at the risk of my displeasure, Albert von Sturmfeder. Obey my order quickly: unfurl my banner, let the trumpet sound! sound and frighten the dogs out of their sleep, that they may know a Würtemberger stands here, and will enter his house in spite of the Emperor and Empire. I say, summon them again, Sturmfeder!"

The young man obeyed the order in silence, and riding close up to the ditch, unfurled Würtemberg's banner. The rays of the moon appeared to welcome it back to its country, and shone full upon it, whereby the four fields with their charges were plainly exhibited to view. On a large flag of red silk were wove the arms of Würtemberg, with its escutcheon and four fields. In the first were the stag horns of Würtemberg, in the second the balls of Teck, the third had the storming flag of the empire, which belonged by right to the Duke as banner-bearer of the empire, and in the fourth were the fish of Mömpelgard: the whole being surmounted by the crown and the bugle of Urach. The strong arm of the young man could scarcely hold the heavy flag in the breeze. He was attended by three trumpeters, who now sounded their wild tones before the closed gate.

A window above it opened, and a voice asked their business. Albert von Sturmfeder answered, "Ulerich, by the grace of God Duke of Würtemberg and Teck, Count of Urach and Mömpelgard, summons for the second and last time his city of Stuttgardt, to open its gates willingly and instantly to him, else he will storm the walls and treat the town as an enemy."

During the time Albert was delivering his message, a confused noise as of a crowd in motion mingled with voices in the streets was heard, which approaching nearer and nearer, at length broke out into tumult and shouting.

"May my soul be punished, if they are not about to make a sortie!" said Long Peter, loud enough to be heard by the Duke.

"Perhaps you are right," answered the Duke, turning abruptly to the startled lansquenet: "close in together, present your pikes, and have the matches ready, that we may receive them as they deserve."

The whole line retreated some distance from the ditch, leaving only the three first companies at the point where the drawbridge fell. A wall of pikes bristled in formidable array against a sudden attack, the guns were presented and the match held at the touchhole ready to fire. The dead stillness of expectation which reigned without the walls was broken by the tumultuous noise within the town. The drawbridge fell, but no enemy sallied forth to repel the invaders: three old grey-headed men alone proceeded through the gate, bearing the arms of the city, with its keys.

When the Duke saw the peaceable mission approach, he rode towards them in a friendly manner, followed by Albert. Two of these men appeared to be councillors or magistrates: they bent their knee before their lord and master, and tendered him the proofs of their submission. He gave them to his attendants, and said to the ambassadors, "You have kept us waiting somewhat long outside: truly we should very shortly have mounted the walls, and have lighted up your town with our own hands, and made your eyes smart with the smoke of it. Why did you keep us waiting so long?"

"Oh, my Lord!" said one of the old men, "as far as the burghers were concerned they were ready to open the gates instantly; but we have some few principal members of the League still among us, who held long and dangerous speeches to the people to instigate them to rebellion against your grace. That is the true cause of the delay."

"Ha! who are those men?" said the Duke. "I hope you have taken care not to let them escape, for I would like to say a word to them."

"God forbid, your highness! we know our duty to our lord, and therefore seized them immediately and put them in confinement. Is it your wish to see them?"

"To-morrow morning in the castle, I'll examine them. Send to the executioner at the same time; perhaps it will be requisite to take their heads off."

"Prompt justice, just what they deserve," said a shrill croaking voice behind the two burghers.

"Who is it that interrupts me?" said the Duke, when looking around, an extraordinary figure of diminutive size stepped forward, carrying a hump with which nature had ornamented his back, and which was concealed under a black silk cloak. His well-combed grey locks were covered by a small pointed hat; a pair of eyes, which bespoke cunning and intrigue, sparkled under bushy grey eyebrows; and a thin moustache, which sprung out from under an eagle-like nose, gave him much the appearance of a feline animal. An expression of fawning courteousness lay upon his wrinkled features, and when he uncovered his head at the Duke's salute, Albert felt an insuperable disgust and a peculiar abhorrence at the sight of him.

The Duke, when he noticed the little man, called to him in a friendly way: "Ha! Ambrosius Bolland, our chancellor! are you still alive? You might have made your appearance before now, methinks, for you must have known we were in our country again; but you are, notwithstanding, welcome to us."

"Most illustrious Duke!" answered the chancellor, Ambrosius Bolland, "I have been laid up with a violent fit of gout, which would scarcely allow me to leave my house; pardon me, therefore, your----"

"Very well, very well," said the Duke, smiling, "I'll soon cure you of the gout. Come to us in the castle to-morrow morning; it is our pleasure at present to ride through the town. Forwards, my faithful banner-bearer!" he turned to Albert, with gracious demeanour, "you have kept your word honestly as far as the gates of Stuttgardt; I will reward your faithful service. By Saint Hubertus, the bride is yours according to justice and right. Carry my flag before me, we'll plant it on my castle, and tread the Leaguist banner in the dust! Gemmingen and Hewen, you are my guests for the night; we'll see if the lords of the Swabian League have left us any of our old wine."

Thus rode Duke Ulerich, surrounded by his knights, who had followed him in his train through the gates of his capital. The burghers received him with loud *vivas*, and the pretty damsels in the windows waved their white handkerchiefs, to the annoyance of their mothers, who thought these salutations were directed to the handsome young knight carrying the Duke's banner, and who, as seen by the light of their torches, recalled to their minds St. George, the dragon-killer.

CHAPTER XXVIII

Oh, may the deeds of those no more,

The glory that they won,

The sire's spirit hovering o'er,

So stimulate the son,

That this day's setting sun may see

Of no degenerate clay are we.

P. Conz.

When Albert von Sturmfeder viewed the old castle of Stuttgardt the next morning, it did not exhibit the same form which it has in our days, the present one having been built by the Duke's son, Prince Christoph. The residence of the former Dukes of Würtemberg stood in the same place; and differed little in plan and appearance from Christoph's work, except that it was for the most part built of wood. Being surrounded by broad and deep ditches, over which a bridge led to the town, a large open space in front served in early times as a tilt-yard for the gay court of Ulerich, whose powerful hand had often rolled many a knight in the arena. The interior also of the building bespoke the customs and usages of the times. High and vaulted halls occupied the lower part of the castle, and were generally used in rainy weather as a place for manly exercises, having space sufficient to admit of the largest lance being wielded without hindrance. Old chronicles mention the size of these halls as being spacious enough to contain between two and three hundred persons at table. A broad stone staircase, capable of admitting two horsemen to ride abreast, and made for that purpose, led to the upper apartments, where the splendour of the rooms, the grandeur of the hall of the knights, and the richly ornamented galleries used for dancing and play, corresponded with the exterior appearance of the castle.

Albert viewed with an eye of astonishment the extravagant splendour of the palace. When he compared the establishment of his ancestors with what he now saw, how small and confined they seemed to him! He recollected the stories he had heard of the brilliancy of Ulerich's court, on the occasion of his magnificent marriage, when seven thousand guests, from all parts of the German empire, caroused in this castle, in whose vaulted halls and spacious court-yards all kinds of games and merrymaking were held for a whole month; and a numerous assembly of noblemen, with all the greatest beauties of the day, kept up the merry dance till late at night. He looked down into the garden of the castle, which, from its beauty, was called Paradise. His fancy peopled the shaded walks and summerhouses, which were scattered about it, with the joyous throng of gallant knights and stately ladies, enjoying themselves with mirth and song. But alas! how deserted and empty were they now; and when he compared their present state with the picture his imagination had created, what a lesson of this world's vanity did it not give! The guests of the marriage feast, the brilliant merry court, all are vanished, said he to himself; the princely bride is flown, the brilliant circle of women by whom she was surrounded scattered to the four winds; knights and counts, who once feasted in these halls, have deserted their prince; the tender pledges of his marriage now in a distant land, in the hands of his enemies; and the lord of the castle is left alone to brood in solitude over his misfortunes, and think only of revenge; and who knows how long he will be allowed to remain in the house of his ancestors; who knows whether his enemies will not get the upper hand again, and, overpowering him, drive him into misery twofold greater than what he has already experienced.

The young soldier attempted in vain to repress these gloomy thoughts, which the contrast between the splendour of the surrounding objects and the misfortunes of the Duke involuntarily awakened in his mind. In vain he summoned to his aid the portrait of that beloved being, whom he hoped soon to call his own for ever; in vain he painted, in the most glowing colours, to his imagination, all the charms of domestic happiness in her company; he was still unable to shake off the gloomy ideas which the sight of the castle had produced on his mind. Whatever was the cause of it, whether it was the Duke's lofty character, which he had so nobly manifested in misfortune, and which had created so deep a feeling of admiration in the breast of the young man, or whether nature had gifted him with an extraordinary perception into future events, he remained riveted to the spot in deep thought. Persuaded that the Duke's affairs were any thing but prosperous, he felt himself in duty bound to warn him against some unforeseen impending danger which irresistibly haunted his mind.

"Why so much wrapped in thought, young man?" asked an unknown voice behind him, and roused him from his reverie: "I should have thought Albert von Sturmfeder had reason to be of good cheer."

Albert turned round in surprise, and cast his eyes upon the chancellor, Ambrosius Holland. If this man had struck Albert the night before, as being peculiarly forbidding by his officious courteousness, his cat-like sneaking manner, he was now more confirmed in his dislike, when he remarked the deformity of his person, rendered more conspicuous by an overladen finery of dress. His dark-yellow shrivelled-up face, with an eternal hypocritical smile upon it, his green eyes peeping out under long grey eyelashes, his highly inflamed eyelids, and scanty beard, contrasted strangely with a red velvet cap, and a gown made of bright yellow silk, which hung over his hump. Under the gown he wore a grass-green dress, slashed with rose-coloured silk, his knee-bands being of the same material, fastened with enormous rosettes. His head was stuck close between his shoulders, and the red cap, which he carried on it, appeared to belong equally to the hump. It was a great joke of the executioner of Stuttgardt, that of all heads, that of the chancellor Ambrosius Bolland would appear to be the most difficult to cut off.

This was the man who looked up at Albert von Sturmfeder with a courteous smile. He addressed him with smooth words, "Perhaps you don't know me, my much esteemed young friend: I am Ambrosius Bolland, the chancellor of his highness. I come to wish you a good morning."

"I thank you," said Albert; "and esteem it a great honour, if you have put yourself out of your way on my account."

"Honour to whom honour is due! you are the pattern and crown of our young knighthood! Truly, you who have stood by my master so faithfully in his necessity and dangers have a claim to my most inward thanks, and my particular respect."

"You might have bought your compliments much cheaper had you joined us at Mömpelgard," replied Albert, who was offended by the adulation of the flatterer. "There is no necessity to speak of fidelity; it were better to reprove the want of it."

A momentary ray of anger shot from the green-eyed chancellor, but he soon regained his fawning manner. "To be sure, I am of the same opinion. For my part, I was so crippled with gout, I could not travel to Mömpelgard; but now, what little power heaven has left me shall be devoted with redoubled zeal to the Duke's service."

He paused a moment, expecting an answer; but Albert was silent, and eyed him with a glance which he did not well know how to interpret. "Well, but you will now be able to enjoy your prosperity," continued the chancellor; "of course it is nothing more than you deserve, and the Duke has well chosen his favourite. Will you allow Ambrosius Bolland also to acknowledge his sense of your services? Are you an amateur of curious arms? Come to my dwelling in the market-place, and choose what most pleases you out of my armoury. If you are a lover of rare books, I have a whole chest full, much at your disposal, and pray select any you may fancy, as is the custom among friends. Come and dine with me sometimes; my niece keeps house for me, a pretty girl of seventeen years; only I must beg of you--hi! hi! hi!--not to look at her too close."

"Don't be afraid; I am already engaged."

"So? ah, that's acting like a Christian; it's very praiseworthy. It is not always that we find such virtue among the youth of the present day. I was quite certain that Sturmfeder was a pattern of virtue. But what I wanted to say was, that we--being the only two as yet who compose the Duke's court--we must keep together, and not allow any one to be appointed without our consent. Do you understand me? hi! hi!--one hand washes the other. But we can talk over that some other time. You will honour me with a visit sometimes?"

"When my time will allow me, Chancellor Ambrosius Bolland."

"I would willingly remain longer in your society, for your presence does my heart good; but I must now to the Duke. He is going to sit in judgment this morning on two prisoners who tried to excite the people to rebellion against him last night. Who would bet that Beltler was not already appointed."

"Beltler!" asked Albert, "who is he?"

"He is the executioner, most worthy young friend."

"For heaven's sake! the Duke surely will not stain the first day of his new government with blood!"

The chancellor smiled bitterly, and answered: "You do honour again to your excellent heart, but you are not fit to sit in a court of criminal justice. Examples must be made. One of them," he continued, with a soft voice, "will be beheaded because he belongs to the nobility, and the other, being a low fellow, will be hanged. God bless you, my dear friend!"

With these words the chancellor departed, treading with light step the long gallery which led to the Duke's apartment. Albert followed him with a look of contempt and disdain. He had heard that this man formerly, either by prudence, or, perhaps, rather by an unwarrantable exercise of artful cunning, had gained great influence over Ulerich: he had often heard the Duke himself speak of the great confidence he had in his cleverness in state affairs. He knew not why, but he feared for the Duke should he put too much faith in the chancellor, for he thought he could read intrigue and falsehood in his eye.

Just as he saw the hump and flowing yellow cloak turn the corner at the end of the gallery, a voice whispered to him: "Don't trust that yellow-faced hypocrite!" It was the fifer of Hardt, who had stolen to his side unnoticed.

"How! are you there, Hans?" cried Albert, and gladly proffered his hand. "Are you come to the castle to visit us? that's very kind; you are more heartily welcome than that humpbacked knave; but what have you to say of him that I should beware of?"

"He is a false man, and I have warned the Duke not to follow his advice, which made him very angry with me. He puts his whole confidence in him."

"But what did he say? Have you seen him this morning?" asked Albert.

"I went to take my leave of him, for I am going home to my wife and child. The Duke appeared moved at first, spoke of the days of his exile, and asked me to mention any act of grace he could confer upon me. But I merited none, for what I have done for him was only paying off an old debt. I asked him at last, not being able to think of anything else, to allow me the liberty to shoot my fox without being punished as a poacher. He laughed, and said I might do it, but that was no act of grace, I must demand something else. Well, I took courage, and said, I beg of your grace not to put too much confidence in the crafty chancellor, for it is my opinion he is false at heart."

"That's just what I think," cried Albert; "he looked as if he wanted to spy into my most inward thoughts with those green eyes of his; but what answered the Duke?"

"'You understand nothing upon such subjects,' was his reply, and became angry; and added, 'you may be a faithful and sure guide among clefts and caverns, but the chancellor understands state intrigues better than you.' It may be," added the fifer, "that I am wrong in my conjectures; I hope so, for the Duke's sake. So now farewell, sir; may God protect you! Amen."

"Will you really go, and not remain for my wedding?" said Albert. "I expect the knight of Lichtenstein and his daughter here to-day. Stay a day or two longer: you were our messenger of love, and ought not to desert us at this happy moment."

"Of what use can a poor man like me be at the wedding of a knight? I might, indeed, sit among the musicians, and take part in the music in honour of the happy event; but others can do it as well as me, and my house requires my presence."

"Well then, farewell," said Albert; "give my salutations to your wife and Barbelle, and visit us often in Lichtenstein. God be with you!"

A tear filled the eye of the young man as he gave the peasant a hearty parting shake of the hand, for he had always found him an honest trustworthy man, a faithful servant of the Duke, a bold companion in danger, and cheerful society in misfortune. He was about asking many questions concerning the mysterious life which this man followed, for he was particularly curious to know the cause of his extraordinary attachment to the Duke, but he suppressed them out of delicacy to his feelings. The natural greatness of mind which characterised the fifer of Hardt, though he were a common peasant, awed him into silence touching those subjects which his friend had always appeared to wish to avoid.

"But, I have one thing more to say," said Hans, as he was going: "do you know that your old friend and future cousin-in-law, von Kraft, is here?"

"The scribe to the council? how did he come here? he's a Leaguist!"

"He is here, nevertheless, and not in the most agreeable position--for he is in prison. Yesterday evening, when the people assembled in the market place, in consequence of the Duke's arrival, it appears he addressed them in favour of the League."

"Good heavens!" exclaimed Albert, "was that Dieterich Kraft, the scribe? I must go instantly to the Duke, who now sits in judgment upon him, or the chancellor will have his head off. Good bye!"

The young man hurried along the corridor to the Duke's apartment. He had been in the habit in Mömpelgard of having immediate access to him at all times of day, and, therefore, the porter now respectfully opened the door. He entered in a hasty manner, to the astonishment of the Duke, who was somewhat displeased; but the chancellor masked his hypocrisy, as usual, under a smile of mildness.

"Good morning, Sturmfeder," said the Duke, who sat at a table, dressed in a green coat embroidered in gold, with a green hunting cap on his head; "I hope you have slept well in our castle. What brings you thus early to us? we have important business."

The eyes of the young man had in the mean time anxiously looked about the room, and there discovered the scribe of the Ulmer council standing in a corner. He was as pale as death; his hair, which was wont to be combed with great care, hung in disorder over his neck, and a rose-coloured gown which he wore over a black coat was torn to tatters. His eyes met Albert's with a most pitiable look, and he then glanced upwards, as much as to say, "it is all over with me." Near him stood other men: one of whom, tall and meagre, he thought to have seen before. The prisoners were guarded by Peter, the brave Magdeburger, and Staberl of Vienna. They stood at their post with outstretched legs, their halberds resting on the floor, upright as candles.

"I say, we have important business at present," continued the Duke; "but why do you look so intent upon him with the rose-coloured gown? he is a hardened sinner; the sword is being sharpened for his neck!"

"Will your highness allow me but one word," replied Albert. "I know that man, and would stake all I possess in the world, that he is a peaceable subject; and positively not a criminal who deserves death."

"By Saint Hubertus, that is a bold speech! You have changed your nature, methinks: my chancellor, the worthy jurist, has put himself forward like a young warrior; and you, my young soldier, would assume the advocate. What say you to that, Ambrosius Bolland?"

"Hi! hi! I adorned my person by way of letting your highness have a joke, for I know, of old date, you are fond of a little fun; and our dear good Sturmfeder, for the sake of adding to it, plays the part of a jurist. Hi! hi! hi! but all he may say or do, he cannot save him in the rose-coloured gown. High treason! he must lose his head, poor fellow!"

"Mr. Chancellor," cried Albert, glowing with anger, "the Duke can witness, that I was never accustomed to play the buffoon. I don't wish to rival any person in this sort of character; but I never play or make sport with the life of a fellow creature! I am seriously in earnest, when I pledge my life for the noble Dieterich von Kraft, scribe to the council of Ulm, now present before you. I hope my bail will be taken."

"How?" said Ulerich, "is he the elegant gentleman, your host in Ulm, of whom you have often spoke to me. I regret that he committed himself so far as to be taken in the act of creating an insurrection, under very suspicious circumstances."

"Certainly," croaked Ambrosius, "a *crimen lesæ majestatis!*"

"Permit me, sir, to speak," said Albert. "I have studied law long enough to know, that in this case it is absurd to talk of treason. The governor and council of the League were still in the town last night, consequently Stuttgardt was in the power of the enemy, and the scribe, who is in no wise a subject of his highness, did not act differently from any other Leaguist soldier, who takes the field against the Duke by the orders of his superiors."

"Ei, youth, youth! How nicely it accommodates itself to circumstances!" said the chancellor; "but my worthy friend, you must know that so soon as the Duke summoned the town, and had the *animum possidentis*, every thing within its walls belonged to him. Therefore, any conspiracy against his royal person, becomes high treason immediately. The prisoner Dieterich von Kraft held very dangerous language to the people."

"Impossible! it is quite contrary to his manner and principles. My Lord Duke, it cannot be!"

"Albert!" said the Duke in earnest, "we have had much patience in hearing what you have to say; but it can do your friend no good. Here is the protocol. The chancellor had examined witnesses before I came, and every thing is proved as clear as day. We must make an example. The chancellor is perfectly right; therefore I cannot hold out any act of grace in the prisoner's favour."

"But allow me to ask him and the witnesses one question--only a few words," said Albert.

"That is against all forms of justice," said the chancellor; "I must protest against it; it is an infringement on my office."

"Let it be, Ambrosius," said the Duke. "He may ask a question, with all my heart, of the poor sinner, who has no chance of escape."

"Dieterich von Kraft," said Albert, addressing the prisoner, "how came you to be in Stuttgardt?"

The forlorn scribe, whom death seemed already to have made his prey, turning his eyes towards him, his teeth chattering from fear, was scarcely able to mutter a word in answer. "I was sent here by the council of Ulm, as secretary to the governor."

"How was it that you appeared before the burghers of Stuttgardt, yesterday evening?" said Albert.

"The governor ordered me to remind them of their duty and oath, should there, perchance, be an insurrection against the League."

"Don't you perceive, he was only acting under orders?" said Albert, turning to the Duke. "Who took you prisoner?" he continued with the examination.

"The man standing beside you."

"Did you take this gentleman into custody? then you must have heard what he said; what did he say?" said Albert to the man.

"Yes, I heard what he said," answered the burgher; "he had spoken but six words, when burghermaster Hartmann threw him down from the bank. I remember what they were, namely: 'Recollect, my friends, what will the illustrious council of the League say!' That was all, and then Hartmann took him by the collar. But there stands Doctor Calmus, who made a longer speech."

The Duke roared with laughter, first looking at Albert and then at the chancellor, who turned pale, and was so disconcerted, that he could scarcely muster up courage to join in his master's hilarity. "Were those all the dangerous words he spoke--is this the charge of high treason--'What would the council of the League say?' Poor Kraft! These few words have brought your neck within a hair's breadth of the executioner's sword. We have often heard our friends say, 'What will folks think, when they hear the Duke is in the country again?' therefore, I will not punish him. What think you of it, Sturmfeder?"

"I know not what reason you could have had," said Albert, addressing the chancellor, with anger beaming in his eyes, "to have pushed the case to such lengths, and advised the Duke to these harsh measures; which, instead of healing past grievances, would only cause the cry of 'tyrant' to be raised everywhere against him. If you have acted from an overheated zeal of duty, you have this once surpassed the bounds of discretion."

The chancellor was silent, and satisfied himself by throwing a furious glance at the young man. The Duke stood up, and said, "You must not blame my little adviser for his zeal in my cause, which has perhaps made him act with too much severity in this instance. There, take your rose-coloured friend with you, give him a glass to expel his ghastly fear, and then let him go wherever he will. And you, dog of a doctor, as for you, who are not worthy of the title of dog doctor, a Würtemberg gallows is too good for you. You will be hung one of these days, so I will not give myself the trouble to do it at present. Long Peter, order your men to bind that fellow on an ass, with his face to the tail, and lead him through the town, and thence let him be sent to Esslingen, to his wise counsellors, to whom he and his beast belong. Away with him!"

The features of the wretched doctor, who had hitherto sat in fear of death, soon cheered up by this happy change in his fate; he breathed more freely, and made a low bow. Peter, Staberl, and the Magdeburger, laid hold of him with savage joy, hoisted him on their broad shoulders, and bore him away.

The scribe of Ulm shed tears of joy, and, impelled by gratitude, wanted to kiss the Duke's cloak; but he turned away, and waved to Albert to withdraw his friend.

CHAPTER XXIX

Stop! stay thy hand, and hear my prayer,--
Ah, do not let it be:
You cannot, must not, will not dare
A deed unworthy thee.

Schiller.

The scribe of the grand council of Ulm did not appear to have sufficiently recovered from his state of terror to answer the many questions his preserver put to him as they passed along the passages and galleries. He trembled in all his limbs, his knees shook, and he often looked back with a feeling of apprehension, lest the Duke should have repented of his act of grace, and the unmerciful chancellor in the yellow gown should sneak after him, and suddenly pounce upon him. Having reached Albert's apartment, he sank exhausted in a chair, and it was some time before he could collect his thoughts to be able to answer his friend.

"Your politics, cousin, had well nigh played you a sorry trick," said Albert; "but what possessed you to set yourself up as a popular speaker in Stuttgardt? And, above all, how could you think of quitting your comfortable establishment in Ulm, the assiduous care of your old nurse Sabina, and fly the vicinity of the charming Marie, to come here in the service of the governor?"

"Ah! she it was who sent me into the jaws of death; she is the cause of all my trouble. Ah! that I had never left my dear Ulm! All my misfortunes began with my first step over our boundary."

"Did Marie persuade you?" Albert asked; "have you not succeeded in the object of your desires? Has she discarded you, and did you out of desparation--"

"God forbid! Marie is as good as my bride; that's my calamity. When you left Ulm, I had a dispute with Mrs. Sabina, the nurse which determined me to demand Marie's hand of my uncle. I was accepted; but, the girl's head being completely turned by your military mania, nothing would satisfy her but that I must first encounter the dangers and hardships of a campaign, and become a man like you. Not until then would she marry me. Oh, merciful Heaven!"

"So now you are formally in the field against Würtemberg? What a bold spirit that girl has!"

"Yes, I am in the field; I shall never in my life forget what I have gone through! My old John and I were obliged to march with the army of the League. What pain and trouble? often compelled to ride eight hours a day. My dress was disordered, everything full of dust and filth; my coat of mail squeezed me to death. I could stand it no longer; and as old John ran back to Ulm, I asked for a place as writer on the staff, hired a litter and two stout horses to carry my baggage, which made my case more bearable."

"Then you were carried into the field like dogs to the hunt," said Albert. "Have you been in an action?"

"Oh! yes; at Tübingen, I was in the thick of it. Not twenty paces from me a man was killed as dead as a mouse. I shall never forget the fright I was in, if I live eighty years. After we had perfectly subdued the whole country, I was appointed to the honourable situation of secretary to the governor in Stuttgardt. We lived quietly, and in peace, until the restless Duke returned once more to disturb us. Oh! had I but followed my own wish, and joined the representatives of the League at Nördlingen! but I feared the fatigue of the journey."

"But why did you not depart with the governor when we arrived? He is now quietly seated in Esslingen, until we hunt him out of it."

"He deserted us shamefully," said Kraft; "and intrusted everything to my head, which has nearly suffered for it. I had not the least idea the danger was so imminent, and allowed myself to be seduced by Doctor Calmus to speak to the people, and warn them against breaking their oath to the League. Had I but succeeded, it would have made a noise in the world, and I should have stood high in Marie's estimation. But the Würtembergers are barbarians, and void of all decent manners. They did not even let me say a word, but threw me down, and treated me like a common vagabond. Just look at my cloak, it is torn to tatters! I regret it, for it cost me four gold florins, and Marie maintains that rose colour becomes the complexion of my face to perfection."

Albert scarcely knew whether to laugh at the folly of his friend the scribe, or admire the stoical composure with which he lamented his torn gown, when he had but a moment before narrowly escaped losing his head. He was going to ask some other questions about his adventures, when an extraordinary noise was heard under the window in the open space before the castle; he looked out, and beckoned to Dieterich von Kraft to come and witness a spectacle of fallen greatness.

Doctor Calmus was being paraded through the town. He was seated on an ass, with his face towards the tail. The lansquenets had dressed him out in a ridiculous manner, with a painted leather cap, at the top of which was stuck a large cock's feather. Two drummers led the procession, on either side, the Magdeburger, Staberl of Vienna, the late Captain Muckerle, and the brave general, marched with solemn pace, every now and then pricking the animal with the ends of their halberts to quicken his pace. An immense crowd of people swarmed around him, pelting him with eggs and mud.

The scribe looked down upon his unfortunate companion in distress with pity, and sighed, "It's hard to be obliged to ride upon an ass in that fashion, but it's better than being hanged." He turned from the scene, and looked towards another side of the square. "Who comes here?" he asked the young knight; "that's just the kind of thing I went to the field in."

His friend looked round, and perceived a train of travellers with a litter in the middle. An old man on horseback brought up the rear of the party, which now moved towards the castle. Albert observing them more closely, cried out, in wild joy, "It's them! it's them! it is her father, and she is in the litter!" One spring took him out of the room, to the great astonishment of the scribe. "Who can it be? what father?" said he. He returned to the window, and looking out, he saw the cavalcade stop on the drawbridge, and in the same moment his friend fly through the gate. Dieterich then observed him to open the door like a madman, a lady in a veil stepped out of the litter, and when she threw it back, to his great surprise he recognised his cousin Bertha von Lichtenstein. "But only see; he kisses her in the public street," said the scribe to himself, shaking his head, "I have never seen such joy before! But, alas! there goes the father to the litter; what angry eyes he will make! how he will stamp and swear! but no, he nods kindly to my friend; he dismounts, he embraces him.--Well, that's very curious, I must say!"

The scribe could scarcely believe his eyes, and to convince himself that he was not deceived, left the room, and went into the gallery, where he perceived the old knight of Lichtenstein coming up the stairs, leading Albert by his right hand, and Cousin Bertha by the left. He thought a great alteration for the better had taken place in her beautiful features, since the time they had made such a deep impression on his heart, and still lived in his recollection.

He had seen her for the first time in Ulm, when she appeared to him like a messenger from a fairy land, so dignified was the expression of her eyes, majesty sat upon her brow, and her whole countenance bespoke a mind far above the common stamp of mortals. The scribe had often puzzled his mind in the attempt to unravel the mystery by which she had gained such influence over him. The damsels of Ulm possessed perhaps cheeks fresher and more plump, eyes more lively, a more attractive smile, and perhaps greater brilliancy of youth. But there was a something in Bertha which he could not account for, which inspired him with awe. Was it the dark eyelashes, which, like a veil, fell over her eyes, and concealed the starting tear? Was it the delicately compressed lip, upon which was encamped the expression of painful grief? or the rapid change of colour upon her features, which appeared to betray suffering of some acute feeling--perhaps of love? Marie's cheerfulness, her easy manners, a certain art of teasing, which imparted life and good will to all around her, had long since driven her cousin's image from his heart; but now that he came again in contact with the influence of the lady of Lichtenstein, poor Dieterich von Kraft felt all his old wounds bleed afresh. What was the power which worked in so different a manner upon his feelings was a question beyond his comprehension. Though there was the same dignity, the same expression, which commands the respect and admiration of the beholder, her eye was now animated with placid joy, a pleasing smile played on her lips, and her cheeks bloomed with unalloyed happiness. Dieterich von Kraft had made these observations in speechless astonishment, when the old knight first noticed him. "Do my eyes deceive me?" he cried, "Dieterich von Kraft, my nephew! What brings you to Stuttgardt? Perhaps you come to the wedding of my daughter with Albert von Sturmfeder? But how you look! What's the matter with you? How pale and miserable your whole appearance, and your clothes hang about your body all in rags! What has happened?"

The scribe eyed his rose-coloured gown in despair and dismay, and blushed; "God knows!" he said, "I am ashamed to shew myself before any decent person. These cursed Würtembergers, these vine-dressers and contemptible shoemakers, have mangled me in this way. Verily, and in truth, the whole illustrious League has been attacked and insulted in my individual person!"

"You ought to be thankful, cousin, that it was no worse," said Albert, as he led the travellers into his apartment; "only think, father, last night, when we stood before the gates, he was exciting the burghers to rebellion against us, for which the chancellor wanted to have his head this morning. It was with very great difficulty I could persuade the Duke to pardon him; and now he complains of the Würtembergers having torn his cloak."

"With your gracious permission," said Mrs. Rosel, the old nurse, and curtsied three times to the scribe, "if my assistance is agreeable, I'll mend the gown, so that you shall not know it has been torn. The proverb says,

'If the young man his new gown has torn,
The old woman can mend it fit to be worn.'"

Dieterich von Kraft accepted the offer with many thanks. He retired to a window with old Rosel, when she pulled out of her large leather pocket all the necessary articles for the purpose of repairing his damages. She entertained him upon the inexhaustible subject of housekeeping, particularly upon the important science of dressing certain dishes not to be found in Mrs. Sabina's catalogue of cookery. At a distance from this couple, at the other end of the room, sat Bertha and Albert, engaged in the confidential whisperings of love. Neither Johannes Thethingerus, nor Johannes Bezius, neither Gabelkofer nor Crusius, though we have to thank them for much important information of old times, have mentioned what these two lovers had to say to each other on that morning. Thus much we know, however, that satisfaction rested upon Bertha's features, expressive of her joy at the near approach of the happy moment to complete her union with Albert.

The reader will thank us if we lead him from a scene of so little historical interest, and of which every one is supposed to know more or less, to follow the path of the knight of Lichtenstein. Having left his daughter to the care of Albert, and his nephew to the ingenious hand of Mrs. Rosel, he himself repaired to the apartment of the Duke. Age had imprinted on his countenance an air of gravity, which at this hour appeared to have received an additional stamp of painful thought, amounting almost to despondency. This man had inherited his love for the house of Würtemberg from his ancestors. Habit and inclination had bound him to the sovereigns who had presided over Würtemberg during the course of his long life. The misfortunes and calumnies which, had been heaped upon Ulerich, had not had the effect of shaking the faithful heart of the old man in the Duke's cause. On the contrary, they tended only to draw the ties of friendship tighter. With the joy of a bridegroom who hastens to the wedding, and with the strength and vivacity of youth, he undertook the long and fatiguing journey from his castle to Stuttgardt, when he heard the Duke had taken Leonberg, and had advanced to the capital. Having entertained no doubt of the Duke's success, he was not deceived in his calculation, and he arrived at Stuttgardt the morning after the establishment of the new authority.

The news which Albert imparted to him as they proceeded up stairs, was not calculated to excite the joy of the old man. "The Duke," he whispered to him, "the Duke does not appear to be inclined to act with prudence; God knows what his intentions may be respecting the government of the country, for he let fall some extraordinary sentiments on the road, which I fear will not be improved in the hands of his chancellor, Ambrosius Bolland." The mere mention of this name was sufficient to raise great uneasiness in the breast of the knight of Lichtenstein. He was acquainted with Bolland; and though he knew him to be expert, and particularly well versed in state affairs, and capable of executing any intricate piece of service, yet he was a man who had often played a deep, if not a false game. "Should the Duke give his confidence to this man, and follow his council, may God be merciful to him! The country is a mere bit of parchment in the eyes of Ambrosius, to be turned and twisted according to his whim. He'll know how to shape and fashion it preparatory to meeting the Duke's eye; but he'll keep the pen in his own hand. But, as old Rosel would say, 'Any fool can cut out; the art is to sew the garment together.'" Thus thought the knight of Lichtenstein, in passing along the gallery. He seized his long white beard in anger; whilst his heart beat with zeal in the cause of Würtemberg.

He was immediately admitted to the presence of the Duke, whom he found in deep; consultation with Ambrosius. The latter was seated, holding a large swan's pen in one hand and a parchment in the other, which was written over with black, red, and blue ink, in many neat columns. The Duke was playing with a piece of sealing wax, which he held in his hand; and appeared in a state of indecision, first casting a penetrating glance at the chancellor, and then looking at the wax, as if it were destined to seal some important document. They were both so deeply immersed in their occupation, that Lichtenstein stood some minutes in the room, contemplating with intense interest the noble features of the Duke, without being remarked. The various sensations which were agitating him were plainly visible upon his countenance and in his expressive eyes. The frown upon his forehead, giving place in rapid succession to a milder expression, bespoke a mind hesitating between an act of severity and one of grace, whilst his companion, presenting him with the pen which he held in his hand, sat before him like the tempter. He turned and moved about like the serpent; and the eternal hypocritical smile, which his little green eyes could with ease convert into the expression of humility when his master looked at him sharply, appeared to urge him to taste the forbidden fruit.

"I cannot comprehend," said the chancellor with an insinuating tone of voice, "why your Grace will not do it! Did Cæsar hesitate to pass the Rubicon? A great man must use strong measures. The present age and futurity will laud your courage in having burst asunder the chains which now bind your hands."

"Are you so sure of that, Ambrosius Bolland?" replied the Duke, with a look of doubt. "Will it not be said, Duke Ulerich was a tyrant: he abrogated the old order of things, which was held sacred by his forefathers; and, having broken the contract which he himself established, treated his country as an enemy, and trod under foot the laws which----"

"Permit me," interrupted the other: "the only question is, who is to be master--the Duke or the country? If the country is to govern, the case is different; for then pacts, contracts, clauses, and such like, are necessary. The nobles, clergy, and commons, would be the masters, and your grace--a mere cypher; but if you hold the reins in your own hand, and wield your own will unrestricted, from that moment you become the source of all law. The sword is now in your hand,--you are lord and master; therefore, away with the old law--here is a new one--take the pen, and, in God's name, sign."

The Duke remained some time in doubtful suspense, agitated between conflicting struggles of conscience. At length, as if impelled by some evil genius, he said, "Am not I Würtemberg itself? the country and laws are concentrated in my person--I will sign!" He stretched out his hand to receive the pen from the chancellor, when he felt his arm arrested. He looked around in surprise, and met the placid but stern eye of the knight of Lichtenstein.

"Ha! welcome, my faithful Lichtenstein; I will be ready to speak with you instantly, only let me sign this parchment."

"Allow me, your grace," said the old man: "having promised me a voice in your council, may I look at the first ordinance which you are about to issue to your country."

"With your most noble permission," said Ambrosius Holland, hastily, "delay were dangerous: the citizens of Stuttgardt are already assembled, and it is requisite to read the proclamation without loss of time."

"The thing is not so very pressing, after all," said the Duke, "that we cannot impart the contents to our friend. We have accordingly determined," he added, addressing Lichtenstein, "to administer a new oath of fidelity, making the people swear allegiance to us, under a fresh contract and different laws. The old ones are null and void from henceforth."

"Is that your determination?" replied the knight of Lichtenstein; "and have you maturely considered what will be the consequences of this act? Did you not swear but a few years ago to the Tübingen compact?"

"Tübingen!" cried the Duke with a terrible voice, his eyes flashing the fire of indignation; "Tübingen! mention that word no more! In that vile city were centred all my hopes, my country, my children,--ha! and on that spot was I betrayed and sold. I begged, I implored them to hold out to the last; I was ready to share my property, my blood with them in its defence; but no! they would not hear of Ulerich, nor listen to his voice. They preferred the new order of things; they suffered me to linger in the misery of banishment, and caused the name of Würtemberg to become the contempt and derision of all the world. But now that I am lord and master again, with my sword in my hand, I'll not allow it to be wrenched a second time from my grasp. If they have forgotten their oath, by Saint Hubertus, my memory is also equally treacherous. The Tübingen compact, did you say? May dire necessity confound every thing connected with that name!"

"But recollect, your grace!" said Lichtenstein, staggered at this burst of passion; "think of the impression such a step will make throughout the country. At this moment you have only Stuttgardt and its neighbourhood in your possession; whereas Urach, Asperg, Tübingen, and Göppingen, have all Leaguist garrisons. Will the country people; stand by you to drive them out, when they become acquainted with the new ordinance to which they are to swear allegiance?"

"I maintain it," said the Duke; "did the country stand by me when I was forced to turn my back upon Würtemberg? No! they saw me hunted down like a wild beast, and sided with the League!"

"Pardon me, my Lord Duke," replied the old man; "but that is not the case. I recollect well that day in Blaubeuren. Who held to you on that occasion, when the Swiss deserted you? who implored you not to leave the country? who offered to sacrifice their lives in your cause? It was eight thousand Würtembergers! Have you forgotten that day?"

"Ay-ay! most worthy sir," said the chancellor, who was aware what an impression these remarks were likely to make on Ulerich; "ay! but that's nothing to the purpose. Besides, we have not to legislate upon what took place at that time, but upon the actual state of affairs. The country has completely absolved itself of the former oath, by swearing allegiance to the usurpations of the League. His grace is now to be considered in the light of a new Lord, having subdued the country by force of arms; and, therefore, as the League instituted their own peculiar measures, the Duke has a right to follow their example. A new Lord gives new laws. He has the privilege at all times to govern according to his own will and pleasure. Shall I dip the pen in the ink, gracious sir?"

"Sir Chancellor!" said Lichtenstein, with a determined voice, "though I have all possible respect for your learning and foresight, you advance that which is positively false, and your counsel is dangerous. The question now is, to ascertain who it is that the people love. The League, by their violent measures, have estranged the public mind from them; this was therefore precisely the most favourable moment for the Duke to appear in the country, for all hearts are with him; but if you repel the good feeling of the people by insidious measures, if you attempt to destroy the ancient laws and institutions, and build upon their ruins your own invented constitution, oh, beware! beware of the consequences, and remember that the love of the people is the only powerful support upon which you can rely."

The Duke stood with folded arms, deep in thought, and made no answer. With so much more warmth did the chancellor reply: "Hi! hi! hi! where did you concoct that pretty little speech, my most worthy and highly honoured sir? Love of the people, did you say? The Romans, in their day, knew very well what that meant. Nothing but soap bubbles, soap bubbles! I thought you possessed more acuteness. To whom does the country belong? Here! here stands Würtemberg, personified in the Duke! it belongs to him, he has inherited it; and besides which, he has now conquered it. The people's love? Bah! it resembles April weather! Had it been so strong as you talk of, would they have sworn allegiance to the League?"

"The Chancellor is right!" cried the Duke, starting from his thoughtful mood. "You may mean well, Lichtenstein, but this once you are in the wrong. It was my forbearance which caused me to be driven from my country; now that I am returned, they shall feel that I am the master. The pen, Chancellor;--I say, it's my will and pleasure, and they shall obey!"

"Oh! my Lord!" said Lichtenstein, "do not commit yourself in the heat of passion: wait till your blood cools. Assemble the states, make any alterations in the constitution you may think proper--only not at this moment--not as long as the League possesses a foot of land in Würtemberg. This rash act may prejudice your cause. Consent to a short delay."

"Indeed!" interrupted the chancellor, "and let them by degrees come round to the old state of things? Do you suppose, when once the representatives are assembled and talk over their affairs, they will concede to your reform with good will? Hi! hi! force will be requisite to compel them, and that's what will create hatred. Strike the iron whilst it's hot. Or is it your grace's pleasure, to stand again humbly under the yoke, and be forced to bend to circumstances?"

The Duke did not answer, but snatching the pen and parchment impatiently out of the chancellor's hands, cast a hasty and penetrating look, first at him and then at the knight, and, before the latter could hinder him, signed his name. Old Lichtenstein remained in speechless consternation; his head sunk over his breast. The chancellor glanced a triumphant look at him and at the Duke. Ulerich seized a silver hand-bell, which was on the table, and rang violently. A page entered, and asked his commands.

"Are the citizens assembled?" asked the Duke.

"Yes, your grace! they are assembled on the meadow near to Cannstadt. Six companies of the lansquenet also are moving in that direction."

"The lansquenet! Who ordered them?"

The chancellor trembled when he heard this last question. "It was only for the sake of keeping order," said he, "I thought of it, because in such cases it is generally the custom to have armed men by way of precaution----"

The Duke waved to him to be silent. An expression in the look of the knight condemnatory of this rash act, met the Duke's eye, and caused him to blush. "It has been done without my permission," said he; "but----if we now recall them, it would create suspicion. However, it is of no great consequence. Bring me my red cloak and hat;--quick!"

The Duke stept to the window, and looked out in silence. The chancellor appeared uncertain whether his master was angry or not, and did not venture to speak; whilst the knight of Lichtenstein continued wrapt in deep anxious thought. They remained some time in this state, until the entrance of attendants interrupted the silence. Four pages entered the apartment, one carrying the cloak, another the hat, a third a gold chain, and the fourth the military sword of the Duke. They robed him in his ducal mantle of purple velvet, trimmed with ermine. His hat was then presented to him, carrying the black and yellow colours of the house of Würtemberg in rich waving plumes, bound together by a clasp of gold, set in precious stones, the value of which was worth a seigniory. The Duke covered his head with his hat. His powerful figure appeared more dignified in this dress than it did before, and his open majestic forehead, with his brilliant eye sparkling from beneath the flowing feathers, inspired awe in those around him. He desired the pages to place the gold chain over his neck; then, buckling on his sword, gave a sign to the chancellor to follow.

The knight of Lichtenstein still uttered not a word. He had observed these preparations with a troubled countenance, and turned away from the scene. The Duke made a slight inclination of the head to his old friend as he passed him in going towards the door, followed by the strange figure of the Chancellor Ambrosius Bolland, who strutted with magisterial step. He did not think it necessary to salute the old man, his master not having done so, but satisfied his malice by casting a crafty triumphant look at the spot where he was standing, accompanied by a scornful smile, which played about his toothless mouth. The Duke stopt on the threshold of the door, and, looking back, his better nature appeared to get the mastery of him; he returned to Lichtenstein, to the astonishment and confusion of the chancellor.

"Old man, and faithful friend," said he, trying in vain to conceal a deep emotion which agitated him, "you were my only friend in my troubles, and I have experienced your tried fidelity on a hundred different occasions,-- proofs sufficient to convince me of your attachment to Würtemberg. I feel this step the most important of my life, and, perhaps, the most hazardous; but where the stake is high we must risk the more."

The knight of Lichtenstein raised his venerable head, with tears in his eyes. He seized Ulerich's hand, and said, "Remain, for God's sake! follow my advice only this once! My hair is grey,--I have lived long, and known and loved you since your thirteenth year." At this moment the drums of the lansquenet sounded in the courtyard, the impatient stamping of horses echoed through the vaulted halls, and the heralds blew their trumpets to proclaim the taking the oath of fidelity.

"Jacta alea esto! was Cæsar's motto," said the Duke, with animated countenance. "I am now going to cross my Rubicon. But give me your blessing, old man,--advice is too late."

The knight cast his eyes around, evidently suffering from intense agony; his voice refused utterance to his feelings, and he pressed the Duke's right hand to his heart in token of bestowing his blessing. The chancellor, observing a momentary hesitation in the Duke to quit his friend, stretched forth his long withered arm from under his cloak, and pointed to the roll of parchment. He looked like the tempter who had succeeded in dragging another victim after him in chains. Ulerich von Würtemberg tore himself away, and went to hear the oath of allegiance administered.

CHAPTER XXX

No furnace ever blazed so bright,
Nor glow'd the burning brand
With half so powerful a light,
As love of fatherland.

An old popular Song.

The apprehensions of the knight of Lichtenstein were not so totally void of foundation as Ambrosius Bolland had represented them to be. A large portion of the country had, indeed, joined the Duke, arising partly from, the predilection of the people in favour of the hereditary house of Würtemberg, but in a great measure from the oppressions of the League, who had forcibly compelled them to submit to their rule. Many were, at first, induced to join his standard, and declare for Würtemberg, when they heard that victory followed Ulerich's path; but the new oath of allegiance, by which all ancient laws were to be abrogated, and the report that the refractory were to be compelled by force to subscribe to these forms, had the effect, at least, of not adding to the Duke's popularity,--a defect, in such doubtful undertakings as the present, often felt too late to be remedied. Urach, Göppingen, and Tübingen were still in the hands of the League, having powerful garrisons in each. Dieterich Spät, the Duke's bitterest enemy, was established in Urach. He recruited so many men in a few days, that he not only kept his district in subjection, but was enabled to make incursions into the country which had submitted to the Duke. The report was also spread that the assembly of the League at Nördlingen had separated, each member hurrying home to re-organize a fresh army to meet Ulerich a second time in the field.

The Duke, in the meanwhile, appeared nowise concerned in the midst of the unsettled state of the country. Ambrosius Bolland was his sole counsellor, with whom he transacted business with closed doors. Many messengers were observed to arrive and depart, but no one could learn what was going on. Judging from the Duke's cheerful mood, it was thought in Stuttgardt that affairs were in a prosperous state; for when he rode through the streets, followed by a brilliant suite, saluting all the pretty females, and joking and laughing with his attendants who rode by his side, every one said, "Duke Ulerich is as merry as he was before the days of 'the Poor

Conrad insurrection.'" He established his court in its former magnificence. Though it was no longer the point of reunion of the Bavarian, Swabian, and Franconian counts and nobles, nor the gay assemblage of princesses who formerly attracted such a splendid train of blooming beauties around them, there was still no lack of handsome women and gay-dressed knights to adorn his court. The atmosphere of the town appeared also to impart additional lustre to the beauties of Stuttgardt at that time, for, when they congregated in the saloons and halls of the castle, the assembly had more the character of a select choice of the fairest belles of the land than one of ordinary occurrence.

The dance and tournament were re-established in all their former spirit. Feast followed feast in such rapid succession that Ulerich seemed to wish to make up for the time he had lost in the misery of banishment. Not the least of these gay doings was the wedding of Albert von Sturmfeder with the heiress of Lichtenstein.

The old knight was some time before he could make up his mind to put his promise into execution, not that he had any objection to the choice of his daughter, for he loved his future son-in-law with the affection of a father; he even felt his younger days revive again as it were in his own person, and could not forget the disinterested sacrifice Albert had made in sharing the exile of the Duke; but, like as the horizon of Ulerich's affairs was enveloped in darkness, so was the old man's brow clouded by anxious misgivings, apprehensive lest circumstances should not long remain in the state they were. He was deeply hurt also that the Duke, who gave his confidence exclusively to the crafty chancellor, did not admit him to his council in the many weighty matters now in agitation. Indecision and anxiety of mind, had caused him to put off the day of joy; but, moved by the expressive eyes of his daughter, in which he thought to read a gentle reproach, and the entreaties of Albert, he at last consented to their importunities, and fixed a day, to which the Duke acquiesced; but would allow of no one making the necessary arrangements for the wedding but himself. Amidst the success which had hitherto attended him, Ulerich did not forget those nights when old Lichtenstein proved his attachment to him by his assiduous attention to his wants, and when the delicate frame of his daughter braved storm and cold to receive him at the gate of the castle, and prepare warm food to cheer him when he came from the cavern. Neither was the sacrifice which the bridegroom had made for his sake obliterated from his memory. His noble mind was fully alive to the fidelity, love, and sacrifices they had each so fully manifested, and, therefore, he wished to prove his sense of gratitude to them. The knight and his daughter had hitherto been his guests at the castle. He now completely furnished a house for them near the collegiate church, and, on the evening before the nuptials, he delivered the key of it to the lady of Lichtenstein, begging her to make use of it whenever she came to Stuttgardt.

The day at length arrived,--a day which Albert had once thought far distant, but to which his most longing desire had ever been, constantly directed. When he rose on that morning he recalled to his mind all the circumstances which had happened to him since his heart had been engaged, and was astonished to think how differently things had come to pass to what he could have at first imagined. Who would ever have supposed, when he rode through the beech wood towards his home, that the happiness of possessing his beloved Bertha was not so distant as he then had reason to fear? When he joined the League's army, in opposition to the Duke, the very last thing that could have entered his mind would have been that this same man, his enemy at that time, should be the instrument of completing his happiness! He could now contemplate in cheerful serenity the agitations of those days when he, with difficulty, stole a moment to whisper a word to his beloved for fear of her father, the avowed enemy of the League, And he thought of that hour in Marie's garden, the most painful he had ever experienced, when he took leave of Bertha, thinking she was lost to him for ever, whereas this day was to bind them eternally together. Every word she had ever spoken to him rushed to his recollection,--he was wrapped in admiration of her firm trust in Providence, who she was persuaded would order all things to work for their good. Though at that time their hopes, their prospects, were veiled in a dark uncertain futurity, she did not despond, but inspired her lover with courage when they took their parting embrace.

The train of these thoughts was interrupted by a modest tap at the door;--it was Dieterich von Kraft, who entered the room, dressed in his very best.

"How?" cried the scribe of the grand council of Ulm, and clasped his hands in astonishment,--"How? I hope you do not intend to be married in that jacket. It is nine o'clock already; the passages and stairs of the castle swarm with wedding guests, shining in silks and satins, and you, the principal performer in the piece, are looking unconcerned out of the window, instead of preparing yourself for the happy event?"

"There lies the whole concern," replied Albert, smiling, and pointing to his dress on the bed, "cap and feathers, mantle and jacket, all of the best quality and make; but God knows, I have not yet thought of hanging the tawdriness on my back. This jacket which I have on is dearer to me than all the rest; I have worn it in worse times, but still in very happy days."

"Yes, yes! I know it well; you wore it when you were with me in Ulm, and I don't forget how jealous Marie made me when she described it to me in glowing terms. But do you call that new dress tawdry? By Jove, I should be happy to possess such smart things the rest of my life! Only look at this white vest, embroidered in gold, and the blue velvet mantle: I have never seen anything more brilliant! truly, your choice has been made with great taste, and the dress matches the colour of your hair to perfection."

"The Duke presented me with it," said Albert, beginning to dress himself; "it would have been much too expensive for my slender finances."

"The Duke is really a splendid man; and now for the first time since I have been here do I perceive that we were too hard upon him in Ulm. There is some difference between life in such a city as this and that in our town. The court of the Duke of Würtemberg sounds much grander than the townhall of Ulm. Still I would not like to be in his skin; you'll see, cousin, his fortunes will go down-hill again with him."

"That's the burden of your old song, Dieterich: do you recollect how big you talked about your politics at that time in Ulm, expatiating how you intended to govern Würtemberg? How stands the case now?"

"Well, has it not turned out as I said?" replied the scribe, with a sagacious look; "I recollect, as if it were but yesterday, that I prophesied the Swiss would return home; that we should gain the hearts of the country people, and that the citizens would open the gates to us."

"Yes, yes! and you helped to accomplish all this," laughed Albert, "when you were carried to the field in a litter: but you also prophesied that the Duke would never be able to return to his country, and now you see he sits quietly and unmolested in his castle."

"Not so quiet as you may think. For your sake and his, I wish with all my heart he may hold his country. The war has done me no good, for the great men take everything for themselves, only leaving us subordinates the honour of having our heads cut off in the cause of the League. But though I wish him success, believe me, his affairs are not in the prosperous state you imagine. The governor and council who fled to Esslingen upon your arrival have petitioned the Emperor and Empire for assistance; the League is again in motion; and a fresh army is already assembling at Ulm."

"All talk,--nothing else," replied Albert; "I know for certain, that a reconciliation may take place between the Duke and Bavaria."

"Yes; but there is a great difference between *may* and *will* take place: thereby hangs many a difficult crotchet to unravel. But what do I see? you are not going to put that old rag of a scarf over your new wedding dress? they will not match together, my dear cousin."

The bridegroom regarded the scarf with a look of intense interest. "You don't understand," he replied, "why I set such a value upon it. It was Bertha's first present; she worked it secretly by night, in her room, when the news came that she was soon to leave Tübingen. It was my only consolation when I was absent from her, and therefore I will not fail to wear it on the happiest day of my life."

"Well, do as you please, in God's name, wear it! And now put on your cap, and be quick with the mantle, for they are beginning to ring the bells of the church. Beware of making the bride wait too long!"

The friendly scribe stood before the young man again, and minutely examined his dress with the eye of a connoisseur. He drew a buckle a little tighter here, he altered a plait of his mantle there, raised a feather of his cap higher, and having satisfied himself that nothing was wanting to adorn the person of the bridegroom, he thought his tall, manly figure, his fine head, and animated eye, were worthy the love of his pretty cousin. "I declare," said he, "you look as if you were created especially for a bridegroom. I would like Marie to see you now; poor girl, she would certainly be troubled with giddiness for a week! But come, come; I feel proud in being your companion upon this occasion, though I shall be fourteen days later in Ulm than I ought to be."

Albert blushed,--his heart beat quicker,--when he left the room. Joy, expectation, the fulfilment of year-long wishes assailed his feelings, as he followed his friend Dieterich through the galleries to the apartment where the assembled company awaited his arrival. The doors opened,--and Bertha stood in all the brilliancy of her beauty, surrounded by many women and maidens, whom the Duke had invited to form the nuptial procession.

When she perceived her lover enter the room, and met his glance, modest confusion spread a deep blush over her features, as she returned his salutation. The intoxicating joy of this moment would have led Albert to impress a morning salute of love upon her lips, but he was restrained by the strict manners of the times upon such occasions to observe a serious distant demeanour. A bride, according to etiquette, was not permitted to touch the hand of the bridegroom before the priest had joined them together, nor were they allowed to approach each other within six paces. To look even exclusively at her future husband before the ceremony was performed was deemed indecorous. She observed, therefore, the precise rule of remaining with cast-down looks, modest and demure, with her hands crossed before her. Such were the customs of the olden times of the country.

To any other person in a similar situation, the position in which she stood might have imparted to the beholder a stiff and awkward appearance;

but as nature endows her choicest daughters under all circumstances, whether in grief or joy, with a charm of interest which attracts even the most superficial observer, so did Bertha, on the present occasion, give to the restrained attitude of a bride in those days, an ease and grace which elicited the admiration of the surrounding spectators. The soft blush which rested on her features, the smile playing about her delicate-formed mouth, the brilliancy of her dark blue eyes, shooting their rays through the dark long eyelashes, like the rising sun dispersing the morning mist, formed a picture of unaffected loveliness, fit for the pencil of the artist.

The Duke entered the room, leading the knight of Lichtenstein by the hand. His eye rapidly passed through the circle of ladies, and he decidedly gave to Bertha the palm of beauty. "Sturmfeder," said he, taking him aside, "this day rewards you for many services. Do you recollect that night, when you first visited me in the cavern, and did not know who I was? Hans, the fifer, gave us a toast, 'the lady of Lichtenstein, long may she bloom for you!' she is yours now, and what is not less true, the toast you gave is also fulfilled, for we are again established in the castle of our fathers."

"May your grace enjoy your prosperity as long as I hope to be happy by the side of Bertha. But I am indebted to your interference and kindness for this day, for without it her father perhaps----"

"Honour for honour!" interrupted Ulerich: "you stood by us faithfully when we first set out to reconquer our country, and therefore we have assisted you in gaining possession of your best wishes. We will represent your father this day; and as such you will not refuse us to kiss your beautiful wife on the forehead after church."

Albert thought of that night when he was concealed behind the gate of Lichtenstein, and overheard the Duke's conversation with his love. It ended by his promise to remind her of his claim to a salute on this day, to which she would not consent then. "Where you please," he replied, "on her lips, if you prefer it, my Lord Duke; you have long since merited it by your generous intercession."

"Who is to accompany you to the altar?" said the Duke.

"Maxx Stumpf and the Ulmer scribe, a cousin of Lichtenstein."

"What, that smart little fellow, whose head my chancellor wanted to have off? Well, then, on your left you'll be supported by the most elegant of men; and on your right by the bravest in all Swabia. I wish you joy, young man; but take my advice, and lean to him on the right, rather than to the other; for if you have him for a friend, you need fear nothing in the world, even if you were as jealous as a Turk. But here comes the right one," he added, as the knight entered the room; "look how his broad sturdy figure shews among the crowd; and how splendidly he has dressed himself! He wore that old faded green mantle at our wedding with Sabina Lobesau, A.D. 1511."

"I don't understand much about dress," replied the brave knight of Schweinsberg, catching the Duke's last words, "neither do I know much about dancing, so you will excuse me; but if the bridegroom will break a lance with me this evening in a tilt, I am his man!"

"So you want to break a couple of his ribs out of pure tenderness and courtesy," said the Duke, laughing: "that's what I call a bridegroom's companion of the right sort. But stop, Albert; I would advise you to hold to your left-hand companion now, for the Ulmer will do you no harm."

The folding doors were at this instant thrown open; when the persons composing the Duke's court were seen stationed along the galleries. Pages of honour led the procession, carrying long burning wax candles, followed by a brilliant train of noble dames and maidens, who had been invited to the ceremony. They were clad in rich stuffs, embroidered in gold and silver, each carrying a large nosegay in one hand and a lemon in the other. The bride was led between George von Hewen and Rheinhardt von Gemmingen, followed by a numerous body of knights and nobles, with Albert von Sturmfeder in the middle, having Maxx Stumpf on his right, and the scribe to the Ulmer council, Dieterich von Kraft, on his left. His whole bearing appeared to be animated by a spirit of elevated joy, his eyes beamed with happiness, and his step was that of a conqueror. His flowing hair, and the waving plumes of his cap, were conspicuously prominent above the heads of those surrounding him. The crowd beheld him as he passed with admiration, the men praising his tall, manly figure and noble gait; and the young girls whispering to each other their remarks upon his fine features and brilliant eyes.

The procession proceeded in this way from the gate of the castle to the church, passing through a broad open space which separated them. The close-packed heads of the worthy citizens of Stuttgardt were all on the stretch to get a sight of the bride and bridegroom as they passed, who, judging by the murmur of applause and admiration which followed them into the church, were flattered by the reception they received.

Among the numerous spectators, a sprightly, plump countrywoman and her daughter seemed particularly anxious to get a sight of the happy. couple. The woman kept curtseying every moment, to the great amusement of the surrounding citizens, who had only paid this attention to the Duke and the bride. She kept up an earnest conversation with her daughter at the same time, who, however, did not appear to heed much what she said. Neither did she seem to be interested in the train of females with their rich dresses, her anxiety being simply to get a glimpse of the bride. As she approached, the young girl's cheeks assumed a deeper red; her red bodice rose and sunk violently, her beating heart appearing likely to break the silver chain with which it was laced. She looked stedfastly at Bertha, and was apparently surprised at the transcendant beauty of the bride, which caused her an involuntary deep sigh. "That's her!" she cried, with peculiar emphasis, hastily concealing her face behind her mother from the gaze of the people about her, who looked astonished at her exclamation.

"Yes, that's her, Barbelle; she is wonderful pretty," whispered the round matron to her daughter, and made a low curtsey; "but now look out for the gentleman."

The girl did not appear to require that piece of advice, for her attention had been long directed to the side whence he was to come. "He comes, he comes!" she heard her neighbours say, "that's him in the white vest and blue mantle, just before the Duke." She saw him; one look only did she dare to cast at him; the blush on her cheek vanished; she trembled, and a tear fell upon her red bodice. When he had passed, she ventured to raise her head again, and look towards him; but it was with an expression of countenance that appeared to indicate more than mere admiration or curiosity.

The procession having by this time entered the church, the spectators crowded to the doors to get in; and in a moment the place which they had occupied was empty. The countrywoman, however, still remained looking at the smart dressed townsfolks, in admiration of their brocade caps, jackets embroidered in gold, and short petticoats. The sight of so much finery awakened in her mind the desire of possessing a dress of the same splendour and shew, only she thought she would not have it cut so low about the neck and shoulders.

Upon turning round, she was startled to see her pretty child concealing her blooming face under her hands. She could not conceive what had happened to the girl; and taking her by both hands, and pulling them down, she observed her weeping most bitterly: "What ails you, Barbelle?" she said, somewhat angrily, but still not without interest, "what makes you cry? did'nt you see him? you ought to be ashamed of yourself! Who ever saw the like? I say, why do you cry?"

"I don't know, mother," she whispered, trying in vain to stop her tears; "I have such a pain in my heart, I don't know why."

"Come, adone with it, I say! or we shall be too late in the church. Hark! how they are playing and singing? Come along, or else I'll not look at you again!" With these words she dragged the girl towards the church. Barbelle followed; and covered her eyes with her white apron, lest the townsfolk should laugh at her. But the deep sighs which she was unable to suppress, made people think she was labouring under some acute suffering. The sounds of the organ and chorus of voices ceased just as they arrived at the entrance of the church. The round matron was aware that the marriage ceremony was now to begin, and therefore endeavoured to push her way through the crowd; but in vain, for as often as she thought to squeeze her plump person into the body of the church, she was sure to be pushed back again with abusive words.

"Come, mother," said the girl, "let's go home. We are poor people, they'll not let us in; come away."

"What? the church is made for every one, poor or rich!" said her mother, indignantly; "make a little room, if you please, we can't see any thing!"

"What?" said the man, whom she addressed, turning to her his well-tanned face, with an immense bushy beard, "what! away with you! we'll not let any one pass. We are his most gracious highness's lansquenet; and our captain has ordered us not to let one soul of you go up to the holy altar. *Morbleu!* I am sorry to swear in the church; but I say, away with you!"

Staberl of Vienna, who was on the spot, interceded for the little girl, but would not consent to her mother entering the church. "Come here, my dear," he called her, "you can see very well here. There; now the priest is putting the ring on her finger, and joins their hands. If you will give me a kiss, I'll get you a better place;" and with these words, without waiting for an answer, he stretched out his hand towards Barbelle. She screamed aloud, and ran away, followed by her mother, who vented imprecations on townsfolk in general, and the unmannerly lansquenet.

CHAPTER XXXI

At last I hold thee in my arms,
My best beloved, my own!
Bestowed on me from war's alarms,
Preserved for me alone.

L. Uhland.

Duke Ulerich of Würtemberg was fond of a good table, and when the glass circulated freely in good society, he was not the first to give the signal to break up. At the wedding feast of Bertha von Lichtenstein he remained true to his habits. When the ceremony was finished in the church, the procession returned to the castle much in the same form as it entered, except that the bride and bridegroom walked hand in hand. The company then separated, and wandered about the pleasure-garden of the castle, where they amused themselves among the shrubberies and artificial walks, some looking at the deer and roebucks in the inclosures, others admiring the bears in the dry ditches. At twelve o'clock the trumpets sounded to dinner, which was held in the tournament-hall, a place large enough to entertain many hundred people. This hall was the pride and ornament of Stuttgardt. It was full an hundred paces long; one side of it, looking to the garden, was occupied by numerous large windows, through which the cheerful rays of the sun, piercing the many-coloured glass, illumined this immense apartment, which, by its vaulted roof and numerous pillars, resembled more the interior of a church than a place for festive joy. Galleries extended round the three other sides, hung with rich tapestry, a space being appropriated to the musicians and trumpeters, whilst spectators, assembled to witness the princely feast, occupied the remainder. On other occasions, such as when a tournament took place, these galleries were set apart for the ladies and judges; when, instead of the clang of drinking utensils, the hall resounded with the applauses of the spectators, the heavy blows of swords, the cracking of lances, the whizzing of spears, amidst the laughter and cries of the combatants.

On this day a display of beautiful women and gallant men of all classes had been invited to celebrate the nuptials of the Duke's friend and favourite. They were seated around tables which groaned under loads of good cheer.

The fiddlers in the galleries flourished their fiddlesticks merrily; the cheeks of the trumpeters were swelled to the fullest stretch; the drummers' sticks beat heavily on their skins; and the spectators who were admitted in the other part of the galleries, joined chorus with shouting and hallooing when the company drank a toast. At the upper end of the room sat the Duke upon a throne, under a canopy. His hat was pushed off his forehead, he looked around him with an air of satisfaction, and did not spare the bottle. On his right, at the side of the table, sat Bertha, who was no longer obliged to submit to the ceremonious restraint of cast-down eyes, and keeping at a respectable distance from the bridegroom. Her glance and the expression of her features bespoke happiness. She looked at her husband, who sat opposite to her, and she could scarcely convince herself her being actually a wife was not all a dream, and that the name she had borne eighteen years was changed to that of Sturmfeder. She smiled as often as she regarded him, for it appeared to her that he had already assumed the direction of her conduct. "He is my head," she said to herself, playfully, "my lord, my master!"

And her thoughts were really verified, for Albert felt all the importance and responsibility of his new position in society. It seemed to him as if the young people already paid him more respect than heretofore, and that the old knights treated him more upon an equality since he had become the head of a family, and stood no longer alone in the world. The notions in the good old times were somewhat different to those in the present day respecting the marriage state, for the designation of nobles and citizens was invariably supposed to include that of wife and children, leaving the state of celibacy to monks alone.

The knight of Lichtenstein, Maxx Stumpf von Schweinsberg, and the chancellor, were seated near the Duke, and the scribe to the Council of Ulm was not far from them, being allowed that honour in consequence of his having been the companion of the bridegroom at the wedding. The eyes of the men soon began to sparkle from the effects of the wine, and the cheeks of the ladies to assume a deeper red, when the Duke gave a signal to his headman, and the dinner was removed. The poor people were not forgotten on this occasion; as was always the case on similar rejoicings, the remains of the dinner were taken to the court yard of the castle, and delivered over to them. Pastry and fruit were next brought in, and the wine jugs were replenished by a better sort of the generous liquor for the use of the men, whilst Spanish sweet wine was served to the ladies in small silver cups. This was the moment when, according to the customs of the time, presents were presented to the new-married couple: large baskets were placed beside Bertha to receive them, and when the fiddlers and other musicians had re-tuned their instruments, and began a solemn march, a long brilliant procession moved forward in the hall. Pages of honour led the train, carrying embossed gold tankards and female ornaments of jewelry, as gifts from the Duke to the happy couple.

"May these tankards," said Ulerich, addressing them, "filled with generous liquor, circulate at the marriage feast of your children, and remind you of a man whom both of you served with truth and fidelity in his misfortune, of a Prince who in prosperity forgets not his faithful friends."

Albert was astonished at the value of the presents. "Your Grace's generosity overpowers us," he replied; "love and fidelity claim no reward but the approval of conscience, else they would be too often the price of venality."

"Yes, truly, unless they spring from a source unadulterated by the alloy of all selfish motives, they are but pearls fit only to be thrown to swine," replied the Duke, casting a look of reproof down the length of the table. "We rejoice the more, therefore, to reward your disinterested fidelity, when all seemed to be lost to us. But look, your bride is in tears! I think I know their cause; they are produced by the remembrance of our late painful fate, which I have now recalled to her mind. But away with these tears; they are unpropitious to the day of your wedding. With permission! of your husband," said he, turning to Bertha, "I will now claim payment of an old debt."

Bertha blushed, and cast an anxious look at Albert, fearing the repetition of a liberty which had once highly offended her. He, however, well knew what the Duke meant, for the scene which he had witnessed behind the door was still fresh in his recollection. Amused with the idea of rallying the Duke and his wife upon the subject, he said, "My lord Duke, my wife and I being now one body and one soul, she has my permission to liquidate the debt which I know she owes you."

"Answered as a fine young fellow," returned Ulerich, goodnaturedly; "and I have no doubt that many of our ladies here at table would have no objection to require payment of a similar debt from your handsome mouth; but my demand being addressed solely to the rosy lips of your wife, it refers to her alone."

With these words, he rose and approached Bertha, who looked at her husband in a state of confusion and agitation. "My lord Duke," she said, in a low tone of voice, and holding her head away, "I meant it only in joke--I beseech you!" But Ulerich would not be deterred from his purpose, and wrung his debt with interest from her pretty mouth.

The knight of Lichtenstein during this scene looked angrily, first at the Duke and then at his daughter, fearing his son-in-law might perhaps take umbrage at the liberty, as Ulerich von Hutten had done in a similar case. The chancellor appeared to enjoy a malicious pleasure upon the occasion, at the expense, as he thought, of the young man's feelings. "Hi! hi! hi! I'll empty my glass to your good health," said he to him. "A pretty woman is an excellent petitioner in necessity; I wish you prosperity, dear and most worthy sir;--hi! hi! hi! there is no harm done in the presence of the husband."

"No doubt of it," replied Albert, calmly; "and so much the more innocent because I was present when my wife promised his Grace this proof of her gratitude. The Duke himself proposed to intercede for us with her father to make me his son-in-law, stipulating for this reward on the day of our nuptials."

The Duke started in surprise at these words, and Bertha blushed again, when she thought of the scene which had occasioned the promise. Neither of them, however, contradicted him, deeming it perhaps unseemly, or rather impossible, to charge him with an untruth, or, what was more likely, suspecting they had been overheard.

The Duke could not forbear asking him aside how he came to know the circumstance. Albert acquainted him with it in a few words.

"You are a strange fellow," whispered the Duke, smiling; "what would have been the consequence had I committed the trespass?"

"As I did not know you at that time," replied the other as softly, "I should have run you through on the spot, and hung your body on the nearest oak."

The Duke bit his lips and felt annoyed; but he took his friend's hand, and said, "You would have been perfectly justified, and we should have been justly carried off in our sins. But look, they are bringing more offerings to the bride."

The attendants of the knights and nobles who had been invited to the wedding, appeared, carrying all kinds of curious household utensils, stuffs for wearing apparel, and such like. It being known in Stuttgardt that the feast was given in honour of the Duke's favourite, an embassy of burghers, worthy respectable men, dressed in black, with swords by their sides, short hair and long beards, had been appointed to offer their presents and congratulations upon the occasion. One carried an embossed silver goblet, another a large jug of the same metal ornamented with inlaid medallions and filled with wine. They first approached the Duke in great respect and bowed, and then turned to Albert von Sturmfeder.

The man who bore the goblet, having saluted the bridegroom with a cheerful smile on his countenance, said:

> May joy attend the wedded pair,
>
> And bliss increasing be their share!
>
> Accept this gift from Stuttgardt's town,
>
> And length of days your union crown.
>
> 'Tis generous wine that cheers the soul,
>
> So come, my comrade, fill the bowl.

The other burgher then filled the goblet with wine from the jug he carried, and whilst his companion drank it out, pronounced:

> A cask full stands before your door,
>
> The best of Stuttgardt's wine in store;
>
> And force of body, strength of soul,
>
> Lie deep within the brimful bowl:
>
> Then drain the cup and find them there,
>
> So Stuttgard has obtained her prayer.

Having finished his draught, and replenished the goblet, he repeated the following lines:

> Be this your toast when you carouse,
>
> "Long live the Duke and all his house."
>
> Drain to the dregs, then, fill the wine,
>
> "To Sturmfeder and Lichtenstein;"
>
> And may we hope that, as you drink,
>
> You will on Stuttgardt's burghers think.

Albert gave the men both his hands and thanked them for their acceptable presents; Bertha saluted their wives, and the Duke also received them graciously. They laid the silver jug and the goblet in the basket along with the other gifts, retiring respectfully and with solemn step out of the hall. But the burghers were not the only ones to tender their congratulations and manifest their regard for the Duke, in this marked attention to his favourite. Scarcely had they taken their departure, when a disturbance was observed at the door where the lansquenet were on guard, which attracted the notice of the Ulerich. Men's voices were heard swearing and ordering the crowd to obedience to their commands, among which were mingled the voices of women, and one in particular the loudest and most violent was recognized by some of the company at the upper end of the table.

"I declare that is the voice of our Rosel," whispered old Lichtenstein to his son-in-law: "what can her business be about?"

The Duke despatched one of his pages to find out the cause of the noise, and received for answer that some countrywomen were trying to force their way into the hall to present their gifts to the new married couple in spite of the lansquenet, who would not permit them to enter, only because they were common people. Ulerich gave orders immediately to admit them, for, having been pleased with the conduct of the burghers, he promised himself some amusement from the peasants. The attendants having made room for them to pass, Albert, to his astonishment, recognized the wife of the fifer of Hardt, and her pretty daughter, led by her cousin, Mrs. Rosel.

When he was passing from the castle to the church, he thought he recognised the lovely features of the girl of Hardt among the crowd; but more important considerations having engrossed his whole attention, this fleeting apparition was obliterated from his mind. He acquainted the company who the women were, and to whom they belonged. The girl excited great interest, from her being the child of that man whose marvellous actions in the service of the Duke had often been a subject of mystery, and whose fidelity and assistance in time of need contributed essentially to Ulerich's return to his country. The girl had the fair hair, the open forehead, and much the same features of her parent; but the sharp cunning eye, the bold and powerful bearing of the father, were softened into a playful kindliness and natural gaiety which shed a charm around the retiring modesty of his child. As such Albert had known her, when he was in the fifer of Hardt's house, but she now appeared disconcerted before so many persons of rank; it struck him also that her countenance betrayed dejection and sorrow, feelings he had not discovered before on her beautiful features.

Her mother, knowing what good manners were, courtesied all the way up from the entrance door till she arrived at the Duke's chair. The blush of anger still rested upon the wan cheeks of Mrs. Rosel, who felt herself highly aggrieved and insulted by the lansquenet, namely by the Magdeburger and Casper Staberl, who had called her an old withered stick. Before she could compose herself, and present the family of her brother in respectful form to her master, the fifer's wife had already taken the hem of the Duke's mantle and pressed it to her lips. "Good day, my Lord Duke," she said, with deep reverence, "how are you since you have been in Stuttgardt? my husband sends you his compliments. But we don't come to the Duke, no, it is to the knight there," she added, as if recollecting herself, pointing to Albert; "we have brought a wedding present for his wife. There she sits, Barbelle, as large as life."

Mrs. Rosel, confounded at the unceremonious conduct of her sister-in-law before such an august audience, checked her loquacity by saying, "I most humbly beg pardon of your grace, for having brought these people here,--they are the wife and daughter of the fifer of Hardt; pray do not take it ill, your highness, the woman means well, I assure you."

The Duke was more amused with the excuses of Mrs. Rosel than with the blunt language of her sister. "How is your husband?" said he to the countrywoman, "will he visit us soon? why did he not come with you?"

"He has his reasons, sir," she replied; "if war breaks out, he'll certainly not stay at home, for then he may be of some use; but in peaceable times, why he thinks it is not becoming to eat cherries with great folks."

The naïveté of the plump matron almost drove Mrs. Rosel to desperation: she pulled her by the petticoat, and by the long tails of hair, but to no purpose. The wife of the fifer went on talking, to the great amusement of the Duke and his guests, whose irresistible laughter, which her answers elicited, appeared only to increase her happiness and good humour. Barbelle in the meantime, playing with the handle of a little basket she held in her hand, scarcely ventured occasionally to raise her eyes to look at that face which she had beheld with such tender sympathy when she nursed Albert during the long period of his fever. The impression which those days had left on her mind still remained in all its vigour, and the sight of him who had unawares made an inroad into the recesses of her heart, made her fearful of meeting his eye. She heard him say to his wife, "That is the kind girl who nursed me when I lay ill in her father's house, and who conducted me part of the way to Lichtenstein."

Bertha turned to her, and took her hand with great kindness. The girl trembled, and her cheeks assumed a deep blush. She opened her little basket, and presented a piece of beautiful linen, with a few bundles of flax, as fine and soft as silk. She attempted in vain to speak, but kissing the hand of the young bride, a tear fell upon her nuptial ring.

"Eh, Barbelle!" scolded Mrs. Rosel, "don't be so timid and nervous. Gracious young lady,--I would say gracious madame,--have compassion on her; she comes but seldom into the presence of quality folks. There is no one so good who has not two dispositions, says the proverb; the girl can be otherwise as merry and cheerful as larks in spring."

"I thank you, Barbelle," said Bertha: "your linen is very acceptable and very fine. Did you spin it yourself?"

The girl smiled through her tears, and nodded a yes! to speak at that moment appeared to her impossible. The Duke liberated her from this embarrassment only to place her in another still greater. "The fifer of Hardt has truly a very pretty child," he cried, and beckoned to her to approach nearer, "well grown and lovely to behold! only look, chancellor, how well the red bodice and short petticoat become her. Could not we, Ambrosius Bolland, issue an edict for all the beauties in Stuttgardt to adopt this neat dress?"

The chancellor's countenance became distorted into a hideous smile: he examined the blushing maiden from head to foot with his little green eyes; and said, "Certainly, a very good reason could be given, by which an ell might be spared in the length of petticoats, for, as your grace a few years back ordered the weights and measures to be reduced, you have also the right, by all the rules of logic, to shorten the dress of females. But nothing would be gained by it, for--hi! hi! hi! you would see that what was cut off from the bottom, our beauties would be obliged to add above. And who knows whether the ladies would willingly agree to that? They belong to the genus of peacocks, who, you know, don't like to shew their legs."

"You are right, Ambrosius;" the Duke laughed; "nothing escapes a learned man! But tell me, my dear, have you got a sweetheart?"

"Ah! what? your grace!" interrupted the round matron, sharply. "Who would talk about such like things to a child! She is a very good girl, your highness."

The Duke paid no attention to this remark; he enjoyed the embarrassment which was visibly manifest in the chaste features of the innocent girl, who sighed softly, and, playing with the ends of the coloured ribands of her plaited hair, sent an involuntary look to Albert, which seemed to claim his kind offices in her present perplexity, and then suddenly cast her eyes down to the ground. The Duke, alive to every thing that was passing, laughed aloud, in which he was joined by the rest of the men. "Young woman," he said to Bertha, "you may now with justice take part in the jealousy of your husband; if you had seen what I just saw, you might imagine and interpret all kind of things."

Bertha smiled, and, sympathising with Barbelle in her embarrassment, felt how painful the taunts of the men must be to her. Whispering to old Rosel, she told her to take the mother and daughter away. The Duke's sharp eye remarked this also, which his merry mood attributed to jealousy on the part of Bertha. She however unclasped a beautiful cross, set in gold and red stones, which she wore on her neck, attached to a chain, and presenting it to the astonished girl, said, "I thank you with all my heart, my dear Barbelle, for your kindness to my husband; remember me to your father, and come often to us here and in Lichtenstein. What say you, would you like to be in my service? I would endeavour to make you happy, and you would live with your aunt Rosel."

The girl was evidently perplexed at this unexpected proposal. She appeared to combat her feelings, and an assent to it seemed to be struggling through an innocent smile on her countenance, only to be withdrawn again by some other contending feeling. "I thank you very much, gracious lady," she at last uttered, and kissed Bertha's hand, "but I must stay at home; my mother is getting old and wants my assistance. May the Lord, with all his saints, watch over you, and the holy Virgin be gracious to you! May you live in health and be happy with your husband; he is a good, kind gentleman!" Bending down again to kiss Bertha's hand, she then withdrew with her mother and aunt.

"Hearken," called the Duke after them, "if your mother ever consents to give you a husband, bring him to me, and I'll fit you out, my pretty fifer's child!"

By this time it was four o'clock, and the Duke rising from table was the signal for the spectators to quit the galleries, which were immediately furnished with cushions and carpets, and arranged for the reception of the ladies. The tables were removed from the body of the hall, when lances, swords, shields, helmets, and the whole apparatus for tilting were brought in, converting this spacious apartment, which had been but a moment before the scene of festive joy, into a place for the exercise of manly games.

In the present day the education of the fair sex gives them a superior claim to intellectual knowledge and accomplishment over those of the times we narrate. The interest they now take in learned discussion and political argument, and the thirst for novelty which induces many to crowd the rooms of the scientific lecturer, would seem, in some instances, to intrude on the more important duty of domestic employment. Not so was the time of the Swabian matrons and young women occupied. The charge of the house was their sole vocation; but, upon occasions such as the present, their delight was to witness the manly exercise of men, whose bloody strifes were even not unwelcome to their sight. Many a beautiful eye flashed with the noble desire of belonging to a brave combatant. Deep blushes adorned many a cheek, not so much from the fear of seeing her beloved in danger as to witness his retreat from the scene of action, when it was attended with disgrace, or when his arm wielded his sword less powerfully than his antagonist.

Horses were even brought into the hall on this evening, and Bertha had the joy to see her husband obtain a second applause for having made George von Hewen stagger two different times in his saddle. Duke Ulerich von Würtemberg was the bravest combatant of his day, and an ornament to the order of knighthood. History relates of him that, on the day of his own wedding, he overthrew eight of the strongest knights of Swabia and Franconia.

After the tilting had lasted some time, the company adjourned to the hall of the knights for dancing, when the victors of the different games had the precedence in the ball, in all respects similar to the one we have already described. The Duke appeared to have pinned all anxiety and care of the future upon the hump of his chancellor, who sat in a window like a demon of evil destiny, looking upon the surrounding scene with bitter smiles. Raging under an envious feeling of spite, by being debarred from joining in the pleasures of the evening in consequence of the deformity of his person, he remained in his position in sullen silence.

At the end of the last dance Ulerich, the crown of the feast, proposed a parting toast to the young and beautiful bride, but neither he nor Albert could find her in any part of the room. The whisperings and smiles of the ladies betrayed the secret of her having been led away by six of the handsomest maidens, who accompanied her to her dwelling, and, as the custom of those days would have it, to perform the mysterious services of waiting maids.

"Sic transit gloria mundi!" said the Duke, smiling; "but look, Albert, your nuptial companions, with twelve others, are approaching with torches to illumine your path home. But first empty a goblet with us. Cupbearer, go bring us some of our best," he added, addressing the attendants.

Maxx Stumpf von Schweinsberg and Dieterich von Kraft now drew near with torches in their hands, and offered themselves to conduct Albert to his house. Twelve young men followed, each with a torch, to do honour likewise to the bridegroom, for that was also the ceremony used on such occasions. The Duke's cup-bearer brought a full goblet of wine, when having, according to custom, first tasted it himself, he presented it to his master, and then to Albert von Sturmfeder.

Ulerich looked at his friend for a time, evidently moved by a feeling of affection for him. "You have kept your word," said he: "when I was deserted by all the world, dwelling in misery under the earth, you made yourself known to me, when those forty traitors surrendered my castle, and not a spot of Würtemberg was left that I could call my own. You followed me out of the country,--you often consoled me and pointed to this day. Remain, my friend, for who knows what the next day may bring forth. I can now command hundreds who will cry, 'Long live Ulerich!' nevertheless, that shout is far less dear to me than the toast which you gave me in the cavern, and which was re-echoed through its vaults. I'll repeat it, and give it you back again. May you live happy with your wife,--may your offspring blossom and prosper for ever,--and may Würtemberg never fail in hearts as bold in prosperity and faithful in adversity as yours has proved itself!"

The Duke drank, whilst a tear glistened in his eye. The guests cheered and shouted his praise,--the torch-bearers arranged themselves in order,-- and Albert von Sturmfeder, led by his two companions, and followed by the rest, was conducted in procession out of the castle to the house of his bride.

CHAPTER XXXII

Hast thou not seen by times the cloudless sky
Sudden illumined by the lightning flash,
And its still, still silence, broken horribly
By the loud music of the thunder crash?
To this we might man's happiness compare,--
To day 'tis present, and to-morrow----where?

Schiller.

The path which the most celebrated novelists of our days generally tread, in their relation of events of ancient and modern times, may be found without the aid of any beacon, and has a direct and fixed limit:--it is the journey of a hero going to a wedding. Let the road be ever so rugged, let him even venture to loiter his time improvidently and inconsistently on his way, he will be induced in the end to hasten his steps so much more rapidly to redeem the lost ground; and so, when an author has at length conducted his reader to the bridal chamber, after having made his hero undergo all the necessary fatigues of his journey with becoming fortitude and resolution, he shuts the door in your face, and closes the book. We might in the same way have ended our story with the gay doings in the castle of Stuttgardt, or included the reader in the torchlight procession of the bridegroom, and conducted him out of our book; but the higher claims of truth and history, together with the interest we have taken in some of the leading characters, compel us to request the reader's patience to accompany us a few steps further, beyond the limit of the bridal-chamber. He will have to bewail with us the destiny of one, who, having begun his career in the midst of misfortune, progressively advanced towards the completion of his best wishes by the energy of his noble mind, until at length his impetuous spirit hurled him again into the depths of misery. His headstrong obstinacy had well nigh involved all his friends in his own sad fate: one alone of them, whose sense of gratitude had indissolubly attached him to the fortunes of his benefactor, preferred rather to risk his life in his service than to desert him in the hour of distress.

Nature's warning voice, which teaches us to be prepared against a reverse of fortune in our happiest days, runs through the world's history.

It is acknowledged by the many, unheeded by the majority, and followed by the few. In all times a troubled spirit has pervaded the habitations of our earth; and, though its influence has been often felt, man has vainly thought to deaden it in the noise of mirth. Ulerich von Würtemberg had heard this warning voice many a night, when he lay on his couch sleepless from a troubled mind. Often times he had started up, thinking he heard the noise of armed men, or the heavy tread of an army approaching nearer and nearer the spot; and, though he convinced himself it was but the night breeze playing through the towers of his castle, a fearful impression still haunted his mind, that his fate was destined to some other awful change. The warnings of his old and tried friend Lichtenstein would often whisper its voice to his mind; in vain he sought to smother it by calling to his aid the artful advice of his chancellor, by which he tried to palliate his own conduct and quiet his conscience. But that faithful monitor upbraided him with having acted without due circumspection and caution since his return to his capital. His enemies, it was well known, had re-assembled a powerful force, with which they threatened the country, and were approaching into the heart of Würtemberg. The imperial town of Esslingen presented itself as a very favourable starting point for their undertakings; being but a short distance from the capital, nearly in the centre of the country: as soon, therefore, as the army of the League could open its communication with it, it became a formidable stronghold, to favour and cover their incursions into Würtemberg. The country people in many places received the Leaguists favourably, for the Duke, by his new regulations, which he had made them swear to, had rendered them distrustful of his intentions. The Würtembergers, from time immemorial, being attached to ancient customs and privileges, handed down through successive generations, regard their old laws and ordinances as so many golden words, though they may scarcely understand their import, or seldom consider whether some reform would not be advantageous.

The peaceable character of the peasant, generally so universal throughout the country, fostered by the tranquil occupations of domestic and agricultural affairs, would lead to a supposition that political strifes were subjects indifferent to their minds; but it was far otherwise: on the occasion of any change or reform in the usages of their ancient laws and customs, which interfered with their ideas of government, they manifested an obstinate caprice, with an ardour and enthusiasm quite out of keeping, and foreign to their ordinary inoffensive dispositions.

The Duke had experienced this love of old institutions in his people, when he some few years back, by the advice of his council, for the purpose of bettering his finances, made an alteration in the public weights and measures. An organised insurrection of peasants, entitled, "The League of Poor Conrad," had made him reflect, and caused the Tübingen compact, which restored the old law, to be introduced. This feeling of attachment to long standing habits was also manifested towards him personally in a very touching manner, when the League entered the country with the intention of expelling the head of the ancient house of their prince. Their fathers and grandfathers having lived under the sway of the Dukes and Counts of Würtemberg, they were filled with dismay and consternation, when a foreign army entered their country to deprive them of their hereditary prince. Their hatred and revenge was excited against the League and their governors; and, though they were compelled by force to submit to their rule, they proved their love to their Lord in many instances of violence towards his enemies.

When their hereditary prince, therefore, a Würtemberger, first returned from exile, the people flocked around him, under the impression that affairs would go on as heretofore. Under his sway they were willing to pay the taxes, to redeem all the state debts, and perform the service done in soccage. There was no murmuring about hard treatment, provided it was done according to ancient usage, and by their legitimate master. But now, the old laws having been expunged by the new oath of fidelity to which they were called upon to swear, the taxes being no longer levied according to old custom, and the whole system being changed, it was no wonder that the people looked upon the Duke as a new master, foreign to their habits, and loudly demanded a return to former rights. They consequently lost all faith in him; not because his hand lay heavier upon them than heretofore; not because he required considerably more from their purses than formerly, but because they regarded the new order of things with a suspicious eye.

A prince, particularly when he lends his ear to such a man as Ambrosius Bolland, seldom learns the true tone of public opinion, and therefore cannot judge whether the measures which his council place before him have been wisely considered. In the present instance, however, the discontent of his people did not escape the penetrating eye of the Duke. He remarked, that he could no more depend upon them, in the event of an extreme difficulty, than he could upon the nobility of the country, who, since his return, had remained neutral spectators of the state of affairs.

He endeavoured to screen from public notice the uneasiness which these observations caused him; and for this purpose he assumed an extravagant tone of gaiety, which often succeeded to blind himself, and make him forget the precipice upon which he stood: and for the sake of instilling confidence into the people, and into the army which he had assembled in and about

Stuttgardt, he determined to revenge himself with double interest upon the League, for the depredations they had committed in excursions from Esslingen. He beat and repulsed them indeed, and wasted their territory; but when he returned in victory from his expedition, he could not conceal from himself, that, considering his own slender resources, the fortune of war might go against him, when once the army of his enemies should be brought into the field. His apprehensions were soon verified; for the rapid advance of the League's troops towards the capital threatened the stability of Ulerich's present doubtful position. Upon the turn of a battle, which now seemed inevitable, depended his very existence.

Little or nothing was known in Stuttgardt of a summons which had been sent to the Duke from the League. The court lived in its usual round of gaiety; tranquillity and joy reigned in the town; when all of a sudden, on the 12th, of October, the lansquenets which the Duke had encamped near Cannstadt, a short distance from the capital, came into the town in confusion, with the intelligence that they had been driven in by a large force of the League. The inhabitants of Stuttgardt were now convinced that an important crisis was at hand; they conjectured that the Duke must long since have been aware of this threatening attack, for he immediately assembled his officers, drew in his troops, which were scattered about in quarters in the villages surrounding the capital, passed his army in review, amounting to upwards of ten thousand men, on the same evening; and in the night marched with a large body of infantry, to reinforce the posts which a division of the lansquenet still occupied between Esslingen and Cannstadt.

The departure of all the men, young and old, who could carry arms, caused many a beautiful eye to weep that night, when they marched out of Stuttgardt with the Duke, to the field of battle; but the wailing of the women and young maidens was drowned in the warlike noise of the marching army, resembling the sobs of a child amidst the raging of the elements. Bertha's grief, though almost overpowering, was silent, as she accompanied her husband to the door, where his servants awaited him and her father with their horses. They had enjoyed the first days of their marriage alone and in quiet, mutually engaged in the affectionate offices of each other's happiness. Dreaming little of the future, they thought themselves safe in the haven of uninterrupted love; and whilst they lived but for themselves, the whisperings, the mysterious disquietude which agitated the public mind, were unheeded by them. Having been long accustomed to see the knight of Lichtenstein serious and thoughtful, they did not attribute the alteration which his features had of late assumed, to any cause beyond the natural anxiety he was known to feel in the present state of the Duke's affairs. Neither did they, for the same reason, apprehend any immediate disaster to disturb their happiness, although they remarked a certain air of fearful anticipation and despair which at times clouded his brow. The old man witnessed the happiness of his children, and participated in it; and, not wishing to interrupt their bliss unnecessarily, he concealed from them his uneasiness upon the state of affairs; but at length the threatening crisis approached. The Duke of Bavaria had advanced into the heart of the country, and the call to arms startled Albert out of the embrace of his beloved wife.

Nature had gifted her with a strength of mind, and a superiority of character, which entered into every transaction of her life, and exists only in that purity of soul which commits its dearest interests into the hands of a higher Power, with implicit confidence. Aware of what was due to the honour of her husband's name, and the relationship in which he stood to the Duke, she repressed her grief, and the only sacrifice which the infirmity of her nature offered for the many dangers to which her beloved husband would necessarily be exposed, was an involuntary flood of tears.

"I cannot believe, dearest Albert, that we are never to see each other again!" she said, whilst a forced smile illumined her beautiful face: "we have but just begun to live; heaven will not cut us off in the bud of a happy existence; I can, therefore, part from you in tranquillity, in the conviction that you will soon be restored to me."

Albert kissed her soft weeping eye, which dwelt upon him so full of tenderness, and whose glance inspired him with consolation and fortitude. In this distressing moment he thought not of the danger he was going to encounter, his only concern was the consideration of the affliction of the beloved being he held in his arms, should he be left on the field of battle. The mere thought of the painful existence she would then lead in solitude, and in the remembrance of the few days of their bliss, unmanned him. He pressed her in his arms, as if to drive away these agonizing ideas from his mind; he gazed with intense love upon her endearing eye, seeking to obliterate the heart-rending feelings of the moment; but his heart, though rent by the afflicting struggle of separation, was inspired with hope and confidence. He at length forced himself from her embrace.

The two knights joined the Duke at the gate leading to Cannstadt. The night was dark, only enlivened by the dim light of the first quarter of the moon and the host of stars. Albert observed the Duke to look gloomy, and wrapped in deep thought. His eyes were cast down, as if to avoid observation, and he rode on in profound silence, after he had saluted them hastily with his hand.

There is something peculiarly solemn and striking in the night march of an army. By day, the sun, a cheerful country, the sight of many comrades, the change of scenery, invite the soldier to beguile time by conversation and the merry song; and, because outward impressions forcibly engage the attention, little is thought among them of the object of the march, of the uncertainty of war, or of futurity, which is veiled to no one more than to the military man. Very different is a march by night. The hollow sound of the tread of the troops, the regular pacing of horses, their snorting, the clatter of arms, only break the stillness of night, whilst the mind, no longer able to dwell on surrounding objects, impressed by these monotonous sounds, becomes thoughtful and serious; joking and laughter cease to cheer the march, loud talk sinks into whispering, and thought, no longer occupied with indifferent subjects, is taken up with speculations upon what is likely to be the result of the campaign.

Such was the complexion of the march of that night, gloomy, and uninterrupted by any shout of animating joy. Albert rode by the side of the old knight of Lichtenstein, occasionly casting an anxious look at him, for he sat in his saddle as if bent down by grief, with an expression of thoughtfulness on his countenance, more strongly marked than he had ever noticed before. Animation seemed almost suspended, and nothing gave indication of life in him, but an occasionally deep-drawn sigh, or when his keen eye was raised in contemplation of the pale moon.

"Do you think we shall have a skirmish tomorrow?" whispered Albert to him, after a time.

"Skirmish!--we shall have a battle," was the short answer.

"How! do you really believe that the army of the League is strong enough now to attempt to stand its ground against us? It's impossible! Duke William must have possessed wings to have brought up his Bavarians so soon, and we know that Fronsberg is still undecided as to his intentions. I don't believe they have many more than six thousand men."

"Twenty thousand," answered the old knight, in an under tone of voice.

"By heavens! I had no idea of that," replied the young man in astonishment. "We shall certainly have hard work, if that be the case; but we have well trained and experienced troops, and the League's army cannot boast of an eagle eye compared to the Duke's, not even excepting Fronsberg's. With such an advantage on our side, do you not think the chances are in our favour?"

"No," was the answer of the old man.

"Well, I'll not give up all hope. We have also a still greater advantage in our cause: we fight for our country, whereas the views of the League are mercenary. That circumstance alone will inspire our troops with courage. The Würtembergs will defend their father-land."

"That is just what I least depend upon," answered Lichtenstein. "Had not the Duke been obstinate in forcing the country to swear to the new oath of allegiance, the case would be far different, he would have had the hearts of the people with him; but now, force alone compels them to fight under his banners. The result is dubious."

"I admit what you say to be true, and that the Duke has lost much by the imprudence of his measures," replied Albert; "but I have great faith in the honest patriotism of the Swabians, and, in spite of everything he has done, they will not desert their hereditary Prince in the hour of need, and in the defence of his lawful rights. Where do you think we shall meet the enemy? Where shall we take up a position?"

"The lansquenets have thrown up a few redoubts at Untertürkheim, between Esslingen and Cannstadt, and have three thousand five hundred men there; we shall join them tonight."

The old man was silent, and they rode on for some time side by side, without speaking.

"Hearken, Albert!" he began again; "I have often looked death in the face, and am old enough not to fear to stand in such a predicament again. We are all liable to the common lot of mortals. If anything happens to me, console my dear child, Bertha!"

"Father!" cried Albert, grasping his hand, "pray do not think of such things; you will still live long and happy with us!"

"Perhaps so," replied the old man, with a firm voice, "perhaps not. It were folly in me to beg of you not to risk yourself too much in the battle; you would not follow my advice; but I pray you to think of your young wife, and do not rush into danger blindly, and without good reason. Promise me this."

"I promise! here is my hand; where duty calls me, I cannot shrink from it; unnecessarily I'll not expose myself; but you, also, my dear father, must give me the same promise."

"We'll not talk about that at present. If I, by chance, am called out of this life to-morrow, my last will, which I have placed in the Duke's hands, will be fulfilled. Lichtenstein will pass into your possession, and you will be invested with the property. My name will die with me in the country; may yours live in its remembrance so much the longer!"

The young man was overcome at these last words of his high-minded, venerable father: he endeavoured to answer him, but the rush of painful thoughts to his mind prevented all utterance. A known voice at the moment called him by name. It was the Duke's. He pressed the hand of his wife's parent, and rode in haste to Ulerich.

"Good morning, Sturmfeder!" said the Duke, who appeared more cheerful; "I say good morning, for I hear the cock crow in the village. How did you leave your wife? was she very much overcome when you last saw her?"

"She wept," answered Albert; "but she uttered not a word of complaint."

"Just like her, by Saint Hubertus! we have seldom seen so much fortitude in a woman. If the night were not quite so dark, I would like to see in your eye whether your heart is tuned to the battle, and if you are inclined to close with the Leaguists?"

"Show me but the path I am to follow, and you'll not find me swerve from it, though it lead into the thickest of the battle. Does your grace imagine, that, during the few days of my marriage, I have so totally forgotten the lesson I learnt of you, namely, never to lose courage in prosperity or adversity?"

"You are right--impavidum ferient ruinæ; we expected nothing less from our faithful banner-bearer; but another must perform that office to-day. I have selected you for a more important service. You will take these hundred and sixty cavalry by our side, choose one of them to show you the way, and trot on direct to Untertürkheim. It is possible the road may not be open, as the Leaguists from Esslingen may have come down to dispute the passage with us. How would you act under such circumstances?"

"I would throw myself with my hundred and sixty horsemen among them, and cut my way through; that is to say, if their whole force were not in the neighbourhood. If I found them too strong, I would cover my position, until you came up with reinforcements."

"You have well said, spoken like a valiant swordsman, and if you deal your blows as heavily on them as you did on me at Lichtenstein, you'll cut through six hundred Leaguists. The people I have given you are staunch. They are composed of the butchers, saddlers, and blacksmiths of Stuttgardt and the surrounding towns. I know them in many a hard fight. Brave, and able to sever the skull down to the breast bone, they will follow you, sword in hand, wherever you may lead them, when once they are well inclined towards you; let them have but one good blow at the brain, no doctor's hand need attempt a cure. That's the right sort of Swabian cut."

"Am I to take post at Untertürkheim?"

"You will find there the lansquenet under George von Hewen and Schweinsberg encamped on a hill. The watchword is, 'Ulerich for ever!' Tell them they must keep the position till five o'clock; before day-break I shall be with them with six thousand men, and then will await the Leaguists. Farewell, Albert!"

The young man returned the salute by bowing respectfully, and putting himself at the head of the gallant band, trotted down the valley with them. The men were powerful figures, broad shouldered and well limbed, whose animated fearless looks beheld their young leader with satisfaction, as he placed himself in their front, and appeared honoured by his command. Having run his eye rapidly through the ranks, he selected one whose penetrating eye and intelligent countenance seemed to point him out as the fittest person to act the part of guide. He immediately called him to his side, and gave him the necessary directions. They approached the foot of the Rothenberg, on the summit of which stood the hereditary castle of the house of Würtemberg, commanding an extended view over the valley of the Neckar. It was but faintly illumined by the glimmer of the stars, and Albert could not distinctly distinguish its form, though he kept his eyes fixed upon its towers and walls. He recollected that night in the cavern, when the Duke spoke in sorrow of the castle of his ancestors, and described the country seen from its towers as abounding in corn, wine, and fruit, all of which he once could call his own. The young man sank into reflection upon the unhappy fate of the Duke, which now again appeared to contend with him for the possession of his patrimony. He dwelt upon the extraordinary mixture in his character, the foundation of which was truly great, but was too often disturbed by rage, malice, and unbending pride. "If you look between those two trees, you will be able to distinguish the points of the towers of Untertürkheim," said the man, who was conducting him on the road. "The road is much more level now, and if we push on, we shall soon be there."

Albert spurred his horse, and the rest following his example, soon gained sight of the village. A double line of lansquenet was stationed outside of it, who at their approach presented their halberds in fearful array, whilst the red glimmer of burning matches was seen scattered about in many points, like the glow-worm sparkling in the night.

"Who comes there?" cried a deep voice from the ranks: "Give the watch-word!"

"Ulericus for ever," answered Albert von Sturmfeder: "who are you?"

"Good friends!" answered Maxx Stumpf Schweinsberg, stepping out of the ranks of the lansquenet, and riding towards the young man. "Good morning, Albert; you have kept us waiting somewhat long. We have been all night upon our legs, anxiously expecting a reinforcement, for in the wood there over against us it does not look pleasant, and if Fronsberg had been aware of his advantage, he might have overpowered us long ago."

"The Duke is coming up with six thousand men," replied Sturmfeder, "and will be here in two hours at furthest."

"Six thousand only, did you say? by Saint Nepomuk, that's not enough! we have but three thousand five hundred here, so that all we can muster in the field will make little more than nine thousand. Are you aware that the Leaguists are over twenty thousand strong? What artillery does the Duke bring with him?"

"I don't know--it was only just arrived when we departed," replied Albert.

"Well, come, and let the men dismount, and take some rest," said Maxx Stumpf; "they'll have work enough this day."

The cavalry dismounted, and laid down to rest. The lansquenet also were permitted to fall out of their ranks, leaving strong piquets on the heights, and on the Neckar. Maxx Stumpf gave all the necessary directions for the remainder of the night; and Albert von Sturmfeder, rolling himself in his cloak, also laid down to repose himself from the fatigues of the past twenty-four hours, and refresh himself for the coming strife. The stillness of the morning, broken only by the monotonous tone of the sentry's call, soon lulled him to sleep, with the last thought directed in prayer to God, into whose hands he resigned himself and his beloved wife.

CHAPTER XXXIII

Enveloped in the smoke,
Both man and horse are hidden;
Away they now have broke,
Now down the hill have ridden:
Across the Neckar springs the steed so good,
And in the valley is the fight renew'd.

G. Schwab.

Albert was roused a little before break of day by the roll of drums, calling the little band to arms. A small border of light was visible on the horizon, the advanced guard of day, when the troops of the Duke were seen coming up in the distance. The young man put on his helmet and armour, mounted his horse, and, at the head of his men, waited to receive the Duke. The stern features of Ulerich had lost none of their thoughtful expression, though all traces of gloom had disappeared from them. From his eyes beamed a warlike fire, and his countenance bespoke courage and determination. Clad entirely in steel, he wore a green cloak, trimmed with gold, over his heavy armour, whilst the colours of his house waved in the large floating plumes of his helmet. The rest of his dress differed in nothing from that of the knights and nobles about him, who, all clad in polished steel, "up to the eyes," formed a circle around the Duke. They saluted Hewen, Schweinsberg, and Sturmfeder in a friendly way, and made inquiries about the position of the enemy.

Nothing was as yet to be seen of the troops of the League, except on the border of the wood towards Esslingen, where a few straggling out-posts were observed to be stationed. The Duke determined to quit the height which the lansquenet occupied, and take up a position in the plain beneath. His army being much inferior in cavalry to the League, who, according to the reports of spies, could muster three thousand horses, he hoped the flanks of this position, having the Neckar on one side and a thick wood on the other, which he intended to take up in the valley, would make up for the deficiency in numbers.

Though the opinion of Lichtenstein, with many others, was against this plan, fearing the army would be exposed to the fire of artillery from the surrounding heights, Ulerich would not be dissuaded from it, and ordered the army to march accordingly. Having arranged his order of battle close to the town of Türkheim, he there awaited his enemy. Albert von Sturmfeder was directed to remain near him with the cavalry, which had been entrusted to his command, to be ready to strike a decisive blow, and at the same time to form his body guard; whilst Lichtenstein, with four-and-twenty other knights, joined themselves to this mounted body of burghers, ready to support them in the event of an attack of cavalry. In those days a battle was often an affair of so many single-handed combats. The knights who followed an army seldom fought in solid masses; but with a quick eye, they marked out an adversary from among the ranks of the enemy, rode at him, and fought him with lance and sword. Such a band of gallant men, headed by old Lichtenstein, was that which now closed with Albert's troop. The Duke himself, burning with the desire of wielding his powerful arm, and proving the renown of his far-famed prowess in single combat, was only controlled in this romantic idea by the pressing exhortations of his friends. A most extraordinary figure was seen to keep his station by the side of the Duke, in appearance more like a tortoise on horseback, than a human being. A helmet, with a large feather, protruded high above a small body, upon the back of which sat an arched coat of mail. The little horseman's knees were bent high up on the saddle, whilst his hand kept a fast hold of the pummel. The closed vizor of the unknown knight concealed his face from Albert's observation; who, curious to ascertain who the ridiculous looking warrior might be, rode up to the Duke to satisfy himself, and said:

"Upon my word, your highness has provided yourself with a marvellous looking animal as a guide. Only observe his withered legs, his trembling arm, the enormous helmet between his shoulders;--who may this pigmy be?"

"Don't you recognize the hump?" asked the Duke, laughing. "Just observe the extraordinary coat of mail he has on; it is for all the world like a large nutshell, to protect his back, in case he has to run for it. He is my faithful chancellor, Ambrosius Bolland."

"By the holy Virgin! what an unjust opinion I have formed of him," replied Albert; "I never thought he would have drawn a sword or mounted a horse, and there he sits upon a beast as big as an elephant, and carries a sword as long as himself. I never should have given him credit for so martial a spirit."

"Do you suppose it is his own free-will which impels him to attend me in the field? No, I have been obliged by force to make him follow me. Having pushed me to extremities against my will, in order to satisfy his wicked intentions, which I fear has placed me upon the brink of a precipice, he shall partake of the soup himself which he has cooked for me. He wept when I insisted on his coming with me; complaining of his gout, and other infirmities, saying his nature was not military; but I made him buckle on his armour, and put him on a horse, the most fiery beast in my stable. He shall have the bitters as well as the sweets of his counsel."

During this discourse the knight of the hump threw open his vizor, and discovered his pale affrighted countenance. The eternal hypocritical smile had vanished, his piercing little eyes had swollen beyond their ordinary size, and assumed a staring look, turning slowly and timidly from side to side; a cold perspiration sat upon his forehead, and his voice had softened down into a trembling whisper. "For the mercy of God, most worthy Albert von Sturmfeder, most beloved friend and benefactor," said he, "pray say a good word for me to our obdurate master, that he may release me from this masquerading gambol. The ride in this heavy armour has most cruelly tormented me, the helmet presses on my brain, setting all my thoughts on the dance, and my knees are bent with the gout. Pray, pray do! say a kind word for your humble servant, Ambrosius Bolland; I will certainly repay it ten-fold."

The young man turned away in disgust, from the cowardly sinner. "My Lord Duke," said he, whilst a blush of high-minded scorn and contempt coloured his cheeks, "permit him to go. The knights have drawn their swords, and pressed their helmets firmer on their foreheads; the people shake their spears, impatient for the signal of attack; why, then, should a coward be counted among the ranks of men?"

"He remains, I say," replied the Duke, with a stern voice; "the first step he makes to the rear, I'll cut him down from his horse. The devil sat upon your blue lips, Ambrosius Bolland, when you advised us to despise our people, and subvert the laws of the land. This day, when the balls whiz and swords clatter, shall you know whether your counsel has proved of advantage to us or not."

The chancellor's eyes beamed with rage, his lips trembled, and his whole countenance was fearfully distorted. "I only gave you my advice,--why did you follow it?" said he; "you are the Duke and master; you gave the orders for swearing the oath of allegiance,--how could I help it?"

The Duke, in anger at these words, turned his horse with such velocity towards him, that the chancellor, expecting his last moment was come, bent himself down in trepidation on his horse's mane. "By our princely honour," he cried, with a terrible voice, his eyes flashing fire, "we are astonished at our own forbearance. You took advantage of the blindness of our anger, when first we re-entered our capital; you knew too well how to ingratiate yourself into our confidence. Had we not followed your counsel, thou serpent, we should have had twenty thousand Würtemberg hearts as a wall to defend their Prince. Oh! my Würtemberg! my Würtemberg! Had I but followed the advice of my old friend! There is indeed a charm in the love of my people!"

"Away with these thoughts," said the old knight of Lichtenstein. "We are on the eve of battle; all is not yet lost; we have still time to repair the wrongs we have committed. You are surrounded by six thousand Würtembergers, and, by heavens! they will be victorious, if you lead them with confidence to the enemy. We are all friends here, my Lord! forgive your enemies; dismiss your chancellor, who can be of no service to you, he cannot use a sword."

"No! remain by my side, thou tortoise! dog of a scribe!" said the Duke. "Seated in your office, you wrote laws with your own hand, and despised my people, you shall now witness how they can fight; how a Würtemberger can conquer or----die. Ha! do you see them on the height there? do you see the flag with the red cross? there's the banner of Bavaria; how their arms glisten in the dawn of the morning, and their helmet plumes wave in the breeze! Good morning, gentlemen of the Swabian League; that is a sight for a Würtemberger! how my heart gladdens at it!"

"Look! they are preparing their artillery," interrupted Lichtenstein; "you must not remain on this spot, my Lord, your life is in danger; go back, go back; send us your orders from yonder tree, (pointing to one at a distance,) where you will be in safety; this position belongs to us alone."

The Duke turned to him, and answered, with an air of proud dignity, "Where did you ever hear that a Würtemberger retreated when the enemy had sounded the attack? My ancestors never knew what fear was, and their posterity shall also, like them, never betray the motto, 'Fearless and true!' Observe how the brow of the mountain becomes darker and darker with their numerous bodies of men. Do you see that white cloud on yonder hill, tortoise? do you hear it crack? that's the thunder of artillery, that pours into our ranks. If you have a clear conscience at this moment, make up your accounts with this world; for no one would give a penny for your life."

"Let us say a prayer," said Maxx von Schweinsberg, "and then at them, in God's name."

The Duke piously raised his hands and eyes towards heaven, and his companions following his example, they said their prayers, imploring the aid of the Almighty in the justice of their cause. This was the general custom of the good old times, before the battle commenced. The thunder of the enemy's artillery contrasted terribly with the deep silence which reigned about this group, now engaged in soliciting God's protection. Each appeared deeply impressed with the solemnity of the few moments which were perhaps left to them in this world, except the chancellor Ambrosius Bolland, who clasped his hands, whilst his eyes were not directed in faith to heaven, but wandered to the enemy's heights. His trembling body, as he observed the fire and smoke of each gun from the League, proved that his soul was not leaning upon Him who makes his sun to shine upon the good and upon the evil.

When Ulerich von Würtemberg and those around him had finished their solemn duty, he drew his sword, which was immediately followed by the rest, and in a moment a thousand blades glittered in the sun. "The lansquenet are already engaged," said he, casting his eagle eye rapidly down the valley. He now issued his orders with a cool determined voice, and, addressing George von Hewen, directed him to support them with a thousand infantry. Turning then to Schweinsberg, he said, "Take eight hundred men to the skirt of the wood, and remain there till further directions. Reinhart von Gemmingen, march with your division, and take position in the middle space between the wood and the Neckar. And you, Albert von Sturmfeder, remain here with your brigade of cavalry, and be ready to advance at a moment's notice. And now may God be with you all, my friends! Should we be destined not to see each other again in this world, we shall meet the sooner in the next." He saluted them by lowering his immense sword. The knights returned it, and advanced with their respective bodies of men towards the enemy, rending the air with loud vivas of "Ulerich for ever!"

The army of the League having taken up the ground which the Duke's men had shortly before occupied, saluted their enemy from the mouths of several pieces of heavy ordnance, moving slowly down into the valley, with the apparent intention of crushing them by superior numbers. At the moment when their last division had quitted this position, the Duke turned to Albert von Sturmfeder, and said, "Do you see those guns on the height?"

"Yes, and they are supported by a very few men apparently," he answered.

"Fronsberg supposes that because we cannot fly over to him, it would be impossible to take his pieces. But there is a path in the wood there," said the Duke, pointing with his hand, "which leads to the left, into a field, which field skirts the hill. If you advance cautiously with your cavalry, and follow the path, you will get almost into the rear of the enemy. And if you succeed, pull up your horses a moment to give them wind, and then gallop up the hill, and their artillery is ours."

Albert bowed to him at parting, whilst the Duke gave him his hand. "Farewell, young man," said he; "it grieves us to send so young a married man upon such dangerous service; but we know of none other better calculated or more determined than yourself to perform it."

The cheeks of the young hero glowed with ardour when he heard these words, and his eyes bespoke confidence in the bold enterprise he was about to undertake. "I thank you, my lord, for this new proof of your consideration," he replied; "you do me a greater kindness than if you had endowed me with one of your most valuable estates. Farewell, father," turning to old Lichtenstein, "remember me to my beloved wife."

"I don't mean to let you go alone," replied the old knight, smiling: "I'll accompany you. Under your conduct----"

"No, remain with me, old friend," entreated the Duke; "do you wish me to follow the chancellor's counsel in the field also? He might lead me into a much worse scrape than he has already done. Stay by my side, old man; make a hasty farewell with your son, for there is not a moment to lose."

The old knight pressed the hand of the young man, who returned it smiling, and, in a cheerful mood, placed himself at the head of his gallant band, when he galloped away with the Stuttgardt burghers, leading them towards the enemy in this critical moment, crying, "Ulerich for ever!" Having reached the skirt of the wood, he had a moment's leisure to run his eye over the field of battle. The Würtembergers were in very good position, their flanks being covered by the wood and the Neckar, and their centre arranged in such a manner as to be able to repel any serious charge of cavalry. It was therefore evident, that any alteration in their present line of battle would subject them to extreme danger. The great disadvantage under which they laboured was the fact of their being inferior to their enemy by two-thirds of the number of combatants and though the Leaguists were unable to bring their whole force into action at once, in consequence of the confined space of the valley, their superiority of numbers compensated for the want of room to manœuvre in, which consideration alone required the most strenuous exertions of Ulerich's small band to maintain their ground. They, indeed, with such fearful odds against them, kept their line unbroken, and their courage appeared to rise still higher as their ranks began to thin. But, though the brave Swabians valiantly disputed every inch of ground, it was to be apprehended lest, by dint of renewed attacks by fresh troops, they would ultimately be forced to give way.

These fleeting observations which Albert had been enabled to make, convinced him that upon some daring piece of service depended the success of the day. The energies of his mind rose in proportion to the difficulties he had to contend with. He felt that Ulerich's destiny was now in his keeping, and that one bold stroke, such as he was about to undertake, would decide the fate of the contest.

His troop having now reached the wood, they proceeded through it in silence and with caution, aware of the advantage which infantry possess over cavalry under such circumstances. But they arrived at the point leading to the field which the Duke had described, without molestation. To the right beyond the wood the battle raged in full fury. The cheers of the attacking part, the roar of artillery and small arms, the noise of the drums, echoed terribly through its trees.

The hill lay before them, from the summit of which several pieces of heavy artillery played upon the ranks of the Würtembergers. The path to the top of it, leading up from the side of the wood, being of gentle ascent, Albert was astonished at the quick eye of the Duke in having discovered the only weak part of the enemy's position, every other point of it being unassailable, at least by cavalry. The guns, as far as he could observe from the place where he stood, were not supported by any considerable force, and, therefore, as soon as the horses had rested a few moments, Albert sounded the charge, and, putting himself at their head, galloped up the hill in gallant style, and reached the summit in an instant, calling to the enemy to surrender. The consternation of the Leaguist troops in thus finding their enemies suddenly among them, paralysed all their means of defence; whilst the brave butchers, saddlers, and blacksmiths of Stuttgardt, taking advantage of their confusion, dealt out the true Swabian cut on the heads of their adversaries, and in a short time reduced the covering party to a small number. Albert threw a triumphant look down the plain towards the Duke; he heard the exulting shouts wafted to him from the throats of many thousand Würtembergers, and saw them advance with renewed courage, being now relieved from the galling fire of the artillery on the hill.

He was obliged, however, to check this momentary joy of victory, in consideration of his retreat, the second and most difficult operation of the gallant undertaking; for the Leaguists, having observed the sudden cessation of their artillery, had ordered a powerful body of cavalry to charge the hill. As there was no time to bring away the captured guns, he quickly ordered his men to fill them with stones and earth, rendering them by this means unserviceable, and then casting his eye towards the line of retreat, he perceived he would have to contend with difficulties he had not anticipated. To retrace the path through the wood by which, he had advanced was his first thought, for, were it even occupied by the enemy's cavalry, he would meet them upon equal terms. But, to his dismay, as he was about to put it into execution, he observed that a large body of the Leaguist infantry had already gained the wood to cut off his passage through it, rendering it thereby impossible for him to join his comrades by that road. To attempt to cut through the enemy's army with only one hundred and sixty horsemen, would seem to be absolute madness. The only alternative left to him, therefore,--and it was one more likely to lead to death than deliverance,--was to make direct for the Neckar, which flowed between him and his friends, and pass it by swimming across. Desperate as this only resource of escape was, he determined to act upon it without loss of time, and once having gained the banks of the river, he thought the passage of it might be easily accomplished. By these means he might hope to join the Duke; though it was but a forlorn hope. Five hundred men of the Leaguist cavalry had by this time reached the foot of the hill upon which he stood. He thought he recognized Truchses von Waldburg at their head, and rather than surrender to him, he would willingly have suffered death.

He gave the signal to his gallant Würtembergers to follow him down the side of the hill which led to the banks of the river. They staggered at the fearful expedient, for it was scarcely to be expected that a fifth part of them would escape, so steep was the descent, and besides which, between the hill and the river stood a large body of the enemy's infantry, ready to receive them. But their gallant young leader, throwing open his vizor, discovered to them his noble countenance, beaming with the inspiration of heroic magnanimity. The whole troop were animated by the same bold spirit, and when they recollected they had seen him but a few weeks back leading a beautiful maiden to the altar, and that he had left this endearing object behind him, for the sake of his Duke and country, they vociferated in loud shouts the practices of their several vocations. "At them!" cried the butchers, "we'll slaughter them like oxen;" "And we'll hammer them like hot iron," cried the blacksmiths; and the saddlers vociferated "They shall be beat as soft as leather." "Ulerich for ever!" cried their bold-hearted leader, who putting spurs to his horse, was the first to gallop down the dangerous declivity. The enemy's cavalry could scarcely believe their eyes when they arrived at the top of the hill, in expectation of capturing their daring adversaries, and saw them hotly engaged with their infantry at the bottom of it. This bold step of Albert's cost many a brave man his life: many were thrown from their horses, and fell into the hands of the Leaguists; but the major part, arriving safely at the foot of the hill, were engaged hand to hand with the enemy, and the helmet plumes of their leader were seen to wave high in the midst of the fray. The ranks of the infantry were soon broken by the impetuous charge of the Würtembergers, who now pushed for the bank of the Neckar, and following their leader, dashed into the water to cross it. Though his horse was a powerful beast he had not strength sufficient to bear the weight of his rider, clad in armour, nor to stem its stream, at present swollen beyond its ordinary height by heavy rains. He was on the point of sinking, calling to his men not to think of him, but to push on to the Duke, and give him his last farewell, when at this critical moment two gallant blacksmiths, having disencumbered themselves of their horses, seized the young knight, one by his arms, and the other taking his horse's bridle, landed him in safety on the opposite bank.

The Leaguists sent many a shot after their flying enemy, but fortunately they fell harmless. In the sight of both armies, this daring band continued its further route unmolested to the Duke. Having passed a deep ford, not far from the spot where Ulerich was stationed, they were received with loud shouts of joy and applause by their companions.

Though a considerable part of the enemy's artillery had been rendered unserviceable by the no less bold than rapid attack of Albert von Sturmfeder, such was the unhappy fate of Duke Ulerich, that even this brilliant feat of arms could not avert the spell which seemed to hang over his destiny. The strength of his people began to fail under renewed attacks of superior numbers. In spite of the experience and bravery of the lansquenets, who gave proofs of the honesty of their promises to the Duke, and though they continued to uphold their accustomed warlike character, and did not cede an inch of ground, the loss they had sustained obliged their commanders to form them into circles to repel the charges of cavalry. The line of battle being thereby broken, the vacant spaces were but feebly filled up and sustained by the country people, badly armed, and worse soldiers, having been brought into the field in haste, and almost without discipline. At this critical moment intelligence arrived of the Duke of Bavaria having suddenly surprised and taken possession of Stuttgardt, that a fresh army was coming up in the rear, and was scarcely a quarter of an hour's distance off. This news was a death-blow to the Duke's hopes, who now perceived there was nothing left to him but flight or death to prevent his falling into the hands of his enemies. What was to be done in this emergency? His followers advised him to throw himself into the hereditary castle of the house of Würtemberg, and there remain until he could find an opportunity secretly to escape. He turned his eyes towards the place, his last resource, which, lighted up by the brilliancy of the day, seemed to look down in stern majesty upon the valley, where the descendant of him who raised it had staked his last hope in one desperate conflict. But when he saw the red flag playing in the morning breeze over the towers and walls of his castle, he turned pale, and pointing to it, was unable to give utterance to the painful feelings which the sight occasioned. The knights directing their attention to it, discovered a black smoke issuing from all corners, a proof that the victorious flag had been planted on its pinnacle amidst the flames lighted up by an avenging enemy. Würtemberg now burnt at every point, and her unhappy master witnessed the spectacle in ghastly despair. Both armies also noticed the burning castle. The Leaguists saluted the event with loud shouts of exulting joy, whilst the courage of the Würtembergers sank in proportion, and viewed the sad sight as the setting sun of the Duke's prosperity.

The drums of the army advancing in the rear were now heard distinctly approaching towards them; the armed peasantry, in many places, began to give way, when Ulerich said, in a firm, voice, addressing those immediately about him, "Whoever means honourably by us, follow me, we'll cut our way through their hosts, or fall in the attempt. Take my banner in your hand, valiant Sturmfeder, and charge their ranks with us." Albert seized the flag of Würtemberg, the Duke placed himself by his side, the knights and burghers on horseback surrounded them, and prepared to open a passage for their lord. The Duke pointed to a weak position in the enemy's line, which appeared the one most favourable to ensure the success of the daring project; if the attempt failed, all was lost. Albert volunteered for the desperate post of honour of leading the determined band; but the old knight of Lichtenstein, beckoning to him not to quit the Duke's side, placed himself boldly in front, and directing one more glance to his lord and son, closed his vizor, and cried, "Forwards! Here's to good Würtemberg for ever!"

About two hundred horsemen composed the resolute band, which moved on in a trot, arranged in the form of a wedge. The chancellor Ambrosius Bolland's heart beat lighter when they departed, for the Duke, amidst the anxieties of the moment, had quite lost sight of him, and he now held council with himself how he could most conveniently dismount from his long-legged steed. The noble beast, however, with upstanding ears and restless motion had noticed the departure of the cavalry. So long as they moved on in gentle trot, he remained tolerably quiet. But when the trumpets sounded the attack, and the gallant crew broke into a gallop with Würtemberg's banner waving high above the helmet plumes, this appeared to be the moment which the chancellor's high metaled steed had been anticipating, for with the rapidity of a bird, he stretched over the plain in the track of the other horsemen. His rider, almost deprived of his senses, and his hand seizing the pummel of his saddle in a state of convulsion, attempted to halloo, but the rapidity with which he cut through the air hindered all further utterance. Though the Duke and his friends had gained some considerable distance from him, the chancellor soon overtook, and then passing them, found himself, much against his will, the leading man in the desperate encounter which was about to take place. The attention of the enemy was riveted to the extraordinary figure of the chancellor, which appeared more like an ape in armour than a warrior on horseback, and before they could make out what he was, his steed had carried him into the midst of their ranks. The spectacle was so highly ridiculous, that the Würtembergers, notwithstanding this moment was for them one of life or death, broke out into loud laughter, which, spreading confusion among the troops of the League, composed of those of Ulm, Gmünd, Aulen, Nürnberg, and other imperial cities, allowed the overpowering weight of the two hundred horses, carrying the chancellor along with them, to break through, and gain the rear of their enemies. They pushed on their march in haste, and before the Leaguist cavalry could be sent in pursuit, the Duke, with his followers, had already gained a long start, and turned off the field of battle by a side path.

The mounted burghers having covered the retreat of the Duke, he effected his escape with a few faithful adherents, whilst they directed their route towards Stuttgardt. The enemy's cavalry only came up with them just as they had reached the gates of the city, when great was their disappointment not to capture either the Duke or any of his principal partisans, whom they expected to find among them. Ambrosius Bolland was their only prize. He, more dead than alive from excessive fright and fatigue, was not able to dismount from his elevated position without assistance. After having peeled his body of its unaccustomed covering, the Leaguists vented their rage and disappointment upon the unfortunate man, by beating him and other ill-usage; for they attributed to his supposed bravery, which appeared to them to exceed all they had ever witnessed, the loss of a thousand gold florins, set as a reward upon the capture of the Duke. And so it happened that the gallant chancellor, not like his master beaten in battle, was beaten after it.

CHAPTER XXXIV

Think on the many gallant deeds
One valiant hand has done,
And follow where your country needs,
Where a hero's grave is won.
Here, here they flee! pursue the way they go:
The light of heaven shows our flying foe.

L. Uhland.

The Duke and his followers passed the night after the day of the decisive battle in a narrow deep ravine of a wood, which, being surrounded by high rocks and thick underwood, offered a safe retreat for the moment, and is called, to this day, "Ulerich's cavern," by the people of the country. It was the fifer of Hardt who appeared again as a saviour in their flight, and led them to this place, known only to the peasantry and shepherds of the neighbourhood. The Duke determined to repose in this secluded spot, and, as soon as the following day broke, to continue his flight towards Switzerland. He would have preferred continuing his route under cover of the night, as being more favourable to elude the vigilance of his enemies. The fate of the disastrous day having given them full possession of the country again, it seemed next to impossible to escape through their numerous patroles, which would now scour the country to intercept his retreat. Delay was therefore dangerous; but the horses being unable to proceed after the heat and fatigue of the battle, he was compelled by necessity to run the risk of taking a short rest.

The party seated themselves around a small fire. Sleep soon came to the Duke's aid, and for awhile made him forget that he had again lost his dukedom. The knight of Lichtenstein also slept. Maxx Stumpf von Schweinsberg, resting his arms on his knees, concealed his face in both hands, and it was uncertain whether he dosed, or whether he was sorrowing over the fate of his unhappy master, which the day's battle had so cruelly decided. Albert von Sturmfeder, though almost overpowered with fatigue, resisted the power of sleep, and, being the youngest of the party, volunteered to keep watch. Beside him sat his faithful friend, the fifer of Hardt, his eyes fixed steadfastly on the fire, and appeared to concentrate his thoughts in the words of a song, whose melancholy strain he hummed to himself with a soft suppressed voice. When the fire blazed up occasionally a little brisker, he cast a sorrowful look at the Duke, to see if he still slept, and then recommenced the same lamentable dirge.

"You are singing a very melancholy strain, Hans!" said Albert, whose attention was excited by the peculiar tones of the song: "it sounds like a death song or mourning dirge; I can't listen to it without shuddering."

"Death may knock at every man's door at any moment," replied the fifer, looking still more gloomily at the fire; "I like to occupy my mind upon such subjects, for it often strikes me, I would prefer going out of this world with similar thoughts in my mind."

"But how is it you think more upon death at this moment than at other times, Hans? You were always a merry fellow at harvest time; and your guitar never failed being heard at a wake. You certainly never sang a death-song on such occasions."

"My happiness is gone," he answered, and pointed to the Duke; "all my anxieties and troubles have been in vain. His star is set, and I----I am his shadow; therefore nothing is left for me. If I had not a wife and child, I would willingly die this very night."

"You were, indeed, his faithful shadow," said the young man, moved at these words: "I have always admired your fidelity. Listen, Hans! it will perhaps be some time before we see each other again; and having now time and opportunity to converse together, tell me, if it be not too much to ask, what has bound you so close and exclusively to the fortunes of the Duke?"

The man was silent a few minutes, and trimmed the burning embers of the fire. A troubled look beamed in his eyes, leaving Albert in doubt whether he had not touched upon a subject which was painful to his friend, whose countenance he thought was tinged with a passing blush. "That question," he at length replied, "refers to a certain occurrence, which I never willingly speak about. But you are right, sir, in your conjecture, and it appears to me also that we shall not meet again for some time; therefore I will satisfy your curiosity. Have you ever heard of the insurrection called, 'Poor Conrad'?"

"O, yes!" replied Albert, "the report spread far beyond Franconia. Was it not an insurrection of the peasantry? It was said, they wanted even to take the Duke's life!" I----

"You are perfectly right, the affair of Conrad was a bad thing. About seven years ago many men among us peasantry were dissatisfied with our landlords; great distress prevailed throughout the country, in consequence of the failure of the crops. The rich had squandered all their money; the poor had long since no more left, but still we were obliged to pay heavy taxes without end, in order to satisfy the exorbitant demands of the Duke's court, where every luxury was carried on in the midst of an impoverished country."

"Did your representatives accede to these extravagant demands?" inquired the young man.

"They did not always venture to say no; for, the Duke's purse having an enormous large hole in it, they had no other means of repairing it than by the sweat of our brow. Many, therefore, struck work, because, said they, 'the corn which we sow, does not grow for our bread, and the wine we make, does not flow into our casks.' They then thought, as nothing more could be taken from them than their lives, that they would live merrily and without care, and calling themselves counts of 'no home,' spoke of their many castles on the 'hungry mountain,' of their wealthy possessions in 'the land of famine' and on the banks of the 'river of beggary.' This was the origin of the insurrection named 'The League of Poor Conrad.'"

The fifer of Hardt laid his head in his hand in deep thought, and was silent.

"But you promised to relate to me your adventures with the Duke," said Albert.

"I had nearly forgotten that," he answered: "well," he continued, "persecution was at length brought to such a pass, that even the weights and measures were decreased in size and quantity, so that the Duke and his courtiers might be the gainers at our expense. We paid the same for a less quantity. The consequence of this species of tyranny gave rise to a circumstance which, commencing at first in mere joke, became a source of bitter hatred and revenge. Many could not bear the thought of this act of flagrant injustice, by which every one else had full weight and measure, whilst we alone, the peasantry, were the sufferers. Poor Conrad carried the weights into the valley of the Rems, and made a proof by water."

"A proof by water,--what's that?" asked the young man.

"Ha!" laughed Hans, "that is an easy way of proving a thing. A stone of a pound weight was paraded to the sound of drum and fife to the banks of the Kerns, and they said, 'if it swims, the Duke is right; if it sinks, the peasant is right.' The stone sank, and Poor Conrad armed himself. All the peasants then rose in the vallies of the Rems and Neckar, and throughout all the country up to Tübingen far over the Alb, and demanded the old laws.

The members of the diet were assembled and harangued them, but all to no purpose, they would not disperse."

"But you--what part did you take? You; don't say a word about yourself," said Albert.

"That's said in a very few words," replied Hans: "I was one of the most violent among them. Never being much inclined to work, and having been inhumanly punished for transgressing the game laws, I joined Poor Conrad, and soon became as desperate as Gaispeter and Bregenzer. The Duke, seeing that the insurrection was becoming dangerous, came himself to Schorndorf. We had been called to that place for the purpose of swearing allegiance. Many hundreds appeared, but all armed. Ulerich addressed us himself; but we would not hear him. The marshal of the empire then stood up, and raising his gold staff said, 'He who holds to Duke Ulerich von Würtemberg, let him come over to his side!' Gaispeter also stepping upon a large stone, cried, 'He who holds to Poor Conrad of Hungry Hill, come over here!' The Duke stood alone among his servants, deserted by his people: we, the opposite party, remained with the beggar."

"Oh, what a shameful transaction," cried Albert, moved by a feeling of the injustice which caused it, "but more particularly so in those who allowed it to go to such lengths! I'll be bound Ambrosius Bolland, the chancellor, was mostly to blame in it."

"You are not far wrong," replied the fifer; "but hear me. When the Duke saw that all was lost, he threw himself on his horse. We crowded about him, but no one was bold enough to touch his person, for we were staggered by his commanding look. 'What is it you want, you scum of the earth?' he cried, and giving his horse the spur, made him bound in the air, by which three men were knocked down. This awakened our fury; the people laid hold of the horse's reins, they thrusted at him with their spears, and I so far forgot myself as to seize him by the mantle, crying, 'Shoot the villain dead!'"

"Was that you, Hans?" cried Albert, and eyed him with a look of horror.

"That was I," he uttered slowly and in a subdued tone, evidently suffering from the recollection of the deed. "But the Duke escaped from us, and assembled a force which we were not able to contend with, and we surrendered unconditionally. Twelve leaders of the insurrection were conducted to Schorndorf, tried and condemned; I was one of them. When I was in prison, with leisure to think of the wrong I had done, and contemplate the approach of death, I shuddered at myself, and was ashamed of being associated with such miserable fellows as the other eleven were."

"But how were you saved?" asked Albert.

"In the way I have already related to you in Ulm; by a miracle. We twelve were conducted to the market-place, for the purpose of being beheaded. The Duke was seated in front of the town-hall, and ordered us to be brought before him again. My eleven companions threw themselves on their knees, causing the noise of their chains to resound through the air, crying for mercy in pitiable tones. He fixed his eyes upon them for some time, and then, observing that I alone remained silent, said, 'Why do not you beg for pardon also?' 'My Lord,' I answered, 'I know what I deserve: may God hare mercy on my soul!' Without saying a word, he looked at us some time longer, and then made a sign to the executioner. We were brought up to the scaffold according to our ages; and I being the youngest, was the last. I remember little more of that terrible moment; but I shall never forget the frightful sound of the axe when it severed the heads from the bodies of the culprits."

"For God's sake, say no more on the subject!" Albert requested; "but pass on to the rest of the story."

"Nine heads were stuck upon the points of spears, when the Duke cried, 'Ten shall bleed, but two shall be pardoned. Let dice be brought: he who throws the lowest number in three throws, loses his head.' The dice-box was given to me first, but I said, 'I have forfeited my life, and I will not gamble for it.' The Duke said, 'Well; I'll throw for you.' The box was then handed to the other two. They shook the dice with cold trembling hand, and threw. One counted nine, and the other fourteen; the Duke then seized the box, and shook it. He looked at me hard in the face, but I did not tremble. He threw, and covered the dice with his hand. 'Beg for mercy,' said he, 'there is still time.' 'I pray you to pardon the rash act,' I answered, 'but I beg not for mercy, because I don't deserve it.' He raised his hand; and behold, he counted eighteen! The effect it produced on me was indescribable; I thought the Duke sat in God's stead in judgment. I fell upon my knees, and vowed to live and die in his service. The tenth man was beheaded, and two of us saved."

Albert had listened to the tale of the fifer of Hardt with increasing interest, and when he finished it, and noticed his bold expressive eyes filled with tears, he could not resist taking him by the hand, saying, "Truly, you have been guilty of a heavy crime against the Lord of your country, but you have also expiated it dearly by being brought so near to death. The terror of immediate death, whilst the sword of vengeance is hanging over a guilty head, must indeed be tenfold more appalling when the culprit is obliged to witness the execution of so many acquaintances, awaiting the slow approach of his own last moment along with them; but you have faithfully atoned to your prince for laying your hand upon his person, by a life of fidelity, sacrifices, and risks of all kinds in his cause. And how often have you liberated him from danger, perhaps saved his life! Truly you have richly redeemed your debt."

The poor man, when he had finished his story, relapsed into gloomy thought, with his eyes fixed on the fire; and had it not been, that an occasional sad smile passed over his countenance when Albert spoke to him, he had all the appearance of being totally unconscious of what was going on around him. "Do you mean," said he, "that I could ever sufficiently repent, and redeem the crime of which I have been guilty? No; such debts are not so easily liquidated, and a redeemed life must be devoted to the service of him who has saved it. To wander among mountains, getting intelligence from an enemy's camp, and finding out places of concealment, are but trifling services, sir, and cannot satisfy the mind under such circumstances. I feel convinced that I must die for him one of these days; and then I pray you take care of my wife and child."

A tear fell on his beard; but, as if ashamed of his weakness, he hastily wiped it away, and continued: "Could but the sacrifice of my life ward off the impending danger which surrounds him--could my death erase that unfortunate oath of allegiance, which he has imposed on the country, and replace him in the hearts of his people; I would willingly die in that hour!"

The Duke awoke. He raised himself up, and surveyed the surrounding rocks and trees, with his companions seated around the faint glimmering of burning embers, with astonishment, as if he had been transported by magic to this wild spot. Covering his face with his hands, and then gazing about him again, to convince himself whether the appearance of these objects were reality or not, he first glanced at one and then at another with painful feelings. "I have this day lost my country again," said he, "but that event has not given me so much trouble as I feel at this moment, for I dreamt I re-possessed it, and saw it in higher bloom than ever. Alas, it was but a dream!"

"You must not be ungrateful, sir," said Maxx Stumpf von Schweinsberg, raising himself from his bent position: "be not unthankful for nature's kindness. Think how much more miserable you would have been, if in sleep, which should give you renewed strength to bear the burden of your misfortunes, you had still felt the weight of them. When you laid down to rest, you were overcome by the fatal result of the day, but now your features assume a kindlier and milder appearance; have we not, then, cause to be thankful for your soothing dream?"

"I would I had never seen the day again!" replied Ulerich. "Oh, that I could have been lost in the pleasures of that same dream for centuries, and then have come to life again,--it was so beautiful, so consoling!"

He laid his head on his hand, and appeared oppressed with grief. The conversation roused the knight of Lichtenstein. He was acquainted with the character of Ulerich, and knew the necessity of not allowing him to give way to his feelings, and, particularly at this critical moment, not to let him brood over the terrible loss he had sustained; he therefore drew nearer to him, and said:

"Well, sir, perhaps you will tell us what you dreamt of? It may, perchance, afford your friends some consolation also; for you must know, I have faith in dreams, especially when they occupy our minds in hours of importance, and are fraught with destiny; I believe they are sent from above to raise our hopes, and arm us with fortitude."

The Duke remained silent some time longer, apparently pondering over the last words of his old friend. He then began, "My brother-in-law, William of Bavaria, has burnt the castle of my ancestors this day, as a proof of his friendship. The Würtembergers have been established there from time immemorial, and the country which we possess takes its name from the same castle. He seems to have fired it with the torch of death, and with its flames to have wished to exterminate the arms, the remembrance, nay, even the very name of Würtemberg, from the face of the earth. He has partially succeeded; for my only son, young Christoph, is in a distant land; my brother, George, has no child; and I--I have been beaten and driven out; they have repossessed my country, and where can I look to the hope of returning to it again?"

Ulerich was again silent. His mind appeared occupied with a subject too great for utterance. A peaceful serenity lay on the features of the unfortunate Prince, and an unusual expression beamed in his eyes as he directed them upwards to heaven. His companions looked at him in awful expectation of hearing some important communication resulting from his dream.

"Listen further," he continued: "I gazed on the charming valley of the Neckar. The river flowed on in its accustomed gentle winding blue stream. The valley and hills appeared lovely, and more luxuriant than ever. The woods on the heights and the meadows assumed the aspect of one continued garden, spreading their rich green vineyards from hill to hill, and in the valley below full-bearing fruit trees without number completed the blooming scene. I stood enchanted and riveted to the view; the sun shone with greater splendour than usual, the blue vault of heaven was lighted up more brilliantly than I had ever witnessed it, and all nature seemed dressed in brighter colours than mortal eye had ever beheld. When I raised my intoxicated eye, and gazed upon the valley of the Neckar, I beheld a castle pleasantly situated on the summit of a hill which rose from the banks of the river, with the rays of the morning sun playing upon its walls. The sight of this peaceful habitation rejoiced my heart, for there were no ditches or high defences, no towers or battlements, no portcullis nor drawbridge, to remind the beholder of the contentions of men, and of the uncertain history of mortals.

"And as I was wrapped in astonishment and delight in the contemplation of the peaceful aspect of the valley and the unguarded castle, I turned round, and beheld the walls of my castle no longer to exist. Here, at least, my dream did not deceive me, for yesterday I saw the battlements fall, and the watch-tower sink, over which my banner had formerly floated. No stone of Würtemberg was more to be seen, but in its place stood a temple, ornamented with pillars and cupola, such as is to be found in Rome and Greece. Meditating how all this change could have come to pass, I observed some men in foreign costume, not far from me, inspecting the country.

"One of these men, in particular, drew my attention. He led a beautiful youth by the hand, and pointed out to him the valley which lay at their feet, the surrounding mountains, the river, the towns and villages in the neighbourhood, and in the distance. Upon a closer inspection, I observed the man had the features of my brother George, and it struck me that he must belong to the race of my ancestors, and be a true Würtemberger. He descended with the boy from the hill into the valley below, followed by the other man at a respectful distance. I stopped the last man, and asked him who the other person was that had described the country to the lad; 'That was the King,' said he, and followed the rest."

The Duke was silent, and looked inquisitively at the knights, as if to hear their opinion. No one answered for some time, at length the knight of Lichtenstein said, "I am now sixty-five years old, and have seen and heard much in the world; many things come to pass which astonish the human mind, but in which a pious man may distinguish the finger of God. Believe me, that dreams also are of his sending, as nothing happens upon earth without some reason. As there were seers and prophets in ancient times, why should not the Lord send one to his saints in our days, to open the dark gates of futurity to the mind of an unfortunate man through the channel of a dream, and give him an insight into coming happier days? Despond not, therefore, my lord! The enemy has burnt your castle--in one day you have lost a dukedom; but your name will nevertheless not become extinct, and your remembrance will not be washed out from Würtemberg's history."

"A King----" said the Duke, thoughtfully, "I dare not presume, now that I am an outcast, to think of a King springing from my race. Is it not possible that Satan may tempt us with such dreams, for the purpose of deceiving us afterwards more cruelly?"

"But why have doubts of futurity?" said Schweinsberg, smiling. "Could any one of your noble ancestors have thought their family would have become Dukes of the country, and their beautiful land have borne the name of Würtemberg? Let your dream console you, which has been given as a hint of the destiny awaiting your family. Believe that your name is destined to nourish in distant, very distant times, in the land of your forefathers, and that in remote ages the Princes of Würtemberg will bear the features of your generation."

"Well, then, I will hope so," replied Ulerich von Würtemberg; "I will continue to hope, that the country will still hold to us, dark as our present lot may appear. May our grand-children never experience such hard times as we have, and may it ever be said they are--fearless."

"And faithful!" added the fifer of Hardt, with emphasis, as he rose from his seat. "But it is high time, my Lord Duke, to set out. The dawn of morn is not far distant; we must pass the Neckar at all hazards before daylight."

They all rose, and buckled on their arms. The horses being brought forward, they mounted, and the fifer of Hardt went on before to lead the way out of the place of concealment. The escape of the Duke was attended with considerable danger, for the enemy sought all possible means to take him prisoner. To gain the road by which he might elude the vigilance of his enemies, it was absolutely necessary to repass the Neckar; and to accomplish this in safety was no easy matter. Heavy rains had swollen the river to such a degree, that it appeared next to impossible to pass it on horseback by swimming. The bridges, for the most part, were occupied by the troops of the League. But Hans had taken the precaution to ascertain by the aid of faithful friends, that the bridge of Köngen was still open, having been given to understand that the enemy had thought it needless to guard it, as, being so near Esslingen and their own camp, they never dreamt the Duke would venture to come that way. This path, therefore, Ulerich chose as the safest, though it still appeared attended with great danger, and the party set out towards the Neckar in deep silence, and with caution.

When they reached the fields beyond the wood, the dawn of morning tinged the horizon; and having gained a better road, they rode on at a brisk pace, and soon got a sight of the glimmering of the Neckar, not far from the high vaulted bridge which they were to pass. At this moment Albert, happening to look round, perceived a considerable number of horsemen coming towards them. He immediately made it known to his companions, who, counting above twenty-five horses, felt assured they could be no other than a party of cavalry of the League; the Duke's men having been dispersed, it was not likely any stragglers were in this neighbourhood.

These men, however, appeared not to remark the Duke's small retinue. To gain the bridge with the least possible delay, before they were hailed and questioned by this party, was of the utmost importance. The fifer of Hardt hastened on before, the Duke and his faithful knights followed in full trot, and as they increased their distance from the Leaguists, each felt lighter at heart, for they all were less anxious about their own lives than to secure the escape of Ulerich.

Having reached the bridge, and arrived on the middle of it, which was highly arched, twelve men sprang forward from behind the walls, armed with spears, swords, and guns, arresting the Duke's further progress. Perceiving he was discovered, he made a sign to his followers to retreat. Lichtenstein and Schweinsberg, being the two last, turned their horses, to retrace their steps, but to their dismay found themselves hemmed in by the cavalry they had first seen, who had galloped up in their rear, and at this instant occupied the entrance to the bridge.

It was still too dark to be able to distinguish the enemy with precision, who were, however, not backward in making themselves known. "Surrender yourself, Duke of Würtemberg," cried a voice, which appeared familiar to the knights; "you have no chance of escape."

"Who are you, to whom Würtemberg should surrender?" answered the Duke, with a furious voice, whilst he drew his sword; "you are no knight, for you don't sit on horseback."

"I am Doctor Calmus," replied the other, "and am ready to return the many kind acts I have received from you. I am a knight, for you yourself created me a donkey knight, and in return I will now dub you the knight without horse. Dismount, I say, in the name of the most illustrious League."

"Give me room, Hans," whispered the Duke, with a suppressed voice to the fifer, who stood between him and the doctor, with his axe raised to his shoulder in attitude of defence, "just stand on one side. Close in, my friends: we'll fall on them suddenly, and perhaps may succeed in cutting through." Albert was the only one who heard this order, for the other two knights were ten paces at least in their rear, already engaged with the Leaguist cavalry, who were unable to force their way past the gallant men to get at the Duke. Albert, therefore, closed with the Duke, with the intention of making a rush with him through the ranks of his opponents; but the doctor, perceiving it, called out to his people, "At him, my men! that's him in the green cloak; take him, dead or alive!" pushing forward at the same time to the attack. He carried a spear of unusual length, and made a thrust at Ulerich, which might have been fatal, for it was still dark, and the Duke did not remark it immediately; but the quick-sighted Hans parried the thrust of the renowned Doctor Calmus, which was on the point of piercing the breast of his master, and with one blow of his axe felled him to the ground, where he lay sprawling among his companions. They were staggered at the deadly blow of the countryman, who, wielding his axe high in the air, drove them back a few paces. Albert took advantage of this moment to possess himself of the Duke's cloak, which he threw over his own shoulders, and whispered to him to give his horse the spur, and force him over the breastwork of the bridge. Ulerich cast a look at the high swollen waters of the Neckar, and then up to heaven, in doubtful despair. Escape appeared hopeless. The fearful leap was his only choice between life or death, or falling into the hands of his enemies. A circumstance, however, arrested his attention for a moment before he decided upon it.

The enemy, with outstretched spears, advanced on the Duke. The fifer still kept his ground, though wounded and bleeding in many places, beating them down with his axe. His eyes flashed fire, his bold features carried the expression of joyful animation, and the smile about his mouth did not indicate despair; no, his noble soul feared not the approach of death, he rather looked to it in proud anticipation, as the reward for all the troubles and dangers he had taken upon himself. As he cut one of his opponents to the ground with his right hand, the halberd of another pierced his breast, that true breast, which even in death proved a faithful shield to his unhappy prince, for whom a more gallant heart never beat: he staggered, and sank to the ground. Casting his dying eye upon his master, "My lord Duke, we are quits," were his last words, which he uttered with a smile upon his countenance, and fell lifeless at his feet.

The Leaguists passing over his body, pressed hard upon the Duke, with the cry of exultation when Albert threw himself in the midst, his sword dealing destruction among his enemies. He was the last and only remaining defence of Duke Ulerich of Würtemberg; had he been overpowered, imprisonment or death to his friend and benefactor were unavoidable. The Duke, therefore, turned to the only means of escape; a desperate one indeed. He cast a painful look at the corpse of that man who had sealed his fidelity with his death, and turning his powerful war-horse on one side, gave him the spur that made him spring in the air, and with one desperate leap he cleared the breastwork of the bridge, carrying his princely rider down into the waters of the Neckar.

Albert ceased to defend himself. His eye was fixed solely on the Duke. The horse and rider plunged deep into the river; but the powerful beast, combating the eddies and current, soon appeared on its surface, carrying his master down the stream with the apparent ease and safety of a boat. All this was the affair of a few moments. Some of the Leaguists were for following him along the banks of the river, to seize the bold knight when he landed; but one of them nearest Albert cried, "Let him swim, he is not the right one; here is the prize, in the green cloak,--seize him." Albert, looking up to heaven in grateful thanksgiving for the escape of the Duke, and dropping his sword, surrendered to the Leaguists. They surrounded him, and willingly allowed him to dismount, to pay the last painful offices to the corpse of that man who had been their fearful opponent. Albert took his hand, with which he still kept a firm grasp of his blood-stained axe; it was icy cold. He felt his heart, to discover if there was still life in it; the deadly thrust of the spear had but too faithfully done its office. That eye once so bold was now lifeless, that mouth which bespoke an unbending cheerful mind was closed, the features rigid; but still the smile, that last dying salute with which he greeted his master, played upon his lips. Albert's tears fell on his faithful friend, as he pressed for the last time the cold hand of the fifer of Hardt; he closed his eyes, and, throwing himself upon his horse, followed his enemies to their camp.

CHAPTER XXXV

Happy the soldier, all his perils o'er,
In peace returning to his native place,
When those who love him meet him at the door,
And gaze with rapture on the wish'd-for face.

Schiller.

After a march of three hours, the troop of the Leaguists' soldiers, with their prisoner in the midst, approached their camp. Though they did not venture to talk aloud, it was easy to perceive, by their countenances, how great was their exultation at their supposed triumph and prize, and it did not escape the acute observation of Albert that the whisper among them referred to the reward they were likely to gain for the person of the Duke. A feeling of satisfaction filled the breast of the young man, in the hope that his unhappy Prince might gain time to escape his enemies by the diversion the bold sacrifice he had made of himself in his favour. But the thought which now gave him the greatest uneasiness was the distress his beloved wife would experience, when she became acquainted with the result of the battle. Though he had informed her, through the medium of faithful messengers, of his having escaped unhurt in the bloody conflict, she was still ignorant of the unfortunate turn in the Duke's fate; still less could she know his own. He could well imagine her state of mind, when, among the prisoners brought into Stuttgardt, neither her father nor husband were found of the number. The thought was agonising to his mind, rendered doubly so amidst the taunts of those who now led him as a prisoner to the presence of his enemies. These, and a thousand other painful feelings, chilled his joy in having been the saviour of his friend.

Could he hope to be liberated a second time by the League, as he had been in Ulm? Taken with arms in his hand,--known as the most zealous friend of the Duke,--his only prospect was a long imprisonment, and harsh treatment. The arrival at the advanced posts of the camp interrupted these gloomy thoughts. One of the troop which guarded him was sent on before to acquaint the commanders of the League of their prisoner, and to receive their orders respecting the place where he was to be brought. This was a painful quarter of an hour for Albert. He wished of all things, if possible, to speak to Fronsberg, hoping that this noble friend of his father might still retain a kindly feeling towards him, and, at least, judge him more favourably than Truchses von Waldburg and many others, who he well knew to be inimical towards him.

The man returned with orders to conduct the prisoner as quietly as possible, and without ceremony, to the large tent in which the officers generally held their council of war. For this purpose they turned off by a side path, and the soldiers begged Albert to close the vizor of his helmet, that he might pass unknown, till he arrived before the council. He willingly complied with this request, for nothing was more painful to his feelings than to be exposed to the gaze of the curious or exulting multitude. Numerous serving men were assembled here, whose different costumes and badges of distinction led Albert to suppose a large assemblage of nobles and knights were congregated in the tent.

The news that a troop of infantry had taken a man of distinction prisoner, appeared to have preceded his arrival, for when Albert threw himself from his saddle, the people crowded around him, and, with looks of curiosity, tried to get a sight of his features through the apertures of his vizor. A page of honour with difficulty made his way through the multitude, having been sent, "in the name of the commanders of the League," to open a road by which the prisoner could reach the tent. Three of the men who had taken him were ordered to follow; their joy was unbounded, and they thought of nothing less than receiving immediately the gold florins which had been offered as the price for the person of the Duke of Würtemberg.

The inner curtain of the tent being drawn up, Albert walked in boldly and with a firm, step, looking round upon the men who were to decide upon his fate. Many known faces were among the number, who eyed him with inquisitive penetrating looks. The scowling glance and inimical front of Truchses von Waldburg were still fresh in his memory, and the scornful exulting expression of the features of this man did not augur him any good. Sickingen, Alban von Closen, Hutten, all sat before him as at that time when he bid the League an eternal farewell. But when he beheld that noble figure, those dignified features of Fronsberg, which were deeply engraven on his grateful heart, he felt self convicted in his own estimation. It was not contempt or triumphant joy which sat upon his features,--no, it was an expression of sorrowing thoughtfulness, with which an honourable man receives a valiant conquered enemy.

Albert now stood before these men, when Truchses von Waldburg began:--"The Swabian League has at last the honour of seeing the illustrious Duke of Würtemberg before them. The invitation which you sent to us was certainly much too courteous, but----"

"You are mistaken," answered Albert, raising the vizor of his helmet at the same time. The members of the League started when they beheld the fine countenance of the young knight, as if they had seen Minerva's shield and Medusa's head.

"Ha! traitors! base villains! dogs!" cried Truchses to the three soldiers; "what cub do you bring here in the place of the Duke? The very sight of him excites my bile! Tell me quickly what has become of him--speak!"

The soldiers turned pale. "Is he not the right one?" they asked. "That was him with the green cloak."

Truchses trembled with rage, his eyes darted fire, he would have executed the soldiers upon the spot, and talked of hanging them; but the rest of the knights compelled him to curb his violence; and Hutten, pale with anger also, but more composed than the other, asked, "Where is Doctor Calmus? let him come forward, to give an account of himself, for he volunteered to arrest the Duke."

"Ah, sir!" replied one of the soldiers, "his account is already settled; he lies dead on the bridge of Köngen."

"Killed?" cried Sickingen, "and the Duke fled! relate the circumstance, villains!"

We placed ourselves in ambush near the bridge, as the doctor ordered us. It was still dark, when we heard the tread of horses approach the bridge, and at the same time perceived the signal which our cavalry on the other side of it had agreed to make as soon as the Duke's party issued from the wood. "Now is the time," cried the doctor; "we instantly got up and occupied the exit from the bridge. As far as we could distinguish, four horsemen and a peasant formed the party. The two hindermost turned back and engaged our cavalry, whilst the other two, and the peasant, attacked us.

"We stretched out our lances, the doctor calling to them to surrender; but they paid no attention to the summons, and fell on us with determined fury. The man in the green mantle was pointed out as the prize, and we should soon have had him had it not been for the peasant,--if it was not, indeed, the very devil himself,--who with his axe felled the doctor and two of our comrades in a trice. One of our party revenged our leader's life by running the peasant through the body with his halbert, which encouraged us to renew our attack on the man in the green mantle. His companion sprang his horse over the bridge into the Neckar, and swam down the river. Having subdued the man who was our principal object, we let the other go, and brought the prisoner with us."

"That was Ulerich, and no other," cried Alban von Klosen. "Ha! to jump over the bridge into the river! no other man in the whole world would have dared to do so."

"We must follow him," Truchses exclaimed; "the whole of the cavalry must start immediately and hunt the banks of the river,--I myself will go----"

"Oh! sir," replied one of the soldiers, "you are too late; we left the bridge three hours ago, so that he will have got a long start, and, as no one knows the country better than he does, there is no chance of finding him."

"Fellow! do you mean to prescribe to me what to do?" cried Truchses in fury: "You allowed him to escape, and you shall be answerable for it. Call the guard--I'll have you hung at once!"

"Pray be just," said Fronsberg. "It was not the poor fellows' fault; they would have been too happy to have earned the money which was set on the Duke's head. The doctor was the cause of his escape, and you have already heard he is not alive to answer for it."

"It was you, therefore, who represented the person of the Duke," said Truchses, turning to Albert, who had calmly looked on during this scene. "You are always coming in my way, with your milk face. The devil employs you everywhere, when you are least wanted. This is not the first time that you have crossed my plans."

"No," replied Albert, "for when you fell upon the Duke, as you supposed, at Neuffen, it was I who crossed your path there also; and it was I whom your men cut down that night."

The knights were astonished to hear this, and looked inquisitively at Truchses. He reddened, but whether from anger or shame it was not known, and said, "What are you chattering about Neuffen? I know nothing about that affair. I only regret that when they cut you down you had ever risen again to appear before me this day a second time. But as it is, I rejoice to have you in my clutches. You have proved yourself the bitterest enemy of the League; you have acted in the service of the exiled Duke both openly and secretly, thereby sharing his offence against us and the whole empire. Beside these crimes, you have been taken this day with arms in your hands. You are therefore guilty of high treason against the most illustrious League of Swabia and Franconia."

"Your charges are highly ridiculous," replied the young man, in a tone of defiance: "you made me swear to remain neuter between the two parties for fourteen days, to which I faithfully adhered, so true as God is my witness. You have no right to require an account of my conduct since that time, for I was no longer bound to you: and as to what you say of my being taken with arms in my hand, I would ask you, noble knights, who among you would not defend his life to the last when he was attacked by six or eight men? I demand then, as my right, the treatment becoming the rank of knighthood; and therefore I am ready to swear to a six weeks' neutrality. You cannot require more of me."

"Would you prescribe laws to us?" said Truchses. "You have learned a good lesson, indeed, from the Duke. I think I hear him speaking; but not one step shall you take to your friends before you own where that old fox, your father-in-law, is, and the road the Duke has taken."

"The knight of Lichtenstein was taken prisoner by your cavalry," he replied; "but the road which the Duke has taken, I know not; and I am ready to give my word of honour upon it."

"To be treated as a knight, indeed!" said Truchses, with a sarcastic laugh; "there you deceive yourself altogether. You must first prove where you won the golden spur! No; such criminals as you, are, according to our laws, thrown into the lowest dungeons; and so I will commence with you."

"I think that unnecessary," interrupted Fronsberg. "I will answer for Albert von Sturmfeder that he has a right to the golden spurs; besides which, he saved the life of a noble belonging to the League. You cannot forget the evidence of Dieterich von Kraft, how, through the intercession of this knight, he was saved from an ignominious death, and was even set at liberty. He has a right, therefore, to the same treatment by us."

"I know you have always spoken a word for him, your darling child," rejoined Truchses; "but this once it is of no avail. He must be sent to the tower of Esslingen this very moment."

"I will stand bail for him," said Fronsberg. "I possess the right of a voice in council with the rest. Let it pass to the vote what is to be done with the prisoner. In the mean while, let him be conducted to my tent."

Albert cast a look of heartfelt gratitude at his kind noble friend, for having a second time saved him from a threatened danger. Truchses muttered an order to the guards to follow the orders of Fronsberg, who led their prisoner through the narrow paths of the camp to the tent of the commander of the infantry.

Shortly after he had arrived at his destination, the man to whom he was so highly indebted stood before him, but Albert could not find words to express his sense of gratitude and respect. Fronsberg smiled at his embarrassment, and embraced him. "No thanks, no excuses," said he. "Did I not already anticipate all this when we took leave of each other in Ulm? But you would not believe me, and were determined to bury yourself among the ruins of the castle of your ancestors. I do not blame you; for believe me the campaigns and storms of many wars have not yet hardened my heart so much as to make me forget the power of love."

"My friend, my father!" exclaimed Albert, blushing with joy.

"Yes, I am truly your father,--the friend of your father. I have often thought of you with pride, even when you stood opposed to me in the enemy's ranks. Your name, young as you are, will always be mentioned with respect; for fidelity and courage in an enemy are always highly esteemed by a man of honour. Most of us rejoice that the Duke has escaped, for what could we have done with him? Truchses might perhaps have committed a rash step, which we all might have had cause to repent."

"And what is my fate to be?" asked Albert. "Am I to remain long in prison? Where is the knight of Lichtenstein? Oh, my poor wife! may I not see her?"

Fronsberg smiled mysteriously. "That will be difficult to manage," said he. "You will be sent to a fortress under safe escort, and given over to a guard, who will have orders to watch you strictly, and from whose charge you will not escape so easily. But, be of good cheer; the knight of

Lichtenstein will accompany you, and both of you must swear to a year's neutrality and imprisonment."

Fronsberg was now interrupted by three men, who stormed his tent;--it was Breitenstein and Dieterich von Kraft, leading the knight of Lichtenstein between them.

"Do I see you again, my brave lad?" cried Breitenstein, as he took Albert's hand. "You have played me a pretty trick; your old uncle made me promise, upon my soul, to make something out of you, which would do honour to the League, but you deserted to the enemy, cutting and slashing at us, and nearly gained the victory yesterday by your hot-brained, desperate attack on our artillery!"

"Every one to his taste," replied Fronsberg; "he did honour to his friends, even in the enemy's ranks."

The knight of Lichtenstein embraced his son. "He is in safety," he whispered to him. Their eyes beamed with joy, in having both been instrumental in saving their unhappy Prince. The old knight discovered the green mantle which still hung on the shoulders of his son, and said, in astonishment, a tear of joy starting to his eye, "Ah, now I understand how everything has come to pass; they mistook you for the Duke. What would have become of him but for your courage and presence of mind in the critical moment? Your bravery and foresight have achieved more than any of us, and, though we are prisoners, we are still conquerors! Come to my heart, thou most noble son!"

"And Maxx von Stumpf Schweinsberg!" asked Albert, "what has become of him? is he a prisoner also?" "He cut his way through the enemy,--for who could withstand his arm? My old bones are powerless, I am of no more use; but he has joined the Duke, and will be of more assistance to him than fifty horsemen. But I did not see the fifer,--tell me, how did he come out of the fray?"

"As a hero," replied Albert, agitated by a feeling of deep regret at the recollection of him; "he was run through the body by a lance, and his corpse lies on the bridge."

"Dead!" cried Lichtenstein, and his voice trembled. "His was indeed a faithful soul,--may it rest in peace! His actions were noble, and he died true to his master, as all should do."

Fronsberg now approached them, and interrupted their conversation. "You appear much cast down," said he; "but be of good cheer and consolation, noble sir! the fortune of war is changeable, and your Duke will, in all probability, once more return to his native country. Who knows if it is not better that we should send him to foreign parts again for a short time? Put by your helmet and armour; your fight at breakfast time will not have spoiled your appetite for mid-day's meal. Seat yourself beside us. About noon I expect the guardian, who is to have charge of you in your confinement; until then, let's be cheerful."

"That's a proposition we can readily satisfy," cried Breitenstein. "Dinner is ready, gentlemen: you and I have not dined together, Albert, since that day in the townhall of Ulm. Come, and we'll make up for lost time."

Hans von Breitenstein seated himself with Albert next to him; the others followed his example; the servants brought the dinner, and wine made the knight of Lichtenstein and his son forget, for a time, their unfortunate situation of being in the enemy's camp, and the uncertainty of their fate, which, according to Fronsberg's assurance, was to be an imprisonment of long duration. Towards the end of the repast Fronsberg was called away, but he soon returned, and said, with a serious countenance, "Willingly as I would wish to enjoy your society some time longer, my friends, I am sorry to compel you to break up. The guard is without into whose charge I must deliver you, and I would advise you to lose no time, if you would arrive at the fortress of your confinement before dark."

"I trust our guard is one of our own rank,--a knight?" asked Lichtenstein, whilst his face assumed a gloomy, indignant frown. "I hope proper attention will be paid to our rights, and that we shall have an escort fitting our station."

"No knight will accompany you," said Fronsberg, "but a fitting escort, of which you shall convince yourself." With these words he raised the curtain of his tent, discovering to the astonished father and son the lovely features of Bertha. She flew into the arms of her enraptured husband. Her venerable father, speechless from joy and surprise, kissed his child on her forehead, and pressed the hand of the honest Fronsberg in token of heartfelt gratitude.

"That is your guardian," said the latter; "and the castle of Lichtenstein the place of your confinement. I can see already, in your eyes," addressing himself to Bertha, "that you will not be too severe with the young man, and that the old man will not have to complain. But let me advise you, my pretty daughter, to have a watchful eye to your prisoners; don't let them out of the castle, for fear of their rejoining the cause of certain people. Your pretty head will answer for their actions!"

"But, dear sir," replied Bertha, whilst she drew her beloved closer to her, and smiled playfully at the stern commander, "recollect he is my head,--so how can I command him?"

"That is just the reason why you should take care not to lose it again. Bind him fast with the knot of love,--let him not escape, for he easily changes his colours; of which we have had proofs sufficient."

"I only wore one colour, my fatherly friend!" replied the young man, looking at his beautiful wife, and pointing to the scarf which he wore, "only one, and to this I remained faithful."

"Well, then! remain true to it for the future," said Fronsberg, and gave him his hand to depart. "Farewell! your horses are before the tent: may you arrive happily at your destination, and think sometimes, in friendship, of old Fronsberg."

Bertha took leave of this worthy man with tears of grateful thanks in her eyes; the men also were overcome when they took his hand, for they were well aware that, without his kind interference, their fate might have been of a very different stamp. George von Fronsberg followed the happy party with his eye until they turned the corner of the long lane of tents. "He is in good hands," said he, as he turned to Breitenstein. "Truly the blessing of his father rests upon him. Not a better or more beautiful wife, and more honourable son, will be found in all Swabia."

"Yes, yes!" replied Hans von Breitenstein, "but he has not to thank his own wits or foresight for it. He who seeks to better his fortune, let him conduct a wife home. I am fifty years old, and still on the look-out for a partner; and you, also, Dieterich von Kraft, are you not upon the same scent?"

"Not at all,--quite the contrary,--I am already provided," he replied, as if awoke out of a dream; "when one sees such a couple, we know what is next to be done. I am going to put myself, this very hour, into my sedan, on my journey to Ulm, there to conduct my cousin Marie to my home. Farewell, my friends!"

When the Swabian League had reconquered Würtemberg, they re-established their government, and reigned over the whole country, as in the summer of 1519. The partisans of the exiled Duke were compelled to swear neutrality, and were banished to their respective castles. Albert von Sturmfeder and his family were included in this mild destiny, living retired on the Lichtenstein; and a new life of peaceable domestic happiness fell to the lot of the loving couple.

Often when they stood at the window of the castle, overlooking Würtemberg's beautiful fields, they would think of their unfortunate Prince, who also once viewed his country from the same spot. It reminded them of the chain of events of their own history, and of the extraordinary means by which their union had been brought about; and which they did not fail to acknowledge, would perhaps not have happened so soon, had their fate been otherwise ordained. But they felt the joy of their existence incomplete when they thought of the founder of their happiness, living in the misery of banishment far from his country.

Some years after the fatal battle, the Duke succeeded in re-conquering Würtemberg. The stern lesson of adversity and misfortune brought him back a wiser Prince and a happier man. He re-established the ancient rights and laws of the land, and won the hearts of his people by judicious measures. He enforced the preaching of holy doctrines, and by his example recommended the practice of them. The religious principles he had imbibed in foreign lands, and which had afforded him the only consolation amidst his sufferings, he now infused into the laws of his country, as the only sure foundation-stone of a people's happiness. Albert and his pious wife plainly discovered the finger of a merciful God watching over the fate of Ulerich von Würtemberg. They blessed Him who thus veils futurity from the eye of mortals, and, as in the present instance, turns dark into light to those who seek his guidance and protection in faith.

The name of Lichtenstein in Würtemberg became extinct at the death of the old knight; but he lived long enough to see his blooming grand-children attain the age of bearing arms. And in this way generation after generation pass over the face of the earth, new comers thrusting out old ones, and after a short lapse of fifty or an hundred years, the fame of honest men and faithful hearts is forgotten. The rushing stream of time drowns the voice of their remembrance, and only a few brilliant names float down the tide of history and play upon its surface in partial glittering light. Far more happy is the man whose actions carry their own silent worth along with them, finding their reward alone in the purity of conscience, and passing through life without courting the praise or flattery of the times in which he lived, nor living for the applause of after ages. The name of the fifer of Hardt and his actions, have come down to us in simple garb, through the medium of successive generations of shepherds in the neighbourhood of the "Misty Cavern." They relate the deeds of the man who concealed his unfortunate Duke among its deep recesses, as they conduct the stranger through their gloomy paths, and talk of the romantic events of Ulerich's life. The writer of history disdains such stories as unworthy of his pen; but they are not the less credible. When recounted on the spot, such as on the heights of Lichtenstein, where the Duke came every night at a stated hour to the castle, and when the place is pointed out on the bridge of Köngen, whence the undaunted man took the fearful leap into the deep waters below for life or death, we listen to the details with believing ears.

The old castle of Lichtenstein has long since fallen into ruin. A huntsman's house now occupies its foundations, light and airy, like a castle in the air, which imagination builds upon the ruins of antiquity. Würtemberg's fields spread themselves before the enchanted eye, rich and blooming as formerly, when Bertha by the side of her lover gazed upon them, and the most unhappy of her princes cast a farewell glance on his country from Lichtenstein's windows. The subterranean apartments of the castle, which received the exile, are still to be seen, in all their pride and glory; and the murmuring streams, gushing through the mysterious depths at the foot of the rock, would seem to relate events long since buried in oblivion.

It is a delightful custom of the inhabitants of the country, and also of the stranger from distant parts, to visit Lichtenstein and Ulerich's cavern on Whitsunday. Many hundreds of Swabia's children are attracted to these mountains on that day. They descend into the heart of the earth, whose crystal walls, lighted up by thousands of wax tapers, are made to reflect their sparkling beauties in numberless fantastic forms; they fill the cavern with the sound of the merry song, and listening to its echoes, which are accompanied by the melodious murmur of the running streams in the depth below, enjoy the wonders of nature's handy work. Having satisfied their curiosity, they return to the light of day, more pleased than ever with the glories of sunshine and the comfort of earth's blessings. Ascending the road leading to the heights of Lichtenstein, they arrive on its summit, where the men, surrounded by their wives and families, with the glass in the hand, overlook the distant fields, displayed to their view in all the lovely colours of the setting sun, and, with grateful hearts, thank heaven for the blessings of their father-land. The halls of Lichtenstein resound again with music, dancing, and the merry song, and the echo from its rocks seems to inspire the jovial guests with recollections of the former inmates of the castle, and with them to gaze upon good old Würtemberg. But whether the spirit of the lady of Lichtenstein, with that of Albert and the old knight, inspires them, or whether the faithful musician of Hardt quits his grave, and, as he was wont to do during his life, mounts up to the castle to cheer it with music and song, we know not. Often have we reposed on these rocks on a still summer's evening, enjoying the landscape, talking over the good old times, witnessing the sun's descent, and observing the castle, standing alone and solitary, lighted up by its last rays. Then it was we fancied we could distinguish, among the rustling of the trees, the sound of known voices, floating on the gentle breeze, wafting to our ears their salutations, and recounting the events of their past lives and actions. We have frequently experienced such like feelings, presenting to our imagination images, which fancy would realize before our eyes, and salute our ears with the whisper of their romantic tales, until at length we verily believed them to be,--the spirits of Lichtenstein.